SAGA OF THE URBAN SORCERERS

BOOK ONE:

THE SUMMONING OF BARKER MOON

I0589618

SAGA OF THE URBAN SORCERERS

BOOK ONE:

THE SUMMONING OF BARKER MOON

ALEX JAMES

Novels by Alex James:

SAGA OF THE URBAN SORCERERS:
Book One: The Summoning of Barker Moon
Book Two: The Reckoning of Emerald Tarragon
Book Three: The Shaping of Cheryl Equiniox (Pre-order)

THE CHRONICLES OF THE TERRAGUARD:
Book One: Maker of Rules

THE ASCENSION SEQUENCE:
VOLUME ONE
The Pandora Sequence
VOLUME TWO
Book One: The Pandora Inheritance
Book Two: The Pandora Arcana (Pre-order)
Book Three: The Daughters of Pandora (Pre-order)

AMAZON SEVEN
VOLUME ONE
Book One: Mission Queen
Book Two: Queen Renegade
Book Three: Intergalactic Ingenue (Pre-order)
Book Four: Princess Executor (Pre-order)

DARK STREETS:
Book One: Agents of Fear
Book Two: Avatars of Wrath (Pre-Order)

www.GalexyTales.com

(or search "GALEXY TALES" at Amazon!)

Dedication

To Whatever it is…
Up there in The Hills.

ONE:
THE LION AND UNICORN

I

It was a dark and stormy night.

It was.

It really was.

But things should never begin that way.

Clem remembered an author telling him that once. The author had stopped in for a neat scotch, nothing less than twelve years old; a tall thin bloke with a grey beard and glasses, slacks and a beige cardigan. Exactly what Clem thought an author would look like, or at least, what one was supposed to look like.

'The night is always dark...' Said Author had opined. '... so there is no point in telling a reader that... the description is redundant! Superfluous!'

It was a stormy night, the night was stormy... that would suffice, apparently.

Clem had thought about that old chestnut since then, on several of the long and quiet nights that had followed, sitting alone behind the bar of the once-flourishing Lion and Unicorn Hotel, as his mind grew weary of the incessant nonsense of the television up in the corner.

The night was not always dark.

Not pitch dark.

He had seen nights when the moon was so bright that the illumination was near enough to daylight.

Broad moonlight, he supposed.

Beatnik beard, stained cardigan, then belting down his regular, ordinary label after lingering over his one shot of the good stuff.

'All tastes the same after the first glass...'

'…and it all comes out the same!' Clem had returned the easy lie with an easy truth.

But it was nobody's fault. The thing that annoyed Clem was when people made excuses like that. If you had fifty bucks to spend on yourself, drinking on a lonely Saturday night, spend it how you like, in whatever time you like. Sit on three glasses of the good stuff for an hour each. Slam them all down in half an hour. Sip the crap stuff at five bucks a shot, mix it with sugar to stretch it out, and sit here all night. Clem didn't care; or rather, he didn't judge. All that concerned him was that you spent your fifty bucks and didn't break anything – or anyone.

Still, it was strange, for a walking cliché to damn the use of such a device, Clem had thought at the time. But Clem's definition of strange had expanded since then, to such a degree that he'd considered writing a book himself.

All he needed now was an ending.

The Lion and Unicorn Hotel had been one of the gateway hotels in colonist times. The main road that passed outside came directly up from the city, from one of the infamous city corners. From there, the road ran straight to the edge of the city plains, then suddenly and steeply up through the ever-increasing gradient of the forested suburban foothills. Then it wound its way continuously up the side of one of the highest and steepest of those hillsides to crest atop the very summit, right outside the door to the front bar of The Lion and Unicorn Hotel. The road then continued over the hilltop and plunged down again toward the inland plains; out to the country, and away. From the 1840s, and well into the 1900s, The Lion had been one of the last stops for supplies and refreshment before those open plains, which were long, and dull, but led to the larger cities, and more thriving communities in the eastern states. Even west, across one of the most boring routes in the world, across the Nullarbor, you eventually arrived in Perth.

But now, the Lion and Unicorn was almost nothing.

Even the television was broken. The Front Bar was essentially as it had always been; a thin rectangular room with three solid wood windows, evenly spaced, that faced the front bar. Eight stools along the bar and, under each window, a table and three chairs. The room, and effectively the hardwood bar itself, was bookended by two massive wooden doors, both original oak; one led further in, to the Lounge Bar and then out to the back balcony. The other, the front door, led immediately out onto the footpath, and the intersection outside, where the hill crested.

The Lion and The Unicorn; the once-proud jewel in the crest of the hills.

There was thunder in the distance.

The thick glass rattled in the old oak window frames.

Clem stared through them and knew that despite even the full moon, the night was, irrefutably, dark and stormy.

That was how he was feeling, too. He could see the halogen-flickering that the low branches were causing, as the trees flailed around the streetlights on the intersection. He could hear the wailing wind, through the thrashing trees, over the dead quiet inside the hotel.

Rain was probably not far away.

Maybe the storm would come right over.

Settle in for the night.

Break something.

Maybe the wind would blast rain, lots of rain, onto the window panes, and save him the effort of cleaning them. The windows would have to be cleaned soon, he thought, if he were to try to make it look decent, get a half-decent price on the place. Although, he had long suspected that any effort in that direction would be futile. He'd never get what the pub was potentially worth. Not even close, after what had happened here over the past few months.

Clem heard a bike approach and pull up outside.

Perhaps this was how it would end? A biker pub. He'd heard other publicans tell stories, how loss of trade for whatever reason had led to a biker gang staking a claim. Then the drugs, then the violence and, inevitably, the police. Pubs usually recovered from such an incursion, but landlords rarely did.

But it didn't sound like a Harley. European, maybe a Beamer. Maybe not.

Nature abhors a vacuum, doesn't it?

What would nature send, Clem wondered, to the empty hole that the once thriving inn, The Lion and Unicorn Hotel, had now become?

II

Barker Moon was not comfortable with motorbikes.

He knew they looked cool, and that the cliché was that they were freedom machines ridden by independent spirits. Hardcore bikers who made their own rules. Zen drifters who travelled for travel's sake. Cheap transport for the young and immortal. Marlon Brando, Steve McQueen, Tom Cruise. Batman, Tron, The Fonz. All sorts; all sorts of minds, and all sorts of independence. He would probably be seen as such, by others, riding this bike now. Or at least, he would be perceived as trying to be one of those types.

Truth was, however, that he had almost no freedom. The bike was clearly choosing to obey him, and virtually steering herself. She could, Barker was sure, change her mind any time she liked, buck him off and roar off in any direction she chose. Far from feeling cool and independent, Barker was extremely unsure of his safety. Still, even so, even given that the bike was haunted and being steered by a ghost of indeterminate nature, age and intention, Barker knew that he was much safer being piloted by a restless, inhabiting spirit than he would have been, had he been driving it himself, independently.

The haunted bike slowed as the insanely steep road peaked at the top of a hill, then turned right into a small township that had long ago formed around and about the summit intersection. There was a church, a town hall, a combined post office and local store, and a pub.

The Lion and Unicorn Hotel.

'Bach, stop here please.'

The bike slowed and stopped, then the stand kicked down by itself.

'Thanks.'

Black. Beamer. Bike. The three B's. Bach, Beethoven, Brahms. Bach had seemed most appropriate.

Barker's memory of the tiny hilltop town had been correct. That didn't happen so often these days. But his memory of The Lion and Unicorn being oddly located was spot on.

'Bach, call Cheryl please.'

Barker's phone was tight in his left breast pocket, but his wireless headset was jammed into his ear against the tightness of the black helmet. There was a click.

'Is that you?'

'Yes it's me.'

'Did you take Gully Road up from the city?'

'Yeah, I did. Well, Bach did. We're near the peak now, looking down into the town.'

'Good. It's a longer drive, but it's easier than the other one… wait; Bach?'

'Ghosts aren't people too, Cheryl.'

Barker smiled as Cheryl sighed. '…ghosts aren't people too…' Barker could practically hear her eyes rolling.

The ghost bike had handled Gully Road's mad, twisting incline easily, then the road had evened out and come up into Warren Road, a notoriously long stretch that covered the back-country side of Adelaide's north-south arcing, all-surrounding, ocean-facing hills.

Barker smiled. 'That other way up looks like a nightmare. I think I remember it.'

'It is. They're both bendy roads, but Gully is less bendy, it goes diagonally along the hill and evens out near the top. The

Nightmare Road just sticks to the side of the steepest side of the summit, just zig-zags right down the gully-face, steep and bendy all the way, and it comes up blind at the five-way intersection.'

'I can see. I'm looking at it.'

There was thick fog rolling in now. But he could technically see it.

'So you can see the five-way intersection? You're at the top of the mountain?'

'Hill, surely?'

'Technically it's just high enough to be a mountain.'

'I'm on Warren, looking down at the hotel.'

Barker surveyed the tiny old village.

'It's mad. Totally mad.'

The Lion and Unicorn had been built right on the edge of the hill, wedged into the dug-out quarter of the incline between Gully Road and the Nightmare Road. The balcony extended out the back, looking down on the city through a long, steep gully.

Cheryl hummed, like she knew that he was looking at it.

'Great view though.'

Behind the hotel, at the peak of the incline, was an intersection that was completely insane. Right beside the hotel, where Warren passed through the village, Nightmare and three other thin country roads collided as one, at dangerously weird angles. One road entered the intersection from a Y-fork that branched after splitting off, just past the main intersection around two blind curves, each prong veering off at about forty-five degrees to vanish abruptly. Into this, Nightmare came up steeply from the city side, right alongside the Lion and Unicorn, then hooked up and descended past the intersection, plunging downward at a hideously steep angle. Both approaches seemed to drop hopelessly into a dark abyss of gum trees, many of which lined each road, surrounded by high shrubs which, it appeared, had been placed purposefully so as to minimize visibility. All exits offered a further nightmare rollercoaster for anyone with a car, let alone a bike, who might be driving home at night from the local pub. This was especially so for Warren, which ran all the way along the back of The Hills, passed at least seven pubs that Barker could immediately think of, and was a notorious speed track for local bogans.

'It's not a true pentagon; but it's a vortex.'

'You already know that.'

'I know it now, but I don't remember it.'

'Try and remember. We used to have birthdays there. You and me and Carlton. Some of the others. Hawker worked there behind the bar, when he was a kid.'

He kind of remembered.

'I don't know... so what's the deal here?'

'Maybe you'll remember when you go in?'

'Maybe...'

It was freezing. He didn't like drinking any more. It fogged his mind, even more than it was already fogged. Maybe they did coffee?

'When was the last time I hung out here?'

'We never hung out. Too far north. But they used to have the best chef in The Hills; back ten years ago. So we'd come out here for special occasions.'

'That long ago?'

'Eight? Nine?'

Barker nodded to himself.

'What are you wearing?' Cheryl asked.

Barker smiled.

'Not like that...' Her neutral smile was apparent in her voice. 'Like, have you found your *thing* again yet?'

Barker knew what she meant. 'No.'

'Not even in that wardrobe? There's a lot of stuff in there.'

'It's all black.'

'You used to wear black. All black, all the time.'

'I know. I've seen the pictures. My hair used to be longer, too.'

'You're stalling.'

'You haven't told me what the deal is.'

'Vanished cat. The owner's depressed. Some kind of dark feeder has moved in and he's losing customers. He's offering five hundred. You should frighten the nasty little spook away just by walking in. Like the one at the old cinema last week. Make some light and smoke if you have to.'

Dark feeder.

What was left of some restless spirit who'd never gotten away. Not the ghost of an actual person as such; just what was left of… all the shadow crap they'd left behind. A gecko's tail, spiritually speaking, that wouldn't stop wriggling. Barker assessed the hilltop intersection again.

'Well Cheryl, once again your information has been accurate, your advice invaluable.'

'Just do your job. Make us some money.'

Barker assessed. 'This is a vortex intersection, a clear, classic and long-standing magical attractor, and you brought me up the safest route.'

'It's just the way the world evolved…'

'…courtesy of our horse-drawn cart ancestors,' Barker smiled grimly to himself.

'Is that a thing?'

'It's been playing on my mind lately… is the landlord expecting me? Will he have the five hundred ready?'

'He's happy to see anyone who says they'll get his customers back. Are you remembering all that from your own mind…?'

'No. I don't think so. It's just the academic stuff. Numbers and angles. Stuff you can read online.'

'Oh…' She tried to hide her disappointment. 'Well, the owner's name is Clem. He's tried a few things. I think even Freyanna has had a go. That's what Angela said.'

'Angela?'

'Angela Lorre. You remember her? She said you'd met.'

Barker hummed. 'I think we went out a while, didn't we? In the dark times?'

'Yeah. When I wasn't here to stop you. Do you trust her?'

'No. But… I don't mistrust her either. She never picked a team. I think that's why we ended it.'

Cheryl paused for a second. Barker could tell she was reconsidering. Then she came back with a little more concern in her tone. 'Look, Barker, you don't have to do this. We need the money, but I can get you another gig. Something more simple. A Tarot reading or something. I'm meeting another potential client tonight, maybe she'll have something that's not so – '

'No… it's okay, Cheryl. I…'

He listened to Cheryl breathing, waiting for him to say something. He hadn't known exactly what he had intended to say.

I have a feeling? I have an instinct that…?

'I want to go in. Check it out. Have a look at the view. I think there's something here for me. And I need a coffee. It's the only place open up here on the hill. I'll see if he's got a machine.'

'If he does have a coffee machine, it's probably broken. You know what it's like when a feeder settles in for the duration.'

He did.

'Nothing works.'

'Precisely.'

'Okay. Bach…'

'Oh God, Barker! I knew it! You're giving the ghost rider free rein, aren't you?'

Thunder rumbled, not far off. Low, but Barker had spent enough time in Adelaide to know; it was something starting. Coming in from the east, across the plains, toward the back of The Hills.

'It's not a ghost rider, Cheryl. I am the rider. Technically, it's a haunted bike.'

'But you don't know who, or what…' Cheryl sighed. 'Look… you know what I mean, right?'

'I know. Listen Cheryl, you'd better get undercover. It's going to start raining soon.'

'How do you know I'm not?'

Barker caught his thoughts suddenly. He'd just seen her.

19

Remote viewed her, very clearly.

'I just saw you. In my mind's eye. Open sky. A cigarette.'

'I'm quitting tonight, Barker.' She went on quickly, before she heard whatever fake tone, in whatever kind but completely fake show of support he'd offer her, upon hearing that shaky, oft-repeated pronouncement. 'Look, that said, can you ask the haunted bike if I can sit on his back tonight? I don't want to be waiting at a bus stop in the rain.'

'Her.'

'Pardon?'

'It's a her.'

'Really?'

'Certain. I'm sure she won't mind. Where are you and when?'

'Barker, don't freak out when I tell you this, okay?'

'No.'

'What?'

'No. You know full well. I never promise that.'

He heard Cheryl sigh, deep. 'Okay. Well, look, I'm at the World Casino, okay?'

Barker knew that. Somehow, in the back of his mind.

He hummed. 'I think I knew that, Cheryl.'

'You did?'

'I think I've known it for a while.'

'But… how? You can't have…?'

'Have you spoken to her?'

Barker heard Cheryl start to say something, then think again. 'Her? You mean Emerald? I've seen her. Once or twice. You can't help but see her, when she's here.'

Barker grumbled. 'I know.'

'Look, I'm not gambling or anything. I meet clients here. It happened by accident, but… you can't see anyone here. I mean, psychically.'

'I know what you mean.'

'I discovered it by accident, but; it's really useful. I can meet clients up here and nobody can tune in. It seems that nothing psychic works here. The Casino has some kind of enormous psychic block in place.'

'We need to talk about this, Cheryl. It might be dangerous. It might be deliberate.'

'I know what I'm doing Barker. But there's something more important than that...'

Barker hated that place.

The World Casino.

But it was a necessary evil, in so many ways.

Now, in a few more it seemed.

'Cheryl, if you don't think you're gambling, you're wrong. You shouldn't be there. You won't be the only one that knows about the block.'

'I think I am. I mean, they ran all the psychics out years ago, right? You know that better than anyone. And witches don't gamble. Even the Black Prax. None of them are stupid enough to gamble. Not in this place, anyway. I really haven't seen anyone else.'

'That's what I'm worried about.'

'I know who's who, Barker. I'm still in the loop!'

'That's not what I mean either; I mean...'

'I know what you mean; you mean that just because I haven't seen any other witches or sorcerers here, doesn't mean there aren't any.'

'Just be careful. I'll get this done and come get you.'

'But Barker, you're missing the most important thing!'

'Bach... take me down to the car park. Cheryl, I'll sign in once it's done. We'll talk about it – ' Bach's engine kicked in. ' – we'll talk about it then!'

The incoming eastern thunder rumbled, and the sky behind the intersection lit up.

'Barker! Y – ca – see – !'

TWO:
NASTY NASTY

I

Cheryl Equinox, for that was her legally registered name, listened to Barker's apparent pet-bike, the newly christened Bach…

'Barker! You've forgotten the most important thing!'

…rev-purr away until the connection was abruptly lost.

'Barker – you can see me! You can see me here, through the psychic block!'

Damn. Cheryl sighed aloud as she ended the call.

How could he see her? That was the kind of thing… that was the kind of power he used to have. Before. Powerful enough to see her in real time, in his mind's eye; and powerful enough to break a casino-level psychic block, without even realizing. So, it was starting again. His powers were starting to return, and… where had that bike come from anyway? So far as she was aware, it had just turned up at the beach-house one day.

Bloody hell, Barker.

She loved Barker, she really did. And Barker loved her too, she knew. They were like the brother and sister both of them never had, despite the fact that they both had plenty of the actual blood-relative siblings. But man, sometimes he was just…

She texted: *Outside 90mins* – and just hoped he'd get it.

Then she sent another – *you saw me idiot!*

The universe had driven him via ghost-bike to the top of a mountain and the edge of a cliff. Well… a big hill, and a gully drop, but still. Still. Surely. *Surely*, he had to see that. What it meant. Either way, it seemed like something was going to happen. Either way, he would get the message. It seemed like, now, he would start to get a lot of things. And that would change things, and then, things would really start happening.

Things, things, things.

It was always *things*.

Things and their happenings.

Things, *changing* things.

Damn you things, and your stupid changing.

Making things *happen*.

Cheryl had made the call to Barker from one of the rooftop bars on the top floor of the World Casino, but now she moved quickly to a small, seldom-frequented unisex bathroom. She had scoped out the entire place when she had first started using the rooftop as her primary location for secret liaisons. There were three rooftops bars, and they existed only to keep smokers inside the Casino, which was a confusing maze, designed to disorient people, that took up the space of two office blocks but was only three floors high.

This rooftop bar was one was the smallest. After a few visits Cheryl had ascertained that the intimacy it offered was too off-putting for the dead-set gamblers, whose repressed shame dictated that they did not want to be seen, or accidentally look anybody in the eye. That, coupled with the cultural weirdness of the unisex bathroom, something to which traditional folks who liked their sports and beer and betting were still resolutely unaccustomed, made it the loneliest corner of the loneliest place in the city.

She entered the bathroom and checked herself, because talking to Barker like that always took her self outside of herself.

(She knew what she meant.)

When you talked to Barker, even this weakened version of her old friend, you got pulled into his orbit and forgot about everything else. Your own world, your own life, and all your shit. At least, some people did, and she was one of them. She sometimes forgot who she was and what she'd been doing. Barker was so intense that way, without trying.

She was even wearing the coat tonight.

The one he'd given her; worn once and made hers.

She forgot that most of the time, but somehow not tonight.

Tonight, as she'd run down the hall and grabbed it, and run out of the apartment, up the foreshore to the tram, the connection was there. She had been aware, somehow, of… not grabbing the coat Barker had given her. Not Barker's coat, that was now hers. But the coat that had come to her, through Barker.

Before Cheryl had made the call to him, before she had thought about anything in this horrible place, anything personal or difficult, she had sent out a spell, a particularly shaped and structured mental signal. This World Casino bathroom was okay, and this open rooftop, of the three on offer, was the least toxic place in it, because it was still part of the original Railway Building that the World Casino had been built within. So Cheryl was able to use the spell to ping through the new plasti-wood veneers, to the true stone walls behind them. The stone reflected the spell back harder, and she absorbed the energy pulse and used it to reinforce her auric shield against the darkness of the general casino vibes that surrounded her. True stone was always good for that. Things worked differently for every witch, every psychic, every sorcerer, but that's how things worked for Cheryl.

In one way, anyway.

Mostly. Sometimes.

She smiled grimly at herself in the mirror. Here she was doing something creative, internal, localized, unprovable, invisible, but definitely magical and totally real, in a place that was dedicated to the financial exploitation of hard maths. The irony was not lost; but neither was it lost on the folks who ran this place.

Even so, despite the stone remnant of a once fine and essentially energetically neutral building, she didn't like to stay longer than a minute or two in here, actually inside the Casino. Just long enough to have a quick pee while she checked her social media updates, then assess herself in the wall-length mirror.

Barsia Swaine was a potential new client after all, of whom Cheryl knew very little. So she had to make sure she looked good, and looked the part.

She thought she'd done okay, although it was getting harder these days to nail the urban witch look. A few too many frills and you looked too sorcery, too seventies, like some kind of Hendrix try-hard, or too mid-eighties, like solo Stevie Nicks. For some reason, in this day and age, that looked too try-hard now, not retro-cool or artisanal. Too dark, too much black, and suddenly you were full-Matrix and stuck at the turn of the two-thousands, and she'd been there, done that, a decade ago now. Too soft with the black and you were a Goth-That-Time-Forgot, or worse, an Emo, identifiably a decade out of fashion. Both looks would come back; they always did. But not today. Today it was; too casual with the urban witch thing and you risked looking like one of Trixie's girls from *Deadwood* (as Barker had nailed her potential clubbing outfit not long ago) but too formal and you risked slipping into Steampunk and people thought you were either a hipster, or cosplaying, or a cosplaying hipster. Too earthy, too hardcore-nature, and people… she'd had a hard time accepting this one… too many people thought you were slightly mental, or politically radical, unless you were exclusively dealing with hardcore feminists and vegans and such, which was indeed a part, but hardly all, of her clientele.

Cheryl was thirty-three and had a good figure. Not fashion, not beachy, but attractive, in proportion, and stable. So she could do… that whole thing, if she wanted, and be normal-hot. But at the same time…

She'd never really settled on a look, past thirty.

So, in that way, she was…

No, she knew, deep down.

In a lot of ways, she was just as lost as Barker.

But, still, here in the mirror, everything looked okay.

'It's too tight on me. Too short. Here; you try. I think it wants you.'

It was dark; a deep navy with a second, rich blue thread that could seem a cool blueberry colour in certain lights, but almost black, and demure, in others. In these terrible lights, the blue seemed to hide even more. And Barker had been right. It had fit her like a glove; one of those wonderfully tailored things, a coat that was more of a thick, long jacket, with cuffs, a high collar and sharp lapel. It didn't really go with anything, but it went a little bit with everything.

So here, in that, in the coat she had grabbed that reminded her of Barker, she looked okay.

Which meant that, outside, away from the harsh bathroom lights, she would look a little more than okay. Public bathroom lights were especially bright, she often told people, especially harsh and revealing.

'Shopping centres, pubs, anywhere where it's good for the public to have low self-esteem, so they spend money, that's where they give the people full exposure; brightly shining, down-lighting, up-lighting, cross-lighting, full-exposure halogen to unveil and showcase all your wrinkles, highlight your spots and deepen the bags under our eyes. Medical-grade dermatological examination levels; scientifically designed to detect and increase visibility of any blemish.'

Cheryl had large eyes, narrow but wide, set far back. With her pale skin, it was hard to hide the dark pigment there, in the shadows of her cavernous sockets. Thanks, Polish mother, grandmother, great-grandmother. If they could get in a TARDIS and all stand side by side at this age, they would look like quadruplets; granted, with radically different diets and lifestyles.

So anyway, she looked okay for now, maybe just better than okay, which was the best she could hope for, given that she had given up on anything more for the time being.

So, Barsia Swaine.

She thought, amongst the general swirl in her head, about the way Barker often said, three times a charm.

Barker, Bach, Barsia.

Ba, ba and ba.

She turned from the mirror, from her Plain Jane Gypsy, okay exterior.

Ba ba ba, ba-Barbara Ann. Four.

What else?

Babar the Elephant. Two.

Out the door, into the courtyard.

Baba. Sai Baba, the Ascended Master. Two.

Ali Baba. Two.

Forty thieves drowned in boiling oil? A thousand stories and… a thousand nights? A princess trying to stay alive. Telling stories. Making shit up. A lot of shit, a lot of nights, a lot of thieves.

In the courtyard.

The three beer garden widescreen televisions were set exclusively to Fox Sports.

A different light out here. High walls, like a prison courtyard, with spikes on the tops of the walls. High, so you couldn't see the beautiful view down to the Torrens Lake outside, so nothing would distract the smoker's compulsive mind from the gambling. Spikes, to stop drunks or known grifters sneaking in if they'd been banned. But also so you couldn't climb up and jump three floors down if you'd lost everything. Well, everything else.

But government health laws, that had banned smoking in all covered areas throughout the city, had meant that the Casino couldn't do anything about preventing punters from being exposed to the actual sky. There were however tall gas burners, ostensibly to keep the enclosure warm against the open air, dictated by the Health Department restrictions that not even a casino could bribe their way out of, but they were strategically placed to block out most of the stellar view.

The last thing a Casino needed was for its clientele to start contemplating, or philosophising.

Baa – baa – baa.

Baba Yaga the Slavic forest spirit… two.

She headed over to the table.

Ba Ba Black Sheep. Two.

There was a girl at the bar. She hadn't been there when she'd been talking to Barker on the phone. That would mean Barsia Swaine was punctual. For a client, that usually meant they were keen, but not especially nervous.

Ba-ba-ba-bahhhh, ba-ba-ba-Beethoven.

Destiny knocks at the door.

But that that was four again. One-two-three-foooouuuuurrr. One-two-three-fooooouuuuurrr. Just like The Doctor. There are always four knocks.

But she needed three.

Barker, Bach, Barsia.

Cheryl sat where she'd been waiting before, in the middle. It was the best seat; there were only two exits, and she was facing one, with the other in her right-side periphery. Because, the sad fact was that even psychics generally never knew who was coming for them. Psychics, witches, sorcerers, whatever, were generally attacked by others of their own kind, those who knew how to shield themselves from whatever abilities others of their kind possessed. Super-nature's even playing field, she supposed.

Whatever; superspy seating position when doing business.

The girl at the bar turned.

'Cheryl?'

'Oh, I thought I saw you there! Are you Barsia?'

Barsia came over and they shook hands. 'Would you like a drink?'

'No, thanks,' Cheryl smiled. 'Is this table okay?'

Barsia sat and Cheryl followed her example.

'That's a lovely scarf.'

'Thankyou. My friend Carlton gave it to me.'

'Carlton?'

'Yes.'

'Not Carl?'

'No, definitely not.'

'Interesting.'

'So what happened to him?'

'Carlton? If it's Tuesday night he's at The Crow. Do you know him? Oh. Sorry. You mean Barker.'

Cheryl sat back and wondered what the hell to tell her. She didn't really know Barsia, nor how well she'd known Barker.

'So, you didn't hear?' Cheryl deflected, as though it was nothing much. As though, you know, nothing at all; everyone's over that now.

'I heard there was something.'

'But not what?'

'No. I just heard that it was something... *awful*...?' Cheryl said nothing, but she smiled, tightly. Barsia shrugged. 'And you really work for him?' She asked as though that in itself was incredible. 'I mean, I never thought he'd run a real business or anything...? Or, you know, have people *work for him?*'

'Really?' Cheryl wasn't sure how to take that.

'No! He just wasn't the type. He was all, like, well-dressed and everything, but such a...'

Cheryl hated hearing about this sort of thing. Barker was like a brother.

'...such a wild, unrestrained spirit!' The woman leaned forward over the black laminate of the sticky-looking square table. 'I can't imagine anything happening to him!' Then she gasped and leaned even more forward. Cheryl wanted to warn her; she was sure there had been beer spilled on the table that hadn't been properly wiped down. 'What happened to him? It wasn't... bad, was it? Like; *bad, bad?*'

Cheryl wondered how much this woman knew about Barker. 'You haven't seen him for, what? Twelve years?'

The woman just kept staring.

'Well, no...' Cheryl allowed Barsia, at length. 'It was... *kind* of bad. But, not *bad*, like what you're thinking.'

'No?'

'No. He had… sort of… an accident.'

'*That is what I was thinking!*'

'No, that's not what I meant; not like that.'

'Oh my God…' Barsia leaned forward again then spoke in a low tone. '…is he… okay?'

'Barsia, how well did you know Barker?'

'We… went out. A few times. He didn't get *scarred* did he? In the accident?'

'Not physically, no.'

'Oh…' Barsia sighed, relieved. 'Good. Because, he's, y'know…'

Barsia waved her hand around her face, smiled and raised an eyebrow.

'Yes…' Cheryl nodded reluctantly. 'I've known him a long time, and I guess I forget sometimes. But yes, he is very handsome.'

'And his body, oh my God!'

'I…' Thinking about Barker like that actually made her feel a little unwell.

'I mean, it's *amazing*…'

Cheryl sighed. 'Well…' She never knew how far to go, what to tell people. 'It's actually a curse, really.'

Barsia gasped. 'Well, of course. I mean, he must have to work out, I mean; what? Four hours every day?'

'No, I mean, an *actual* curse.'

'Oh, don't get me started Cheryl. I've known fitness freaks before. Oh, I wish I could stop! I wish I didn't have to look so hot! I wish I could just totally not want this gorgeously toned body anymore! Wah-wah-wah. Sure, cry me a river. But bend over for me, just a little more, while I'm practising my ping pong stroke off your Michelangelo-marble butt.'

Cheryl stared at her. Didn't want to hear it. Okay.

'And you two aren't…?'

'Me and Barker? No, we're not.'

'*How could you not?*'

Cheryl shrugged. 'One of those things. I know him too well.

He's like my brother.'

'Oh yeah. I know that. I've had that.' The memory seemed to calm her down. 'So where is he? Is he in Adelaide again? He was heading out, that last time.'

Yes, Cheryl thought to herself, her dry inner monologue rising up.

He is in Adelaide, and so am I.

He came over here, and I came with him.

I get him work, he does the work, he cuts me in.

That's the rub. And as soon as he's done what he came here to do, I'm going to go back with him, and getting out of this suburban hell-hole where they don't have any big musicals, or anything to do really at all, except fish around to get Barker another job while he builds up the courage to go and see – her. You know it Cheryl. You know that's what he's doing here. You know there's no other reason he would come back here.

'Yes, he's here. So you dated a while?'

'He seemed... so tormented. I was living in the Riverland back then. I mean, he was just passing through, but you could tell he was troubled. I was attracted to troubled men, back then. He was reading Tarot cards and traveling. He said it paid his way, because he was real and the others were fakes. I always wondered what he meant by that. It's so funny that we should meet and you should mention his name.'

'Not like there's more than one Barker Moon.'

Cheryl had put the word out the day they'd arrived.

That there was a proper psychic for hire.

Since then, there had been a few calls, and she'd passed the information on to Barker. Barker had accepted most of the jobs. He'd retrieved a couple of lost dogs, sorted out a couple of infidelities gone more wrong than usual, cleaned a recently purchased hundred-and-fifty-year-old brewery with surprisingly little supernatural activity, and tracked down a couple of curse sources. Nothing any well-practised, low-level sorcerer couldn't manage.

'To tell you the truth…' Oh God. Barsia was going to make a confession. 'I thought it might have been a made-up name.'

'Oh. Well, no. It's not,' Cheryl smiled. 'He gets that all the time.'

'So… he was scarred…?'

A waitress appeared suddenly.

'Sorry.' She was completely insincere as she wiped down the table. 'Can I get you ladies anything?'

'Large latte thanks,' Cheryl smiled.

Barsia nodded. 'Mocha decaf…?'

The waitress smiled again and departed.

'Scarred…' Barsia tapped the side of her head. '…upstairs?'

Cheryl sighed. 'How long ago did you meet him?'

'I was twenty… so I suppose, eight years ago?'

'He won't remember you.'

Barsia's pretty eyes widened. 'Oh really? I think he might…'

'No, no, I'm sure he *would* remember you… if he didn't have amnesia.'

'That memory thing?'

'The accident happened to him about seven years ago. If you met him before then, he won't remember. Or he might, but he won't remember anything about why he knows you.'

'Really? But; how long have you known him?'

'Longer than that. He remembers me, and his family, and other people he's known a long time. But, nothing specific. And certainly nothing he learned as a sss-…' How much did Barsia know, really? '…ssstudent. At university. Was that how you met, Barsia? At university? Or did he just… read your cards?'

'No, I told you. I was up in the Riverland. He said I should go to uni. Come to think of it, that's how I ended up here. I hadn't thought of it before. Nobody had ever suggested anything other than… retail. He just read my cards, told me to go study. And… you know. There was the weekend. A long weekend.' She sighed. 'I knew he wouldn't stay. I knew he was passing through. But then, after that, I knew I was leaving too.'

Cheryl smiled. Classic Barker. Old Barker.

'He said that he usually only did readings by appointment, friend-to-friend sort of thing...' Barsia smiled. '...ummm, word of mouth?'

'He still is. I'm kind of his unofficial manager.'

'But sometimes he bumps into people who need him...?'

'That's right. Or I do. Which brings me to...?'

Cheryl slipped her Cintiq pen from her Galaxy Note and raised her eyebrows expectantly, prepared for anything. The really pretty ones quite often had no idea how much danger they were in. Just the way things went sometimes.

'Still...' Barsia probed, ignoring both the device and Cheryl's promt. '...I'm sure he would remember *me*.'

'No, really. I've known him a long time, and he remembers that. He knows I am his oldest friend, just about. But he doesn't remember any actual details about our friendship, not until seven years ago. Everything before the accident is a blur. I didn't think it was even going to be that. It took him three weeks to recognize me after the accident.'

'Oh?'

Barsia went quiet and stared over Cheryl's shoulder.

The ever-present jingling of the thousands of poker machines, just a few rooms away, was distracting in the worst way, and Barsia was taking in everything she'd just heard. Still, it was getting late, a stronger than usual chill seemed to be settling in, and Cheryl was getting anxious. She wanted to call Barker again. Preferably to see him. Tell him forty-five minutes, not ninety. She had a weird feeling about Angela Lorre, and the Lion and Unicorn. Barker would be there now. He'd be doing it now.

Hurry up, something's not right.

Since Barker had asked her to come back to Adelaide with him, some six weeks ago now, they'd been staying at his mother's empty beachfront apartment, down at Glenelg. They'd never really lived together, but Cheryl had commandeered his mother's main bedroom on the top floor of three, Barker had gladly accepted the spare room on the second, and they had quite peacefully shared the classic open-plan kitchen-living area on the ground. Sometimes they hung out. Sometimes they had their own thing going on. Both had agreed not to bring people home.

They both liked watching serials, but when they went out Barker went to the movies, or to see spoken word, stand-up or lectures, whereas Cheryl preferred live music or theatre. But they always co-ordinated if they could, and she knew that if she could nail this Barsia booking and call Barker in time, she could hitch a ride back home to the apartment on the back of Bach...

Great, now she was doing it too...

...as Barker passed through the city.

They could get some dinner from the local fish and chip shop before it closed, sit on the balcony and talk about...

He had to have felt it, right?

Since last weekend, something had been...

Cheryl checked Barsia. It had been more than a few seconds now and she was still checked out to the jingle-jangle. Processing. She lit a cigarette. Barsia just kept staring out, past the unisex toilet, down the corridor that led to the cathedral of machines. Then she sat back a bit, without moving her eyes, still transfixed, as though unconsciously shifting away from the pungent blue-grey sliver of toxins.

Cheryl really wanted these to be her last cigarettes. It might have been a malevolently concocted trap for compulsive gamblers, but this bar was, amongst other things, one of the last places you could still go and have a drink, or a coffee, and smoke while sitting down at a table.

But what had they done?

They'd done something.

You could enter and not be far-seen, or remote viewed, or detected in any kind of supernatural, psychic, or metaphysical way. At least, not that she'd found, and she'd asked several trusted souls who were very well-practised at such things to try and find her, psychically, while she'd been here. That really did make it the perfect place to meet clients with metaphysical concerns. If you had a problem with a witch, sorcerer, demon or angel; whatever, they would not be able to tell you were plotting against them while you were within the walls of the World Casino. She didn't know who else knew; didn't know if Barker had already known, given his past association with this place, or if the block was deliberate, accidental or what. She might have asked Emerald. There was no bad blood between them after all, and Emerald had to know that she was here, using the bar to meet clients. Emerald was brilliant; she would have sniffed that out in a minute flat. But she hadn't asked Emerald; the block, the bar, was too useful to risk losing, assuming Emerald was prepared to let it go, so long as Cheryl did not draw attention to herself. And besides, she and Barker would be gone before long, and then it wouldn't matter. By then, most likely, one of the people she'd asked to test the theory for her would have twigged, and then word would get out, and everyone and their wolves would be here.

The flipside of course was that it was a depressing, soulless place, and more than twenty minutes spent here was an energy-depleting, if not a completely exhausting experience that lingered long into the next day like a hangover. Maybe that had something to do with the metaphysical and supernatural not working here, but at least this bar was endurable for perhaps half an hour longer, almost certainly because it was open to the sky. There was still an inescapable funk though, like the whole building existed within a space that had been hollowed out from rot, and the space within cauterized against something fetid and dank that had continued to rot, unabated, just outside its perimeters.

She hated walking through the main arena to get up here; that was the most exhausting part, she had come to realize after... was it six, or seven client meetings now? And she still had to get back out, tonight. She had a secret relating to that, a trick she had often employed in the newer dark places, similar to the one she had employed with the walls in the bathroom. But...

35

tonight it felt like she would have to walk back the six kilometres to Glenelg, not just down two flights, across two gambling floors and outside, just to get home.

She looked across at Barsia again, who was still oblivious to all of this. She knew though that this woman was remembering her fling with Barker, how hot and amazing it had no doubt been, with his supernaturally toned body and easy-going charm. Right now, she would be wondering what it was that was keeping them apart. Maybe it was her; maybe it was Cheryl? A lot of the really pretty ones thought like this; competitive, desirous, covetous.

Cheryl wasn't any of those things; not for Barker anyway. And she was sure that Barker was not interested in reviving old flames. Not even one as dark, and pretty, and well-turned-out as Barsia Swaine. She was so Barker's type, ten years ago. Barsia would have been a pretty kid he could have impressed with real sorcery, but could rest assured would vanish like a banished spirit once she caught wind of the *really* real.

Just the way Barker had liked it back then.

Distance.

Yes, Barsia was Barker's type back then.

Before the corporate witch.

Before Emerald.

Barsia suddenly turned, refocussed, and started talking.

'Well, it's delicate.'

'That's okay. We're very discrete.'

Barsia sighed. 'Well, I have this boyfriend…'

Cheryl groaned inwardly. Of course you do.

'And, sometimes… not very often, I go out with the girls and we have a bit of fun. Sometimes, a bit too much fun, if you know what I mean…'

Cheryl was tired. 'You like to sleep with someone else every now and then?'

Barsia made a pouty face. 'It's not like we're married or anything. I wouldn't if we were, I mean, I *believe* in marriage and all that, but we're not; and it's not very often…'

I don't care, Cheryl wanted to say. *I assumed it was him, but it's you. In these cases it's always one or the other but somehow, when it's the girl, I think you're letting down the cause. Not that anyone really knows what the cause is any more. There are as many versions and interpretations of the cause as there are women, and people. So just fucking tell me, Barsia, so I can get out of here, out of the cold, and go home to my batter, lemon juice and tartare sauce...*

'Did he do something to you?'

'He drew on me. Here...' Barsia touched her jacket lapel about her left breast. 'He said it would come off, and I was so drunk...' She laughed uneasily and rolled her eyes. '...but when I woke in the morning, it wouldn't come off in the shower. And the tattoo guy I went to said it's not a tattoo, and then my doctor wouldn't believe that it isn't. He thinks I'm in denial or something.'

Please tell me this isn't just a dumb hot chick who got a tat on a girl's night and thinks the reason it won't come off is something to do with magic, Jesus please.

'The thing is...' Barsia lowered her voice now. '...ever since he drew it on me, I'm just horny. Horny, horny, horny. All the time. I mean, I'm horny now.'

'Really?'

'No, I mean, no, not like that. Oh! Are you gay?'

'No, I meant...'

'I mean, you're really cute, for sure, and I have a friend who's looking, and you would be – '

'No, no. I have enough men... I mean, enough trouble with the men in my life as it is; I mean, enough *to deal with*, without introducing the idea of dating women as well, on top of men, or a man, or a *relationship*...of any kind... I mean, *Jesus*, who has the time anymore?' Cheryl took a deep breath. 'I mean, no, thanks Barsia. But really, no.'

Barsia shrugged. 'Okay. No worries. So; this guy? When I am horny, and like I said, *horny all the time*, I just think of him. And only him.'

Cheryl couldn't help herself. 'You think I'm *really cute?*'

Barsia was slightly surprised. 'Yeah. I mean; of course. My friend, she would, for sure.'

'What about me is…?' Cheryl caught herself. Barsia stared at her curiously. It made Cheryl think that there was some quality about herself, about her looks, that she hadn't seen, or realized yet. Then Barsia looked her up and down. Cheryl was surprised. Barsia's gaze was judgmental, clearly, but she was not mean.

'You're not the first psychic I've seen.'

'I'm not…?'

'But I think, you probably have a killer body under all those rock and roll gypsy clothes. Am I right?'

'Rock and roll…?' Cheryl let out a massive sigh of frustration. 'Really? I was trying to get away from that! I mean, that was exactly what I *wasn't*… fuck!'

'You sort of… almost have. But I think…' Barsia was checking out her bust, then her shoulders. '…you've been in that look too long to, like, simply, *adjust it* and make the most of it… you know?' She was looking at her bust again; or what she could make of it under the three layers of pseudo-rock-gypsy layers, then at her hair, which was shoulder length, thick, and light biscuit-brown. It had always been her best feature; lush with a natural shine. '…I think you have the look of someone who needs a completely new look.'

It was as though the universe had spoken.

Cheryl sat back.

'I do, don't I?'

'The other psychics I've seen; they don't look messy anymore.'

'Messy?'

'I'll give you a number.'

'You will?'

'I have a friend.'

'You do?'

'I saw her downstairs when I came in. She said she'd be here a while.'

Cheryl suddenly felt a little ill-at-ease.

'Who is she?'

'She's like you, but older.'

'Like me?'

'Not older. A different generation.'

'A different…?'

'She was the one who told me to come and see you.'

'She told you about me…?'

'She does astrological charts. Huge ones for your whole life. She tells you where the ley lines are, and the energy lines, and what places on the planet are the best for your lifetime, and when you'll have ups and downs. And they totally work. I had mine done three years ago. This was supposed to be a dark period.'

Cheryl nodded. 'I think I know who that is…'

'No. She said she'd never met you.'

'It's not an old woman named Freyanna?'

'No. It's a friend of my Mum's, called Shirley.'

'Okay.' Cheryl stared at Barsia for a few seconds. Very pretty. There was no indication at all that she might be something other than…

'Okay!' Barsia threw up her hands. 'So, back to business?'

'Okay!' Cheryl threw up her hands as well.

Maybe Barsia was crazy?

'So, this guy I shagged…?' Barsia proceeded in a weird tone that suggested the other part of the conversation was anything but over. 'He had this weird red sharpie, with a feather tied to it. Like, in the old days.'

'Like a quill?'

'Yes! I knew it started with a 'q'! A quill!'

'A quill? Really?'

'Yeah. And afterwards, now, I keep bumping into him all the time. At the supermarket, outside work, even once at the end of my street.'

'But what does your boyfriend say?'

'I told him it's fake, that it will wash off in a week or so. Like, I just wanted to see what one would look like. He hates it, and it's not even starting to fade.'

'Okay.'

'I see him. Here and there. Almost every day now. I just go out and there he is. Sometimes I walk around for an hour before I see him. And he walks past me in the street while I'm window shopping, and I try not to follow him, but I can't resist. Like, really can't resist. And we just end up pashing in the back corner of a lounge discounters, or making out in the back row of a computer store. I let him cop a feel, and one time in Myers I pulled his dick right of out his pants and…' She kind of looked a bit scared now. '…now I say it out loud… I don't even like him. I mean, sober, he's not even my *type*. I mean, I've been through that kind of passionate fling before… well, three times actually…'

'Three times?'

'Well… yeah.'

'Okay…'

'…and this isn't like that.'

Cheryl didn't like this at all. None of it, but the supernatural stalker most of all.

'Barsia, you haven't told anyone else about this have you?'

Barsia shook her head.

'I told Shirley I thought I'd been… cursed, maybe? And she gave me your number, and said you'd help.'

It was clear that verbalizing Barsia's experience had brought it into terrible focus for her; that suddenly magic was real, and that nasty people could employ it. Had employed it. On her.

'This is… like, more than a curse, isn't it? It's like I'm marked or branded or possessed or something, right? Really possessed. I mean, I'm sneaking out, but… not in that nice way, that exciting way, where you can't wait to sneak out and see them and nobody else knows…'

Cheryl looked at her, tried not to judge her. Barsia continued.

'This is different. It's sneaking around… in a *weird way*. In a nasty way. Not good nasty. Nasty nasty. And I know that if I don't stop it, we'll end up doing it again… it's all I can manage to tear myself away before it starts getting…' Barsia smiled uncomfortably. '…y'know, really heavy…'

Cheryl was scribbling on the Cintiq to avoid meeting her eye. 'You haven't actually had sex with him again?'

'No, no, and I don't want to. But I keep going to him! I find excuses to go out. He's like a magnet; he finds me wherever I am! But the scariest thing is this; if we do, if I let that happen, I know there won't be anything else to do but stay with him. I just know it. Stay forever, and never leave him.'

She'd seen this before. She could tell Barker in one word what it was, and he would know exactly what to do. But she still kept scribbling mindless spirals, so that she wouldn't have to llift her gaze and look Barsia in the eye.

Mother Goddess, there were some real creeps around.

Cheryl looked up.

And there it was. The viJlated look.

Cheryl gulped. 'Three hundred bucks, before I go on. We can force you to secrecy, if we do proceed, but we prefer not to. Your word is enough.'

'Yes.' Barsia's voice was breaking as tears formed. 'I can afford that.'

'You have what's called a reetree. The symbol over your heart, is it like this?'

Cheryl deleted her spirals and went to draw the reetree on the screen, but thought better. She went to her coat and took out the magic marker she carried around, and drew the symbol on a napkin.

'That's it,' Barsia confirmed.

Cheryl lit another cigarette, then used the lighter to burn the napkin in the ashtray. A wind passed over them after the paper started to fire up, but seeing as they were two of only eight patrons, and the others were all staring up at the sports screens as though their lives depended on the results, no-one saw.

'Primal urges are the easiest to manipulate. Basically what he's done is the equivalent of a love potion that works with your guilt and self-loathing.'

'My...?'

'We can get it removed in no time. I could do it myself, but it's better if it's removed by a bloke. In a way it's better that you've had past involvement with Barker, because... well, you don't need to know about all that. There are equations, and that will help balance things in your favour. I don't really know that I get it myself.' That was a lie; she understood it perfectly. But sometimes people had a reaction at this point and bailed. It was better, as Barker's agent, that she maintained the mystique from here. She held up the screen again.

'Is this your number?'

'Ummm. Yeah.'

Cheryl went to work.

'I just texted you my account details. If you can transfer half the fee up front, I can book you an appointment now.'

'Ummm... okay.'

Barsia didn't seem to hesitate as her colourful nails flickered over her iPhone.

Barsia was a bit younger, but Cheryl was an eighties child and a nineties teen; old enough to still find the tiny computers everyone carried around more magical than magic itself. Magic had always been there; these hadn't.

'Done.'

'Okay. Thanks. We're for real, this will work. You'll need to be in your own home, alone. Three in the afternoon is a good time to do this. I don't know what day, specifically. Sometimes Barker's work tires him out and he needs a day. I'll call you one morning later this week; can you get away from work and be in your home at three PM?'

'I run my own shop.'

'If we don't call back, wait. It just means some other job's taking more time. You're third in the queue.'

The SIM she was using was specifically for Adelaide jobs. Different numbers for different cities could make tracing either easier or more difficult, if things got weird. Considering her line of work, it was surprising how seldom things did.

'We're good people, we'll get back as soon as we can.'

'Okay.'

Barsia looked around as she collected herself, preparing to leave with her life, in some way she couldn't fully yet understand, somehow completely changed.

'You're clever.'

'Huh?'

'This is the least magical place in town. I get it.'

Cheryl smiled. Barsia smiled back, tightly.

'Barker. He must be nearly forty by now?'

'Mid-thirties. We all grew up together. He trusts me. Will you trust me, Barsia? He's not the man he used to be. But he absolutely will help you with the stalker.'

Barsia nodded and stood. Then she leaned down and touched the back of Cheryl's hand.

'I want to help you somehow.'

'Help me? But...?'

She spun Cheryl's phone around and had the pen out, like magic. She was maybe ten years younger, a nineties child, a millennial teen; not born with one of these in her hand, but educated with one in sight.

'I'm sure she'll still be downstairs.'

'Your friend? But I don't need my chart done. I have more than enough – '

'It's not for the astrological chart. She's a consultant too. Do I look good to you?'

Cheryl looked her up and down.

'You look amazing.'

'That's what she does. She looks at your chart, sees who you're meant to be, and dresses you like you're meant to be now. Not, like, a kind of pale imitation of how you were supposed to be ten years ago.'

'Is that how you think I look?'

'Isn't it how you think you look? Honestly?'

Cheryl wasn't sure what to say.

'Listen to me, Cheryl Equinox.' The smile was earnest, but it looked as though she was going to cry the instant she left her sight, and stay home crying until Barker showed up and fixed her. 'Call Shirley. She's downstairs. Tell her it was me.'

She spun the phone back around.

Underneath the phone number, she'd written; *Lightwork Fashion. Shirley. Bars sent me.*

'Tell her you're up here. And when you come to see me, I want to see a new you.'

Barsia smiled at her. Then she smiled broadly, tears already forming, and departed quickly, for which Cheryl was grateful.

She called Barker but he didn't answer.

It was past nine in midwinter, long since dark already. If she'd missed Barker, at least the remnants of the old Adelaide Railway Station were still underneath her here, underneath the World Casino, and she could get a train from there back down to the beach; Brighton or Seacliff or somewhere, and walk back to Glenelg. There were buses too; that was easy in Adelaide. Buses in Adelaide were like trams in Melbourne or trains in Sydney. Even at night, there was at least one every hour to wherever you needed to go.

She found that her hands were restlessly juggling the phone.

Then she found that she was looking at Barsia's message.

She didn't even really realize that she had entered all the digits and pressed 'call', until she found that she was disappointed to get a message bank.

'This is Shirley Swansong. Leave a message.'

'Hello. This is Cheryl Equinox. I'm upstairs. Bars sent me. She said we should talk. About... I think... a makeover? Text me if you want me to come down, or, I'm up here at the Aces High bar. On the roof. I'm expecting someone in about... thirty minutes? If you get this message, before then... Or, look... I'm sure we can catch up some other time. Thanks.'

She hung up.

She thought about Barsia as she waited in the cold for Barker or Shirley Swansong to call back.

It was a weird business. It wasn't always the victim who hired them. Sometimes it would be a practitioner whose spell had gone wrong, the victim completely unaware. Sometimes an anonymous request and accompanying cheque, or sometimes a tip.

Like yesterday.

Angela Lorre had told her about The Lion and Unicorn. A friend of a friend she'd forgotten she had, practicing in a coven she'd never heard of. Strange that; that only now did it seem...

And the story. The owner was so bummed out about losing his cat that some presence had managed to ingratiate itself into the hotel and feed off his despair...

The customers were so depressed by the aura it was spreading that trade had gone dead...

Like she'd told him, Barker would only have to walk in the door.

Little spooks like that didn't take much warning.

But for some reason, now, it all sounded like... complete bullshit.

She stared at her phone.

He'd only have to walk in the door...

Had Angela said that?

Why had she said that?

Maybe because Barker's reputation preceded him. Back in 'the day', Barker had faced all sorts of things, bigger and madder and more powerful.

But this was not 'the day'.

Now, Barker was just okay.

Just an ordinary sorcerer.

Good for the three to six hundred dollar runs, but nothing more. Good for breaking simple spells and curses, good for a few psychic scans... good.

But she'd known Barker back then. Before the accident, before the amnesia. She'd seen him open portals and banish demons. Real demons. Not the guys in rubber masks from the telly. Sure, some of them had taken human, or semi-human form. But real demons were fucking scary. They didn't sit in bars, or congregate in secret societies, or serve as neat metaphors for the disenfranchised or cultural minorities. Real demons, it was all you could do to stop yourself pissing in your pants when they were even in the next building.

That Barker... he'd been the best.

A natural with the supernatural.

Seven years ago, he'd scared everything.

Except for one.

Except for whatever the hell it had been, at Bridger Mansion.

THREE:
CLEM AND BOB AND BAZZA
AND JAN

I

Barker listened as the connection scrambled, then cut out as the thunder repeated.

Three times a charm.

Bach idled down the street and turned right, down a steep gravel drive that led beneath the city-facing hotel balcony. He saw that the wide car park had another access route, in from Nightmare, opposite this one. Nightmare passed at forty-five degrees and the short, dirt road in looked weather worn, like a natural run-off, eroded into the earth by heavy rainwater, as much as it did an actual, deliberate access route. There was even a catchment and water tank, down the hill on the other side.

There were traps for new players everywhere, Barker recognized, even in the car park. Blind spots, weird angles, high speed, metal, glass and flesh. But from here he could see that the balcony surely did hold a spectacular view of the giant Adelaide plain and the forty-kilometre expanse of city and suburbia within it.

After all, what good was a trap for falling into, without a decent distraction?

Bach parked herself.

There were only two other vehicles. The landlord and a customer, Barker surmised as he dismounted. He pulled off the black and lime green leather gloves and stuffed them into the soft innards of the matching helmet. Sometimes he carried it, but tonight he secured the helmet to the back of the bike. The black bike with bright lime green streaks.

He looked up. The fog had descended past the intersection, over the hotel roof, and was lingering just under the balcony. To his immediate right there was an entrance to a front bar, and some permanent tables and benches along the front of the lower section, but it was dark inside, and all locked up. He'd seen illumination upon his approach but it had all come from above, in the larger of the two bars, leading in from the street.

Gravel crunched under Barker's off-the-rack black runners as he walked into the fog, back up the gravel drive, and onto Warren Road again. There was an absurdly thin footpath that led to the hotel entrance. Logic, and a flash of memory, suggested that this was the front bar. The lounge bar being closed… that seemed pretty good work for a feeder, especially with the beautiful view that would surely keep people coming for sunsets and dinner, no matter what. And it was odd, too. Dark feeders needed people. It needed them to be miserable, to have a bad time. Dark. So they could feed. Hence the name. An empty bar was no good to them.

Barker paused now, once again on the edge of the foggy, five-fold death trap. Standing this time, no bike, no helmet. Thunder rumbled, and it was becoming very cold all of a sudden.

A guru had once told him, in relation to meditation, that one must always pass through the front door before one can enter, more leisurely, though the back. Know the road before you take the shortcut, Barker had thought. He'd since begun to interpret the advice in another way as well; know who's at home before you enter uninvited. Some echo of the notion had always remained with him in regard to hotels, and places of accommodation or hospitality.

He assessed the mad intersection. Up close now, he saw, as he knew he would, three separate memorial wreaths. Seven years ago, he said to the victims, I could have done more than chase away feeders. I could have told you who you were, and how it happened. Maybe even why, why this had been part of your longer journey, for the shorter one to end here, so abruptly, so painfully.

Seven years ago, I could have…

Exactly.

Could have.

He pushed the heavy oak, and entered through the front door.

II

Clem knew that his anxious look had been spotted by the newcomer.

What the hell.

One other customer on a dead Friday night, what was to hide?

The stranger looked at him, and looked at Bob. Bob was so quiet these days, Clem had almost forgotten he was there, sitting in his regular stool. He stared back at the newcomer, in the way a well-domesticated dog would become alert to a stranger entering his house.

The newcomer was not a biker. That much was immediately apparent. Clem sighed. He didn't know whether to be relieved or not. If a gang moved in, he might at least make some quick cash.

Tall, dark and handsome. Another cliché.

Strikingly good-looking, in fact, but a bit dark around the eyes; the bone structure of a soap actor. Which was why, after a few more seconds, Clem realized there was something odd about him. Odd, if not wrong. The man's thick, dark brown hair was too long to be fashionable. It was swept back but uncut. At least, it hadn't been cut for a while. Men who looked like this almost always had hair, with a style, and product. His shoes and his jeans were cheap, and old; the brands generic, the blue denim too light, too faded, the cut too unflattering. These were the garments of a working class stiff; all off-the-rack at K-Mart. The old grey jumper looked okay, almost deliberate, but the old black tee underneath probably doubled as the pyjamas he'd woken in this afternoon, and the round neck didn't suit the sharper angles of his chin and jawline. The only thing that half worked was a long black wool coat; which was decent, classy. Was someone else dressing him? Or no-one else? Was he a recovering junkie from an outreach program, dressed in whatever mix he'd dug out of a Goodwill store? Lucked upon the coat? No. Too well-fed. A depressive? Perhaps. Had he been riding in The Hills like this? In that outfit? Unprotected?

Something had happened to this bloke.

This was a man who no longer knew who he was.

'Evening…' The man seemed friendly enough as he eyed a barstool, gently swept the coat tails aside and sat, like any other bloke. 'Coffee machine working?'

Clem shrugged. What the hell. Something to do.

'Sure. I was just gonna have one m'self.'

Curious, Clem thought. The voice didn't suit him. He was a bit gruff, vocally. Deep, but not particularly so. But he had the voice of a commander, a good leader. With the body of an actor… the way he carried himself, there was tone under the outfit. Muscle and physique. But the clothes? Maybe he was an actor? He wouldn't know any more, hadn't followed any of that stuff for years. One of those ones who went off the rails every now and then, went native in whatever city it happened. There were always a few of them, at any given time.

The customer sat a few stools down from Bob.

Bob had not taken his eyes off him.

'Heard your bike,' Clem said as he hit the buttons to make the machine start. People drank coffee in pubs these days. Coffee and soft drinks and water. Times were changing. He'd like to change with them. Serve lolly water, and just water, at five bucks a bottle.

'Espresso?'

'Latte thanks. Mug if you've got one.'

'To go?'

'No… I'll have it here.'

Clem nodded. That was okay. Bob was ignoring them. He could talk to this guy. Get his story. Like he used to. Size 'em up as they came in, see how much he'd guessed right.

'Was that a BMW I heard pull up?'

'Yeah.' The customer shrugged. 'Was that a guess?'

'I knew a bit about bikes. A while back. They're good bikes. Reliable.'

'I don't have anything to compare this one with. Someone left it to me.'

'Lucky you. They purr, the Beamers.'

'I think they were killed on it. At least…someone was.'

The customer gave him a strange look, then started to shift a bit, to look around; taking the place in, seeing where he'd ended up tonight.

Okay. A weird one. Weird ones always had trouble keeping jobs. Making money. Mystics, creatives, savants. Making and then keeping money seemed impossible for most of them. No matter how good looking, they needed someone. So; this guy's someone was buying his clothes for him on a low income. So if he was a weird one, had he come here to try and…? Wait. What?

'Someone was killed on a bike, and left it to you?'

'I think so. I'm not sure. The thing is, it's new. Just a few months. But the thing that came with it… isn't.'

Clem stared. What the fuck did that mean?

The customer smiled. It was a very charming smile.

'I'm sorry. I weirded you out. I forget myself sometimes. I haven't been myself lately. Well, years. So I'm told. No sugar by the way…'

The machine was essentially push-button. The steam was starting. You could do the milk yourself… but Clem hit the button for it to do it automatically. Suddenly he didn't feel like turning his back. When he looked back, the customer had turned from him. Suddenly Clem found himself caring what this new, odd character thought. But he knew what he would be thinking. It was what Clem himself would be thinking, what anyone with a bit of awareness would be thinking, if they happened across this place and decided to take stock.

Rustic, was once very charming. Very old; back to the first

days of colonization. Tables, chairs, stools and a fireplace, all empty. Only one other customer. Barman, about fifty-five, weary looking, probably the landlord. A feeling about the place… no-one's making the effort here.

Something is wrong.

There is no apparent reason, this guy would be thinking, that this pub is not thriving.

Thunder rumbled again, close-by. They could hear all the glasses and bottles rattling on their shelves.

'Was there thunder before? Hard to tell on the bike…'

'Yeah…' Clem nodded. 'Has the fog come in?'

'Yeah… there was fog down to the balcony…'

'It's gunna rain,' Clem confirmed.

The thunder ceased abruptly.

But the glasses and bottles kept rattling. Clem watched the customer as he realized.

'That's not an earth tremor, is it?'

Clem didn't answer. The barstool, one down from him, lurched out from the bar with a fourfold, scraping squawk.

Two stools down, Bob groaned and slumped forward.

Both he and Clem knew; it was starting.

It always started with that one, that particular stool.

For some reason the customer didn't look at the stool that had moved by itself. Instead, he looked up. The feature lights above the bar hit his face, just as the thunder came again, as though suddenly right on top of the hotel…

Thirty-five, Clem guessed, but he'd seen more than most his age. And before long, Clem knew, the customer would be gone and he would never see that face again. Just like all the others.

Behind the bar, one of the fridge doors swung open and slammed by itself.

Bob threw Clem a look.

Oh no, said the look, weary yet afraid.

Oh no.

Not again.

Barker waved a finger at the coffee machine, acting as though nothing were happening.

This wasn't a feeder.

'I think that might be ready?'

The bartender quickly attended to the machine, then turned back. In his hands was a large mug of frothy latte. The barman placed it on the bar before Barker. He was trying to keep his hands from shaking; older hands but nimble still. The latte was perfect, though the froth trembled a little as well.

Okay.

This... really wasn't a feeder.

'Your name's Clem, right? Short for Clement?'

People's names were right at the front. Mostly, they wanted to tell you, wanted to be known. Naming something was the first line of defence, of separation, but also the first establishment of a shared reality.

'That's right. Did someone send you here? Are you with the creditors?'

'No... but yes, I was sent here. On a false pretence, it seems.' Barker clearly picked up a residual thought; *he speaks too well for someone who dresses cheaply.* 'Clem, you don't own cat, do you? I mean; you didn't own one, and then lose one, did you?'

'No. Not a cat. I was thinking about getting a pub dog. Until... I didn't.'

'Your pub is haunted, isn't it?'

Barker watched Clem's face change.

'Oh...' Clem grunted. 'I guessed, when you said about your bike. You're one of them, aren't ya?'

Barker smiled to himself.

'I...'

He decided to try something and shifted slightly, reaching out to his side, stretching his open palm down over the stool that had moved. He let his hand hover.

He'd tried doing this a few times since he'd lost his memory, and his powers. It had been so many years since there had been any kind of response, or reaction, that he'd stopped. But tonight…

He was really assessing.

Was he really…?

Yes, yes he was.

He could feel it again.

Then it was totally obvious; that this was the centre of it all. Right there. It was like a cold breeze blowing into his palm, where there was no breeze. No cold. Right into the centre of his hand, and up through it, out of the back of his hand. He'd done this before, felt this before. Known it before; a lot. But he hadn't been able to do it, not even remember how, in ages. Memory was like that; forgetting was like that. You took something away, or strayed from something, and it was as though, gradually, the knowing of it faded. But here he was, doing it again. Remembering it again. The echo of the forgotten; a phantom breeze, a temperatureless cold.

Seven years since…

The other customer, the weary one, growled. Actually growled at him, with a sneer, then continued to watch with a suspicious scowl. He was a regular. Anyone could see.

Barker leaned into the bar again as grasped at the handle of the mug.

Holy crap.

He was remembering.

After all this time in Sydney, reading cards, cleansing auras, half-pretending at clairvoyance…

As he took the mug of latte in his hand, the fridge doors started to open and close, slamming furiously, repeatedly and then in unison. Behind Clem the bottles on the spirit rack poured themselves out, simultaneously splashing vodka and brandy and bourbon and scotch all over the rear counter, then each empty bottle shattered as though a sharpshooter were taking target practice across the room. The other unattended barstools shot backwards across the bar, smashing into the tables and chairs, overturning some of them, then the chairs scattered independently of each other around the room, as though an enormous invisible child were having an almighty tantrum.

Then it stopped, and there was silence.

Even the wind outside seemed to have stopped.

Barker saw that the regular, Bob, had taken cover. He was crouched tightly with his back to the bar, his hands gripping his stool in front of him for protection. Clem had taken cover with his arms over the back of his head, face-down on the rubber matting behind the bar. It had been like a drill for them, well-practiced. He didn't blame them.

Barker however had forced himself to remain still throughout.

Appearances had to be maintained, after all.

Bob stood quickly and made a mad scramble for the front door, half-falling over himself, as Clem rose slowly to a stand.

'I'll fix it.'

Barker had made the statement squarely, deeply, with supreme confidence.

Bob stopped, statue still, his hand gripping the front door handle so tightly and with such a mad grimace that it might have been electrified.

Barker looked across the bar, stared Clem directly in the eyes.

'One thousand.'

Despite the deliberate intensity of his gaze, Clem made a scoffing sound.

This made Barker like him.

'You want your customers back, Clem?' Barker asked, more softly, but still confident. It was a total act, the confidence, but he could do that. He could act.

The glasses, those that remained, started to shake again.

Bob took a few steps back toward Barker, watching him, sneering a bit.

'We've had all sorts in here,' Clem told Barker. 'They all run.'

'I won't run.'

'A geologist, a kid who claimed to be psychic, and a heavy bird, with too much makeup, in a white fur cloak. Claimed to be a witch.'

'Freyanna.'

'Yeah. You know her?'

'I know her. She'd not very good. Not at this sort of thing anyway. I won't run, Clem.'

Clem proceeded regardless. '…a medieval fair wizard, a "real life" vampire, and a man from the brewery with a dowsing rod. Just to name a few.'

Barker nodded. 'And, they're just happy to let the place go? The brewery?'

'They don't own it. It's one of the last ones they don't own. Original family kept it for generations. Then another bloke, then me. No corporation wants a place like this. No corporation wants to fix it. Too many cracks, too many stairs. I own it, lock stock, for my sins.'

'And only a few more barrels left. Right?'

Clem smiled. Tight, sideways. 'You a mind reader?'

'Kind of. The mind talks to itself all the time. When the emotions are big, it's like you're shouting at yourself. You have an internal transmitter and an internal receiver. Some people are born with external receivers. External transmitters. It drives you mad.'

'It does?'

'Until you learn to decode it. Or someone teaches you. Two barrels. But you don't care because it's only Bob at night and two stoners in the afternoons and between them it's going to take a month to exhaust your supplies.'

'Those were my thoughts exactly as I had them.'

'I know.'

Clem reached down to a small freezer, removing a bottle of ice cold vodka, and swiped two shot glasses from the shelf as he turned back. He quickly poured himself one, then raised an enquiring eyebrow at Barker.

'I'm driving.'

He poured just the one.

At the front door, Bob remained glued to the door handle, still watching.

'Now...' Clem stated firmly. 'I have seen a few things since this started. Real things we're not supposed to think are real.'

Barker held his gaze but gave nothing.

'I've been up and down the United Kingdom on pub tours, private ones, landlord to landlord, side to side, top to bottom...' Clem leaned forward, on one elbow. 'And I've spoken to enough pub landlords in my time to know that there are only two kinds of haunted pubs...'

Barker smiled sideways and nodded slowly. 'The ones that attract punters...'

Clem nodded back. '...and the ones that keep 'em away.'

Barker smiled a little more, just a bit.

'One K, Clem. Up front.'

Clem nodded again. Barker could see. He was tired of all this. But beyond all that, what only Barker could sense was; he was still hanging on, still willing.

'You're the first weirdo, forgive the phrase, who hasn't opened with a song and dance number. Given me exactly what the movies make me think I wanna see.'

Barker smiled a bit more. He shrugged.

'Sometimes, it is like in the movies, Clem. Then, sometimes it's completely different. It can be as different by as many degrees as there are people, and things, and reasons to die and be angry, or stay and watch over. And that's just the ghosts.'

Clem shrugged. 'Sure mate. But, I'm gonna need to see... something.'

Barker nodded. 'A teaser.'

Clem nodded. 'Okay.'

Barker turned to Bob.

'Why are you still here?'

Clem turned to Bob as well.

'You won't do anything,' Bob responded.

Barker looked at him oddly and Bob knew straight away that he had misinterpreted the question.

'I don't mean; if you don't expect to see anything, why have you stayed here watching me. I mean, why do you still come here every night? You're the last evening customer. The last night time regular.'

It was a guess, but Barker knew he had the kid pegged.

Bob's reply was shaky with nerves. 'You're here.'

Barker returned to his latte.

'He's either an idiot...' Barker spoke softly, directly to Clem. '...or he's frightened out of his wits.'

'He's both...' Clem uttered.

'You don't know what's happening!' Bob cried, releasing the door handle and lurching another step toward Barker. Then he stood there, shaking.

Thunder rumbled again.

'Clem, beyond people shouting at themselves, I'm not great at reading minds. I'm told I never was.'

'What did you say your name...?'

'I didn't. But the big spell, Clem, that's my curse. Apparently, I made that a kind of going concern. Took on a lot, it seems. Focussed will and transformation. And in the end, apparently, I became quite good at bringing things through...'

'Bringing things though?'

'Apparently. And almost, *almost* as good, at *sending things back*...'

'Used to be?'

'I thought maybe I was meeting you tonight, in this place, near the end of my story, Clem. Sort of; this is what he does now, and he's okay with that, and... that's what he does, for the rest of his life. Fade to black, as I smile, bittersweet but self-resolved.'

'I know that feeling.'

'I'm okay with it, I suppose. I've met people like me, like that.'

'And we've all seen those movies.'

'Right. Most of them are pretty good, if you like that kind of thing. But now Clem, now, I'm starting to get that old feeling. The old feeling that you don't even remember you've lost. But when it comes back, it's like; ah – that's what I've been missing. Without even realizing you've been missing it. Because when it went, it went so suddenly, and so completely, that it left no trace of what it actually was. So you convince yourself... you never had it.'

Clem threw back his vodka.

'You know who I am, don't you Clem?'

'You're that guy. You used to live up here. Then the thing happened. At Bridger Mansion. All those people died. And you got off, then you left.'

'Clem; in a minute, you're going to go to the register, and with a few beeps, you're going to lift out the float tray and take out some notes. Ten hundreds. Then you're going to place them on the bar, just out of my reach. Just to let me know you have it, and to see if I go for it and try to do a runner. That's what you're thinking, anyway. It's part payment for the delivery guy tomorrow, but you've put him off so many times now... it won't make a difference. It's the last grand you have to throw at this place. And you will. You will throw it at this place. One way or another. Because when you've thrown that last grand down the toilet, you can say you did everything. Took every last loan, borrowed every last cent, and threw it all at this place. And then you can go. But if you go, and take that grand... it's tainted. It will always be the last grand you could have used, and it might have saved the place. It might have been the Miracle Money, the last grand gesture that the Pub Gods recognized. You want to walk out of here clean, with the fruit of the poisoned tree all rotting away at its roots. And nothing rotten in your pockets.'

Clem had grown pale as Barker had spoken. But now, suddenly, his cheeks flushed.

'Okay then.' Clem made the register beep. He lifted the tray and took out the float. Ten green Australian one hundred dollar notes. He placed them on the bar, just out of reach, as though daring Barker to take it, to ruin his story, his act. 'Fix this here and now, and you can have that grand. Don't fix it, and you, and me, and Bob walk out of here, I lock the door, and the rats can have it.'

Bob's voice trembled. 'Wha-what are the rats gonna do with a thousand bucks, Clem?'

'The place, Bob. The rats can have the place. Jesus…' Clem looked back at Barker. '…there's nothing to say the landlord has to go under with his pub…'

Barker could see that Clem was serious. He wasn't too old yet. He could walk out, and start again. Someone would give him something for the place, down the line. There was a sign on the wall behind him. It was Heritage Listed, couldn't be demolished. But he could, and would, walk out… and wait.

Barker chuckled shortly and stood, calm.

'Alright then. Let this be the day. The hour.'

'The end…'

'…or something else again?'

Clem smiled grimly, then nodded. He and Bob watched as Barker closed his eyes, folded his arms, took a deep breath and slowly released it. He knew the place to go, within. It was like remembering something from childhood. A dark room in an old relative's house. Somewhere haunted, in the middle of somewhere totally safe. Then he turned and stretched a hand toward the facing wall, between two of the old wood-framed windows, and opened his eyes.

There were framed photographs there, Barker saw.

Black and white and sepia prints of the hotel in the days gone by, of the horse-drawn cart ancestors. The crazy roads weren't their fault. They'd just done their best, negotiating The Hills;

found the path of least resistance, and followed each other until the recurring tracks had become roads.

Nobody's fault...

Then he let his power flow.

IV

A rough wind shook through the bar, despite the fact that Clem knew that no ordinary door or window had been opened to let it in. He was suddenly made sharply aware that he knew every inch of this place. How much he'd loved it when he'd first bought it. Enjoyed it over the years.

It had been so quick, the descent.

The old photos, the ones that had come with the place, fell to the floor. The glass smashed. Rain hit the roof with a sound like a dump truck unloading a mountain of stones. The lights went out and a weird succession of images illuminated the bar, shocking Clem to the spot. There was a face, a ghostly face, pale with sunken black eyes, half-familiar, centred within a whirlpool of eerie purple light. The pattern, like a satellite photo of a hurricane, spun about on the wall to where the sorcerer's hand was reaching, his long black coat flapping madly behind him, slapping the bar in the hurricane wind. The sorcerer stood resolute; eyes shut. Clem saw a fallen stool right itself and levitate, rising in mid-air. He saw glass shards spinning about like mad dragonflies. Clem snapped out of his paralysis and took cover as he heard the stool thud into something then everything stopped as the glass shards from the pictures smashed into the bar and fell all around him.

Then lights came back on.

The sorcerer was rising from the floor, just as Clem was. He was wincing, his coat ripped down his left arm, shoulder to elbow, where he held it across his chest. Then the rain stopped. It simply shut off again. There was a new sound now though. A hum, as though a ghostly rock band in the corner, the echo of the kind that had once played regularly here, had just kicked an amp up

61

to eleven.

'Lord strike me...' Clem uttered.

The bar was trashed, totally trashed, worse than ever.

'What happened?' Bob was still on the floor, his arms over his head, speaking into the carpet.

The sorcerer spoke.

'He's ready.'

'Who?' Bob looked up. There was wild panic in his eyes. 'Who's ready?'

'Your friend...' The sorcerer smiled. 'I brought him back through.'

Bob stood slowly, still shaking. '...my ...friend?'

'Your mate. He's been haunting this bar since he died, hanging around on the lower astral and refusing to leave until...' The sorcerer's shoulder drooped a bit and he huffed. '...it must be very frustrating. But anyway, I've opened a portal so he can communicate properly.'

'Bullshit!'

'Three weeks ago, your friend Barry Ridge left this bar in an extremely drunk and agitated state...'

The sorcerer cocked his head, as though listening.

'He says you called him Bazza.'

Suddenly a convert, Bob spun about to Clem.

'How could he know that!?'

Clem exchanged tired glances with the sorcerer.

'En route home...' The sorcerer seemed to listen some more, to the supernatural hum of the invisible amp. 'Bazza had a car accident. He made it half way home but ran the Warren lights, like he always did that late at night. But this time, he ran out of luck. He swerved to dodge a tow-truck but ran straight into a Stobie pole. He died straight away, but he died angry, with something on his mind. Before Bazza left this pub, you and he fought over... a matter of popular culture. Bazza wants you to know you were wrong.'

'I was not!'

Clem knew it was true, even as he heard himself exclaim, incredulously:

'Bazza? All this time, it's been Bazza's ghost wrecking my pub?'

The sorcerer turned to him.

He looked like shit now, not thirty but fifty, an old fifty, drained and exhausted.

'The timing didn't strike you...?'

Clem stammered. 'I... suppose... I...'

'Clem, I haven't done this for a very long time. I'm not sure how long the portal will remain open. So...' The sorcerer turned back to Bob. '...Bob, settle this matter as quickly as you can.' The sorcerer gestured to one last upright stool. 'He'll go peacefully, and I can get to a hospital to see if he didn't crack any of my ribs.'

Bob approached the stool, looking queasy.

'That was his regular spot... right?'

Bob gasped. 'Bazza? Is that you? Are you really a ghost?'

The sorcerer commanded him now.

'Bob! Bazza! Settle the matter! Lay your argument to rest, now and forever more!'

'Okay, Bazza...' Bob choked a little. 'You were right. I... I *bloody knew... I bloody knew you were right, mate!*'

The sorcerer cocked his ear. Clem got it now. He was somehow tuned in.

He could decode the music they were playing, through the amp from the other side.

Then the sorcerer guffawed.

'You're kidding...' He turned to Clem. 'Do you know what this is about? What they were arguing about?'

Clem just popped his mouth.

Bob continued, tearful now. 'You were right, Bazza! I'm sorry mate! Eve Plumb was never in *The Brady Bunch Variety Hour*. It was a different Jan, I know! I'm so sorry mate! I always knew! Dammit, it was a different Jan! *It was a different Jan!*'

63

Bob's body started shaking as tears of grief and shame and regret poured down his cheeks.

The sorcerer responded softly. 'He says thank you.'

Clem couldn't believe it. 'That's it?'

'He's satisfied.' The sorcerer shrugged. 'He says goodbye. He says you were a good mate, Bob.' He moved toward Bob and stood in front of him. There was compassion in his voice. 'His best mate.' The sorcerer placed a hand on Bob's shoulder. Bob's body sagged in stages, like a marionette having its strings cut one by one, as he started weeping hugely, until he was barely able to stand. Clem wondered if the sorcerer's hand on Bob's shoulder was propping him up. Or maybe, somehow, his hand was the one with the scissors, cutting the strings. Then the sorcerer looked up, sensing something.

'He's gone.'

The sorcerer removed his hand and Bob collapsed over Bazza's old bar stool, buried his face in his arms and continued to weep. The sorcerer smiled sympathetically, nodded and headed for the door.

Clem tried to say something, but couldn't find the words. Then the sorcerer turned back, just a few steps from the front door.

'Strange, right?'

Clem swallowed. 'Strangest thing I ever saw...'

'No; I mean – a husband of fifty years dies, the wife isn't haunted. A son loses the father he's fought with for twenty years, not a peep. Even children – they die young and have to cross over without their mothers. Not so much as a distant cry in the night.'

The sorcerer sighed, long and hard.

'But this kind of crap...'

Bob was still sobbing.

' – brings 'em back – *every damn time!*'

The sorcerer swung the front door back and a howling wind blew in, blew back his coat, then whistled and wailed through the front bar and down the stairs as the sorcerer exited.

Clem glanced at the bar.

The ten green notes were gone.

v

Clem ducked out through the back of the front bar, turned left and trotted down the private stairs, into the private hall on the lower level, right into the lower bar, coming out behind it, along the second bar, around the corner there, through the empty bar itself, and on to the main public entrance. The keys were in his hand and he fumbled with the lock, then turned the key as he hit the security codes.

The sorcerer was out there, by his Beamer bike.

He turned to see Clem rush out.

'Hey!'

The sorcerer held up both his hands.

'Clem, we agreed. That was a fair – '

'No, no that's okay. I mean; I know. It's like…' Clem frowned. '…that was real, wasn't it?'

'If that's what you want to call it.'

The sorcerer unfastened his helmet and took his gloves out. Clem was surprised at the bike. Its racing stripes were as bright green as the lights inside had been bright purple.

'I mean, *you're real*, aren't you?' Clem asked. 'A sorcerer? Like I saw in Ireland?'

'Yeah… I'm a sorcerer,' he told Clem.

Clem watched as the stranger raised the helmet over his head.

'At least…' The sorcerer paused, the helmet high, like a king awaiting coronation. '…I think.'

Clem watched him as he donned the helmet, started the bike and turned about the car park. He was still watching as he roared off down that terrible bendy road, back to the city.

'You… you *think*?'

FOUR:
THE CROW AND KINGFISHER

I

Carlton Craven knew that something bad was happening as soon as the woman had walked in. They'd shagged for a few weekends. What, a year ago now? He was okay looking but she had been way out of his league. Not, way out. Just…

What was her name again?

Fff-fff…

Efff… faaa…

Hmmm.

Feff?

Or something. A few cold Saturday-into-Sundays, around this time last winter; three weekends in June-July.

She was a rich girl, you would say. Slumming it. Not necessarily with him, but certainly around this part of The Hills. He'd thought she'd been after a bit of rough, a bit of strange. Like, really strange. His kind of strange.

Occult strange.

And now here she was, at his front bar, a Pound and Silver lounge bar girl (especially since the renovation) drinking at the Crow and Kingfisher, flicking glances across the room at him.

Yes, this was bad.

Something bad was happening.

Why?

Why was she here? She had a boyfriend, didn't she? Wasn't he some kind of well-regarded local sports dick? Some sort of local wanker captain? Drank and worked out? Did she do this once a year? Was she looking for another working class bloke to have a fortnight's variety with, then drift back over the hill?

They'd been careful back then. Nothing had been said, but they'd both known that it had just been stomping out a fire; all her, her fire, his kindling. It had happened to him once or twice, some out-of-his-league local babe with a strange crush, and although he generally far-from-objected when it happened, he had never made a habit of looking for it, nor trying to maintain it when it came upon him. Carlton wasn't an adrenalin junkie by any means; she... he still couldn't remember her name... was going to get him beaten up or something. That's how those dudes rolled, wasn't it? Those local cricketers were fucking hardcore, mate.

Jesus Christ.

She was coming over.

'Carlton.'

'Look, I'm sorry I never called you.'

'No you're bloody not.'

He shrugged. 'I just... what?'

'You're okay Carlton, we like some of the same stuff, but it doesn't make up for how weird you are.'

She spoke well. He remembered now. Like, she was aware of every single word. Nothing she said had not been considered, composed and filtered; her tongue was as sharp as her eyelashes, her annunciation as refined as her cheekbones.

'What?'

'I'd just... I had always wondered. Since high school. What it would be like. We talked about that. Pillow talk. You had wondered as well. But this is not about that.'

There was something amazing, almost brazenly defiant, about somebody well-spoken who still had an Australian accent.

'Not about what...?'

'I am not here...' She stated clearly, speaking seemingly with only her lower lip, her sharp chin jutting slightly. '...about that.'

'No?'

He looked at her. He wished her could remember her name. It was an F but it was, like, three names or something, depending on where she was and who she was with.

She smirked, smiled an edge. 'You're rather like the Freaker Fonzie, sitting here…'

Carlton pulled his head back and frowned, as though incredulous.

'That a lot of F's.'

She smiled. 'It's two. Two is not a lot. Like I kept telling you.'

Her eyes flicked down to the front of his jeans. Carlton scoffed. Was she flirting?

'Two's usually enough for one man, darling. Three would freak most women out.'

She smiled. She liked him, still. And she knew that. She knew that she liked him. Carlton knew that too; they'd had a good time. Three weekends, but then, *my boyfriend.*

'You're Freaker Fonzie, and this is your office. This corner of the Crow and Kingfisher, Mondays, Tuesdays, Freaker Fonzie, and it's *fucking freezing* in here.'

She shivered a little, contained though, despite the fact she wore an enormous camel coat and black leather gloves. All you could see was her face, still framed with the same Rachel-from-*Friends* cut she'd been rocking since she'd become obsessed with it, like all the other girls in her clique, near the end of the nineties. It still looked good on her, although she was styled-blonde now, not the natural dark blonde he kind-of remembered from back then. That cut had been something; it had worked on her, and on a whole sub-section of women from their generation who, like her (and from what he had seen, Aniston herself) had stuck with it all this time.

'Freaker Fonzie fucking freezing…' Carlton smiled. 'That's even more F's. I should come here on Fridays.'

'Only in February.'

He took a stab. 'That's even more F's than you have in your name…'

There was a pause as her face changed, then hardened as she stared at him.

'Oh. My. God.'

Carlton squirmed a little. 'Isn't it?'

He knew there was an F in it.

'You've forgotten my name, haven't you?'

'No, I...'

'Haven't you, Freaker Fonzie?'

He deflected. 'I'm not even wearing my leather jacket. And if I were, it wouldn't be like that. I don't even have my hair pushed back; look, there's another guy... I mean he doesn't look like Fonzie either, but he wears black and, well, at least he used to... I think, at least, *he* should be the one to get called – '

'Your Barker friend.'

'You know him?'

'We all hung out at the same pubs back then, Carlton. Everyone knew everyone. But I never *knew* him, no. I just saw him around. He didn't go to school with us, did he?'

'Kind of. For a while, but not really. He had a different kind of education.'

She acted like she hadn't heard that.

'People talk about him though.'

'They do?' Carlton was wary now. Of course they bloody did. But hardly anyone ever mentioned him to Carlton. Carlton protected his mates. You didn't talk shit about Barker, not around Carlton.

'They do. People say he's even more mental than you are. That he flipped out and killed all those people. I don't think anyone really believes it though. Nobody who knew him.'

'I thought you said you didn't know him?'

'No. I mean; I knew who he was. We said hi. I knew him enough to say hi, how's it going, did you watch... I don't know, *The X Files* last night? Jesus, was it that long ago? Anyway, I knew he hadn't done all those things.'

'Just like that?'

'I have good instincts, Carlton.' There was a short, tight smile. 'I trusted you, didn't I?'

Carlton returned the smile. 'It was mutual.'

She glanced behind her at the only other people in the bar, a group of older men gathered at the far end. 'Being accused of that by everyone...' She was frowning when she looked back at Carlton. 'Having to vanish like that. People said he totally freaked. "More freaked out than even that other guy, his friend, Freaker Fonzie", they said.'

Carlton stared at her. 'No they didn't.'

'No, they didn't. But I can get them to call you Freaker Fonzie. If I want.'

Carlton smiled. She probably could. People in the clique still took her lead, and the clique still had social power. But he knew that she was just stirring. Maybe she was actually flirting. But he wouldn't go back. Back then in the day he'd seen it; some poor bastard from the city flirting with a cricket boy's girl. She'd been flirting back, too. Big time. They'd ganged up, pushed him outside onto the street, roughed him up when he'd stood up for himself. Nothing too bad, but nothing you wanted, and nothing that made you like them. He'd seen that thing a few times, before the renovations on the Pound and Silver.

The other, older blokes were staring at her. The five of them played darts on Mondays. Sometimes here, with another five blokes turning up. Sometimes somewhere else. Out north or down south. A different five each week, but rotating. They all got along. It was some kind of local network, a long-running, never-ending Hills tournament. Carlton knew enough to take it seriously; he'd seen people who could use sorcery to level mountains just laying low, playing darts in bars like this. He'd watched games where more than a tin cup was at stake. Then again, he'd seen enough of them to know; these guys weren't that.

Well, maybe the one with the beret was something; Carlton hadn't decided yet.

The men were staring because they were old school, and she, with the multiple F's, was a very rare sort to come into this pub. Usually it was just some guy in a hot car, taking his mistress or new girlfriend or third wife for a spin down Warren Road, stopping off here, at random. They had behaved accordingly, as though she were coming in for just a second, to buy a lighter or something. As though their old-school brand of 'different time' male bravado, their cheeky-chappy, male-bonding 'different time' sexism, would be okay, as though she wouldn't care about their little bit of fun; this wasn't her world, and she would be gone in a second, they assumed, with a story to tell whoever was in the car with her. He would be some lucked-into-money bloke with a square chin and a few million bucks in the bank, and when she got back to him, she'd complain about how much she hated those horrible old places with the disgusting old drunks, and why the hell didn't he go in himself? There had even been a 'cwoar...' when she'd first entered, in just a coat, with the black boots and gloves poking out.

But it was her face, really. It wouldn't matter what she wore, her face would always give it away; all sharp-featured and striking, with the hair, bright blonde...

The men would never consciously register any of the specific details that had led to their Pavlovian response, but what they were seeing essentially was a combination of health and wealth and good genes over several generations. Her glowing skin, the sheen of her hair and spark in her eyes, her manner and attire all suggested this. Carlton saw the same woman as they did, but the older men would see her through their generation's veneer; a rich man's daughter, now protected, if not outright owned, by another, younger rich man. Carlton, on the other hand, saw an independent woman, with a good job, maybe with a boyfriend, perhaps even a husband, also with a good job; a woman who was taking good care of herself as she negotiated her way to the top of the material world, in which she was very much at home. Regardless of her heritage, her lineage, F clearly possessed the kind of physical radiance, and carried herself with the natural self-confidence, that all those elements provided for a pretty woman.

Carlton knew her to be a descendant of local colonists

71

who'd done well for themselves, and those colonists' children, who'd inherited and started a main street business, and now the successive generations of their kids, who'd all profited from fresh food, country air and exercise. She was the product of third or fourth generation well-nurtured stock, combined with the lotto win of being naturally aesthetically attractive; F's ancestors, both male and female, having been selected by wealthy men, or hatched from the various combinations of them, because that was something wealthy men had always been able to do,;to select, breed and collect beauty, even harness its power within their own greedy gene pool. That process had become institutionalized.

And now, she was moving still upwards in an age of new possibilities for not just women but especially upper-middle women, rising by virtue of birth into some realm of the genuinely beautiful; perhaps, even into true wealth. He didn't know for sure; he remembered that her boyfriend was wealthy too. Yes, he did remember that.

Was that really how things worked? Carlton wondered. Did F's genes really just want to be a senator, or senator's wife? A corporate princess, or a business queen? The sociopathic genes of ambitious men, combined with the equally covetous traits of the most beautiful women; women beautiful enough to be the wives and mistresses of rich men, who could, as the cliché went, have any woman they liked?

Archetypally, Carlton supposed, all of this had entered the pub with her and expressed itself with one glance. He'd certainly seen it, registered it, even the first time they'd met as adults, perhaps even as children. The ancient darts team had simply felt this in its most primal, aggregate form, and responded with a virtually unconscious chorus.

But F had not simply turned and vanished, having bought her rich boyfriend a cigarette lighter, after throwing them a look of disgust. (Which might, in some cases, have gotten them going even more, Carlton supposed.) No. Instead, she had ordered a neat vodka, then taken a barstool. Not quite sitting. Just the edge of a buttock, balanced under the coat; one foot on the barstool rail, the other toeing the vile carpet, uncommitted. That had made them all a bit uncomfortable; an edge embarrassed, and a little confronted.

Then, she'd started casting glances over her shoulder at Carlton.

They really hadn't known what to make of that. Carlton was not a known womanizer. Not to them anyway. He sighed inwardly. Not to anyone, really. Then he chuckled inwardly. It was all done in the dark, with him. Then she'd been silent a while, then seemed contemplative. When she'd stood again, then walked over to him, the darts elders had reacted as though a movie they'd been following on the bar television that they thought was going to be crap, or best case really ordinary, had just taken a good twist. They were into it now. No talking.

'Is it true though?' F asked. 'That Barker was involved? With what happened? All those deaths?'

It occurred to Carlton suddenly that she might be one of those Barker freaks from the internet, playing the long game, looking for him. Little did they know, he was doing nothing more than hanging around Sydney, locating lost wallets and wedding rings. Still, people up here in The Hills *had* heard of Barker, because of what had happened at Bridger Mansion. Even though the dust had long since settled, his urban mythology still hung around, like the fog on Mount Lofty. People were still interested; nutters mostly, but a few with genuine concern for him, or legitimate business with him. Then of course there were the websites, and forums. Always things like that to keep the memory alive, inevitably just whenever it looked like it might fade away and leave them all alone for good.

Memory. Huh.

Carlton regularly posted on most of the boards to keep people confused and off the scent.

Nobody asked him to, he just did it.

It seemed the thing to do.

'I've seen Barker do some things…' Carlton smiled.

'Like the things you can do?'

Carlton smiled. Maybe he couldn't open portals, and banish demons, the way Barker once had.

But seriously, who the fuck would want to?

He and Cheryl had been there once when Barker had done it, just before it had all kicked off at Bridger Mansion; but no fucking way. He did not want to see that again. Barker could do plenty of other stuff, sure. But what Carlton could do was way more subtle. And in the long run, more useful. Which was why, when Barker had been here in Adelaide, the three of them had made such a great team. And that was why, he supposed, he screwed with the people online; to keep people away from his old mate, when and where he could, so that one day they might all get back together again, and figure it out once and for all.

'Yeah, I've seen him do some things…' Carlton's smile broadened. 'But murdering people? That's not one of them. Nah, that's one of those urban myth things. There's probably something at the root of it, but then people made shit up and added to it. Bored kids and ghost-hunter crews got hold of it, then it went viral. Who knew what the internet was capable of back then?' He smirked. 'Barker couldn't handle it. He went a bit off his nut. I think he's in Darwin now. Or New Zealand. That's not even his real name, so who knows where he is.'

'Really? Well. There you go, hey?'

Wait, what? That wasn't the look.

The look on her face was genuine; she couldn't have cared less about Barker.

Unless she was *that good.*

He tried to remember.

Yeah; he had been sober, pretty much, and consciously present when they'd done it. Had she been curious about Barker then? He couldn't remember. Present but still a bit pissed, but he remembered most of what they'd talked about.

'Everyone knows, Carlton.'

'Knows what? About us? Last year? Does your boyfriend know?'

'No, not that! I *told you* I wasn't here about that…!'

'Good, because, I mean, like, I *knew* there was bound to be one, a girl like you, but I really didn't *know*, if you know what I mean…'

She stared at him. Her eyes were huge, and ice blue, and their laser sights zeroed in on his brain.

'Carlton, Jesus. No. For the last time. It's not that.' She paused, staring. 'Okay?'

'…okay…?'

She kept staring but dialled it down a notch.

'Look. What I know is; what everyone knows is; if you want to talk weird, or you want something weird done, you come here to this old dive pub on a Monday or Tuesday. You'll be sitting in the corner here.' Then she frowned, as though challenging herself slightly with what she was about to add. 'If I wanted to keep… *seeing you like that*, I could have come by. Any time since.' She leaned in a bit more. 'So chuck those tickets you've got on yourself mate, the show's over.'

Carlton blew hard through pursed lips.

'Okay F, you got me there.'

'Really? F? That's the best you've got?'

'Fiona?'

'Yes, Fiona, but that's just a guess.' She leaned back again. 'Holy fuck, Carlton. It's only been a year, how many other women have you had since then? That you can't remember my name? I mean, how many do you go through in a year? Three, four? Seven, Eight? I mean, is it every weekend for you? Or just every other? Should I get myself *checked*?'

Behind her, the five-man darts team made a few noises. Some pained groans, and a low whistle, like Carton had just taken some serious hits.

'Checked?'

'I told you the story, Carlton. You asked, so I told you. For some reason in university people started calling me Fifi. I hated it. So when I graduated and came back here, I started trying to get people to call me – '

He remembered. Praise the Gods!

' – to call you Fiif. That's right! Fiif. And it stuck.'

Fiif folded her arms. 'Well. Done. I jogged your pickled memory.'

'No! I actually remember!'

'How do I spell it then?'

'Spell it?'

'Fiif. There's a way I spell it... with letters, like in language, and literature?'

Carlton clicked his fingers. 'So it doesn't look like Feet. Eff, eye, eye, eff. Fiif. Like Wiig. Like Kristen Wiig, that's where you got the idea – but you don't pronounce it the same way.'

Fiif kept her arms folded.

'Right?'

Why the hell was he *trying so hard?*

'Am I right?'

'Yes.'

'Well, that's that out of the way. So, what can I do for ya? Eff?'

'Don't call me that.'

She seemed pissed off now. He didn't know why. He didn't care. He was beyond trying to figure out why women got pissed off. But she was F'ing him off, too. More F's than she had in her three F'ing names. If they were going to F again, which seemed, to be quite F'ing honest with himself, quite F'ing far from a dead cert, she'd better lay off it with the fucking F's.

'Go buy me another drink.' Then she uttered a coarse addition. 'So it looks like we might be shagging.'

'So it looks like... we *might* be shagging?'

'No offense. I just don't want anyone to know I'm coming to you for the weird stuff.'

Carlton sighed. The weird stuff. Truly? Were people still like that? He wondered half a second, then laughed to himself. Of course they were. They were always like that. Always had been, always would be. He got up, gestured broadly but gentlemanly for her to sit at his table, then went to the bar.

So, he considered. A year later, and Fiif was back. Back from her world of upper-middle normality, where the boyfriend would be angrier with her if she'd spent her money on some supernatural sham-shaman, than if she'd let a bogan from the wrong side of town into her bed.

The bartender was what had once been called a barmaid, and still was in this pub, but was supposed to be called just a bartender now. Or if you had to, a female bartender. She was new, and she didn't know him yet. He couldn't remember her name either, which was surprising, because they hadn't shagged yet.

Boom-boom.

But still, because she was new, and they hadn't talked, she still looked at him weirdly. He ordered two beers, nice ones, and was promptly served. Fiona-Fifi-Feef-Fiif was nice enough, even posh-cool in her way, but Carlton was pretty sure she was still a Hills Chick at heart, and would still like a beer. The fact she'd been playing him as well, for those three weekends, impressed him. He liked a bit of a game. But the fact remained; she had a boyfriend. Had the sports dick cheated on her, and he'd been her revenge? Was he supposed to have been found out and beaten up, back then? Was Fee-Fie-Fiona that sort?

He didn't think so, but he supposed he'd soon find out.

Carlton returned to the table and Fiif accepted the beer with an eye roll, like; typical bogan. Buy a girl a *beer*. But then she saw the label and smiled, and took a polite swig.

'Thank you, Carlton.'

'So, what do you think it is that you know about me, Fiif?'

'I'm sorry. I didn't mean to be rude before. I'm not here to get seen, I'm not here to have some kind of guilty secret finally exposed.'

'I hadn't thought of that one.'

Fiif nodded. 'But you were thinking.'

'Who wouldn't? I mean, I thought you were out of my league last year. But I knew what it was. To be honest I thought you handled yourself extremely well. I thought we both did.'

Fiif smiled.

'What I know about you is this; half is what you told me about yourself, and the other half is what people say about you.' She smiled tightly. 'About half of that meets in the middle.'

'What I told you?'

'When you were drunk. Those three times we were together. You told me…' She leaned in a bit. '…you don't remember?'

'I… might.' He leaned in as well. 'Tell me… what do people say about me?'

Fiif sighed and leaned back out. 'Do we really have to go through all this occult master spy crap?'

'No.' Carlton shrugged and leaned back out as well. 'I thought we were flirting.'

'We're not. Look, you said once, when people have a hunch, a strong hunch, they almost never act on it. But when they do, for whatever reason, they're usually right. Well, last night I got a hunch, a big one. My friend Tess…'

'Tess the cute one?'

'Yeah. I suppose. Probably. You remember her. Went to school together.'

'Yeah. I remember. Hot Tess. Sure.'

Fiif looked at him strangely. Girls couldn't help themselves, Carlton thought. Now she's just a little bit jealous, a little bit in competition with the absent friend she's here to help.

'You said that you could track things, using your psychic powers? You did some things back then, when I asked, but I thought you were just doing clever…' She frowned. It was adorable. '…not stage magic, the other thing.'

'Cold reading.'

'Yes. That. But I asked around, and it seems to be true. You've helped people.'

'I have.' He allowed himself an edge of pride there.

Why not? He had, after all.

'And you said… you can't do it when you're drunk?'

'Yeah. That's true too.'

'So… how much have you had to drink tonight?'

FIVE:
DROPS

Barker rode Bach down Nightmare as she negotiated the multiple hairpin corners with road-racing precision. He felt like a mote of dust on a drop of wine as it drizzled down a corkscrew. On the first hairpin bend, as the halogen headlight illuminated a shimmering carpet of sturdy, blue-grey, mid-twentieth century asphalt before him, he straight-away felt as though shuttled through some kind of Ichabod Crane ghost-ride, along a twisting tunnel of high and overhanging gum forest, with jagged rock on his left, and nothing but a steel guard rail on his right to prevent a plummet into blackest oblivion. His mind seemed desperately to want to take his attention from that, and reminded him that the road had been christened after an early settler. Nightmare Road had a proper name. He wondered whether or not he, for it was surely a he, would have wanted such an insanely twisted and dangerous road to bear his name… whoever he might have been.

On the second and third bends, which came roaring in with ludicrously quick succession, Barker noticed several little Christian crosses, here and there on the corners and curves, just as there had been back at the vortex intersection, indicating where there had been crashes. A red crucifix on a black stake for an accident, a white one on a black stake for a fatality; the local government, desperate to remind people of their own mortality.

After the third hairpin, he realized that the road was heavily haunted.

To further take his mind off it, he considered Googling it, the settler whose name had been lent to this potentially deadly road, nee random-ploughed mountainside horse-track, using the bike and the screen in his helmet, the one that had helped him map the route here. But then again, reception was notoriously patchy through these gully roads, and… history could wait. It was all too often way too grim.

Of course, when the track had been carved out from the least-resistant natural rock formations, into the steep hillside and all the way around the side of the hill itself, the fastest any vehicle could have travelled was probably something like galloping speed. And hardly that really, Barker had to assume. Not here, so steep was the incline, so precarious the decline. Surely anything over a steady, patient pace would have invited disaster? Still, he wondered if, back in the days of his horse-drawn cart ancestors, there hadn't been collisions with high speed riders coming downhill and slow speed wagons going up. Tired horses slipping and going over, or slicing with jutting stone along the hill-face.

He supposed so, but he also supposed it would have been rare.

But then of course, as he rounded the fourth bend, he realized that the reason that thought had come up was because it had happened, right here where the bike was turning. All along The Hills behind him, the length of Warren Road, there were peaks from which a lookout could gain a fair view of the ocean; from the offing straight up to the horizon. Back then, lookouts and messengers had often posted themselves at the inns around the time that longships were expected, trying to get an advantage, and a forewarning of incoming cargo, over the less-elevated towers in the ports. Especially on foggy nights, The Hills views were often valuable; literally, as the first with the news was handsomely rewarded by grateful merchants who could get a head start to port over their competitors. Sometimes there was competition between messengers, sometimes even from the same hilltop lookouts or inns. Sometimes the merest hint of a glint on the horizon was enough to start a race down the hill. And sometimes on a foggy night, an awaiting messenger would drink too much, out on the balcony. Sometimes fall asleep, wake with a start and set off in hot pursuit. Sometimes dash, then fall off his horse. And once or twice, fall down the ravine to his death.

Barker could see him on this fourth bend, in the fog. There should have been a bridge, a short bridge, but there wasn't. Instead, the thin road continued down at about thirty-five degrees, the sharp bend followed the hillside inward at a right angle and hair-pinned one-eighty, then the road came out again along the other side of the indent and vanished down around the hillside mountain again. The ghost stood at the first corner, on the outside of the jarring right angle, on the edge of the drop, staring up at Barker as he came down.

The fog was thick, but that seemed to render him almost more clearly, like a film projection, in the moonlight, with something more solid to rest upon. He seemed to consist of greys, whites, and some navy almost; and the weird pale blue of the moonlight itself. Barker recalled what his mentor had taught him so early on; starlight, moonlight, fog, mist. All of these things rendered spirits more clearly. There were daytime equivalents as well, but people did not look for ghosts in the light. This one was just standing there, in the dark, the moonlight, in the cold and fog, on the bend, on a high, flat rock. Shirt and trousers and boots, hair tied back in a short ponytail. Mournful, watery eyes. Just watching Barker as he passed, the bike's headlight seeming to make no difference at all, the ghost never taking his dead eyes off him, never breaking his gaze. As Barker passed right by, as they were less than a meter apart, there was a connection made from the translucent young man's pale-blue, ethereal eyes.

Bach made the right angle, and then the hairpin easily, purring high and low, then the road caused Barker to face the ghost again, and Barker looked up now, at him, and wondered how he'd died. As though in response, the messenger seemed to corpsify, was suddenly a vision of himself as dust and bone, with a huge crack on the top of his skull; breaks, fractures, punctures and rips all over him. Barker understood that the man had been a little tipsy, but mostly tired. The horse had started when he had not turned the bend in time, and the man had been thrown over his horse's head, down the ravine, between the bends, head first.

Spiritual contact is fast, Barker remembered suddenly.

Like wifi or something; a packet of condensed memory can arrive in less than a millisecond but can sometimes take days to unpack. People without psychic abilities who saw past death, saw something like this guardian spirit, freaked out. Quite often, so did people with supernatural abilities. But the people who freaked did so without the benefit of communication, without the positive side of gaining the information that the spirit, no matter how confronting and even terrifying, had remained here, on this plane, to impart.

The ghost did not want sympathy. It wanted to protect. To warn people. Most people would feel his presence here as an extra urge to slow down; several jolts above any normal common sense warning that anyone with common sense would automatically give themselves. The earthbound imprint of the death messenger was, in the end, a self-appointed traffic cop from the spirit world, and Barker wondered how many lives he would have to convince himself that he'd saved, before he could rest.

For a second then, just a few seconds before he completely passed from Barker's view, the messenger boy returned to normal, and looked relieved.

Bill, his name had been.

In the very last second, as Bach rounded the end of this hairpin and lost his rear view, Barker saw Bill the ghost turn sharply, as though startled, to look back up the hill toward the summit.

To look at something.

Something was coming down behind him.

Back in those days, it would have been easier to hear the danger bearing down, echoing through the gullies from miles away. But on a bike, in a helmet, even one that purred, it was difficult to hear anything.

And now… down a couple of bends… two or three down, near the bottom of Nightmare, through a gap in the trees, Barker saw a truck on its way up. Just an old farm-worn flatbed, but big, and taking up a lot of space; two thirds probably.

It would have seen Bach's headlight, surely.

Barker started to worry now, and had to wonder; what was it about roads? What was it about the interconnectedness of public thoroughfares and the collective unconsciousness that so often made the only two vehicles in shouting distance connect at the single most dangerous point of a road simultaneously, and not pass individually, minutes apart? Even seconds? Why, when he saw the truck down the gap, negotiating the lowest of the seven hairpins, the one that first curved up, onto the steep hillside, did he know that after this one coming up, number five, there would be number six, and that would be the sharpest hairpin yet, and then, after all these long minutes of undoubtedly spooky, and yes, very steep, but essentially unhindered descent, with he and Bach the only ones on the road, that that, there, number six, right on the bend, would be where he and Bach, and the farmer's flatbed, and whatever it was that was coming down behind him, that had startled Messenger Bill, would all three meet, and turn the hairpin corner at precisely the same time?

'Bach!'

Rrrr.

'Bach, you got this?'

Rrrrr.

Barker tried to calm himself. This had happened before, many times. It happened to people switched in to the magical grid, the spiritual source; it was one of those common synchronicities to which he'd eventually become accustomed. Usually the incident passed; the other people on autopilot none the wiser.

But what worried him now, more than anything, was… whatever it was that was coming down behind him. He'd started to feel it, at the back of his neck.

Hairpin five went out; a long, extended piece of hillside, a jutting blind corner like a ship's prow on a voyage to oblivion. Three black crosses, one red, two white. There had been a collision here. Two dead, one forever maimed. And here, a second warning spirit, hovering, watching, protecting. Staring straight at him, balanced on the furthest extension of the guard rail. A seventeen-year-old boy who had gotten drunk at the Lion, and sped away into the night, driving on his own for only the third time on his Provisional License, drinking under age with a fake ID, drunkenly daydreaming of all the places he would go in his newly purchased third-hand car, soaring around the bends like a fighter pilot.

Barker got the story; he'd hit an oncoming vehicle and rolled over the guard rail, right at the place where he stood. He'd killed himself, swan-dived into oblivion, and killed the other passenger in the process, leaving the other driver unable to ever walk again. What remained of his earthly presence was bound here out of shock, then anger, and finally guilt, ready with all those weapons in his arsenal to warn those who were prepared to listen to their own better-selves, the government commercials, or take note of the Hills Council's warning markers. How many people did this one, or whatever was left of him; the powerful fraction of human personality that had been compelled to remain, feel that he had to save before he could dissipate into etheric memory?

Barker suddenly checked himself.

Into... *what*?

Barker knew that phrase, but... what did it mean?

Why the hell had he come down Nightmare in the first place?

To dissipate into etheric memory?

You know why, Barker.

Because it's starting again.

It's starting again.

Rrrr – *rrrrr.*

Even Bach knew.

Could she see these spirits?

There wasn't that much left of the boy's image of himself,

Barker saw as he passed right by; he looked more like a slender white bird now, but Barker read his story in his energy field all the same. Then he too turned sharply, as though jolted by the sudden presence of something, and the white bird suddenly becaame the boy again; Led Zep tee, black jeans and black ripple-soled sneakers, and the boy cast his startled gaze toward the road behind Barker, up at something coming down from the summit.

The bike helmet felt tight now, tighter than ever, like it was smothering him. He wasn't actually driving but he'd gotten used to trying to use the rear-vison mirrors, to at least assessing the road for himself. But he saw nothing, just the red glow of the tail-light illuminating the black rocks and trees.

'Bach! This is a trap! This whole night is a trap!'

He didn't know where that had come from.

Rrrraaaarrrr!

As Bach turned, Barker saw the ghost boy look up suddenly, as though something had shot into the air above him, then turn and look at Barker, back through the mirror; a distant but direct glimpse of panic. Not panic for himself though. For Barker.

Around the edge of the hairpin, Barker saw that the upcoming old flatbed had gained speed, passed the lowest hairpin, and was making its way up around the curve. They would pass easily on the forty-five degree decline between the last two bends that hugged the side of the lower, broader hillside in long, graceful S-stretch. But Barker has accepted this too soon. Just as Bach curved around the tip of the hairpin, something crashed down the side of the hill, rolling and pitching, then smashed onto the road right before him. Bach skidded to a halt, her back tyre spinning them about perpendicular to the road. It was a branch, maybe even a trunk; at least six feet long. It should have just kept rolling, bounced or pitched over the guard rail and continued on its way to be smashed to kindling down in the ravine. But it had landed oddly, almost flat, and jerked around until it had come to a rest diagonally, blocking the road.

Bach remained steady, having also come to rest diagonally

across the road.

The truck was coming.

Barker had no choice.

'Bach! Stay!'

He ripped off his helmet as he disembarked, thrust the open visor onto the left handlebar and ran down the road to the branch. As he reached it, he waved down at the truck; it was coming slowly, still a good one hundred meters away, but Barker knew that if the old truck halted there, now, it could very well be stuck there all night, trading one hazard for another. The truck flashed its lights, twice, as the driver indicated that he could see what was happening. The truck was very loud, becoming even louder as it approached, straining on the incline as the engine sounding off one continuous, long, low blast, like a terrible fog horn on the misty road.

Barker was at the branch now, but he could see immediately that it wasn't just a branch. It was a log maybe, probably a trunk, but weird. Weird, in some way he could not define at a glance. Then the sound of another vehicle, a car, this one coming fast down the hill, came to his ears. There was another crash from high up the side of the hillside, and through the darkness another log came crashing down, this time carrying smaller, leafy branches and a few rocks with it. It landed in a similar fashion, with a similar odd bounce, perfectly across the road, right around the first sharp bend. By its sound, the approaching car above was picking up speed. It would swing around that bend and hit the log, and the rocks, then there was no telling how it, the car, or the driver would react.

He bent down and tried to grasp the log on the end closest to the guard rail, to pull it closer to the drop, with the idea of then pushing it over. But it wouldn't budge. He squatted and tried to roll it, further to the other edge, just out of the goddamned way at least. He used his muscles, the muscles he had, but had for the longest time not wanted; had been given but never asked for; the muscles that were now part of him and, he had to admit, he was finally starting to appreciate, despite the tiresome cost. But the fucking thing would not budge.

The texture was odd, like stringybark but withered; too dry and yet too leathery to be anything like actual bark. It was like no tree Barker had ever come across. He kept trying to lift and heave and push, shifted weight and angles. Nothing. That was almost impossible, and the odd, leathery feel of it was really starting to creep him out. And his ribs, where Bazza the Brady-obsessed ghost had swung a bar stool right at him, hurt like hell. But Barker was unusually strong, unusually toned, and put everything he had into it, against the pain.

'Jesus!'

It was like the thing… it was almost as though it was *digging in*. Like it was bracing itself, not to be moved, and was just as strong as he was.

'Bach!' Barker stood and staggered back, exasperated. 'People's lives are at stake! Do what you can!'

Bach purred, unsure.

'Nobody will care that you move on your own if you save their lives!'

Bach roared, swirled around completely on her own and drove right up to the log. Then she spun again, gaining momentum from almost a full donut, skidded and slammed her spinning back tyre into the log. The rear rubber squealed immediately upon impact as Bach kept the pressure up, but while the collision had budged the log slightly, there was no movement after that.

'This is it!' Barker cried out. 'Bach! This is the trap!'

The trunk flinched. It was starting to shred, to burn at the pressure. But Bach's tyre was taking heat as well. Suddenly the log started rolling down the road, as though it had been clinging on somehow as long as it could, but just then had reached its limit and decided to throw itself off. Bach swung wildly around as Barker smelled – flesh. He'd smelled it before, burning flesh. This was the same.

'Bach!'

She pulled up right against the side of the hill, bumping her rear hard on a massive stone but not damaging herself. Barker could have sworn she'd growled, properly growled in that second, then she virtually pounced after the log like an insane cat attacking a fleeing snake.

There was a sliding shimmer of bright red in Barker's high peripheral vision. He turned and looked up behind him; there was a red sports car up there. He hadn't been aware that, elevated across the ravine between the hairpin, you could see traffic on the previous hairpin; but there it was, a sleek, curving red-lipstick Porsche, speeding the corners like Le Mans. Ten, fifteen seconds away.

Behind him the truck's sustained trumpet-like engine raised an octave as the driver doubled down and power-up against the weird rolling log that was hurtling down the road toward it, chased by a riderless lime-striped Beamer.

'Bach! The car above!'

Bach seemed to understand, one-eightied instantly, and powered back up to Barker. He was on her instantly, and she tore back around the ravine hairpin like a maniac.

There came a tremendous clap, like thunder right above them, and a primal force gripped Barker. Terror, and shaking. Bach was turning the apex of the bend when another two logs came down, behind and before them, but this time they remained upright. They were humanoid now, with arms and legs and faces; horrifically withered people with leather-bark skin, but clearly extremely strong, with striking sinewy muscles that stood out like prime athletes.

'*Nofuckingway!*'

The creatures had descended; no, attacked, Barker decided, as an earth tremor, or something very like it, had struck the ravine. More rocks fell, tumbling down the edge of the hillside and hitting higher outcrops, bouncing out, high over Barker's head. Bach lurched forward and slammed sideways into the edge as more fell straight past them, then another massive one, smashing the trunk-thing in the head, sending it staggering to a fall down the middle of the ravine. The other was coming up behind them; Bach kicked in and they roared up to the higher edge of the hairpin to the rock where the ghost of the boy had been, but rocks and branches were careening down around them. Stones and pebbles were striking Barker around his shoulders, pelting Bach, but then a big one connected with the edge of his elbow as he was putting his helmet back on and Bach kicked it again, this time around the corner. Once around, from the higher vantage, two things struck Barker almost at once; the situation to his left, down the hill past the hairpin, and the situation immediately to his right, up past the bend.

To his left, the first trunk-thing had given up pretending and was standing in front of the truck, in humanoid shape, as the bull-nosed flatbed, in humanoid shape, as the truck was coming right up on it, its speed significantly increased. The trunk-thing actually, Barker was sure, glanced back at him to make sure he was watching, then launched itself onto the bonnet and smashed a root-knot fist through the front windscreen of the vehicle as it impacted. The truck veered sharply to the driver's right and crossed the middle of the road. There was a smashing sound, and the high-pitch of screeching metal, as the right headlight and bumper were demolished along the rock hillside, then the passenger door scraped savagely along the rock-face as well. The driver then over-compensated and veered wildly to their left, crossing back and immediately smashing into the guard rail, nearly demolishing it right through, and coming to a precarious halt with the front left tyre spinning over the black edge. Barker heard a man crying out and girl screaming. The root-thing hung on, its arm stuck in the shattered glass of the windscreen. But as Barker took that in, another scream came from behind him.

Just ten or so meters up the hill, the red Porsche had stopped. There was a woman sitting inside, gripping the wheel. The fourth of the trunk-things – fourth. Barker spun around as the one behind him came up the road, trundling over the rocks toward him. Then came a second tremor. Bach fell to the side. Barker fell with her as the thing lunged forward and took a swipe. There was a huge crack from high up the hillside; not another earthquake or tremor but more like a cacophonous rip, a series of deep tearing sounds, and from above an entire tree, a massive gum, seemed to dislocate from its bed and slide, to surf on its unmoored root-base, down the side of the ravine.

It was big, Barker saw as he ripped his helmet off, and descending in one piece.

The trunk-thing was staring up in shock. Barker wrenched Bach upright and ran; ran with her, rolling her to the guard rail as a hail storm of twigs and gum nuts, of debris and even animals; possums and rats, came down around him, falling, rolling and scattering; an owl soared down, then straight up, even as the tree somehow still remained upright. It was level coming down; the branches were wide and thick; it blocked out the moonlight as, miraculously, the whole massive tree continued to slide and for a second, then two and three, remained fully upright with its enormous, broken, pythonesque roots right there as it impacted with and steadied on the road before them. For a stunned moment Barker thought; it's going to get up and walk like one of those CGI jobbies in *The Lord of The Rings*. But it did not, it remained, a tree, with the tops of its branches somehow hooked into the rocks above, remaining a whole trunk-level lower, like a giant canopy. The thing had come down right beside the trunk-thing, and it was staring at the tree, shaking, terrified at the mass of roots and soil before it, almost as wide as the road. Several snakes dropped out of the soil and started slithering toward the trunk-thing with amazing speed. It reacted with a jolt, with odd, reflexive movements that conveyed absolute terror and panic. The snakes were enormous; four of them, two meters long, dark brown and furious. One raised up and slashed out at the trunk-thing, biting him three times so quickly that it was utterly horror-inducing, even from where Barker stood on the rock a good fifteen meters back. The four snakes wrapped themselves around the creature with shocking speed, all four around his legs, biting, then they all went backwards over the guard rail, into the sliver of the ravine.

There was a snap from above, from somewhere high up in the rogue gumtree.

Barker looked up; his attention there alerted him to the other trunk-thing, which had taken the woman by the hair and was dragging her out of her car, over the windscreen, as it advanced toward Barker, reaching out with its other wood-knotted hand. But a big branch, carrying something huge and round and heavy, furry and grey with a burned-orange stripe, smashed into the thing's head and shoulder, jarring it sideways before hitting the ground. Then another, like a huge rock, fell from the tree and pummelled the thing's head again. But this one didn't fall onward. This one grasped hold, and suddenly the trunk-thing, to Barker's utter amazement, was dancing around the debris-strewn road with a huge koala grasping its head, the furry creature staring down intently, furious, shredding the thing's wooden-leather face up with its long, black claws. The koala was trying to kill the thing. Did koalas even attack? The other one had hit the ground hard, and it had blood down the side of its face, but it was up again, on its four legs, and charging the trunk-thing's feet like a bull-elephant. The huge nugget of fur smashed into the creature's legs, one then the second, and the wood-thing stumbled. Then it too toppled over, tumbling down the ravine, taking the still-shredding koala with it. The first koala charged on regardless, as though in a daze, until it collapsed at the side of the Porsche, by its front wheel, and lay still.

Barker's heart almost broke.

'No!'

What the fuck was happening!?

The tree above him groaned.

Bach growled her engine.

'Bach, stay!'

The woman from the car was staggering toward him, looking

for his help, but Barker ignored her. He scooped up the branch that the first koala had fallen with and ran in the other direction, past the trembling tree in the middle of the road, down the hairpin, around the hairpin corner, and back along the other side, then down again, sprinting with the branch in his hand, his black coat blowing out behind him, right at the trunk-thing with its arm still pinned by the broken glass to the windscreen of the bullnose flatbed.

Barker's hands found easy purchase, flowed with easy movement along the branch as he grasped the end with both hands and brought it down with a savage blow onto the head of the last trunk-thing. There was a flash of white light and the head jarred down and rebounded, cracking right open, straight down the middle as though Barker had hit a log with an axe, breaking it clean in half.

A girl jumped out of the passenger side, then, as the truck tottered fatally toward the drop, an older man struggled halfway out behind her. Barker dropped the branch and went around the open door to him, holding out both hands, grasping both the older man's hands as they reached out, then tightly maintaining the grasp as the truck fell away around him, and was gone as both he and Barker fell to the road, free of constraint.

The girl ran to the older man and embraced him, face down where he lay, trying to get up. She helped him up as Barker turned back and saw the blonde woman in front of her red Porsche, back up around the hairpin ravine.

'What is happening! What is happening! *What is happening!*'

Barker felt a powerful hand on his shoulder, and he spun around.

'I don't know what is happening; but you and your crazy bloody bike saved our lives.'

'What were those things?' The girl was wide-eyed, alert and demanding. 'Who are you? How does that bike go by itself?'

There came sounds of rustling; loud and en masse. Then the huge tree simply fell forward, and in a series of surprisingly simple, short snaps, rolled to its side and was gone, vanishing down the ravine, banging and crashing and finally, still.

When it was done, Barker could hear himself, the man and the girl, all breathing heavily. Barker turned back and looked at her again, then to her father. He had to be; they looked almost identical except for their noses, hair-colour and height. He addressed him squarely.

'My name is Barker. Barker Moon. Have you heard of me?'

'No.' The girl clearly wondered why she should have.

'Yes. You're that guy. The murderer, they say.'

He looked deeply into the man's eyes.

'I always maintained my innocence. There was no proof, no DNA, and they let me go. Now, you saw those things. I didn't kill anyone. Do you believe me?'

The man kept looking at him. Then he looked down the side of the hill, where his truck had gone.

'There was a rock slide. You saw it all from up there, on your bike, and you came down and helped. We owe you our lives. Pretty sure we're covered for that kind of thing.'

Barker smiled. He looked at the girl. 'You okay with that?'

The girl looked back and forth. 'Okay, I get it. We need a new truck. And nobody needs to think we're crazy. But I want a real explanation.'

Barker nodded. 'Okay. Okay that's fine. Meet me up there…'

The Porsche started up. They all exchanged glances.

'I'll talk to her; but I meant, meet me up there, at the Lion, okay? Tomorrow night. It's an anniversary, and I want people to know the story. Then you'll get your proper explanation. Okay?'

'You really are that… Barker Moon bloke?'

Barker assessed the older man. 'Yes. But I need to go now.'

'Stop that woman blabbing. We'll be at the Lion. If you can explain all the… weird shit that's been going on around here for the past few weeks?'

'That's exactly what I intend to do.'

'I'm Terry Buttress, this is my niece Krystal. We'll clear the road so nobody else gets hurt. Once you're gone I'll find some-where with reception and call the emergency services; and we'll meet tomorrow night? At the Lion?'

'You have my word.'

'And if I go down the ravine and look for my truck, and find what's left, what am I going to find, stuck by its arm to the windscreen?'

Krystal spoke up. 'It was a withered man. But he was made of wood as well. He had a face; and proper eyes, almost. He was staring right at me the whole time, but his arm was stuck on the glass.'

'How?'

'What do you mean?'

'It was windscreen glass. It doesn't shard…?'

The Porsche kept revving.

'Write down everything you can remember!'

He started running backwards. The poor kid. She would see that face in her mind for a long time; and if she came with her father to the Lion, she would not have slept by then. Barker knew how these things worked.

'I'll be there!'

He turned and started moving, running faster back up toward the Porsche. His body was tensing. He could hear Bach purring as he ran. He needed the potion, or he was going to get… nasty.

'Don't go!' Barker shouted at the woman.

But the road both in front and behind was covered in sticks and branches, rocks and stones, and massive clumps of soil. She wasn't going anywhere, and by the time Barker reached her, she had reached that conclusion herself.

'Are you okay?'

She was clutching the wheel, gripping it tightly and staring straight ahead. She hadn't even looked at him.

'Are you Barker Moon?'

Barker froze.

'Who the hell are you?'

'I was sent. I was told to follow you.'

'By who?'

'I'm going to tell you. But I want you to promise me something.'

'What?'

'I want you to promise me, that if I tell you, you'll fucking kill them for me.'

'Holy shit!'

'Oh come on, Barker, I know your god damn history! You can't tell me another body or two is going to – '

'No; I mean – holy shit, I think this koala is still alive!'

SIX:
KNOT TO BE

'Master Shilling… what is that thing?'

Shilling barely acknowledged him as he responded, dry as ever.

'What thing, Mister Gong?'

Burley Gong was stunned. Shilling could not be serious; the thing was right there. Right in front of them, crouched in the far corner of an otherwise empty dining room, pacing back and forth in a tight arc, in a manner that suggested it was clearly unhinged.

'Right there, Master Shilling. That *thing*. In the corner.'

At first Burley had thought it to be a shadow, created by Shilling as he'd opened the double wooden doors, cast by some sort of candlelight behind them. But the mind plays tricks, as Burley well knew. It plays tricks and makes fast assumptions. There was no sort of candlelight behind them, just those lightbulbs that made everything slightly more white, yet more weird and fluorescent. Now Burley was thinking that the flickering thing in the corner was part of the sorcery he'd been promised, and finally come to see; perhaps a shadow come to life, a shadow-spirit, unhinged?

He and Fenner Shilling had walked what seemed a long way to reach this room, but the strange layout of the giant house was disorienting, no doubt deliberately so, and to be honest they might have been walking five minutes or fifty by now.

Burley had only been here once before, six years ago when the place had last been up for sale. He had walked through this floor and ventured into a bare fraction of the floor above, but had not stayed any longer than it had taken him to broadly assess the place and guess the number of bedrooms and bathrooms, to be written up for a quick sale. When it had come to exploring the second floor he had essentially balked at the top of the stairs. He had scanned quickly and never dared even glance at the thin central steps behind him, that led even higher into strange darkness. To this day he did not really understand the floor plan on the first floor, and never intended to even try, not for one second.

Back then, it had only been a year since all the murders had occurred, and it still had not felt right to even set foot in the place. It had not felt right walking in, and it had not felt right a few minutes later, flooring his car through the gates at the end of the twisted, overgrown driveway to get away from the grounds as soon as he could. Nobody, it seemed, ever hung around Bridger Mansion very long. Nobody except Fenner Shilling.

The whole time he had wanted to ask questions.

Do you know what happened here?

Did you know any of the people who were killed?

After the murders, when the cops were through, and they had made whatever they had made of the massacre, there had still been furniture here. Burley remembered it; creepy, turn-of-the-century stuff. Edwardian stuff. But some interesting, almost warm Victorian pieces as well; the kind you might expect to find in an explorer's house. It had all been very dark however, heavily draped, dusty and cobwebbed. The last remaining heir of the family that had owned the mansion since colonization had been well into her hundred and eighth year when she had passed, but she had been well beyond maintaining the mansion by herself. Although still financially self-sufficient, and able to walk with a cane, she had chosen only to maintain the cleanliness of the three front rooms, in which she had lived exclusively for the last two decades of her life. Now, so far as Burley Gong could tell, at least the whole of the first floor of the enormous house had been completely emptied of all that furniture, and divested of all those fittings.

Nobody had lived here since the old woman. So, presumably,

all of those contents had long ago been gutted and stored, perhaps even sold off. He assumed that it had been Shilling who'd bought the house, after Burley's own crude assessment that fearful day he'd fled without properly doing his job. Certainly after that somebody else much more senior in the real estate franchise, the grand old bastard of the firm, had handled the actual sale, which had been totally private.

As Shilling's tour had progressed, Burley had seen the occasional red brick feature wall, or a bluestone mantle, but very little else other than the ever-present polished wood surfaces. All of the floors they had walked, the staircases and landings, and the occasional balconies they had passed, including the massive one just inside the front parlor, erected there as though straight out of some old Louisiana mansion; all the paneling and the built-in shelves and empty display cabinets, the high ceilings and the massive wooden beams, all of it, had been hard, dark-stained timber. The colours were consistent as well; blood-amber, with slight black-chocolate variations here and there, all clearly ancient, yet polished and dusted as though well-maintained for centuries. There was so much of it, so little variation, and the house was so huge, that Burley was truly starting to believe that if Shilling led him to the center of the house and left him here, he might conceivably have become lost for hours before finding his way out.

But they were not in the center. They had walked down a long hall, once or twice diverting to different rooms, or circuits of rooms, but always returning to the main hall. Just a few minutes ago they had taken a wide corridor to the right, taking stock of whatever newly-placed, lone and stark occult-style statues had been positioned within the house (or at least, those that Shilling deemed him worthy of him seeing) that had clearly been selected to replace all the rustic relics that had been there until a mere few weeks previously. The one they had just passed was so fluid, so erotic, that it was almost impossible to stop oneself from not simply becoming aroused in its presence, but from fully embracing, if not attempting to fuck the gorgeous thing right there and then.

He was prevented from such an indulgence when he heard another of the sounds that once or twice had echoed through to them, down from the higher floors, perhaps even echoing in descent from the high rafters, suggesting rather disconcertingly that they were not alone. But until now he had seen no one, or no *thing* else.

Is it true that there were more people here than the police let on?
That some of them were not killed, but simply vanished?
Or, were allowed to vanish?

Three floors, he had thought upon approach, staring up at the house, named a mansion, as he'd driven down the crazy jungle of a driveway that he had sworn never again to trespass upon. The overgrown mess had looked three times worse this time than it had six years ago. Maybe a loft or something on the top. Maybe something else again. But the sounds now, here within the house, indicated that there were others, probably mortals, other beings at least, also within these walls.

Higher up.

That the killer might not be locked up, might still be at large?
Were you *here, Fenner Shilling?*

'What is it?' Burley winced, still attempting to assess the thing in the corner. 'Is it a man?'

'No.' Shilling was quietly confident. 'Maybe it was, once.'

'Once?'

'There are ways of turning men into things.'

'Slaves, you mean?'

'Well, of course. But there are many varieties of slave. Tiers. Degrees of oppression, toward degrees of inevitable soullessness.'

Burley assessed the ex-man thing again.

'If that's true, then that thing must be very low.'

It was still loping, like an ape on its hind legs, back and forth in the wooden corner. Yet the room was big. Deep and long. Perhaps it had escaped from somewhere, where it had been confined for a prolonged period, and was now intimidated by even the limited, but open space of an old dining room.

'This is one of the things you were going to show me? One of the accursed magics?'

'Majicks.'

'*Majicks*. Ah yes. I see.'

He immediately regretted the tone of self-satisfaction, of becoming aware that inflection was important when pronouncing the vocabulary of the occult. Shilling picked up on it immediately of course.

'That's nothing, Burley. Just a trick of speech, of accent.'

'Of course.'

The creature, for that is what Burley was starting to understand the thing in the corner to be, nothing truly resembling a man at all, shifted and grumbled and growled. He saw that it was not completely solid, and that it seemed to be almost part of the wooden walls. Attached somehow, with some kind of flimsy, mist-like lead or chain, directly from the low center of its stomach, where the navel or umbilical cord would be, to a great knot of dark wood in the pattern of the boards behind him. Then, as it moved, as it passed back and forth before the knot to which it seemed attached, he saw that the wood-knot seemed to be a reflection of its shape somehow. It gave him the chills and he turned away.

'What are you going to do with it?'

Shilling shrugged. 'That remains to be seen.'

Shilling took him gently by the upper arm and guided him back out of the room, though the open, hardwood double doors. Except, when they were out, back in the mansion hallway, it was clear to Burley that Shilling hadn't touched him at all. Burley was beginning to understand now; this was something Shilling could do. He could suggest things, and they would feel real. Real enough to provoke a response.

'Did I tell you, Mister Gong? Several years ago I was almost killed in this house.'

'So you were here. Somehow I can't believe you were the first.'

'A man betrayed me. Man! Well, no more than a boy really. Killed several of my friends. Well, I say killed...' Shilling looked absently up and down the cavernous hallway as though he had misplaced his keys. '...now, there was something else...'

Burley looked at Shilling. The way he turned things back on you; with words. And yet; Burley would not get caught in that. Shilling had just told him something. It had been one of those things sorcerers tell mere men, obfuscated but there, so that later they could turn it back, and tell you; I told you. This is not my fault. I warned you, but you did not listen.

'Killed, Shilling?'

Shilling smiled, tightly. He was a handsome man, middle-aged but vital, and Burley was starting to realize that he was very attracted to him.

'Yes. That's what I said. Many opt not to hear that.'

'How? How did he kill them?'

'He went against me. Many deaths resulted. I was lucky to escape myself.'

'Escape... yourself?'

Shilling smiled again and uttered softly. 'Well done...'

'That's what you meant, isn't it?' Burley felt himself swallow hard, felt that his mouth and throat had gone dry. 'What did – did you...' He swallowed again. '...did you *go too far*?'

Shilling let out a tight sigh. As though he had considered this long and hard, and was almost but not quite yet sick of explaining himself.

'I trusted the wrong people to support me, when I decided to go further than we had planned. I simply wanted to proceed, they did not. From that perspective, I went too far. From my perspective, however...'

'They betrayed you. Weak!'

'Frightened. But yes, weak.'

'Weak, Shilling! I see it all the time. Nobody willing to make the hard decisions to stay ahead of the pack. What happened to them?'

'They were consumed.'

Burley screwed his face up. 'Consumed? How? By what?'

Shilling looked suddenly down the hall, deeper into the house.

'This was a betrayal Mister Gong. Things, the doings here, had gone far, but not as far as I had desired them to. But it had gone far enough, so that it could not be undone by those who had tried to stop it. After the betrayal cut proceedings short, things were simply allowed to settle, and bide. But, all good things, all good things. And now is the time to resume. For things to become unsettled once again, for intents to be made clear, ransoms demanded, and prices to be paid. We had to bide our time, now the time is right. Now, time is with us, and we are ascendant. Come with me.'

Burley Gong could do little else; not only had he never been aroused by another man, but he had never been *this aroused*, not ever. Fenner Shilling was the real deal, he could tell. A genuine black magical player. There would be no stopping him this time, no going back; time was with him, with them, and he, they, would ascend!

Then they were walking again, just two men on their way through an old house.

The floorboards creaked, with the occasional reverberation down a whole series of planks and panels to indicate that this ancient place was unaccustomed to footfalls. Everything snapped, everything echoed, both at the sudden cold outside that had settled in this afternoon, and from the lack of furnishings that would usually absorb sound. Then they turned and were walking down a thinner hall, not quite a corridor. Near the end Shilling placed a firm grip on an old-fashioned door handle, then flicked an old-fashioned light switch.

There was a person in this new room. An actual person, a girl, a woman. Like the weird wood-knot creature, she was in the corner, but unlike the creature, she was huddled tight.

'Where is the door?'

She asked the question in a shudder.

Burley wasn't sure if she were terrified or frozen to the bone. Probably both.

'Why is she here?' Burley had not meant to demand anything, certainly not an explanation. But she was pretty and, quite irrationally, he suddenly saw her as a rival, as another who could service Shilling's desires.

The other side of his mind, the side that retained his connection to normality, to his pride in his hitherto rock-solid heterosexuality, his bigotry and homophobia, his belief that this was all part of a business plan, to steal the top dog position in the real estate company from his last remaining rival, before securing the love and respect of the sick old bastard who had been his overlord for twelve years, but still looked at him through his narrow, racist eyes, with the still slightly-sneering way he said *Gong*, that was, whenever he could swallow hard and bring himself to say it...

That side of him, that rational part of him that didn't care that he was risking prison to kill the old fucker, even if it was with unprovable, untraceable, *nonexistent* sorcery... that part asked; was Shilling one of those true maniacs? Not just someone who would knock off an old prick a few years ahead of his inevitable heart attack to get ahead when the time was right. Was Shilling the *other* kind? Did he kill, for blood ritual?

'Are you going to kill her? Is this ritual sacrifice?'

He was surprised at his own coldness, and the cruelty of asking that question in front of the girl-woman. But now that Burley had come, finally, with Shilling to the house, he found that he was completely committed. Just like that. He would kill for Shilling, kill this person here and now if he requested it, for what Shilling had to offer.

'Kill her? Oh, no. This house doesn't want blood. Not anymore, anyway. Oh no, no we don't kill people Mister Gong. Killing people brings police. Not only do we not want the ordinary police in here, poking their snouts around where they're not wanted; quite equally, we don't want our good and solid and stable allies within the police force to have to do anything that might compromise their positions. When people get killed, bodies turn up; investigations commence. Nobody wants that. Tedious, tedious business. When people go missing, on the other hand; perhaps a cryptic message, a clue left behind that they have chosen to vanish, maybe a hint that they might even come back sometime; anything can happen. People fill in the gaps. People invent fantasies; where their beloved is, how they are happier there, and think fondly of them sometimes. Do you see?'

'Did you kidnap her? Is she a sex slave?'

Shilling laughed. 'Oh no, Mister Gong! Sex slave? What a grim mind you have, what a squalid imagination! This young woman is here of her own free will. She wanted me to teach her something; I told her that I would tell her what she wanted to know, provided she could find her own way out, as I was rather busy at the time.'

'But… the way out is back there. Back down this corridor, down the big hall. To the parlor with the stairs and the landing.'

'Of course it is. Did you hear that, Angela?'

Angela stared at him.

'Where? Where is it?'

'Down this hall, to the end, left to the bigger hall and straight down…'

She was the kind of woman Burley would have considered sexy, had he not been in the presence of Fenner Shilling. She had that gypsy look; she was probably Eastern European, slender but with curves; strong, sharp features, full lips and big brown eyes. Her long, black hair flowed past him as she bolted between them, out of the room, muttering crazily under her breath. Burley watched her run, practically a scamper, and turn the way he had told her.

'Will she find it?'

'Does she want to? Surely, she would have found it by now?'

'Is that why she's here? To enact some kind of inner turmoil? When she finds the door, will it be in her mind? Or, in her vagina where the bad man touched her? Or, some other such nineteen seventies navel-gazing nonsense?'

Shilling smiled. 'She's here to learn, and to trade. She's been outside. She was outside yesterday. She ran an errand for me. Planted some seeds. But she keeps coming back. She keeps wanting to know more. And I tell her; I will tell you more, but you must always find your own way out.'

Burley wondered. Maybe this was a cult after all? Was the girl, Angela, drugged? But no; that wasn't it. Shilling was head-tripping her, mind-fucking her, but she would be better for it at the end. She had asked for this; she had asked knowingly and now one of the great dark occult masters of the entire human race was teaching her. What was a little time, lost in your own mind, lost in a haunted house? When true occult wisdom was the reward?

Some of the echoing voices became clearer now, down the hall, closer. Shilling seemed pleased to hear them. They sounded like kids. Teenagers. Shilling figured this out simultaneously, and for a brief moment an expression of disappointment crossed his gaunt features.

'I see...' Shilling growled, quickly accepting whatever change in his situation that these young voices had brought forth. He stared at Burley a second.

'Apparently...'

Burley couldn't take his eyes off him. You could see he had been a proper ginger once, a proper freckled-bright-orange, but his mane, biblically long and swept back to his shoulders, and his facial hair, a thick but ordinarily trimmed beard and moustache, were more white now, so that he had a kind of aging-Pitt look beneath the hippie hair. The strange thing though, and now Burley was starting to see, the beautiful thing, was that he had black hairs, dispersed throughout as well. They looked thick, tough. Almost pubic. He wanted to –

'...apparently, you are supposed to see this.'

'Supposed to?'

'Follow me.'

Shilling was easily six-three and long-limbed, but unlike others of such stature Burley had seen, he carried himself gracefully, walking with his height rather than against it. It made Burley realize how high the ceilings were in this place; very old school, like Shilling himself, who seemed oddly ageless, if not timeless. The three times they'd met, Shilling had worn a gray wool, three-piece suit, with some kind of expensive brown leather lace-ups, a long, loose burnt-orange scarf, and a jet-black pork pie hat. The hat's flat top had always seemed to level out his great height, like the intimidating level of intensity he maintained. But there was black and orange weaved into the gray waistcoat this time, with a black shirt; Burley was sure he'd worn different combinations of this outfit (as all of those connected to some higher source tended to) but this one made him forget all the others. This was the combination Shilling had worn the first time Burley had truly *seen him*.

'This house was built specifically to attract and channel energies. Some time ago, something came here, was attracted to it. Nobody knows what happened to it. But I have a theory. It was my theory that the house seemed to want to prove that theory; but now I believe that theory is no longer valid. Now I theorize... that the theory is trying to prove itself!'

Shilling seemed very pleased with himself, so Burley smiled appreciatively, even though he had not really understood. They had come to the end of the hall now, to a huge door with carvings all around it. Past it was a square room with a fireplace facing the door. A strange, pale light was coming from above, but that was all. Burley barely noticed; Shilling was going to show him something, and that was all he could see.

'Remove your clothes. Leave them outside. Go to that corner. The corners are designed so that you cannot be seen if you do not move.'

Shilling was pointing to the inside corner to their left.

Burley obeyed. He was not ashamed of his body. He swam twice a week, ran an hour every morning, and trained at the gym, weights and everything, Mondays, Wednesdays and Saturdays with a real dude who knew his shit. He had sex with his wife afterwards, every time, when he looked his physical best. He banged hookers on Tuesdays and Thursdays, paid them to show him things, so she would stay interested, so she would never be bored, so he would not be just some kind of sex machine to her. He was doing it all for her; Gong was only half Korean but she was full, and if he could prove himself by taking control of the business from the old cock, her well-respected family would come on board, and there would be money fountains to fuck in for eternity.

There were two doors on either side of the fireplace. As Shilling moved like a pale specter, unseen to the corner of the room on the other side of the door, four people filed in slowly.

'See?' A young man spoke. 'I fucking told you!'

There was a girl giggling, but Gong could see, another who was definitely not. They were all four of them young, all under twenty. The pale light from above was almost ultraviolet. Strongly violet, at least.

'This is where the murders happened?'

Nobody answered.

'Fritz?'

Fritz spoke as though startled out of a deep mood.

'What? Oh yeah. This room. This was where the ceremony took place.'

'What's that light? That weird light? How…?"

'Skylight…' The apparent guide seemed way too sure of himself. '…catches the moonlight off the clouds.'

'Does anyone else ever come here?' The girl who was not giggling was not frightened either. That was strange.

'No-one's got the balls…' This was the boy who was holding hands with the girl who was, still, giggling.

'You have…' Giggling Girl uttered. 'I've seen them…'

Before Burley knew it the boy, the Hot Boy, was pushing Giggling Girl toward him, and she was allowing it. It was playful, and when she backed into the wall behind her, right beside Burley, they should have been able to see him. The Hot Boy tripped over something on the floor, maybe some part of the floor that was raised, and came at her hard, but planted both hands heavy on the wall each side of her shoulders and laughed in her face, catching balance, uncaring. They started kissing, right next to Burley. Every part of him was suddenly stiff and excited as he watched them, almost shoulder to shoulder.

The other couple were across the room, in front of the fireplace, watching them. Fritz stood behind the thoughtful girl, his arms around her from behind, her arms up over his. Burley knew this one; the couple who weren't ready, but liked to watch the couple who were. Oh! The things couples got up to when there was no-one else around.

Beside him, passions were escalating beyond heavy petting. Harl (she had uttered his name) was unzipped and very much out, and Marsh (he had uttered hers right after) had taken matters into her own hands. Burley had almost laughed at his little internal witticisms. But he didn't; he knew better than to spoil it.

Suddenly the virginal voyeur, who would not even allow Fritz to touch her breasts with her coat and sweater on, gasped and stepped forward. She had her left hand on her heart, on her breast, over her coat and sweater. But then the coat was coming off; she was panting, like a hot flush. Burley saw that the skin on her cheeks, and on the backs of her hands, was… or wait? Was it the violet light? Was it the violet light making her hands glow…? Or was it the glow from her skin, her face and hands, and now with her coat off, her neck, making the violet light in the room even stronger…? Yes, yes he did believe it was. The violet light was reacting with her skin, and her skin was glowing and making the violet light… not brighter, but more dense. The way fog seemed brighter in moonlight, the thicker it became.

'Nell?' Marsh demanded. 'What the fuck?'

Fritz raised his hands. 'I didn't do anything!'

'You're the one who knew about this place! Did you drug her so she'd come here?'

Harl turned around, his full erection jutting out of his unzipped pants.

'What's with the fucken lights?'

Fritz was staring down at Harl's cock, clearly never having seen another man erect before. But then he pulled his eyes away and stared back at the person who was, nominally, presumably, his virgin girlfriend. She had just tugged her sweater over her head, ripped it off her body like a rag, and thrown it onto the floor. She was now pulling off the ratty white tee-shirt that had been exposed underneath. She had a curvy body; in this strange current youth culture, curves had not quite yet returned to normality, and one so young would probably have been wise to hide them from a potential suitor, at least until she had become sure of his serious intent. But it was almost comical that any woman should ever be ashamed of a young body such as this full-figured one, inhabited by this 'Nell' creature. Especially when she was glowing, literally glowing, with supernatural power. But people, especially young people, were morons.

Nell kept glowing with supernatural light. At least, he assumed that's what it was. It felt like; that was what it was. This room, something in it, brought this out. That was what this room was for. Already the rude boy, Harl, was starting to glow violet as well. Nothing like Nell, but it was there. Fritz and Marsh, hardly at all. But along with the teenagers, the room itself was changing. The atmosphere was different. There was a different energy coming in from the walls. Burley looked closer. Were they? Yes. Yes, they were. The wooden walls were now blood red.

The four youngsters started moving toward the center of the room, staring into each other's eyes, each moving from one to the other, but circling around Nell, touching each other's faces, touching Harl's cock, touching Nell's barely-contained cheap-bra tits, as though they were all suddenly high, as though they were performing in some terrible, amateur encounter group from the worst end of nineteen-sixties counter-culture. As they did this, they were also ripping off their clothes like ballet performers, gracefully, but with a powerful sexual urgency, like the Rites of Spring or some such toss. They were all naked now, the other three walking around Nell, Nell looking from one to the other, barely able to breathe she was so excited, and then as though she were floating ocean prey and they were sharks, they swooped in on her and devoured her. Nell was glowing ultra-violet now, all over as they bit and kissed and tongued her like mother-animals washing their young. She fell to her knees, as Marsh came up under her with her mouth wide open, as Nell opened her mouth for the two boys. Then, after a minute or so of this hungry mouthing, Fritz was suddenly on his back, for Nell to descend on top of him. Beside them, Marsha was on her back, Harl's toned and tanned footballer's bottom humping into her, facing Burley as he began to pleasure himself at the shocking brightness of the pure, violet, primal sexual energy that was now filling the entire center of the room. There was another shift and Nell stood, dripping wet all over. She raised her hands and looked up. Burley saw, all of a sudden, that the light was coming from very high up, and that the room had no ceiling. There was a balcony around where the ceiling and the floor of the next level should have been, surrounding the whole room, and there seemed to be figures there, lined along the thick wooden rail, looking down and observing with... Burley had to admit; it seemed to him like nothing more than passing interest. There were some people, he thought. Normal people. Others seemed like light beings, glowing and almost camouflaged within Nell's shocking violet aura, others still seemed to be stick-like beings, thin and twisted and dark.

How could this be?

How could the house do this?

Even just this one room?

How many of these… creatures?

Living here?

He sensed that there was more than one major supernatural event occurring, that this huge house had been made able to do something, something special and amazing; but not exactly this. This was all being manipulated somehow, warped beyond the original pure purpose toward something crooked. Despite the violet energy incurring some kind of pleasurable height, some kind of apex-state of sexual build-up and ever-cresting ecstasy, this room was not meant to be this way, not exactly.

Then he saw Shilling. Shilling was moving in with them.

Shilling had done this, made this.

Naked, Shilling stepped up onto the square; that was what it was, a raised square that took up most of the room. Shilling was holding a huge white dagger, a good eight inches long, with a strange, pointed tip. Ceremonial, no doubt, for this very purpose, low in his right hand, coming up behind Fritz.

But while he had been watching Nell, as Nell realized that they were all being watched from the balcony, Fritz had entered Harl from behind. Such was their combined ecstatic state; it had simply happened. Now Shilling was behind Fritz, the dagger still low and – it wasn't a dagger. Shilling was erect. As he entered Fritz, Burley realized that Shilling has some kind of long, tapered, albino –

Fritz threw his head back and screamed.

The room exploded with tendrils of jagged, blood-red bolts of energy that had been kick-started across the floor from the soles of Shilling's feet and spread right across the room like an undrewater explosion of blood. These new, violent, blood-red energies knocked the swaying, curvy Nell to her feet again, then rebounded up the walls, to the balcony and beyond, then slammed back with a lightning strike of power, right into Fritz's crown as he was fully, violently penetrated by Shilling. Then Shilling pulled out, once, like a slash, and blood poured from

Fritz as though he were simply a sack filled with liquid that had been shot through with a bullet.

Shilling stepped aside as Fritz's scream continued, but diminished, then the boy fell fully, flat onto his back like a rump steak dropped off a meat counter by an intoxicated butcher.

The ethereal light in the room was no longer violet or red now, but the worst mix of both; the colour of a bruise, an ugly, swollen, dark-brown-edged purple. The room had changed suddenly and drastically, as though they had been at sea but just then encountered a terrible cyclone that had set down right on top of them without warning. They were surrounded by streaks of white lightning, red lightning, swirls of red and purple and brown and black blood, and the sound of horrified screams. Not just from the four victims. Above as well; some of the witnesses were apparently just as terrified and appalled as the children were down here.

Others though, hooted in appreciation.

Burley found that he had stepped forward.

Nell saw him and ran to him, her body hitting him full force, embracing him in terror for some kind of humanity, any kind of safety. Burley was shocked. Her embrace was so fully empowering that he felt for a second that he had not yet ever been fully alive. Her violet energy seemed to flow directly into him, as though her need for him, to quench her fear, served him directly. He grabbed her, embraced her, and the energy kept coming. It was amazing, amazing.

Through this, he watched Fritz gradually whither, his body thinning as the fluids ran out of his anus like a forgotten-running tap, flowing into the floorboards and becoming absorbed into the house. Shilling went to Harl, who it seemed could not stop humping Marsh, even though his expression of complete, bewildered terror clearly suggested that he would like nothing more than to stop. He was still glowing violet, only one third, maybe less than that of Nell's lovely expulsions. Shilling pulled Harl's head back by the hair and stared down into his face. Harl screamed up at him, baring his teeth like a wild animal helpless in a trap. Shilling threw Harl aside. Harl rolled to a halt, prone by the fireplace, and was still. Shilling lowered his wiry, fatless body down to his knees, then leaned over Marsh. The girl was spent and delirious, lost in an incomprehensible nightmare like a druggie novice on a brown acid trip, and she did not try to stop him. Soon she too was bleeding her bodily fluids into the floorboards.

The purple ones were batteries.

The red ones were fuel.

Yes.

Burley understood.

And they all lived upstairs, with Shilling's coven.

Shilling came over to him.

The swirling purple bruise of an energy cloud now seemed to surround him, but somehow the cloud still enveloped the whole room.

'As I said, Mister Gong. Killing, it's such a complicated waste...'

There was movement from within the cloud and the wood-knot creature from the dining room suddenly emerged and was standing behind Shilling. At least, he assumed it was that one. Had there been – more? Upstairs? No; no it was a different one. Solid. More fully... grown?

'What... what's it going to do?'

'It's going to help me.' Shilling turned to it. 'You have two new friends. Find them rooms of their own where they can settle in. Rooms with quiet corners. Explain what's required of them.'

The creature nodded and moved away.

'Required?'

'They are to do my bidding.'

'Your... to what end?'

Nell suddenly turned her head from being buried in Burley's shoulder and looked up at Shilling.

'Keep me here? Like this? In the light? I'll do anything to stay in the light!'

Shilling ignored her.

'They are going to bring back the man who betrayed me. The man who knows the combination of the lock.'

'The combination?'

Shilling was pleased with Burley. Burley knew; most would ask; *the lock?*

'The violet occurs here naturally. The red must be cultivated; it feeds the being that is here.'

'How? How do we do it? I will go now, I will find this *vile traitor*, and bring him here, kicking and screaming. I have people, I have money, I have –'

'I have all of those things and more.'

'Then how?'

'How else, Mister Gong? We're going to threaten everything he holds dear, we are going to summon him, and re-summon him, until he agrees to return…'

'And then?'

'And then, it can't be helped.'

'What can't?'

'Well, then, Mister Gong, the police won't matter. These four children, they can be covered up. They've gone backpacking, joined a cult, become Scientologists… whatever. We have the people and the money and the means. But for what we have planned…'

'What, Shilling?' Burley was so excited now he could barely contain himself. 'What can't be helped?'

'The killings, Mister Gong. Oh yes, on that day, Mister Gong, you will see some killing. Oh yes. By then, Mister Gong, we will be way past caring, about trivial matters like morality, or law…'

'Yes?'

'Oh yes. On that day, we will be Gods.'

SEVEN:
CLOSE

Carlton exited the Front Bar via the creaking old dark-hardwood door that directly accessed the wide, plain, concrete-floored veranda. He took a few deep breaths of the freezing cold air. There was a dim but serviceable light just over the door, with a little more light from the main front bar window to his right, two halogen carpark lights further out, and a streetlight even further up Warren Road. The huge door behind him released only a modicum of light from a tiny trio of windows set in a line at peak eye-level, as though the nineteenth century barkeep were still wary of approaching strangers, lest they might be bushrangers. Combined though, there was enough illumination to navigate drunk to one's car, generally parked no more than a dozen steps away, right outside. Carlton waited, guzzled down the last of his beer, then placed the empty bottle upon the closest of six hardwood tables, three each of which extended out along the veranda to either side of the front door, all of which had been bolted to the walls, and down into the ancient crack-riddled concrete of the well-worn verandah, with their long benches fully attached and immovable, many decades prior. Carlton was alone out here. Only the smokers braved the cold this time of year, but most of them favoured the benches on the balcony out the back.

'Concrete. Steel. Glass. All neutral…' Barker had told him once. '…in essence.'

On the other side of Warren Road, immediately facing the hotel, was a rocky hillside. Warren curved along this broad hillside, a steep gradient of right-to-left decline, heading down toward Stirling then continuing down and around, eventually out of view to the left, towards the unseen freeway, two k's away. The Adelaide Hills were not particularly high, with just one central barely-mountain, but they were big, forming a long, wide arc around an expansive basin, the flat plains of which the city and expanding suburbs were built upon. Warren Road formed the central part of the larger extension of roads that followed what was referred to as the back of The Hills, the side that didn't face the west-facing, sunset coastline, right around, north to south, pretty much from one end to the other. All the pubs along Warren were like this; the entrance directly in from the road, the balcony out the back, and there were as many pubs as there were old passes up from the city (which was five, Carlton knew all too well, and one each in between, like the Crow and Kingfisher, bringing the total to nine.) Some of the original roads were major suburban thoroughfares now, leading into the thriving Hills suburbs. These colonial-era pubs were the stops where, in the olden times, you could have a last drink, or a last night's rest, or get last provisions, top-ups or forgotten items before a potentially very long and dangerous journey to another town, or even another city, hundreds of miles away, often in another state. Sure, there would be other towns along the way, but nothing was guaranteed and until then, by horse and cart, these pubs, just over the rise of The Hills, had been it.

They had also been amongst the first public structures built in the young nation, along with the churches. They had both thrived of course; just as the towns that had formed around them had thrived. That was where Fiif was from; a long established family, right at the heart of one of those towns, the town of Stirling, where the Pound and Silver Hotel, her local, had long ago taken down its dart board and hired a five-star chef.

Then there were the pubs that had evolved for different reasons. Those that had not evolved along main thoroughfare intersections, specifically for travellers to restock, but as purpose-specific gathering places for townsfolk, the pubs in-between, deeper within the expanding communities.

The Crow and Kingfisher was one of these; the 'dive pub' between the Pound, three k's south, and the Lion, five north. The Crow had now become more secluded than any other Hills pub, virtually forgotten and generally avoided by anyone who was not already a regular, and thus had barely changed since the early settler days; still privately owned and out of the clutches of the corporate breweries, still primarily servicing its local, traditional clientele, a loyal member of which Carlton was, very much so, and had been all his life.

The old place definitely needed some work though, the rustic darkness of the vibe notwithstanding. The Crow was older even than the Lion, and somehow... darker, Carlton supposed? He was a sorcerer, and he supposed he should have a better word than that. Not evil, certainly. Just... more occult? More hidden, and secluded? After all, he'd practically lived in the front bar for a while, seven or so years back, after the disaster at Bridger Mansion, and nobody had bothered him. Nobody had known, really. The bar had become a second home to him now, or at least a second living room, and he felt comfortable within its weird echoes of working class colonial darkness, and its – some said – creepy, insular, local vibe.

Several times he'd heard new visitors throw quotes around from the comedy-horror film, *An American Werewolf in London*, or mention the fictional dark-comedy town of Royston Vasey.

He would laugh.

He supposed he could see it.

The balcony here, just around the corner from where he stood at the front door, looked east, inland, back over the hilly, undulating planes, toward the outlying ranges. Even the near-midnight view from the back of the Crow hinted at the distant, infamous outback, as opposed to the more metro-romantic view from the city, out across the distant ocean, that the Lion offered, and Carlton genuinely preferred it. He stretched a few casual steps along the creaking wood. It was stunning, but with no ocean-sunset view and without a major township surrounding it, the view had become forgotten over time.

Although… he had been hearing weird stuff about the Lion for the past few weeks. How that had been empty, too. He was surprised that he hadn't been approached, given that this was, essentially, his turf. If what he'd heard was true, then why had nobody come here, to the front bar on a Monday or Tuesday night, and asked him to fix –

Someone exited the hotel. Fiif came around to the edge of the balcony, down to the corner, to where she'd told him to wait.

He smirked. 'Afraid to be seen with the local psychic?'

'What? No. I needed to pee.'

'You said wait outside.'

'I said, do you want to wait outside?'

'Oh.'

He saw her clearly now in the carpark light; he realized that he'd never really seen her just normal. She'd been really hotted-up, the three times he'd seen her before. The time they'd bumped into each other at the Pound and Silver, the first time the chemistry had happened between them, the first time they'd seen each other for a few years, she'd been kitted out as the leader of the local sports WAGs. Then, the other two weekends after that, when she'd come right over to his place after going to the pub first, then making her excuses, she had presented herself very well. She had gift-wrapped herself, even. Just for him.

But now here she was. Just normal. Probably been at work all day, a little extra makeup before throwing on the huge coat, borrowing hubby's car and telling him she was going – somewhere else. Under the centrally parted halo of long, thick but dead-straight bright-blonde hair, the long locks of which remained splayed over the huge coat, Fiif had a pale complexion with light freckles over a thin bone structure ending in a sharp chin. Her lips were normal. That is, for a woman of her strata, she was surprisingly natural and free of collagen. They were not full lips. Straight, almost severe, but that was part of what happened when she smiled, or gave you one of those smirks. It made her look knowing, calculating, and to Carlton, distractingly sexy. Her blemish-free skin glowed evenly now, and her huge, wide, black-lined eyes, all white with brilliant teal-blue at the core, looked right at him, then away.

Where was the boyfriend, the husband, tonight, he wondered?

Where had he been back then?

Did they live together?

As she turned away, he saw the element that really made her something. Head-on, she was hot. Simply, hot. You could put her on a cover. The bridge of her nose was two perfectly symmetrical crescents, from the inner edge of her dark eyebrows to the edge of her barely-visible nostrils. But that was because, in profile, her nose was really something. Long, sharp, defined. Narrow, so it was invisible head on, but from the side it quite simply stood out, and she was infinitely more stunning because of that. The darts crew probably wouldn't see it that way. Ordinary folk wouldn't see it; they would process it as part of her package that *was hot*, and allow the nose to go unnoticed, unless someone, probably cruelly, decided to make a point of it. But it was there, and Carlton found it a thing of infinite fascination. A hot beak. Go figure.

He remembered kissing the hot beak, once or twice, affectionately. He remembered her touching it after, puzzled. Almost blushing. He remembered it all, when he wanted, but it all seemed like a dream now. He hadn't asked questions, he'd just allowed it to unfold without any well-formulated query really occurring. Like some corny chick-flick. Her father owned a business, she had money and a career, and a boyfriend who could say the same. But *he*, Carlton, was unshaven pub scum.

'So how do we do this?' Fiif asked.

Professional face. 'Where was this party?'

'I'm not sure that's important.' Fiif sniffed in the cold. 'They never got there.'

'And this was last Saturday night?'

'Amanda, she was with Maz. They'd only just started.'

'Amanda? What happened to Hot Tess?'

'Tess is distraught. We're looking for her little sister. Amanda.'

'Oh, right.'

Fiif exhaled heavily. 'Really.'

'They just met? Her and the new boy?'

'No; it's one of those things. They've known each other forever, ignored each other their whole lives, until suddenly a few months back…'

'The planets aligned…' Carlton mumbled.

'You believe in all that?'

'All that?'

'I mean, isn't that part of the whole thing?'

'The whole thing?'

She looked away from him, like she had no time for him being a prick about her simple questions. Like, she knew he wasn't actually like that. After all, he wasn't, and he wasn't sure why he was being that way. She must have been getting to him.

'I don't suppose it has to be…' She glanced back, then looked away from him again. Vapour blew around her mouth. She was cold, and worried. 'You can be occult without believing in astrology. Like you can be spiritual without being religious. Believe in Christ without believing the Bible. That sort of thing.'

The fog was thickening around the carpark, enough so the lights were falling on it.

'Sure…' Carlton shrugged. 'The Abrahamic religions have a monopoly, but on the mystical cosmic scale, they're…'

What was he doing? Was this what she wanted to hear?

He looked out at the road again. The long and twisted path of Warren Road took it through just about every socio-economic district possible; from high views and money houses, where everybody could see; through the ordinary nice homes, where nobody cared; past little shanties, and down valleys, where nobody knew. That was where they were now. A stretch with dirt drives that dived immediately from one side of the road, or jutted up without warning from the other. Tiny letterboxes. House numbers nailed to gum trunks. Otherwise ordinary suburban-brick three-bedroomers that sometimes quite startlingly clung along a ridgetop as though deposited there by a cyclone.

'…the Abrah's; they're like the Pound and Silver. They started small but positioned themselves to be on a major thoroughfare. But really, it's just supposed to be one stop on a long and winding road. Not something you build a civilization around. You really don't, really shouldn't, have to spend your whole life there, even though once you've settled in, it feels like you might want to. And the owners, certainly, want you to.' Carlton looked at her. 'Is that the kind of thing you want to hear?'

Fiif made a little scoff, not unappreciative, and looked further out to the blackness of the Crow and Kingfisher's balcony.

'So what's this? Crowley Corner?'

Carlton smiled. 'It can be.' She could see that he was impressed. He let her see.

'I can Google you know,' Fiif shrugged. 'I know about all that. I listen. You made an impression. Anyway. She was seeing another guy. Older. Said it was something to do. Maybe it was just the sex, but he was a real douche. Maybe…'

She walked a little way down the balcony. The wood boards creaked as she took a few steps in. The single bay window beside her looked into the unlit, L-shaped dining room that ran the length of this side of the hotel, then right along the back. Deep within they could see a glowing orange upright rectangle, where light seeped through from the closed inner door to the front bar.

As soon as someone else bought it, Carlton knew, that room would be filled with poker machines. This was one of the last hotel dining rooms in Australia not to fall prey in that manner. The room, the whole pub really, at least most of it, still belonged to a completely different time, a different world, a different sensibility, and for reasons that he kept well to himself, Carlton was quite proud of that fact.

'Maybe that's got something to do with it…?' Fiif shrugged her thick coat shoulders, and the thick hair that lay upon them.

'How old are these people we're looking for?'

'Thirty, around.'

'So she's thirtyish? And she left an older guy for a guy her own age?'

'He's our age. Thirty-five.'

'The douche?'

'Yeah. And he is. A real...' She sighed. 'Douche is so American. He's a fuckwit. A real fuckwit.'

Carlton followed Fiif along a few steps to the wide valley view, centrally dissected by the bright freeway lights that curved down from The Northern Hills; two bright-white strips of two, centrally separated, receding way into the distance, far along the valley floor. Beneath the view; a steep, five-hundred-meter descent into a rocky ravine.

Fiif looked out with what appeared to Carlton to be a wistful gaze of deep appreciation, but really could have been anything.

'Do they still call it Donger's Tramp?'

Carlton laughed. 'Poor Donger.'

'Whatever became of him?'

'He stopped drinking. Moved away.'

Donger had been a perfectly ordinary looking bloke who had such illogically low self-confidence that he would have to, almost routinely at the end, get so hopelessly drunk in order to ask any given female customer for a dance, or a snog, or whatever, at the end of any given Saturday night, that after the inevitable drooling, indecipherable proposition had been delivered, it would inevitably be refused. As a result, Donger would then drink even more to drown his sorrows, and talk himself into believing he was some kind of hideously unlovable beast that no woman could or would ever fancy, which at this point in the evening, with his blotchy skin, red eyes and slurring speech, it had to be said, was sadly a self-fulfilled truth. Donger would then walk out to the balcony and state to anyone out there with all due heightened emotion that he intended to end it all by throwing himself off.

The first time he'd done it, the locals had all been fairly sure that he'd been serious. But what Donger hadn't known, this being the mid-eighties and all, was that due to new health and safety regulations, the pub's then-owner had some time ago been forced to place a strong net below the balcony's sheer drop. This had been one; for this exact reason, and two; to protect any person standing upon the hiking trail beneath from the ignominious fate of having a beer bottle dropped on their head from such a height; it was said that just a five cent piece would reach terminal velocity from here.

Not every Saturday night ended with a Donger jump, as a sympathetic woman could often be found talking him down for hours, perhaps giving him part of the attention he so sorely required. However, locals had long ago assessed that by the time Donger hit both the wagon and the road, he had launched himself off, into the net, some fifty or sixty-odd times in six years, and that he had long ago started to enjoy, if not look forward to it. Such was the casual acceptance of the group-alcoholic front bar that constituted Donger's peer group, that the name Donger's Tramp had come, and stuck, no later than the night of his fifth attempt.

'That's what people assume, anyway. He was always talking about quitting, moving away. He said he was stuck, and he couldn't help it. Alcohol does that to some people. Every pub has one. That guy who can't leave, but should. Who's perversely become content somewhere he can't be happy, because he's too scared to leave, and start again somewhere else, where nobody knows him.'

Fiif sniffed hard, and looked around, all around.

Carlton seemed to have touched a nerve.

'I know that. He came to the Pound one night. He couldn't even talk to anyone. I gave him a pity chat. But, he was so weird by then. All he could do was take out a Swiss Army Knife. Said he'd bought it because one day he'd get out, go traveling. Seemed to think he'd need it. He might have been perfectly nice; but his brain was stuck in a terribly limited perspective. He was just so scared of everything.'

Carlton stared at her. 'He went to The Pound?'

Fiif shrugged. 'A few times. It was very brave of him. If I saw him around, I'd always ask how he was. He was different sober. But he was still very awkward. So shy, poor boy. I hope he did leave. I hope he found somewhere to be. Some people are just born in the wrong place.' She took a few more steps into the darkness. 'It's been a long time since I was out here. I forgot. They really should do more out here, make more of it.'

'They've had offers.'

'What do you mean?'

'I thought that's what you meant; developers want to turn it into a modern pub. Pokies and a bistro. Proper chef. Nightclub vibe. Like the Pound. Watch the cars race down the freeway, into the valley and beyond, racing toward their destination while you sit, content, right here on the balcony with your wine already in hand.'

She gave him a blank look then stared back out.

'Nothing wrong with that… in its place.'

'This isn't its place.'

'I didn't say it was.'

Carlton stared out too now, silent.

The valley vista remained low but hilly way off to either side, throughout the further expanse of which the web of the Adelaide Hills suburbs was spread, just as the path of the freeway lights itself still undulated as it receded for tens of kilometres. Usually you could clearly see the great stretch of land that led out to the vast horizon; the harsh country with its lush pockets, expanding to the cruel, craggy, haunted outback and eventually the unforgiving ochre of the blistering desert. But not tonight. Tonight, despite the moonlight, the full vista was bordered by a vast bank of storm clouds.

'That's unexpected…' Fiif uttered.

'Is it?'

She walked on, a few more steps, a third of the way down.

'Huh.' Carlton didn't know where the fuck he stood now. Perky, almost flirty; interested, if not educated, then melancholy, now curious again. Was she luring him? He knew from experience, from coming out here with people who secretly smoked weed, that at this time of night, if the balcony lights were out, and the dining room was closed, you could not see a soul, not past half way down the side of the balcony. Still, he had no idea. Was this for real? Was she really seeking the wisdom of his occult experience? Or was it just an excuse for another fling?

Or both? He made a play anyway.

'So how's things with…' He pulled something out of the air. '…Old Rectangle Head?'

They always did. Square heads, rectangle heads. Hexagon heads, some of them. They always had them.

'Rectangle Head?'

'Old Tiny Ears Rectangle Head…'

She stared at him.

'…isn't that what all the guys call him?'

He really had no idea. He'd never even seen the guy.

She laughed. Just a short one, accompanied by a huge puff of vapour.

'Okay. Well, Old Rectangle Head watches the weather.'

'For sports…?'

'Keeping an eye. Preparing for Saturday. Cricket in summer, footy in winter. It becomes an obsession…'

'The sport or the weather? Don't answer. All of it, right?' She didn't answer as Carlton continued to stare ahead. 'That really is a hell of a storm front. Can't see past it in any direction… don't think it's a dust storm…'

'Does that mean something?'

'In the occult? Sometimes. Mostly though a storm is just a storm.'

'But…?'

'This wasn't predicted on the news, was it?'

'Carlton, seriously. Don't pretend like you don't have a weather app on your phone. It's going to be cold all week. Light rain Saturday. But they didn't expect the storm last weekend either, all that rain. This looks much worse.'

Carlton walked out, past her. He couldn't take his eyes off it now.

'That's right. There was a bad storm on the weekend, wasn't there? And... that's when your friends went missing...'

Out there now, it was as though a massive cliff-face of white and greys, and deeper, darker greys, close to blacks even, had been suddenly erected over the distant countryside. It certainly had not been there when he'd arrived a few hours previously.

'You don't remember? Last weekend? It thundered down.'

'Yeah. I mean...' He kind of remembered. 'Of course I remember...' He'd been sleeping off a long day at the races the day before. But this massive low pressure system seemed to have rolled in hard, and fast, from deep in the far outback, and was now roaring up and bearing down on Adelaide, horizon to horizon.

'It's like...'

'It's like a big metal wall...' Fiif uttered. 'Like aliens have landed and fenced us in or something...' She scowled. 'It's like the front of a massive wave...'

'Like a...' Carlton fell silent a second.

'What?' Fiif demanded. 'You're on to something. What is it?'

It was, Carlton thought... like; like a...

He looked north and south. He couldn't tell. But it felt bad. It felt... awful. It felt as though it were not just one bank coming in from the east, across the plains toward The Hills, but just the part of it they could see; part of a massive whole, a massive circular weather formation.

'Freak weather can be just freak weather. But sometimes... *sometimes*...'

'It's summoned?'

'Yes. But; not the way you think. Not like a rain dance to bring in the rain. More like, there has been a mystical quake, here in the city. And this is the result. After all the energy has been exploited, and sucked out, this is the tsunami, coming in. That's what I was thinking. A tsunami.'

'A mystical quake?'

'A ceremony. A destructive ceremony.'

'Black magic?'

'Cheryl calls it Moxic.'

'Moxic?'

'She's very politically correct. And she doesn't like the connotations that black, or night, or the unconscious, or the hidden, or the occult, or the guarded, is evil. So she's trying to get people to call it toxic magic. Moxic.'

'Really? Moxic?'

'She'll settle for Togic as well. Maxic sounded too cool. I think it'll turn out that the "Old Black Magic", as it were, is Moxic. She's hoping one or the other ugly words will stick.'

'They won't. If Maxic sounds cool, it will probably end up being that. It's cool to be bad, Carlton. You should know that.'

Carlton stared are her. 'What do you do, Fiif?'

'What do you think, Freaker Fonzie? I'm the Media Coordination Exec at Wicca'd Inc. I do their PR.'

Carlton kept staring at her, as best he could in the moonlight.

'Wicca'd Inc?'

'Sure. Why not?'

Carlton let it drop. 'I'll tell you later. But look, Cheryl wanted something new, for the new millennium.'

'Didn't we all?'

'Well, she tried. She kept trying. It's what she does. She knows what she wants, Cheryl. You got people to change what they call you, didn't you Fifi?'

'I got a dozen people in a closed circle to drop on syllable at the end of my name. And even that took six months. Your friend wants to rebrand 'black magic'. Do you know how long it took for people to start referring to 'the universe' the way they do, when they mean non-specific, non-institutionalized, non-affiliated-with-established-religion-God?'

'No.'

'Actually neither do I. But I'm sure it was more than a decade. What's reception like here, I might Google it…?'

'That's how it starts though, Fiif, right? A small group of people in the right city, the right cultural enclave? Or, those people individually infiltrating many enclaves, at once?'

'I don't work for the CIA, Carlton.'

They had remained half way down the side-balcony, and from what Carlton could tell, the storm had remained still too. But surely, it just seemed that way. Something that huge, from this distance, more than one hundred k's away… it was sure to be closing in, whether they could see it from here or not. Carlton didn't feel the cold, not like Barker and Cheryl. But when this kind of thing happened, even the first sweeping breezes, the initial chills, gave him cause to cover up beyond his open shirt, tee and jeans. He had his long leather jacket in his car, but for now he didn't want to go back. And it wasn't just that it would reinforce the Freaker Fonzie thing. He was missing something; and now Fiif stepped into the shadows, her eyes fixed on it.

'Warm enough?'

She looked back and shrugged. 'Sure. I don't mind sightseeing. It's majestic and… I don't know. Maybe that giant wall of steel cloud is what you think it is. Maybe you have to watch it a while…? Maybe that's the real reason we're here?'

'You're here to hire me. Let's not forget that. But, I can do both,' Carlton gave a tight, sharp shrug. Then he walked past her, right to the end. It was black everywhere; right down into the valley. Aside from a few houses above The Hills, here and there up late; golden, homey, warm and deceptively distant, the full moon on the banks, and the four streaks of freeway were the only lights that stood out. Then one flicked out, even as he had the thought. The boards creaked and echoed as Fiif walked down behind him, right to the back rail.

'So…' Carlton heard himself say. 'You're pretty sure…?'

'I woke up…' She was standing beside him now, staring out into the long, foggy valley. '…Zinco asked me what was wrong.'

Zinco.

His was genuinely surprised, just a tad, to feel his heart sink a little. So much for John Hughes.

'I asked why, and he said that he just felt that there was something wrong with me. I'd just woken up weirdly, he said. I hadn't intended to say anything. Zinco's not superstitious. And I said that I felt it; like something really bad had happened. And it was… all about Amanda. Like she was gone… and it hadn't been nice. I thought…'

Carlton watched her face in the shadows and moonlight now. This was part of it. Some people just got a bad feeling in their heads and ran with it; turned it into a premonition. If it happened to coincide with reality, then they were suddenly psychic and sometimes even parlayed that into a cottage business. Other people were flat-out fakes, but some, not even that rarely, just picked up on a wave of something. They connected with… maybe a burst of mental energy sent out at the moment of a trauma? People said that the brain wasn't a receiver any more than it was a transmitter. But Carlton had seen enough to know that it was. At least, for some, it was. One or the other, sometimes both. But he'd also read enough to know that nobody could prove it, or even if they thought they could, didn't know how it really worked. Drove themselves mad trying to explain, to prove, to the point where it just all shut down. He didn't care, really. He just did what he could. That way, madness lay.

'…I thought she'd been in an accident. But both of them are missing.'

'Missing is a broad word, Fiif.'

'Well, okay, look; they didn't tell anyone where they were going. I mean, she runs the café on High Druid Lane and he's a contractor. Her assistant opens up if she's not there and his crew goes on working whether he's there or not. Everyone thinks they've just gone off on a romantic weekend and don't want to come back.'

Carlton hummed. 'Tuesday night and they're still not back... that's a long weekend, given that it's not a long weekend...'

'Exactly. Her phone's still ringing, but it's not going to message and nobody's answering. He's the same, apparently.'

A car went past behind them on Warren. A quiet roar, and as Carlton glanced back through the developing fog, he saw the bright ice-blue lights of a high-class European car. He looked across the valley again, to the plains beyond. Those clouds. Darker and higher... maybe closer. Maybe faster. All perspective.

'Reception here is terrible. Two k's that way is the biggest, highest phone tower in the state, but down here – nothing. We really should check the weather, it's better out in the carpark, let's – '

They fell suddenly silent as they realized that the dart guys were leaving. They could hear them speak, joking in rapid succession, two or three at a time over the top of each other. Carlton and Fiif retreated quickly around the balcony corner, then leaned about a third down.

They heard;

'... shagging in the bushes!'

Then raucous laughter. They saw the glow of a phone, then a second phone, then both went out within a second of each other.

'Night Maxine!'

They heard further cries of goodnight, then slamming car doors, motors starting, tyres on gravel and all the cars at once headed out. The cold night was so silent, they could hear each car individually, for more than a full minute each, quite distinctively heading home across the hillside roads. When they were gone, Carlton headed back to the balcony corner, then walked half way back along the side. There were three cars still there, nested in the side of the essentially circular, white-gravel parking bay. His, Fiif's and another. One of the five old blokes must have driven another home. Maxine, the new bartender, seemed to have gone as well, there was no light at all from within the pub. Fiif walked up behind him. Each step of her elegant leather boots sounded like the sharp chop of an axe, then she stopped beside him.

Carlton was feeling edgy. Nothing felt right.

'So, he killed her? Right? The boyfriend killed Amanda? Or, she killed him? Whichever, the killer disabled messaging, put the phones somewhere satellites would have a hard time finding them, tossed them at least, and ran.'

A possum cried out. A horrible squawking that sounded like long, croaking, mocking laughter.

Waaaah, wah-wah wah-wah.

Waaaah, wah-wah wah-wah.

Fiif ignored it and stared at him. 'I hardly think so. You'd crunch them, destroy the chip.' Carlton laughed low to himself. He knew that. Fiif went on. 'Not leave them to ring, like, murder evidence with its own built in locator and unique theme song that plays by remote. Maz is no genius but he wasn't totally thick.'

Now Carlton was fully chuckling. His eyes were becoming more accustomed to the moonlight, still emanating from high above the incoming cloud bank. Then another chorus;

Waaaah, wah-wah wah-wah.

It seemed to mock their good humour.

'People never believe that, though, do they?' Fiif sounded as though she were reconsidering something. An important element of her assumption. 'Even though it's…'

'What?' Carlton asked.

'What is it? Eighty, eight-five? Ninety percent of the time, it's the person closest to the victim who ends up being the murderer.'

Carlton shrugged. 'Doesn't matter, we'll find out.'

'We will?'

'If something has happened to her, I can tell you.'

'How?'

He looked at her, enquiringly.

'I mean, what do we do? How... do we go about it?'

He considered a second. They heard a car roaring in the distance, from the Stirling side.

'So, they never got to the party...?'

'No.'

'Did anyone see them together that night?'

'She called Tess before she left.'

'Tess.'

'Her sister. Hot Tess. Remember Hot Tess?'

'So Maz and Amanda were going to leave from Amanda's place, and walk to the party. Walk where? How long? Where was the party?'

'A scout hall; one of those ones they hire out for twenty firsts. You know, there's basically one in every town.'

'Which one?'

'Verdun? Lobethal? I can't remember.'

'Twenty first? A bit old for that, aren't we?'

'No. It was a big one. All ages. That's generally what big twenty firsts are, Carlton. That's why you hire a hall. Especially up here; the way everyone drinks. Besides, Amanda was a surprise. She's eight, nine years younger than us, than Tess. The party was for someone Amanda used to babysit for, or something. Amanda still drinks, still goes to all those mad binge parties with the cricketers and footballers and whatever.'

'Isn't your boyfriend one of those?'

'Zinco is the main one of those. Which is how I know.'

Carlton felt his brain pinch, above his right temple; that always seemed to mean he'd hit a raw nerve.

'Know what?'

She gave him her hawk profile.

'That she was supposed to be there. That she didn't show.'

Carlton nodded. 'Come on, I need reception.'

She nodded and they walked back out to the carpark. With

their eyes adjusted to the darkness, and only the streetlights and moonlight now, it was okay.

But then again, to Carlton, it still seemed very dark.

What was it? If there was any genuine animosity between her and Rectangle Zinco, he couldn't detect it. Their three-weekend fling must have happened during a bad patch with her and Zinco. Or maybe he'd been a genuine wild oat. She still had her gloves on; he couldn't see any rings. But then again, he would not necessarily have heard about it, if they'd gotten married.

'I know it sounds bad. But look, Maz was driving to Amanda's place, and they were going to walk from there. Maz got there, Amanda was on the phone with Tess, her sister, and she said they had to get going because they were walking.'

'Walking to avoid drink driving?'

'Maz was in an accident a while back. Now he walks everywhere, if he's drinking. And, everyone in that sports crowd drinks everywhere they go.'

Carlton nodded. 'Sure. I do the same. You drink too much, you walk home, you hope it all balances out. I'm about three k's, uphill all the way. So where does Amanda live?'

'Why?'

'We need to go there. If they connected there, then went together, I can follow the way they walked.'

'Follow them?'

'I can get an emotional signal…' Carlton told her.

'A what?'

'It's like…' Carlton huffed. 'It's like, if something happened to them, if there was a rock dropped in the psychic pond of their lives…?'

'Yes…?'

'If I can get to the edge of the pond, before the psychic waves stop lapping up on shore, then I can… see.'

'See?'

'Where the waves are coming from. Trace the ripples back to where the rock impacted. But, three days later… if I can still pick up waves, ripples on the shore, it won't be good. It will have been a big rock. Hit hard. An awful splash.'

Fiif regarded him squarely. 'We'd better go then.'

'Now? You're okay with that? It's ten o'clock on a Tuesday night, sweetie. Won't your hubbie – ?'

'No, he won't. That's my car.' She pointed to something large and shining, bottle-green. It looked powerful, and safe, and cool. It was probably Zinco's.

'I'll drive,' Fiif assured him.

Carlton heard a strange noise above them. The roads all through The Hills were lined with Stobie Poles, a kind of above-ground power pole virtually unique to Adelaide, named after the man who had designed them. Each consisted of two upright steel girders, held together with a long central slab of cement. There was a roadside Stobie on each side of the carpark; the one on the left was painted with a kingfisher mural, the one on the right with a crow. Carlton looked from one to the other then up to the top of the poles. Atop each were a dozen wires, connected by two short horizontal poles, like the top of a ship's mast.

Two grey possums, presumably the ones who had been calling out not long ago, ran up the Stobie with the painted crow totem and leaped in turn onto the electrical wires. Anyone who had lived in Adelaide, anywhere near The Hills, had seen this many times. The wires were fully insulated.

'Oh, look…' Fiif aired. 'I love it when they do that!'

Each of the possums froze, briefly remained clinging upside down to the wires, then dropped twenty-five meters to the ground, almost simultaneously with a sickening double thud-thud.

Carlton and Fiif stood still.

'Oh. That's horrible. Poor things!'

'It happens sometimes…' Carlton offered.

'I know. But…? I mean, there's a 'but' coming, isn't there?'

'Your friends…'

Carlton looked squarely at Fiif.

'I think they're in real trouble.'

Suddenly the car in the distance sounded incredibly loud.

'Or...'

'Or...?' Fiif demanded.

'That car's on Warren...' Carlton uttered. 'It's coming here...'

'Hoons, this time of night,' Fiif groaned. 'Even after all the – '

'Or; *we're* in real trouble.' Carlton grabbed her hand. '*Come on.*'

He turned and led her with all due haste back down to the edge of the balcony. They had only just rounded the dark corner as the car, rapidly peaking in volume the entire time, skidded off of Warren and onto the gravel of the Crow carpark, narrowly missing the fresh possum corpses.

'Stay back!' Carlton warned as she peeked around the corner.

She ducked back. 'It's Zinco!'

'Oh. Christ.'

'Hardly!'

They heard two doors slam and shuffling footsteps on the gravel.

'Fuck! She's not here!' The first voice was gruff and immediately irritating.

'That's my car.' The second voice was Zinco. Calmer. Much calmer. 'Who else do you think was driving it?'

'Yeah, but...'

They heard more gravel scuffling as they clearly attempted to see inside, and empty clunking as they tried the door handles.

'There's nobody in the fucken thing, Zinco!'

'Jesus Wombo. I can see that.'

Carlton whispered, extremely low. 'Wombo? As in, William 'Wombat' Bathurst?'

She nodded.

'He's your *friend?*'

'I just know him. He's my husband's *friend.*'

'*Husband?*'

'Zinco and me are married. Seven years.'

Carlton couldn't even look at her now. Zinco and Wombo. Two people he never expected, wanted nor deserved to see again in his entire life, who just happened to both live in the same town.

'Fucking Wombo has fucking hated me since primary school!'

She nodded again, with a little shrug, but not the slightest hint of apology.

'Hey!' Wombo snarled. 'This is that cunt's car.'

Carlton let out a slight groan.

'That arsehole who drinks here.'

'What; that Carlton bloke from high school?'

'Carl-*tun*. *Tun-tun-tun!* Fucking Cunt-tun, the Craven Raven. Rark rark rark! Fark fark fark! Fark the Cunt! Fark the Cunton!' Wombo gave an angry chortle. 'Fucking arsehole. Learned to take a fucking joke about as well as he learned to take a fucking beating.'

Carlton could feel Fiif's eyes upon him now, different, another level of energy. He could sense her heartbeat increasing, racing. She seemed to inch closer.

'Carlton Craven. So what? He was dealt with years ago.'

Dealt with? Carlton was confounded at this man's choice of words.

Zinco went on. 'Now he's a fucking derro, drinks here every night.'

'No I...' Carlton murmured. 'Mondays and Tues –'

'Ssh.' Fiif shouldered him in the back.

'Wombo, Craven Raven's an idiot. He was caught up in all that shit at Bridger Mansion. I was told all about it by people who were there. He couldn't handle himself. Him and all his fucking idiot witchcraft mates.'

'He's in on this with her!' Wombo insisted, sounding, it had to be said, more than a little mentally unstable. 'Listen, mate, your fucking wife is hiding my fucking girlfriend so you come clean about your fucking mistress. This is un-fucking-acceptable, mate. We all know he had the hots for her after that night he came to the fucking Pound, we all saw the way they were talking –'

'Wombo, she likes talking to weirdos, she says it makes them feel better…'

'Fuck that! She's got a fucking thing for 'im, we all know it! She always had, right back to fucking high school!'

'Rein it in, Wombo. High school was a long fucking time ago and that's my wife you're talking about.'

'It's fucking true, Zinco! That's why we sent 'im off, last time 'e came through, an' 'e never fucking came back, did 'e? But if Fiif were gonna do something mental, like real batshit mental, like kidnap Amanda and give 'er some money to run off with that fucker she thinks she's in love with, then who's she gunna get to help 'er? We all know he does drugs from here Tuesday nights!'

Carlton watched as Zinco cast his gaze around the rim of the carpark, running his vision over a wall of darkness, bordered only by night-shaded trees, the hotel frontage, and the dark asphalt of Warren Road. Carlton knew what he would be thinking. Did he go looking, into the dark? Out the back here, to the balcony? Stoners, lovers, junkies, UFO-spotters… you could run into anyone; chilling, thinking, plotting, scheming, whatever, out here after midnight. Even the ghost of old Donger, dead after his last jump, but still trying to find a sympathetic woman to convince him to stop.

'Look, you need to come clean with 'er about bloody Tess mate! That's all she wants!'

Even under her coat, Carlton felt her whole body tense.

'Fuck this, Wombo. Tell me again, and talk more slow this time; what exactly did your Dad tell you?'

'Dad rang me. Right? When he was leaving the pub tonight. Here, this pub. And he said; "Son, you know your mate Zinco? Well, his hot fucken wife's only been in the front fucken' bar of the Crow, all bloody night, chattin' up some rough fucken trade, makin' a real fucken spectacle of 'erself, an' just before closing, they both went off outside together!" And I said, "Right! Right, Dad! Thank you, mate! I am getting in the car as we speak and getting Zinco and driving right fucken there! Right fucken now!"'

There was silence for a few long seconds until Zinco spoke

again.

'Both their cars… are here.'

'And that's my Dad's. He gets a ride with The Baron when he's three sheets and knows it.'

'So he was pissed?'

'He knows who Fiif is, Zinco. Fucken everyone knows who Fiif is!'

Fiif whispered in Carlton's ear. 'The hot babe with the big nose who's married to The Captain.'

'The hot *fucken* WAG, with the big *fucken nose*, and the big *fucken tits*, who's married to *The Fucken Captain*.'

'Shut up a minute Wombo. For fuck's sake! She doesn't have a big nose! Let me think for a second!'

Carlton whispered. 'Yes you do. It's part of what makes you beautiful.'

She whispered back, with a slight scoff. 'Like, *I know*.'

There was some clatter as Wombo started picking up fistfuls of gravel and throwing them onto the road.

'Wombo! Jesus!'

Wombo spun about, furious. 'They're probably still fucking here, Zinco! They're probably still fucking out the back on the balcony! They probably jumped down onto Donger's Tramp and are still fucking, fucking laughing at us, Zinco! She's probably frozen in the bushes over there with his limp cock still in her mouth!'

Wombo pointed right at Carlton. Zinco took a few steps toward the balcony. Carlton's head was just poked around; there was no way he could be seen, but he could see that Zinco was livid. Properly livid.

Carlton allowed himself an utter. 'There's something wrong…'

More cars became apparent in the distance, one each approaching fast from either side.

Zinco turned back to Wombo. This time, he sounded properly angry.

'I said not to!'

'If she's with Cunt Craven, we need to teach that fucker a lesson!'

Carlton and Fiif whispered very low now.

'Oh God, Carlton, can you fight?'

'No.' He hissed through his teeth. 'I mean...'

'Can you throw a punch?'

'Not since... no. I don't know. Is there a skill to it?'

'Fuck.'

'Look, a sorcerer can defend, and fight if needs be, right?'

'Sorcerer? Carlton, this is beyond –'

'But there are rules...'

'Wombo and his mates don't fight to any rules, Carlton...!'

'Not like that; the thing is, if we don't choose the path of the warrior priest, we can only fight properly, with sorcery, wielding our nominated weapon.'

'Nominated weapon?'

'Which is in the boot of my freaking car!'

'Fuck.'

'Look, I might have to go out there...'

She suddenly embraced him. They were down low and she was locked into him, kissing him with an open mouth. He felt her lips press his mouth open, her nose against his, and her tongue inside his mouth. He kissed her back, then she pulled away suddenly, and was staring into his eyes.

She seemed a little sad.

'Now I know why you slept with me.'

He didn't know what to say.

'I'll get us out of this. Stay here.'

She was up and around the corner, and walking back down the balcony toward the carpark as the other two cars arrived.

EIGHT:
ANIMAL RESCUE

It wasn't far, but Barker was trusting Bach to be stupidly, emergency-level fast while he lay back, his hands not anywhere near the handlebars, cradling the unconscious koala in his lap, hammocked by his buttoned-up coat and further supported by his left foot being hooked up over his right knee. He was quietly praying that the enormous furry thing, easily taking up the whole of his lap, was okay. It was breathing, but it was also bleeding from its head, and it still hadn't woken up. But he was also, a little less quietly, praying that if it was okay, it would not wake up until he got it to safety. He had never held a koala before but he'd seen several around The Hills, and like most Australians he was well-aware; a koala's claws were potentially deadly, razor-sharp grappling hooks made for clinging for long periods onto gum trees, hundreds of meters high, in all weather conditions. Also, their limbs were relatively dextrous, extending way longer than anyone had the right to expect, especially given the cute, fluffy balls they appeared to be in most of the Adelaide Hills tourist propaganda. The fact that his very solid unconscious passenger also seemed to weigh a metric tonne also reminded him that male koalas, when they fought for territory, like any animal really, could be awfully brutal. He'd heard of them biting, as well as scratching, and the size of this one… well, it was no petite femme.

Phone reception on Nightmare had worked for once. At least, it had worked long enough for him to access, briefly study and retain the route to the place that held up its hand to be ready to help wounded koalas twenty-four-seven, just two long bends, one stretch and a couple of corners away at the bottom of Nightmare.

Bach had sped down and around the last hairpin, to where Nightmare evened out suddenly, and Barker felt as though he'd piloted a light plane through a storm, only to have the clouds part and see the runway appear before him, wide-open and long. Although Nightmare continued under another name directly into the city, in a hugely ironic completely straight line, just before it did, just before it reached the edge of the outer grid of roads that surrounded Adelaide's inner-grid, there were perhaps half a dozen off-shoots that headed out toward other areas of the foothills. Or, back up another crazy road, or into a hidden batch of foothills streets, a clutch of houses that constituted some tiny, hidden-away suburb; if Bach mistook any of these they could become lost, or lose precious time. But no, there it was. He remembered it now, an ordinary street parallel with the oncoming outer-grid intersection, and there, on a large white sign: 24-7 VET AND WILDLIFE EMERGENCY, strategically located at the base of the foothills.

Bach pulled into the small carpark. Adelaide's eastern foothill suburbs consisted of many small villages, pocketed strategically between enormous main-road shopping precincts. These villages, like this one, were most often clusters of small businesses: cafes, take-outs, local surgeries, boutiques, craft shops and post-offices. They were almost always surrounded by tall gums and as many native wattles and bushes that could feasibly be maintained. This veterinary surgery was nestled unobtrusively near the edge of one of these villages, one that seemed specifically to cater to the problems that Nightmare Road presented, located cosily between a crash repair and a non-franchised hardware store that specialized in farming supplies. The wildlife surgery had been built beside an old brownstone home that had been split into a duplex, with the surgery a separate and relatively modern add-on. It was located to the left side, where the front lawn and side-garage had once been, and presumably extended right into the back in the manner that many other similar houses in the area had added on a sun-room or a granny flat. The windows were dark-tinted and covered in pet care posters, so it was difficult to see inside, but there was a light from the back; at least, Barker thought.

He carried the injured koala, which he guessed to weigh in at about twelve kilos, across the small four-car parking space, past the massive white Ghost Gum trunk, right up to the door. The entire block was shaded by the broad white branches, several of which lay strewn about from the recent wild winter weather. He pushed the creature's furry but rock-solid muscular back into a large night bell button and waited to see movement past the posters and dark glass. Immediately there were shifts in the light that suggested someone was getting up out of a chair in reception.

Barker shouted.

'I've got an injured koala! A big one!'

The lock shifted and the door opened. It was dimly lit inside, with a backlight on reception from down the rear hall, and the glow of a laptop or tablet on the desk. The girl was perhaps sixteen and dressed casually in an oversized pullover, track pants and ugg boots, all a brighter shade of lavender with a dark-violet four leaf clover brand, as though she might be ready for bed.

'Oh no! I'll call Mum!'

Her phone was already at her cheek and her mother seemed to have answered immediately.

'Koala.' The daughter looked at Barker, then at the koala he was cradling. 'Was it run over?'

'No. Up on that nightmare road, a tree fell. One went straight over but this one came down on the road.'

The daughter gasped with a sorrowful expression.

'Oh no! Poor thing!'

'Can I put him down? I think it's a he; the big ones are he's and he's really big.'

'Yeah, yeah, oh, poor, poor thing; bring it in here…'

She led him down a corridor at the side of reception to a standard veterinary consulting room with a large, high, central steel table. Barker lowered the koala onto the table then slowly unbuttoned his coat and released the creature onto the shining, cold, reflective surface. Then the koala rolled onto his side and lay still.

'It's bleeding…'

She put her phone down on the bench and touched its head. The phone had the brand as well, Barker saw; not a four, but a five leaf cover.

'It was still clinging to a branch as it fell. The branch broke its fall when it hit… hit the side of the hill, then it fell the rest of the way.'

'A tree fell? On the road?'

'Never seen anything like it. There were others there. A woman, a bloke in a truck, and his niece. We were lucky nobody was killed.'

Except that other poor koala, was the thought both had but neither expressed.

'Wow…'

There was a sound outside and Barker turned to see a plump but healthy-looking woman with short brown hair, bright brown eyes and a button-nose moving quickly down the corridor toward them. She flicked a smile at him as she finished throwing on a white lab coat, over an open-necked floral pattered blouse that was undone one button slightly too low, a sensible pair of black slacks and a pair of black ugg boots, all of which looked as though they had just been pulled on in quite a hurry. The smile was just a twitch; serious but friendly over the whole of her wide mouth, stretched across a round, rosy-cheeked face that had inherited perhaps a hint of… Barker guessed without trying; a Korean mother?

'I was half asleep; nearly fell off the couch. Still trying to finish *The Wire*. This one fell out of his tree?'

Barker nodded. 'Hit the hillside, then down to the road.'

'Will he be okay, Mum?'

The vet began to examine him. 'They haven't evolved for forty million years to be killed every time they fall out of a tree, sweetie.'

She glanced at Barker. 'She's new at this. I let her use the wi-fi if she mans the station.'

'Forty million years?' This Barker had not known.

'Give or take. It's like Hooper says in *Jaws*, to paraphrase; they're a miracle of evolution. All they do is sleep and eat and make little koalas, and that's all. Forty million years, thanks for coming, nice view, have a chew.' She smiled at Barker to make sure he understood, and then she smiled again, realizing he did. 'They have extra fluid around their brains to protect them if they fall. Not much brain to protect; more helmet than head if you take my meaning, but they're very good-natured, and adorable looking; they're the symbol of our country and the whole world loves them.' Her nimble fingers reached the blood on the koala's head. 'No, it's not a head injury, not that kind at any rate; looks like he's split his ear...'

'What about his chest there; that cut?'

'No, that's a scent gland. Right down the middle of his chest there. Territory marking. Definitely a bloke. Maybe five years old; one this size has at least a decade left in him, if he's okay. Yes, he's a very large one, even for South Australia. Beautiful specimen; look at that burned red coat on his back, a real handsome chap. Not sure why he's...? Maybe he is brain-dam – oh no, here we go...'

Just as she began to speculate, the koala opened his eyes and blinked a few times. Then he rolled over to a sitting position on the bench, lifted his head high and looked down his giant black-oval nose at them.

'Coo-eeh!'

Barker's heart skipped a beat. For a second he thought the koala had spoken. But then he realized that someone else had come into the surgery.

'Barker!? Anyone at home?!'

Barker turned to the vet and explained. 'That's me. I'm Barker. I think this is the woman who was behind me on the road, when the tree fell.'

'It just fell?'

'Yeah. Just, slid down the side of the hill, hit the road, stayed a few seconds then toppled.'

Right when the tree-men attacked. In fact, it was as though the sliding gum, and the koalas, were trying to kill the tree-men. But we won't mention that, will we koala mate?

The koala kept sitting, watching them speak, watching Barker think. Then the woman with the red Porsche entered then room.

'Oh! Oh, there he is! Alive and well! He is well, I assume?'

Barker smiled. 'Probably. He might be slightly concussed. But he was wearing a helmet.'

The woman ignored him and extended her hand to the vet.

'Kerry Steward. You must be the vet.'

Barker regarded Kerry now, in the full, bright light of the surgery. She was a natural auburn-redhead; not fiery or ginger, but a glowing reddish-brown. You didn't see that too often. She had light brown freckles all over her pale, Gallic features, with a long nose and a sweeping, soft-pointed jawline, punctuated with a tiny, almost mouse-like mouth. It was a cute face, the frame of auburn hair flowing thick and vast from a central part, essentially a shoulder-length fringe, straight down beside big, natural dark-green eyes. The mane was real, a natural feature with no extensions. It flowed, splayed and rested over her shoulders and high, small breasts, braless and obvious with her slender figure tightly outlined under the absurdly unseasonal red dress, complete with an almost shockingly plunged décolletage that revealed her top and mid-section of her pale, fashionista rib-line. Her only concession to the freezing night appeared to be a long matching-red coat that she wore back on her shoulders like a sweeping cloak, and knee-length red-leather boots. The high heels, Barker determined, made them roughly equal height.

'Essa Tiger.' As she introduced herself, Essa the vet politely refrained from critically assessing Kerry's costume, at least openly. 'You're both so terrific, really, bringing him in here like this. We can keep him under observation overnight, then I'll get him to the Wildlife Hospital in the morning.'

'Your name's Tiger and you're a vet?' Kerry guffawed. 'That's so cool!'

'Is it?' Essa smiled widely, politely.

Barker wasn't sure that she hadn't meant to sound condescending. But Essa probably didn't see what Barker saw; this was a cute face in her early thirties who somewhere, somehow had lost all but the actual visage of cute. He saw as she swallowed, hard. As her gaze darted, the second nobody saw, taking in the whole room, the whole practice, storing. Taking in Essa, and her daughter. Barker knew the look; would she ever have to come back, break in? Take this woman on? For whatever circumstances she would have told whoever she had told; I know somewhere we can *get*... what? Pain killers? Needles? Animal blood?

The daughter seemed anxious.

'Don't we need to sedate him, Mum? He might get away? Should we put him in a cage overnight?'

The koala looked completely sedated as it was. He hadn't moved from his seated position, nor his seemingly continual assessment of them.

'I think...' Essa spoke absently as she started a further examination. '...I'll just...' The koala didn't seem to mind. It just kept watching. Watching Barker, it seemed.

'Barker?' The daughter asked. 'Is that right? You've cut yourself. Your arm... right down; look, it's, like, straight down your coat, and wide open.'

That was right. Barker had forgotten.

Essa was examining the koala's eyes with a pen-torch.

'Tiny little eyes. Not great vision, our friends the koalas. Tremendous hearing though. Strange this one...' She glanced at Barker's arm, at the rip straight down his coat. 'I can stitch you up if you like. Reward for your good efforts?'

Barker shrugged and pretended it didn't hurt. 'The coat or the arm?'

'The arm is free. The coat, I'll have to charge.'

Barker liked her. 'To be honest I haven't really looked. I forgot, with... everything else. But I'm sure I'll be okay, I'm sure it's just a scratch...'

Essa turned from her examination again and stared at Barker in a way only female doctors can stare at male patients who know that they are hiding something.

'I can take a look if you like.' Her voice went up an octave, to benign schoolmarm. 'It's no effort.'

'No, really, I – ' But even as he spread his arms to look unaffected, Barker winced.

'Jesus, Barker. You really are hurt!'

Barker turned to the new arrival. 'Thank you, Kerry, but – '

He winced again.

'Okay, get that coat off.' Essa waved at him as she prepared an injection for the koala. 'Let's at least see what you're pretending you're not dealing with.'

Barker winced a third time as he raised his arms to drop the coat, but Kerry moved forward behind him and slipped it off his back.

'It smells of koala...' The daughter informed him, placing it on a chair by the door. 'You probably do as well.'

Barker had no idea if that were a good thing or not. He was starting to feel decidedly overwhelmed and outnumbered, suddenly open to a sixteen-year-old girl's opinion of him, as she moved around and daintily opened the cut in his jumper with two pincer-like hands. Barker glanced down; it had indeed gone right through the coat and the old grey jumper, right through to his flesh.

'Oh... Holy Shit!'

'Language, Tallulah!'

'But Mum he's cut himself right open, right down his arm!' She looked up at Barker, horrified for him. 'How could you not know? Did the tree fall on you as well?'

'I suppose it must have – I guess there were branches and… it all happened so fast…?'

Branches.

Damn. He'd used that branch and just left it there.

That wasn't good; he didn't know why, but he knew that.

Barker glanced at the koala. It remained sitting up, staring at him, despite whatever sedatives Essa might have given him. Essa noticed their shared gaze.

'I gave him something to prevent infection. I think he's in shock. He'll most likely fall asleep soon. If he starts moving around, I'll sedate him. But they only move four hours a day, on average. Cover a lot of ground, four to six k's some of them; no problem for one this young and fit. But when they find somewhere they can eat a few hours, they nod off and sleep the other twenty.' She waved at Barker. 'Can you take the jumper off, let me have a proper look?' Then she eyed him up and down. 'Not shy are you? Seem like a fine specimen…? Nothing to be ashamed of?'

'Mum!'

'Oh, he's heard it all before, sweetie.'

Barker smiled wryly, sighed and shrugged. He slipped his right arm back through the jumper, then gently did the same with the left. They all watched as he carefully looped it over his head, then turned to assess the damage.

'My God…' Kerry gasped.

Barker saw the slice. It was right down the outside line of his upper arm, the whole middle third, gaping open perhaps half an inch deep.

'Well, it's not *too bad*…' Essa stared. 'Clean slice. I can stitch so it won't leave a scar…? It must hurt like billy-oh.'

'No…' Kerry protested, as though in a world of her own. 'Not that. I mean, my God, Barker, *your body*…'

Barker sniffed. He was accustomed to this, but it always made him uncomfortable.

'What do you… like, work out as much as a koala sleeps?'

Barker looked down at himself. Even under the old tee, you could see his pecs, like plates of armour. And now his shoulders were exposed, like some kind of flesh robot.

'Well?' Kerry demanded, with a hint of a suppressed laugh, like she simply could not believe her luck, running into him, even though luck had apparently very little to do with it.

'I inherited good genes,' Barker uttered. 'It doesn't take much work, seriously. Some people are just lucky. Low body fat, high metabolism.' He knew if he threw out a few junk-terminology terms like that, most people generally accepted it. Essa glanced at him to indicate that she certainly had not. 'Just a fluke of birth,' Barker added for good measure.

'A fluke...?' Kerry gasped, then fell silent, perhaps overwhelmed.

Barker sighed. He did, indeed, possess what most people would describe as perfect muscle tone. Very low body fat. But he didn't have to like it.

'Mister Barker likes to work out...' Essa smiled as she prepared another needle.

'It's... more of a diet thing...' Barker offered. 'Genes and diet.'

Kerry came around behind Essa, making no effort to hide her stare. Her eye-line was gliding over his body as though he were some kind of perfect cupcake, and she didn't know where to bite first. Tallulah was pretending Kerry wasn't doing this, as though fighting the urge to ogle Barker's shoulders and chest herself, while Essa seemed to take it all in her stride as she planted the needle in his arm.

'Strong antibiotic. I'll give you a pain killer, then stitch if you like.'

Barker flinched again, and his free arm went up to his ribs.

'But; you're bruised, up here.' Kerry reached in and touched his ribs, where Bazza the ghost had...

Barker flinched. '*Pol* – tergeist!'

...had hit him with the bar stool.

'They're broken, Barker. That one and …'

Essa softly lifted the old tee and assessed. He flinched again as Kerry's fingers brushed the wound, as though she couldn't keep her hands off him. The bruising and the swelling seemed only to encourage her.

'Please don't do that,' Essa scolded. 'You need a hospital, Barker. And you shouldn't be driving your bike. What exactly happened to you up on that hill?'

'I really don't recall. I just wanted to save…'

The koala was still staring at him.

'Doctor Tiger…'

'Just Essa, please.'

'Essa, I've been hurt before; something for the pain would be fine, a stitch or two, but I can get to the hospital fine from here. Straight down the Nightmare Road… a straight line to that hospital on North and East Terrace. But, if I'm honest, what I could really, really use right now is a decent coffee. A latte, a strong latte with lots of milk.'

Essa huffed, just a little. 'We're tea drinkers here, I'm afraid, and lactose intolerant. But if I were you, Mister Barker…'

'Barker's my… it's Moon, Barker Moon.'

'Mister Moon, I'd forget the caffeine and get to a hospital to check for internal bleeding, as fast as I could, Mister Moon.' She stared at him shortly, but very seriously. 'I'll clean and bandage the arm; the hospital will stitch it better when you get there.'

'Well, okay. Thanks.'

'Go and check the phones, Tallulah.'

'Okay.' She pointed at the koala. 'Stay still there, Mister K!' Then she picked up her five-leaf phone and smiled at Barker, really not knowing what to make of him, but somewhat more flustered and girlish than when he'd first walked in, and departed.

'Kerry, was it?' Essa glanced at her as she searched a shallow drawer beside her computer. 'I wonder if you could do something for me?'

151

'Oh! Well...?'

'The tree outside. It's a big old lemon-scented gum. Drops branches like mad. Could you just pop outside, see if there's one on the ground? Just what our little mate here needs to send him to sleep, a nice big meal of lemon-flavoured eucalyptus leaves.'

'Oh! Oh, of course!' She smiled, a big red lipstick smile, and gave a little laugh. 'Kerry the Koala Nurse! I'll be right back!'

Then she too turned and departed.

'Disinfectant...' Essa told Barker as she sloshed some liquid from a plastic bottle onto a swab. She dropped the lid, then bent down to pick it up. She remained squatting a second, and looked up at Barker. Barker was looking down her cleavage, right down the neck of the one-button-too-open floral shirt, and she was looking up. She saw Barker's body tense, saw his hands grip the side of the table, saw his jaw expand and contract as his molars ground powerfully, involuntarily.

Essa stood slowly.

'You're Cheryl's friend, Barker, aren't you?'

'I...'

'It's like a fever, isn't it? Like flu. Glandular and aching.'

'Look, I'm sorry...'

'The Ox? Isn't that what they call it, in sorcerer land?'

Barker ground his teeth, but didn't answer.

'Withdrawals, driving you crazy? Yes? Stupid man. What did you do to get it? Wanted bimbos like Kerry chasing you around all night did you? Got what you wanted? Stupid men and their stupid –'

'It's a curse,' Barker snapped. 'I didn't want it, or this stupid, grotesque body; it was –'

They heard the front door open.

'Here we are! Lovely leaves for our lovely boy!'

'And it doesn't work like that...' Barker uttered. '...I don't know why she's following me.'

Essa applied the bandage and started carefully wrapping.

'There's all sorts of oddness happening; up in The Hills, flowing down into the foothills. Last few weeks. Look at that koala. The way it's looking at you. Are you anything to do with it?'

'No. Maybe. Not delib – I don't really…'

Kerry entered, carrying a branch the length of her arm, covered right at the end in pale green eucalyptus leaves.

'Here we go! Shall I just give it to him?'

'See if he takes it.'

'Okay.'

Kerry went to the table and extended the branch to the koala as though she were offering a mate a cigarette from a packet. The koala regarded the branch for a second, then reached out a long paw and gently took it.

'Isn't that gorgeous!' Kerry explained, wide-eyed.

'Will you go outside and get another for me, Kerry? I just want to try one more thing.'

Kerry put her best face on it, trying to think of an answer that did not make her seem like she was taking orders.

Essa grinned politely. 'You're being so helpful, Kerry. Barker's bandage will be on, and then you can go off and get on with whatever it is you two have planned.'

Barker smiled tightly at Essa, as Kerry gave her a quick salute.

'Koala company, yes ma'am!'

And she was gone again.

Barker immediately started talking again, low and frustrated.

'The tree came down, she was there. Said she'd been sent to keep an eye on me. How do you know Cheryl?'

'We mixed in the same circles a while. Neither of us liked the choices of coven around the city, so we hung out. Then she left. To find you. Barker.'

'I'd be dead if she hadn't.'

Behind Essa, the koala was still watching Barker, even now as the leaves rustled and crunched in his paw, and chomping teeth. He seemed to be eating very fast; he'd nearly finished the whole branch by the time the front door reopened.

'Colonel koala, reporting for...'

'Take her away. If she's Black Prax I don't need her blowing my cover!'

Kerry was moving fast down the corridor, as though she suspected she might be missing out on something.

'...oh my!'

The koala had almost finished eating.

'Nearly done here, Kerry. You can almost have him back.' Barker threw her an almost dirty *thanks* look. 'Just one more thing, Kerry; can you break off a bunch of those leaves please?'

'Break...?'

'Just pick a bunch off the branch. That's such a great branch, Kerry. You're so good at this, natural vet instincts, I'd say.'

Kerry obeyed.

'Now, just put them down on the table in front of him, just loose off the branch. That's it. There you go Barker; good to go!'

She was already holding out his old jumper.

The koala watched as Kerry laid the leaves out before him, in a line as though he had some kind of choice.

'Why are you doing this?' Barker asked.

'Koalas are gorgeous, essentially harmless, iconic and heartwarming. But they are also incredibly thick. Like Hooper says; eat, sleep, reproduce. They just never evolved the need to develop more cognitive function. So when leaves are not on a branch, they don't recognize them as leaves, or food, or anything useful. They just don't. It would have to be the world's...'

The koala reached forward, grasped with its clawed paw along the line of leaves on the table, and collected a clump. Then he raised them to his mouth and started eating them.

'...the world's smartest koala, to know how to do that.'

NINE:
ROCKS

Carlton obeyed.

He wasn't up for this. He was an adult, but these people, maybe even Fiif too, were children in adult bodies. They still thought it was okay to punch someone, probably to beat someone up, and just walk away as though it was something that happened every now and then. This was not his world, these were not his people, and now he would simply wait here until they had all gone away.

What had she meant? Why he'd slept with her?

From Carlton's limited automotive knowledge, the two new cars looked about the same as Zinco's car, the one Fiif had come in. Two more rectangle heads got out, although one was more oblong, and the other more a rectangle head with huge ears, not tiny like Zinco's.

Carlton smirked to himself. *'So I was right about that…'*

Oblong-head was a bit cross. 'What the fuck's going on Zinco? We were binge-watching *Breaking Bad…*?'

Wombo shook his head. 'You are so fucking behind, Bourkey.'

'It's 'er fucking night off, Zinco! She's fucken livid!'

'We're all fucken livid mate!' Wombo declared. 'His fucken woman's gone off the deep end! Kidnapped my Manda and sent 'er off with that Maz fuck!'

Then Bourkey, the oblong-head, saw her. 'Hi Fiif.'

And they all spun around. Fiif was walking up casually, but with haste.

'What the hell are all you guys doing here!?' It sounded like they'd really put her out. 'You're making enough noise to wake the fucking dead!'

Zinco was stunned as Fiif demanded. 'Zinc, what's happening?'

'Been here the whole fucking time have ya, Fiif?' Wombo accused.

'I've been having a giant wee off the balcony, if you must know, gentlemen.'

'What are ya doin' here? Where's Cunto?'

Fiif sighed, as though Wombo were the most despicable thing in her life with which her marriage had forced her to endure. 'I came here to buy some weed. And yes, it was off your old friend Carlton. He might be a weird derro but everyone knows he's got the best gear in The Hills.'

'Yeah? Where is he then?' Wombo demanded.

Carlton could see; Zinco was watching her with an intensity that was unnerving.

'And where's Amanda?!' Wombo demanded on top of it.

One thing was for sure; if Carlton had still been married, despite what his wife had put him through, he would never have let any of his friends talk to her, even look at her, the way Zinco was allowing Wombo to speak to her now.

'Ah, bloody hell Wombo,' Bourkey moaned. 'Not more of this shit! She's fucking five years younger than you! She fucked you when she was pissed! She's moved on, she's not interested!'

Wombo went up to the fourth man. 'That's *your* fucking woman talking, Zinco! Fucking women's talk, all of it!'

'Easy Wombo,' Zinco commanded.

Wombo sneered. 'I want that fucken' Amanda. She's the fucken one for me!'

'Wombo…' Bourkey moaned. 'You better listen. He's right, mate.'

'About what?! That we stayed in bed for a whole three days, fucking? That as soon as she met his bloody wife – ' Wombo stabbed a long, stiff finger directly at Fiif, but then almost comically made a brief aside to Zinco, ' – sorry mate, but it's bloody true – she talked her out of it!'

'Why would she?!' Bourkey demanded.

'Because it's Amanda's sister that he's –'

Wombo bit his tongue. It was right there. Zinco had a mistress. That mistress was Tess, Amanda's sister. But everyone was pretending...

'You're all off your rockers...' Fiif laughed. 'This is completely nuts!'

She walked between them, and Carlton saw that Fiif was heading to his car. Why? Then he saw; she had his keys. Jesus! The kiss! The tight embrace! Holy fucking shit, she was going to get them all killed! She was going for the weapon, because he'd said he could... but she wouldn't know what it was!

But Jesus, she was really something though.

'It's bloody true Fiif, and you bloody know it! And that Mazhar bastard came along and now she won't even fucken look at me! Well, she looked at me for those three days, I tell ya! And your wife's been here, and that Cunt Craven has been helping her – turn my Manda against me! Using his weird occult shit to –'

'To what?'

Carlton walked out.

'Get high?'

'He fucking *is* fucking here!' Bourkey gasped.

As Fiif reached for the boot of Carlton's car, Slacka's hand shot out and grabbed her upper arm.

'What the hell do you think you're doing!?' Her voice was high, genuinely shocked. 'Let go of me!'

Carlton was equally as appalled.

'Let go of her,' Zinco ordered, his voice totally even.

Slowly Carlton's guts started to twist. The way Zinco had just given that order, for his enforcer to release his wife; not outraged that another man had dared to physically bully her. No; this was a mate, acting on behalf of a mate, who took precedence over his wife. It spoke volumes and was totally horrifying.

Fiif snatched her arm away and continued back to Carlton's car boot.

'I just want to get my weed and go home! Jesus Slacka, I swear if you ever fucking touch me like that again...'

Her hand was shaking as she fumbled with the keys. Then she took a deep breath, and let it out in a deep sigh.

'Fuck you, Slacka.'

The key slid right in and she popped it. The car was a burnt orange 1995 Ford Falcon, and the boot was huge, and filled with...

Fiif turned back and looked at Carlton.

'Where is it?'

'Where's what?' Wombo sneered.

'He gave me the keys, said there was an ounce in the boot.'

'You paid him yet?' Zinco asked, still icily calm.

'No, you think I'm stupid?'

Zinco turned to Carlton. He was closest, about six steps away, but Wombo was just across from him, blocking his path to his car. Bourkey was behind them but Slacka was still standing right near Fiif. They were all big men; Zinco was tall, with a strong build, and clearly worked out. There did not look to be an ounce of body fat on him. He was handsome, no doubt, but his eyes were small, in big sockets. It didn't affect how handsome he was; it was that brute handsome look that many women, not surprisingly, found fascinating on some primal level. But they looked dead, Zinco's eyes. Like a predator. And he was regarding Carlton in such a way that made Carlton think that it had been a long time since Zinco had needed to assess a genuinely unexpected scenario. But he was definitely assessing; a certain kind of man assessing in a certain kind of way. For flaws, tells, gives. Weaknesses. Carlton had seen these men all over. Seen them here, in The Hills, all his life. And that was how he knew, instantly, that Fiif had been cheated on, multiple times, before she had even been engaged. He knew this guy, on several levels. And on every level, this guy was very, very dangerous.

'Where is it, Carlton?' Fiif enquired.

Suddenly Wombo was upon him, had him by the scruff of his tee.

'Where's my Manda!?'

Carlton was pushed back a few steps. Panic set in as he felt the rock-hard fist in the centre of his chest. Wombo was a nugget. In certain parts of Australia, wombats, like roos and emus, were deadly road hazards. Wombats were cute, sure, but they were all muscle-mass; hitting them in a car was like hitting a giant rock. People who hit wombats over a certain speed would be flipped and probably killed. This was Wombo. Carlton hadn't seen him, not really, since primary school. He'd threatened him one night at the Pound, not that long ago, and freaked him out a bit. But Carlton went to the Pound every now and then, when there was a band, or a party for a friend, and every now and then some tiny drunken mind flared up for a second, confronted by something about him. Sometimes that was the tiny, basically unaltered mind of someone he'd gone to some kind of school with. Generally, such an incident did not freak him out at all, and if so, not for long. But then, on that night, as now, what did freak Carlton out was that Wombo seemed to believe that he still had some kind of –

Pain seared up Carlton's right arm and shoulder as Wombo twisted and locked him up.

'Ow, fuck!'

Wombo was behind him now, his other hand clamped onto his left shoulder, his hot breath in his ear, sniggering. It was disgustingly intimate.

'Hey Cunty Cunty Craven?'

Carlton grit his teeth. 'Are you even drunk?'

'*What?*' Wombo jarred his arm back.

Fuck that hurt.

'If you're not drunk, you need help. I mean, you need help anyway, but if you're doing this sober, you need serious, I mean serious, they build mini-housing estates in loonie bins for nutters like you to stay in for months at a time, because you need so much – *help.*' There was no response. 'A lot of help, is what you need, is what I'm saying.'

Wombo's other hand kidney punched him and he fell to his

knees, with his right arm still in the ape's clutch.

'Crying for help again Cunto Crayfish!?'

Then he released him.

Carlton was aware that the three other men were exchanging glances but none of them seemed to be acting with any sense of reason or adulthood whatsoever.

'What does that even mean you fucking bottom-feeding groper?'

Fortunately, Wombo hadn't heard this, because Fiif had chosen that moment to become unable to contain herself.

'Fucking hell, Wombo…!'

Oh no. As he looked up, Carlton could see the pain in Fiif's eyes. It had been emotional, a kind of gasp. Everyone had turned; everyone could see it. She cared about him; it was in her eyes, it was obvious. But she continued.

'…he works with his hands, Wombo, he'll fucking *sue you* if there's any damage!'

'Who's gonna tell?' Wombo spat.

'I fucking will, you mental fucking ape!'

There seemed to be an infinitesimally small gesture between Zinco and Slacka, then Slacka had Fiif by the back of her hair, and was yanking her backwards. Fiif was startled, then quickly shocked and terrified.

'Zinc! Help!'

Zinco did nothing. She squealed again as Slacka yanked her back further, but none of the men moved to stop her.

'*Zinc!*'

Carlton knew he had one move. So did Fiif.

Zinco suddenly addressed him. It was like a war movie, where the resistance had been caught and the troops were beating them up; and suddenly the superior officer speaks. Only, it was outside his local pub. *Was this how it started?* Carlton wondered grimly, not un-panicked about the prospect.

'What are you doing here with my wife, Craven?'

Of course it was.

'We were finishing our drinks and she was buying some weed.'

Fiif protested, almost a shriek. 'People come here to smoke on the balcony Zinc! It's a thing! At night!'

'Is it? A thing? Then why don't I know about it?'

'Zinc, tell him to let me go! Slacka, let me go!'

Zinco nodded again and Slacka let her go.

She was panting, full of adrenalin.

'That fucking hurt, you fucking psycho!'

Slacka slapped her hard across her face with the back of his hand. She spun about, staggered and fell, as fate would have it, with her face in the boot of Carlton's car. Zinco hadn't ordered that. Carlton was certain now; this was routine. They'd all done this before. But how? Why? And; how could Zinco ever expect to come back from this? Was he going to break a leg? An arm? Was he going to kill him? Kill her? This was very bad but it could turn worse, and potentially fatally bad at any second. He could get out of it, but Fiif? Could he get her out as well?

'Just take the fucking weed!' Carlton cried out. 'What's wrong with you fucking people!? We know each other! We were talking!'

He was up again, also adrenalized, when he felt the moron behind him try to grab his arm again. He wrenched free, Wombo almost catching his cuff. But Slacka was in the way now. Carlton was starting to see; Wombo was the muscle, but Slacka was the enforcer. These were definitely not ordinary people. These were not even the ordinary tough kids that had bullied him in primary school, nor the yobbo sports wankers who thought they had a say in who did and who didn't frequent their local pub. Something else had happened to them. Now they were small time gangsters, some kind of locally endorsed unit. Something in that vein had pulled them all into the dark. The question was; to use this kind of violence with impunity, were they being paid by white-collar dealers, or were they ruled now by the Togic Moxic?

Or; both?

But why? Why either?

Didn't matter.

It just made what he needed to do, to get them both out of this, so much easier.

'Let me get the *goddamned* weed, you can *goddamned* take it, and we can all go fucking home and forget this *goddamned* night ever *fucking happened*!'

Fiif's hair was everywhere as she pushed herself up, her eyes streaming with tears. She had something in her hands, something in each hand, but Carlton couldn't see. Was it...? How could she have known...? Surely...?

'Who are you!?' Fiif roared at her husband.

'It's for your own good.'

They both reacted to that one; both of them flinching to stare right at Zinco with contempt, almost simultaneously.

'For her own...?

'For my own...?'

Zinco smirked. 'I told you to get another tattoo.'

'I don't want bloody another one Zinc! I didn't bloody want *anything else* from you!'

'That was *your choice*. Every time I told you, and you went against me, I told you; well, it's *your choice*...'

Both Carlton and Fiif whispered in unison, in disgust.

'...*what?*'

'I told you to go up a size. C's are fine, but I want Double D's. You said no, I said, okay, it's your choice. I said I wanted to watch you with another guy. You said no, I said...' An elaborate shrug. '...*okay*, your choice.'

Fuck, Carlton thought. He seems so reasonable. Like, *he actually thinks he's being reasonable.*

'But baby, when you refused *the nose job?*'

She uttered beneath her breath at Carlton. 'Christmas present.'

'Told you...' Wombo grunted.

'That was when I knew; you were lost to me. Of course, I knew we were finished long before that. We both did. You must have been so bored with the sex?'

Wombo suddenly jabbed Carlton in the back, pushing him past Zinco and closer to Slacka. 'Get her to tell us where Amanda is!'

He saw Slacka clearly now, saw his eyes. He was not dissimilar to Fiif really; a dark version, could be her cousin. Long face, gaunt cheeks, piercing blue eyes with a long hawk-nose that was quite distinguished, kind of like Prince Philip. But his hair was dark, and curly, and medium-length. He was wiry, dressed like Carlton in jeans, with a shirt over a tee, a Jim Beam tee and a matching black, white and red Western shirt, and similar running shoes. Zinco was the smiling face, Wombo was the fist; but this guy was the dagger.

What was it? They'd been... okay guys? In a certain social structure, within a cultural norm, they'd been, to employ an Americanism... they'd been 'okay jocks', hadn't they? Sports nerds? Hick athletes? Footy bogans? Cricket derros?

Wombo had been a bully, and an idiot, but; not a killer, surely? That in the least you could say about him, couldn't you? The others; he'd even said hello to, every now and then. Same high school, different cliques, but all adults now, over that? Recognize each other in the supermarket? Polite?

But no. Again, this was clearly not the first time these four had acted in unison. Wombo had clearly taken the childlike entitlement of his bullying nature into adulthood. Had he been like this the whole time? How could Carlton know? He'd only seen him the once, with blazingly red drunk-and-stoned-eyes, when he had drunkenly mumbled at him that this *wasn't his pub*, and that he should *get the fuck back where he belonged*.

Carlton was struggling with it now. He'd never seen this. The aging local sports team as enforcers.

Carlton turned to Bourkey.

'What do you say?'

Bourkey was a Germanic blonde, as tall as Zinco and basically his negative-image counterpart; where Zinco was a more round-ed build, with essentially dark, pleasant-features, Bourkey was blonde and severe, with an oblong head and tiny ears, wide shoulders and a more apparent muscular physique.

But; aha.

There he was. The conduit.

'Why would I say anything?' Bourkey responded. He had a slight, crooked smugness to his mouth as he spoke. 'I just want my mate to be happy.'

'For his fucken wife to act like she's bloody supposed to! Not like some disrespectful slapper from the outer northern suburbs!'

'Fuck you, Wombat cock!'

Wombo immediately grasped at his groin, unzipped his Levis and flopped out his flaccid penis.

'Look like a wombat cock to you?'

'Holy shit…' Carlton uttered.

Fiif was momentarily speechless.

Carlton guffawed. 'Looks like it's meant to be hung and dried for a week, then sliced and served on a platter with a selection of fine cheeses.'

'Serves twelve,' Wombo sneered, gloating. 'Wait; are you saying you want to eat my cock you fucking poof!?'

'Enough Wombo!' Zinco snapped. 'Put it away!'

'For fuck's sake…' Slacka uttered. 'Any bloody excuse…'

'That's what she said,' Wombo kept sneering as he tucked it back in.

Carlton saw that Fiif was trembling now.

Zinco sighed, like he'd suddenly had enough.

'Fiif, get the weed. We're leaving.'

'I'm not going anywhere with you.'

'You need to be rebranded. There are places in town open until midnight. I promised Dad kids, and I don't have the patience for divorce and remarriage. I've been too lenient; I should have insisted. You won't care about any of this by Friday.'

'You think I'm coming back? You've been screwing Tess behind my back for – '

'You don't know that; that's just what my friends think. There are much bigger plays on the board, and if you start – '

'Plays on the board?' Carlton snapped.

'Give her the weed. And don't interrupt me again or he'll break your finger, Works With His Hands.'

'Here…' Fiif suddenly raised her own hands and took a step forward toward Carlton. '…work with these.'

The two staffs slipped into Carlton's palms so easily that they might have been baton racers who'd rehearsed it for months. Both Wombo and Slacka made a move but Carlton was suddenly so activated, and so immediately adopted an attack stance, that they both froze.

'What the fuck?'

Zinco sighed. 'This idiot bogan doesn't know how to use kali sticks. Just take them from him. Get him on his knees.'

'Wait, what?' Carlton guffawed. 'You think I'm the bogan?'

'Fiif…' Zinco sighed. '…you'll pay for all this over the next few weeks. Once again; your choice. Come with me now, and – '

'You *truly* can't *believe* that I'm coming with you? You won't see me again after tonight until we're sitting across from each other in a room filled with lawyers.'

'You do not understand, Fiif. I have told you many times. I'm not sure if you don't listen, or don't understand. Fiona; I am your father's son now.'

He could feel her tense; Carlton himself tensed. He couldn't place it. Vaguely Freemasonic? But then again, maybe not?

'That's a threat, right?' Carlton queried.

'Fuck you…' Wombo snarled. He looked down at his feet and scooped up a white potato-sized rock that he could barely contain in one fist, totally completing the caveman look, the edge of which he had always skated so closely toward, then scuttled apishly a little further away to grab another.

'You're almost literally playing straight into my hands, you fucking moron.'

Wombo was outraged. 'Wot did you just…?'

Carlton swiped back at Bourkey with one hand, then across at Slacka with the other as they simultaneously tried to move in. Both were surprised, and were forced to dodge, but Carlton didn't hit either of them. He'd simply repositioned himself to the outside of the dynamic; he was now at the tip, facing them all in a rough diamond. Then he pointed one of the sticks at Wombo, the other at Bourkey, who was closer.

'Bourkey. Leave. Drive until you find your favourite food. Eat your fill, then go home and watch your favourite movie.'

'Fuck you!' Bourkey shouted, laughing, even as he moved to his car and took out his keys.

'Bourkey!' Wombo cried out. 'What the fuck! We can beat the shit out of him! The Devil said we could! This isn't the one he wants!'

The…?

Even as Wombo had shouted, Bourkey had opened the door, gotten in and slammed it shut again.

'He's one of them…!' Bourkey cried out from his car window, as he turned the key. Then he shouted over the revving engine. 'This isn't over! You don't understand; you're not wanted here anymore! Your kind…!' The engine revved higher, angrier, as the car began to move. '…your little magicks! They have to go…!' Bourkey accelerated slowly, then drove up to the road, still shouting back behind him out of the window. 'Your pathetic little magicks; they have to be wiped out!' The car disappeared into the darkness, to the left, toward Stirling. 'You were never meant to live! *You were never meant to live!*'

The total weirdness of the moment had frozen them all; then Carlton looked back to Zinco.

'So he's the one with the knowledge. What's in it for you?'

'Money. Power. Women like her, forever.'

Carlton groaned, deep at the back of his throat.

'Such a stupid word, forever. Stupid word for stupid people.'

Slacka pulled a knife as he spoke the word stupid for the third time; Carlton used the right-handed kali stick to break his index finger, whereupon Slacka dropped the knife and screamed in pain, falling to his knees. Fiif stepped forward, grabbed his head by the hair, pulled his head back, spat in his face them kneed him right in the nose. There was blood everywhere as she stepped back, avoiding it all.

Carlton was impressed.

Zinco was standing still, but panting through his teeth and nose, like a trapped and confused animal. Then his phone rang.

'Who is that?' Carlton demanded.

Zinco slipped the phone from his pocket and looked. He answered.

'Bourkey? What the fuck?'

Zinco listened a few seconds. 'I know he's one of them. What? You called…?' Slowly, a smug smile dawned. '…he did? Oh *really*?'

Fiif picked up a rock; a nice big one as Wombo used the distraction to take a few steps back, tensing his arm.

'Wombo, I swear, make another move…'

He immediately threw the first rock at Carlton's head. He had big, powerful arms and it was close range. But the counter-throw from Fiif's hand was much faster, and more powerful. Both rocks exploded halfway between Carlton and Wombo, spraying them all with shards. From his whimpering kneel, Slacka cried out.

'Baaah!'

Then Wombo threw the other rock. Fiif was slower this time because she had to kneel and scoop, then throw another. But Carlton was ready, and staggered backwards as Fiif's projectile, startlingly rapid, again self-destructed as it destroyed Wombo's in mid-flight.

'Bitch!' Wombo cried out, oddly high-pitched, scooping up more rocks with both hands, throwing them once, twice, with all his might at the two of them, not caring for the cars behind them, nor for Slacka on his knees beside them. Slacka screeched in pain as several hit him in the head. But Fiif had again mirrored Wombo, and again, all his best-aimed projectiles met with hers, exploding like fire crackers and leaving a mass-plume of white dust in the air.

Now Carlton was truly impressed.

'So, that's how...'

Carlton pointed the left kali stick at Wombo.

'Over the edge; Donger's Leap.'

Wombo's face filled with fear, but he said nothing as he ran off along the balcony, into the darkness.

Now only Zinco remained.

He was still on the phone, but he was hanging up now.

'He knows now.'

'Who?'

'The boss. Our employer. He's been setting this up for years. Decades.'

'What?'

'Point your stick and tell me to tell you the truth.'

'It doesn't work like that.'

'I know. Because you're not willing to tell me any truths about yourself. Bourkey called him, told him; he told Bourkey and Bourkey told me how they work. Clever. Basic rule; nothing the wielder, *nothing you*, wouldn't do yourself. So now you have to go eat your favourite food and watch your favourite movie. Or it will drive you mad. Now you have to jump over a balcony; or fate will make you.'

'They dispense karmic punishment too, Zinc. I'll save that in case we meet again.'

'Right.' Zinco smiled. 'Understood. But you'll be taken care of before we ever have the chance to meet again.' He turned to Fiif. 'Have you got Amanda?'

'No.'

'I didn't think so. Wombo's crush is going to have to be butted out.'

Fiif nodded, staring at her husband as though he had grown two heads.

Zinco was considering now. 'Slacka was willing to break her

finger...'

'So it broke his finger.'

Zinco smirked. 'But I was the one who allowed it...?'

'It doesn't know about *just following orders*.' Carlton smiled, just an edge. It was as though Zinco *wanted* the thing to take retribution. As though he'd have *earned* something. 'At least...' Carlton added dryly. 'Not unless I make a point.'

'All that *allowing* was *just you*, just *you*, Adrian.'

'Adrian, now?'

'Oh yeah...' Carlton uttered. '...that was your real name, wasn't it?'

'So feisty...' Zinco ignored him, scoffing at his wife. 'I haven't seen that side of you in a while.'

Carlton was fed up with him now, Adrian. 'That's because you've controlled her with the Moxic for... how long, *Zinc*?' He turned to Fiif. 'Tattoo every year, is that it?'

She pulled up her coat cuff to reveal, beneath the rim of the black leather glove, a bangle-design tattoo around her wrist.

Carlton's eye popped. 'Oh, Zinc. You sick puppy.'

'Every year...' Fiif uttered, starting to realize. 'We hooked up on that day. I had sex for the first time, I mean. Then we were engaged, he proposed the same day, two years later. Then we were married on that day, a year later.'

'I need to call Barker...' Carlton uttered. 'Only he knows...'

Zinco laughed. 'Don't worry! Fuck me, Craven! You don't even realize, do you? He'll find you! He's just over there, Carlton, just over there!'

Zinc was pointing out and up, at the general direction of the Lion and Unicorn.

He knew; he was supposed to run there now. Find him.

But...

If Barker was back and hadn't told him...?

'We need to go there now,' Carlton lied. 'Fiif, you need to come with me!'

Carlton slammed his car boot.

'Slacka!' Carlton pointed the left-handed kali stick at him. Slacka looked up, mournfully, covered in blood. 'Feel better. Go get mended. Try and understand and forgive.'

They ignored him as he got up and walked away to his car on the other side of the white gravel.

'And what about me?' Zinc demanded, softly, but with implied menace.

'You might as well give him the keys.' Carlton smiled at Fiif.

Fiif shrugged, and threw the keys at him, which he naturally caught without trying.

'I'll have you back. I'll keep fucking everything I can behind your back, and you won't care, because I will own your family's future. He has three daughters, and no sons. I am your father's son now.'

Fiif shuddered.

'Order him to shut up.'

'No…' Carlton lowered both kali sticks. 'He's got something else coming.'

Zinco went to his car and got in. They watched as he reversed, then steered toward the road, but paused beside them, lowering the passenger window to speak with them across the car's interior.

'You'll be dead,' Zinc told Carlton squarely. 'That's just a fact.' His burning eyes locked onto Fiif. 'And you'll come back. When you do, I will use you as a super-fuck-doll until it's me, me who decides it's time for a divorce. Then we'll see who has the most lawyers. And who gets the Double D's…'

He wound the window up, maintaining eye contact with his wife, who was not really his wife at all.

She spat on the passenger window, a slight spray that was, Carlton knew, a fine effort considering how dry her mouth must have been.

Then Zinco, the car, and all three minions, were gone.

They stood there a while, silent, making sure nothing else was coming.

'So...' Carlton ventured into the crisp night air. '...where'd you learn the stone-chucking thing?'

'You mean the magic?'

'Yeah. Where'd you learn that?'

'I didn't learn it.'

Fiif turned around and grabbed him with both hands by the collar of his shirt, pulling his face in, close to hers.

'It was you, you fucking idiot! I never had a thought of my own, never had an idea of my own, until we fucked that weekend! Until you, you fucking idiot, *fucked the magic into me!*'

TEN:
HAUNTED

I

Barker replaced his jumper, then his coat. Nobody had said much since the koala had grabbed all the attention, then Kerry had unexpectedly gone to check on her car.

'We should talk.'

'No, Barker. Things are getting weird. I have a daughter. If there's a darkness in The Hills again, I need to keep out of it.'

'Again?'

'Barker, I am grateful for your soft spot for The Hills' wildlife, but seriously –'

'Okay. Okay, I understand. Thank you, Essa.'

'Just get to a hospital before that woman does whatever it is she needs to do with you.'

'I told you, it isn't like tha –'

'I don't care. You saved the world's smartest koala from being run over. Well done. Go get your reward.'

Barker smiled. 'Okay. Thanks. Really. Thanks.'

Kerry was waiting for him at reception, edgy, and not talking to Tallulah, who was resolutely wearing Apple earbuds.

'Thanks!' Barker stated loudly. She grinned at Barker as he gave her a thumbs up, and opened the door in gentlemanly fashion for Kerry. They heard Essa cry out, then a thump, then again; but it was surprise in her voice, not fear. Then they heard the trundling as the twelve kilo koala, probably more like fifteen now Barker got a good look at him on the move, came galloping down the hall and into reception. Then it was still, watching Barker as he held the door open.

'I'm holding the door open!' Barker yelled.

Essa came up behind the koala; he ignored her.

'I think it's okay…?'

'He doesn't seem distressed.'

Tallulah chirped up. 'He seems distressed that you're leaving.'

It was innocent enough, if irrational.

Barker still stood there, with the door open.

'Maybe if we leave, it will leave?' Kerry suggested.

Barker shrugged. 'Okay.'

Kerry went through the door, then Barker followed, but remained outside with his good arm still holding the door open. The koala obediently trundled forward, and exited. Then he sat, just outside, and looked up at Barker as he let the door swing slowly closed.

'Are you okay, buddy?' Barker enquired.

The koala just kept looking up at him.

'You wanna – ?'

Then he moved. He trundled past Barker, across the small car park, and half way up the trunk of the lemon scented Ghost Gum.

'Gained a taste for it, I guess?'

Essa and Tallulah had come out to watch. None of them said anything as the koala regarded them once again, now at eye-level, for a few seconds more, then proceeded up the tree again, this time right up and into lower branches.

'He's so cute…' Tallulah sighed.

'Okay sweetie…' Essa declared sympathetically. 'Lock up. Switch the office over to mobile. That's all for us tonight.'

II

Barker watched the veterinary team retire each to one of the two units on the block beside the clinic, Tallulah glancing back coquettishly before closing her front door, Essa not glancing back at all, done with the pair of them.

'Nice set up.'

Kerry had parked right beside his bike, not quite blocking him in.

'Barker...' Kerry started up straight away. 'Barker, I'm telling you the truth. They told me to follow you.'

She was tense, speaking in a strange kind of tone; a normal volume, but low, as though she were containing something, huge emotions like she could strike out and hit something, maybe him, any second.

'They?'

'I do that for them. Sometimes.'

'Follow me in that car? You know they still make black cars. I mean, even white is less obvious.'

She wasn't listening. She was retracing her steps. 'I just came home. He was there, with my husband. They're not even trying to hide it any more. They sent me back out, in a hurry. Like I was nothing; a fucking intern. Now I know why.'

'Who was with your husband?'

She heard, but ignored the question with an air, as though it were simply foolish for him to ask.

'You don't get it, Barker. You have to understand. They want me out of the way. I didn't see it until now. I really didn't. I didn't think they would do that to me; not to me. They must have sent me to be killed by those things...'

Barker suddenly flashed to Kerry in the car, back after the attack, her hands grasping the wheel, tense and furious. She couldn't have cared less about the wounded koala. This wasn't a new quality that she was exhibiting; her genuine personality had returned. The whole bubbling enthusiasm act, which in the end had been for nobody but Kerry herself, had been dropped completely. She'd been livid about something else; some *one* else.

'They told me to follow you down to that beach house.' She was speaking through her tiny mouth, her jaw out but clenched, her tone low. 'They even gave me the address in case I lost you. They told me not to sleep with you, not to fuck you, just to lead you on. But, those things… they played me; they wanted us both dead.'

'You don't know that for sure; what are those things? Your friends control them?'

'In a way…' She looked away, at the Ghost Gum. '…but I didn't know they were going to…'

'Who, Kerry?'

He saw it even more now. The cute party girl, but grown up, dealing with her compromises; maintaining the cute mask but eventually, after years and years of never giving up on the score, whatever it was for her, realizing that the mask was all that remained.

'If I tell you…'

'You said; you want me to kill them.'

'Really kill them, Barker. Not any of this supernatural bullshit; where they seem like they're dead but they come back. Kill them really fucking *dead*.'

Seem like…?

Okay. He was dealing with someone here. Dealing with someone from his old world; of powerful mystical energies, of true sorcery. That real, occult world was encroaching once again on his current world, his normal world of harmless Tarot and burning sage sticks to banish bad vibes. Returning, with the coldness in Kerry's eyes that Barker thought was familiar. The chill that he knew was… inevitable here, in the occult world. There was that chill, that coldness, that beautiful women like Kerry possessed, he knew, just from being alive. Not all beautiful women by any means traded their beauty; but those who did had that cold look when they thought you were the most powerful, or influential, or best bet in the room, in any given room. Until they saw something else enter; someone or something up a rung, and that high beam of charisma they'd been employing just one millisecond earlier, just for you, to enchant you completely, you and you only, like you were the only other person in the room, was suddenly – gone. That cold-eyed look, in the gap between switching it off for you, and on for another, every man knew. Every woman knew, from the male equivalent.

But that coldness could be even bleaker still.

Barker had only ever-so-slightly brushed up against a version of it, within the world of organized crime; those women had another layer of fear, of desperation behind their eyes that they carried below the other coldness. But Kerry; she was a deeper layer again. Chillingly, Barker's wellspring of memory was now sadly reminding him, even as he regarded her with increasing intensity, that it was an icy layer with which he had once possessed more than a passing familiarity.

Somewhere, down another rung or two, Kerry had traded with the Black Prax.

For sex or a high. For a house, or a place; a promotion or even a person; in fashion, in the media, in the world. Women who'd seen that, who'd been that, who'd been within that for their... what? Their requisite five or ten years? Those women had the cold, and the fear, and the deep, sustained haunted emptiness, right to the very back of their pupils. The look that let you know; not one second was passing, had passed since, that they were unware that nothing, absolutely nothing for which they had traded, whatever it was that they had traded it for, had been worth it.

'Who are you, Kerry? What the hell is all this?' He was suddenly furious with her. 'Tuesday night, red Porsche, red dress, red lipstick?' His hand was up on her long Gallic chin, holding her face there, tight. 'What am I supposed to make of that? I can't figure out who you're supposed to be.' He stared into her green eyes, exposing only black-pit pupils in each, receding back and back and back. 'I can't figure out who you think you are; who or what I'm supposed to think you are?'

She met his gaze; she had met his gaze before.

She had met sorcerers.

'My husband sent me. He called me in a hurry. Usually it's

something more planned, discrete. He told me he wants me to keep an eye on you. To keep up with you...'

'To lead me on but don't fuck me.'

'It's not the first time in the past few weeks he's put me in harm's way.'

Barker kept his grasp on her chin. Her husband. She would be just a toy to him, if he were Black Prax. She was not magical, had no talent; one look in her eyes had told Barker that. It made him angry. 'Nobody told you they were setting those things on me, did they? Is this something your husband does? A regular Tuesday night? Throw you to the wolves and watch you charm you way out of it? Does it make him hard? To know you worked for it?' He was getting really furious now. Irrationally furious. He wanted to fuck her now. Because hubby had said not to. Because even if hubby had said to her, tell him I told you not to, then fuck him to make him feel power; he would do it anyway, to make her feel power. And then he knew; he never thought like that. He had the Ox; he really did have the Ox. And he could fuck her and her douchebag sorcerer husband would know. It would be all over her for days, like a whole bottle of perfume. He would fuck her so it was like kerosene. Let these fucking Black Prax know; *I know what you want me to do and I will not do it*. He was squeezing her chin tight now; the pale skin around his thumb and forefinger plain white. She hadn't broken his gaze.

'I need protection, Barker. He's not going to be there for me anymore. He's got someone else. I'm thirty-two. I don't have the power. Not what he wants. You saw those tree-things, Barker. They tried to kill you as well as me. You were sent as bait. They're against the natural order of things. I saw that tree; that real tree, it dislodged itself. It killed itself to kill those things. The things of nature, real nature, all attacked those tree things because they are an abomination to the true order of nature. That's what they do, my husband and his friends; they pervert nature.' Barker hadn't let go. 'Barker, please. Please. I need protection.'

She wasn't crying. He's seen this act before, but she wasn't crying; this was where they always cried. He usually gave in, took them in a while, but they always went back.

'Barker...'

The haunted look. Now, it was like he couldn't look away. He was seeing it. The haunted eyes; the reality that she had seen real spiritual darkness, had witnessed and been affected by it, and that it had lingered, deep, to haunt her.

'...you know, Barker. You can see. Others have looked, looked like you're looking. I haven't done anything. Never done anything like that. Just seen. It's not too late for me. You can take me. Claim me, Barker. I will give myself to you. My husband will dispose of me, I've seen him do it to others. Claim me Barker, I will fuck you as long as you like. Please Barker, please. Fuck it out of me, Barker, fuck the darkness right out of me again, so I can go home...?'

No tears. Just the direct gaze.

'...I just want go home, Barker.'

'Go back to the beach house. You said you knew where it was?'

'Yes...'

There was no relief in her eyes. This was just an order. Just another order from another sorcerer. Not the thing she was looking for. Not the promise of safety, the passionate response that sealed the deal. And yet, she had not lifted her arms, hadn't touched him, tried to turn him on. She was making her play; a moment ago, she had realized for sure that her husband was trying to kill her. In that moment, her charismatic gaze had left him and locked onto Barker, onto her better bet in the room.

'Wait for me, at the back, don't go inside. Wait.'

He let go of her.

She didn't break the gaze as she took a few steps backwards. She pulled the red cloak back over her shoulders, wrapped it around herself properly, as though sensing the cold for the first time that night; as though her protection from the night had just departed. Then, snap, the gaze was gone. Kerry got in the car, the keys still in the ignition, started it and drove away, toward Nightmare. Barker stared after her long enough to see her turn right; down toward the city, and the beach.

He heard a click behind him, and from one of the front doors of the apartments came a voice.

'You'd better come in.'

ELEVEN:
WRONG

Maz Anders had not learned much in his twenty-nine years on planet Earth.

But in some ways at least, he and Carlton Craven were the same.

Carlton knew this as he picked up Maz's psychic scent, as Fiif drove him along the path that Maz would have driven last Saturday night to Amanda's place; a path that had led Maz, he was fairly certain now, to his ultimate fate.

Carlton focussed.

Within his busy social life as a sporting local of the Adelaide Hills, it went without saying that Maz had certainly been to every hotel and every sports club there was up here, multiple times. But Maz had also been to the home of every family and individual involved with his football and cricket teams, been to every victory party or commiseration gathering for his club, every week they played (which between the footy and the cricket was almost every week of the year); partied in every shed, back yard, scout hall, town hall or designated country paddock, by virtue of attending every sixteenth, eighteenth, twenty-first, twenty-fifth and thirtieth ever held (and even a fortieth or two), and in short, attending any event, celebration or party held for or by anyone in the wider local area who had anything to do with any of the organized sports that The Hills had to offer. He'd even been to most of the homes and parties of most of the teams with which they regularly sparred, and been to *their* clubrooms and bars. He'd been out doing this just about every Friday night and Saturday night and most Sunday afternoons too, just about every week he'd been alive and permitted, which had been, give or take, since he'd been about fourteen years old.

In his time, in his teens and twenties, Carlton had done that too. He had not been a sportster; he'd been a jester, a larrikin. Enough people liked having him around that usually someone remembered to invite him along. They had no idea he was a sorcerer. They thought he just ran the local second hand book store that more than half of them didn't know was there and the others never went into. Most of them, a decade on, still didn't know, and still didn't read. He'd occasionally seen his old bullies; the foursome from tonight. But they had been primary school bullies, not high school, and when they had started growing up and attending the local hills pubs, there had been barely any recognition between them. Yet, tonight?

Things had changed, it was fucking weird.

And not in the way Carlton liked.

Fiif pulled up outside Amanda's house and parked Carlton's Falcon on the other side of the road. It was an eighties house, pale brown brick with olive gutters, set on a small block from when the urban sprawl had started to move through the hills like some kind of sentient, mock-colonial, kitsch ivy. Before then, everything had been simple red brick, or hippy eco-houses.

'Was she renting?'

'Does it matter?'

'No.'

'She didn't see the point in buying without a partner. But then one day she just went and got a loan, and bought the house she was renting. She was a sensible girl, but she cut loose when she drank.'

Carlton nodded. 'I guess that's normal.'

They hadn't spoken much at all in the fifteen minutes it had taken Fiif to drive there, an option they both seemed happy to adopt. Fiif's, or Zinco's car had looked so expensive and modern, so sleek and beautiful and comfortable, and so far outside of Carlton's world, that to him it might as well have been a spaceship. But here, even secure in the driver's seat of his 1995 Ford Falcon,

Fiif looked so elegant, rugged up with her sharp profile, that he couldn't believe he had once had her, even for a short time. She made any car seem like it was impossible to be in; as remote to his reality as the worlds her spaceship-car would take her to.

'See there's a street up there? It's a cul-de-sac. There should be enough shadows on the curve to hide the car. We'll walk back, take a look. You okay with that?'

She nodded and proceeded as he'd requested. After they'd parked, she turned sharply to him, earnest. 'So, you're like a bloodhound for psychic trauma?'

Carlton stared at her.

'What?' Fiif recoiled. 'I'm sorry, I... was that – ?'

'No!' Carlton was impressed. 'That's good. I like that.'

He was a little angry he hadn't thought of it himself.

Bloodhound for psychic trauma.

Jesus, that was cool.

They got out of the car simultaneously and it was about as freezing cold as they had both expected it to be.

'You okay?' Carlton asked over the car roof.

Fiif shrugged. 'No.'

There was little else to say so they walked back down the cul-de-sac and back three blocks to Amanda's house.

'Where's Maz's car?' Carlton asked.

There were a few other cars parked up and down the road, but Carlton remembered from the psychic trace he was following that Maz had parked in the driveway, behind Amanda's car. It was eerie, Carlton felt, what he and Maz had in common. To begin with, because of his social life, Maz had been forced to learn one thing in his twenty-nine years, very well indeed. He had learned his way around the Adelaide Hills, on foot, without GPS.

'He... Maz. He was twenty-nine? She was twenty-eight?'

'Yeah. Was?'

'I was just...' He could feel the trauma up ahead already. It was bad. '...that was unconscious. But you didn't drag yourself all the way back down here and risk the wrath of Zinco to see me, just because you think they're really okay.'

Fiif didn't reply.

The lawn and the bushes were overgrown but that hadn't happened in just a few days of neglect. Not a gardener. A short cement drive down the right side of the house led to an open corrugated carport, fenced off at the back, adjacent to the neighbour's corrugated fence, where two cars would easily fit, bumper to bumper. They stood there and looked. Carlton had put his leather coat on now, so they looked, perhaps only just, like investors inspecting property.

'Both cars gone. Hers was here too.'

'Stolen?'

'I guess.'

'Why else would...?'

'Listen, we need to talk about what happened, Fiif. That ape fucker Wombo was talking like he was *owed* Amanda. And your husband, and that creepy guy Bourke, he had a foot in my world. Wombo even mentioned The Devil.'

'You know where he got that name?' Fiif uttered, putting it together. 'I mean they all have these club names, and they always stick because they always stick together; but his is because nobody knows where he comes from. He won't say. Apparently once, someone said he came from the Back of Bourke and...'

'It stuck. Right...' It could mean anything. But... 'That's not good, Fiif. None of this bodes well at all.'

Fiif nodded, then she removed her left glove to reveal the ring of tattoos. Despite the cold, she put it in her pocket.

'I just didn't love him anymore. That's why I said no.'

'Seven years is...' Carlton shrugged. 'You must have, once. Those things have to start somewhere.'

'Things?'

'Well...' Carlton approached, looking at them under the ambient light; the full moon and a street light two houses off that was half blocked by the branches of a massive liquid amber. Fiif lifted it for him as he approached.

183

Her wrist was slender, her hand and fingers thin, with pronounced tendons.

'I thought it was just Celtic. You know, it interlocks. I like that.'

'So do I. But that's just a base. The symbols that are on it…?'

'Yeah?'

Carlton looked around.

'Can we get in the house? You don't have a key do you?'

'No.'

'We should go round the back at least. It's possible there are cops watching, or worse. And I don't want to be answering questions in court on a missing person case.'

There was a gate at the carport fence, over which they could see a back yard that was bland; just an uncut lawn and a clothesline with a few rags hanging miserably in the cold. There were some under-watered roses along the far fence, but the rest hadn't been tended for maybe a year. It was taking on the classic unmaintained mini-jungle appearance that Carlton quite liked. Regardless, there was clearly nobody around.

'Cool…'

Carlton jumped the fence, then Fiif. Her hard shoes made the only real sound as they hit the concrete on the other side.

'Not a straight line person?' Fiif enquired.

Carlton smiled. 'I like it when nature plays jazz.'

She smiled back and looked around. Carlton picked up on her notion.

'You're a woman, you know this woman, and you're switched on. It's probably exactly where you think it will be.'

Fiif nodded. She took a few steps toward the back of the house, as though the spare key she was looking for might have been somewhere in the garden, then turned sharply and looked down, to the corner between the fence and the house. There was a stone frog down there, just small enough to sit on the side ledge of the house's concrete foundations. Carlton saw it; there were no other garden decorations, and no apparent reason for it to be there in particular. He was closer so he leaned down, tipped the base of the frog, and there was the key. Bright silver, as though freshly cut and never used.

He handed it to her, and she accepted, grasping it tightly in her un-gloved hand.

'You think this is all connected, don't you?'

'Maybe.'

'What if...' She couldn't look at him. 'What if, I was promised to Zinc, to Adrian, the way Wombo thinks Amanda is promised to him? Like, there's a Devil here? Is that possible?'

'An evil entity calling itself a Devil. Sure. That's possible. Casting spells on beautiful women, making them fall in love with complete fuckwits, in return for... I don't know. Loyalty? What they think are their souls? Vital energies? The list goes on, and I've seen it all. I've never been out of Australia, and I've seen it all. Cities are built on such deals. Power rests on it. Loyalty can absolutely be bought. People think conspiracies can't be sustained, because it would take hundreds if not thousands of people to keep a secret. But hundreds of people working on television series, on movie sequels, in production offices and on sets keep secrets for months, all the time; because their livelihood depends on it.'

'You think that's true?'

'Look; if you receive an extra payment of a thousand bucks every year, or fifty a month, to shut up about something you've seen, and that's been keeping your kids in college, that's been keeping your mistress in a nice apartment, been keeping your medical bills paid; I dunno, maybe it's been supporting your model railway collection and that's the only thing that gets you through your shitty desk job; in the end, for most people, who gives a shit that something evil happened to someone else? Something that can't be changed, can't be reversed, that there's no point in reporting, going to jail for; *getting killed for*? These guys we just ran into; they rough a few people up for money, and in return they get a hot wife who's brainwashed to look the other way; while they fuck another brainwashed bimbo every weekend until they get bored and swap her for...'

He saw the look of hurt strike across her features.

'I'm sorry; I'm angry. Fiif, I'm sorry.'

She nodded.

'I was brainwashed. I get it.'

'Not like the CIA. Well, not like the CIA admits to. Fiif, this is serious. I'll follow the trail, but after tonight, I have some friends I'll need to call in. Barker is already here, apparently. But if he's here and he hasn't told me, it's to protect me. And it'll mean Cheryl's here too.'

'He said that The Devil had been sorting this for years, Carlton. Decades.'

'One of them said I'm not the one The Devil wanted. Like...' Carlton felt himself frown, felt his whole face compress. '...I was supposed to go and find Barker. And, that was what they wanted.'

'Why?'

He'd been staring at the concrete, but looked up. Fiif's expression was filled with concern for him. She looked adorable. Nobody had looked at him like that in the longest time. But they were in danger, out here.

She moved forward and kissed him again, pressing him back against the wall with both her hands on his chest. Carlton was okay with girls in his league; he'd never made a move on a girl out of his league in his whole life. But now, again, the girl who was out of his league was moving on him; *this was happening*. He was pressed against the corner, where the key had been hidden, half his back wedged against the fence, the other half against the wall of the house. He reached forward and put his hands on her hips. She came forward a little more, and he felt her leg moving in, between his.

Over his shoulder he saw her eyes bulge at something down the drive.

She retreated suddenly, grabbed his lapels and yanked him back around the corner of the house. Again, they were peeking around a dark corner from which they could not be seen. Again, they were staring at an oncoming car.

'It's him, isn't it?'

This time they were standing, and she was closer to him, pressed tight against his back with her hands hooked tight, up around his chest as he peered around.

He could see who it was before the driver's window had passed the neighbour's fence, and he ducked back. It was the car; the car Fiif had driven to the Crow and Kingfisher, the car Zinco had driven off in.

They listened. The car went further up the road. To the cul-de-sac? If you were looking, turning your headlights up there, would you see Carlton's car? Where they'd tucked it against the curve? No, Carlton told himself. That's exactly why they had put it where they had. So that could not be done. They listened as the car u-turned and came back. He peeked around again; the same headlights on the road, returning. He felt Fiif rest her head, sideways against the back of his shoulder.

'Go away go away go away…'

Then they both shifted back, and pressed themselves against the wall of the house. The car stopped and idled a while.

'Don't look.' Carlton spoke gently, despite the fact that there was no chance Zinco could hear them over his engine. 'He's staring right at this corner…'

Fiif took him at his word.

The car passed the house slowly again, then stopped at the top of the driveway. Carlton could sense him; staring, right at the corner where they were. He didn't want to get out, didn't want to face Carlton again. Then he revved, sharply, twice, then abruptly sped away. Once again they listened, as though the crisp cold of the evening carried the sound further and more clearly.

'He's still looking for us.'

'At least we know he's not tracking your phone.'

'I'll leave it somewhere. He's gotten someone to do that before. One of the guys that works for him was bludging – maybe he already... oh, I don't know.'

The pause that followed was like a white light, like the start of a migraine headache in Carlton's brain. One massive white flash, pain, like a hit. But it wasn't a migraine, and he had not been concussed.

Fiif was crying.

She was staring at her hands, up in front of her eyes, one gloved, one not, one marked, one still concealed. Her hands were shaking. Her whole body was trembling. The white explosion in Carlton's field of vision was dissipating, and he saw tears forming in her eyes like two shower drains, suddenly blocked, pooling, then overflowing; more water more quickly than he would have thought possible, and a terrible whimper, increasing to form a cross between a groan and a squeal.

He left her, just for a second, walked in a quick crescent around her to the back door and tried the screen. It was open. The hardwood door and the lock behind swung inward with the turn of the key and he left the door open as he returned to Fiif. She hadn't moved but she was shaking uncontrollably now, mucus coming from the long nostrils of her wonderful nose, her blue eyes totally red, with just the black pupils visible. The long bright locks of her golden hair were shaking, quivering, lank but jangling as her whole body became overwhelmed with convulsions of...

What?

Shock? Grief? Anger? Terror? Disgust? Irrational shame, irrational guilt? Carlton had heard of such things; he'd seen it happen and been overwhelmed by it himself, so he'd spoken to people about it, tried to understand it, to be prepared for the next time.

He put an arm around her and guided her by the shoulders to the door, then inside. The huge coat fell behind her, by the back door, and he had to be careful not to trip on it as they passed through a small back-parlour laundry and bathroom that exited directly into an open kitchen. He released her and she walked across a white-tiled floor and spread both her hands on the kitchen bar, tensing her shoulders like a defensive cat, and pulsing out a few more bursts of furious sorrow.

There was an unwashed cereal bowl and a half-finished coffee right before her. The half-mug read in writing that covered the whole vessel: A TRIPLE ESPRESSO NEVER KILLED ANYONE!

'Fiif?'

She spun around, as though in those few seconds she had forgotten where she was, and who she was with. She made choking sounds with her sobs, like she couldn't catch her breath. Carlton moved into the kitchen as terrible sounds started coming from her throat; like panicked jungle animals. Then she caught herself, sucked in her breath and stopped. All of a sudden; still. She looked at Carlton, behind her now, over her shoulder, with her sharp features accentuated in profile. For a brief second she resembled a stereotypical hag, or an evil witch, as she spoke with bitterly precise annunciation.

'He raped me. For seven years.'

Carlton felt like someone had kicked him in the nuts, stabbed him in the guts, and cracked him across the back of the head with a hammer.

'Fiif...'

'I remember. I took a gamble. I thought; he's not the one but we have good sex and I can live with him until...' She looked away, into the darkness beyond the kitchen bay, then swung back. 'I could have had...'

'Don't go there.'

'You know, don't you?'

'I know what he's done. I know how to –'

'No; you don't. You don't know, you never did. It was the only thing I didn't like about you. If only... all those times I came in, and bought a book you recommended. And I came back, and we talked. If only, just once…'

'But you were… always with someone…'

'Someone, Carlton. It's not your fault. It's not my fault. But; I'm starting to remember.'

'That will happen. They can't last forever. Even that many. They're not even tattoos. At least I don't think. They're magical symbols. That type; you could draw them with pencils, and they wouldn't come off. But once you break his influence, if he doesn't keep drawing them, there's nothing you can do. When you find the one you're meant to be with, they'll just vanish. Overnight.'

She held up her wrist. The Celtic chain was still there. But the other symbols were nearly gone.

'Retrees are like that…'

She stared at him, still bent, still over her shoulder.

'Don't you understand Carlton? He came in, right when we would have…'

'Would have?'

'All these years. Carlton. It should have been you. *It should have been you.*'

TWELVE:
CHECK-UP

The door closed behind Barker and he stood there as she regarded him with a kind of mildly grim, but not unfriendly expression of inevitability.

'So what was it? An accident? An attack? Or... what did she say? A tree?'

Barker didn't answer, just kept looking at her, although he wanted to look around to see where he was, assess her home. Essa hadn't moved since he'd closed the door behind him and she was effectively blocking him into a square meter of corridor just inside the front door.

'It'll be okay tomorrow.' He didn't sound convincing, even to himself.

She shook her head. 'It was only a matter of time, I suppose.'

'What was?'

She ignored his question.

Why did women always ignore his questions?

'You've got the Ox? But you said it's not what I think it is?'

Barker shrugged. 'I didn't realize I had it, until I was trapped in a small room with three women.'

Essa scowled a little. 'I'm sorry. But, my daughter, she's nineteen going on nine.'

'I thought sixteen.'

Essa gave him a look; *so you see what I have to deal with.* 'I know what she can be like around charismatic men. Still, I shouldn't have behaved that way. I shouldn't have judged.'

'Look, that's okay. I'm way past chasing teenage girls.'

'Well from the look of you, you don't have to be.'

'Is that another judgment?'

'Why else would you do that to yourself?'

'I told you, I didn't. The first man to train me…he did it.'

'He did it to you?'

'He was perverse.'

'What? He made you this way so he could…?'

'No, not that. Although, I think he might have done that with others. Later. I think I was just starting to find out about all that when…'

'When what?' She'd interrupted like she really didn't want to hear about his bad uncle sorcerer. 'Cheryl said you couldn't remember things. She said you might have been lost somewhere, with amnesia. Or worse.'

'She was right. I was lost. But she found me. If you're a friend of Cheryl's…'

His mind started drifting.

'What?'

'We were related, the man who gave me this body. At the time, he still thought he was on the side of the angels. So, that kind of taboo breaking didn't interest him.'

She shook her head. 'Holy Christ, they really think like that, don't they? Those men? Taboo breaking?'

'It's a myth that it's just men. It's mostly, but not only; and getting more equal year by year.'

'It's disgusting.'

'I don't disagree.'

He broke her gaze and looked left and right. There was a small bureau; the corridor was a dissected central hall from the original house. The walls between must have been thin because the corridor was a good six boards wide. Key bowl, lamp, something framed. But right beside him was an RAAFNS certificate for service in the Korean War. Sergeant May Sullivan. That was the nineteen-fifties. Early fifties.

'Was that your grandmother?'

'Lu's great grandmother. She gave birth to my mother in 1957. Thirty-two, pregnant by a South Korean General who followed her out here, emigrated and everything. Thirty-two was getting on to be carrying a child back then. Mum said it was the Korean genes where we all got the – '

She seemed edgy all of a sudden. Barker could practically see her stop her own thoughts and reverse.

'I listened to you talk to that woman. Kerry. I've seen women like her, acting like that.'

'So have I.'

'Seven years ago.'

'So have I.'

'They all end up hanged, in hotel bathrooms; all the Prax concubines, the black-Wicca WAGS. Or they end up locked away for their own protection, if they could get to the right kind of asylum in time; just like your friend Heather.'

Barker locked in with her gaze again.

'There are some terrible people out there, Essa. Terrible people. But you and I know, there's a point, witch or sorcerer, magician or sage or druid or whatever; there's a point where the energies overwhelm us. Some people are lucky enough to recognize that straight away. We let it flow, because we know there is something else, something that's a reflection of everything that we can't take in, not in any other way than the abstract, and we acknowledge that. And it overwhelms us; but then it keeps going and we observe it and follow it and watch it and if we're lucky we get to help it. After that, it's a wide open road with more detours and roadside attractions than you can count. But it's the people who think they're controlling it; they're the problem. And the people who actually do control it; for a while, stem the tide and dam or bottle or even distil it, they are the real nightmares.'

'Men and their power games.'

'You know as well as I do, there are covens that take young girls and indoctrinate them into believing all men are monsters; all men are rapists waiting to happen. There are covens that specialize in finding a man's psychological profile, finding his type, his sexual weakness, knowing his mind and what he wants to hear, and becoming that, becoming something beyond a concubine; some of them summon the energy of the succubus, embrace and become it, and they do this to men they think can one day manage a position of power; they help them get there. They leave men destroyed when that doesn't happen, an empty shell when it does. All of them, men, women and boys and girls, they all belong in the same camp as the psychopaths who use terror rituals, and ritual sacrifice, to maintain the imbalance that we see in the world today, the shocking disparity of education and wealth and – '

'Are you going to go on like this all night, or do you want me to do something about it?'

Barker held his breath. In the back of his mind, the image of Essa, of looking down from the table at her looking up, had been there the whole time.

'There are many things I need to do something about tonight. Ranting isn't one of them, but neither is…' He wondered for a second. 'Wait. What are you actually suggesting?'

Essa stared at him again and hummed suspiciously. She'd removed the white lab coat, done up her button, and her arms were folded tightly over her breasts. They had been folded like that since she'd let him in.

'I know about those covens, Barker; Cheryl got my sister out of one. That's how we met, how I became interested. How I discovered myself;, my potential with energies. That's why I live here, why I do what I do.'

'Cheryl is a very good deprogrammer. Very good witch too.'

'I told you before, for weeks now there's been something going on.' She gulped. 'I don't want any part of it. But I still know people. I still keep in touch. My old coven, they say they won't go up there now. Not for weeks.'

'What about Freyanna?'

'She's old. She had too many protégées who think they know better. She's losing control of the city; after what happened at

Bridger Mansion, she has to be losing control to allow anything like this darkness to start rising again.'

'Who's in charge now?'

'Nobody knows. But rumour has it, one of them is spending a lot of time in The Hills. The Dark Hills. They've been seen near Red Gully and Sleepy Creek. Where Argent was.'

'One of them? Freyanna doesn't know which of her protégées has gone over to the Black Prax?'

'Someone said.'

'Who said?'

Essa huffed. 'I can't say. I'm still sworn to some basic oaths. I hardly know you.'

'That's okay. I wouldn't know Freyanna, or her protégées, if they flew in here on broomsticks crying their names out loud.'

Essa smirked. 'Well it's going to be a long and bitter battle when she passes. And she won't be the only one. A lot of the old guard are fading. They want to go. They don't understand the past decade, don't want to. They'd rather die and come back with a pre-implanted chip in their infant brain than grapple with a smartphone in their eighties.'

Barker hummed. He wasn't ready to even consider what the world would be like when he was an octogenarian, whether he would be able to cope or not, or want to. Not yet anyway.

'There are power struggles coming from the witches and the sorcerers, and all that crap energy filtering down the hill from the black forests is just the start. They say it's too dangerous to go out past Hahndorf at night. Crime in the satellite towns has spiked. The dark energy is too dense for light-workers to think out there; impenetrable some say. They say that there are people going about, behaving like they know. Like they know the occult, like they know the old ways, like they're protected somehow. And not just kids. Adults who would never even *think*...'

'How long?'

'Look, Barker, I don't know how much you remember, but you must realize; something very bad is going to happen. They say it only gets like that, when it leaks out and people start behaving like it's all *normal* for them, they say that only happens when people are doing blood sacrifice, when they don't care who they're killing anymore.'

Barker thought about it then; then and there. For the first time he thought about it, for real. Doing exactly what they wanted. Going back to Bridger Mansion. Finishing what he started; whatever that had been – although he had a pretty good idea now. Killing them all, all those who were left, and razing that place to the ground. Salting the Earth...

'Essa, why did you leave the coven?'

'Cheryl didn't tell you?'

'No. If she told me I don't remember.'

Essa shrugged. 'They wouldn't have anyone who'd been touched by what happened at Bridger Mansion...'

Barker heard himself groan. 'And Cheryl left to find me? After they kicked you both out?'

'Look, it wasn't such a big deal. Not to me. But she lost friends, and people she thought were family. She hung around a while. She lived in Lu's place next door. Then she went to find you. Said she was angry with you but you were the only family she had left.'

Another reason to be angrier. 'Look, why did you bring me in here? I mean, obviously you're not trying to seduce me, given –'

'Witches call it The Itch.' She turned and walked into the house.

Barker regarded her curiously. Regarded her shape, lustfully, despite himself.

'Before I met Tallulah's father, I was sexually more fluid.' She turned at the end of the hall. 'A lot of people in the alternative scene fall in love with people, they say, not gender. I think you need to be in that world, though, for it to work. The world of fluid people. But I met her father outside of it. And, we played family for a while. Then I realized, he was not playing fair.'

Barker walked down to her.

'Is he one of them?'

'Black Prax? That's what you sorcerers call them, isn't it? Black Practitioners? Probably, by now. But he's not here; he runs a recording studio. Here in Adelaide, but down south, in the middle of a winery at McLaren Vale. Fucking Black Prat, more like. But, he wants this place, the land, not the practice, in the divorce settlement; and he has better lawyers.'

Barker nodded. 'A lot better, no doubt.'

'So, The Ox? If it's like The Itch, it's a build-up of occult energy. An excess. It makes you angry and irritable and...'

Barker looked around. He didn't know Korean culture, but he didn't see anything particularly Asian here that would speak to her heritage.

'It has a life of its own, some think. Supernatural energy. The occult practice, magical systems, it's just a way of channelling it.'

The living room interior was decorated with whites and creams, contrasted with limes and emeralds; the drapes and curtains and scarves, oil burners and bowls were all in this scheme.

'We need to channel it though our bodies and sometimes our bodies get confused. It's a bit like being drunk; when you get drunk, you relax, and your body wants to release stress. But once you've let your body de-stressed and relax, you've lost control of all that emotion the stress was keeping at bay. There's no rational place for it; it's been stored up over time and the things that caused it are either gone or far away. So your drunken, out-of-control psyche reverts to the primal; it looks to create the big stuff. It wants to channel the emotional energy out, through fighting, or laughing, or crying – or fucking.'

She smiled grimly. 'Sometimes all of the above.'

Barker returned the tight smile. 'That's the angry ape; sometimes it's controlled by a dark passenger, but mostly it's just the inner moron. Out of control drunk people are generally the most arseholeish or duncelike version of themselves.'

There were beautiful framed landscapes of rainforests, of mountain woodlands, and some nude sketches over a grand piano that must have taken up a quarter of the living room, behind a massive couch facing a wall-mounted widescreen. The room, the house, he suspected, was very new age; there were statues of fairies and dragons and elves scattered about, but there were also animal sculptures.

'The Ox is similar; if you don't have a spell or a function to use the magical energy, you start getting tense and irritated. Lower spirit entities start following you around, but good things find you too; the difference is because you're not drunk, or high, you can just hold on, and manage it, until something does come along, and allows you to use it properly.'

She seemed to be fond of chameleons, but in this room they were all various shades of green. He sensed there was a live one, too. Somewhere here. He stepped over the dark hardwood floor, toward a beautiful light stand that looked as though she might have purchased it from the set of one of the *Avatar* movies, at a fan auction or something... But everything in that world was digital. This was real. Art. Sculpture; or...? Then, no; it looked like a *Matrix*-thing, then... Geiger, or; *what was it?*

'What...?'

Essa sounded very anxious all of a sudden.

'The koala... is that what you mean? Is it possessed by a lower entity?'

Barker kept staring at the lamp. It was definitely an occult object; it was too deliberately crafted, too endowed with sensual, mystical energy not to be. It was like a slender woman, backlit by a full moon so bright you could...

'Barker? The koala? Is it possessed?'

...it seemed to be calling him. It seemed to want him. It seemed.

She was behind him now, and they were in the middle of the room. Her hands had come up and touched his chest, parted the coat and placed themselves on his pecs. He could feel her heavy breasts pressing into his back. Her head wasn't high enough to kiss his neck, or she would have; she would have started in there and then, and that would have been it.

'My husband wants this place. He wants Tallulah to go down and live with him, be part of his world, with all the music-makers. She'll lose herself there. You know she will. I've heard; I know, the Ox, making love to a sorcerer with the Ox, some of it, the glamor, it transfers, it rubs off...'

Barker spun around and she gasped.

'You're in my aura. You have your facts wrong. That was stupid.'

'I can't move...'

Her hands were raised, halfway toward wanting to touch him again.

'The Ox; yes, it makes the recipient of its attention glow for a few days. But your ex will know what you've done. You think it will make you more able to charm him, into dropping the case; it would, if he wasn't empowered, but he is. You need to step back.'

'I can't.'

'You need to step back or I will devour you.'

'I...'

'You need to employ all the willpower you have. The Ox is base and sexual, it's blue-balls for men, for a while. But if you keep turning that down, it goes beyond. It starts taking more energy. From anyone who raises its interest. I will happily help you, I will happily keep Tallulah safe. Any friend of Cheryl's. But if you do not back away, I really don't know which spell Kerry's sexual energy; the energy she poured into me out there, trying to seduce me, will activate. Do you...?'

It was as though a hand had touched him on each shoulder, and gently guided him to step back.

He did; he stepped back.

He was free.

He thought, and said aloud; 'I need to go.'

'I'm sorry...' Essa gasped. 'I didn't know. I didn't mean to...'

'It's okay.'

It was, after all. Just okay. It just... wasn't all that *good*.

Then Barker realised; Essa hadn't been addressing him. She was talking to whatever was standing behind him. To whatever had been camouflaged beside the lamp. It was telling him, whispering silently in his ear; he was not allowed to see. But it was helping. He tried to ignore it.

'You need to come to the Lion, tomorrow. The Lion and Unicorn. You know it?'

'What? Yes – at the top…?'

'Tomorrow morning. As soon as it opens. Bring Tallulah. Once you're there, don't leave. There will be others there who know me; tell them, stay, don't leave. It will be dangerous to leave. Tell Clem to get the rooms ready.'

'Clem? What's happening?'

'I'll help you, Essa. I promise, if we all live through this.'

'If we…?'

'Someone's got to be here for the koalas. Go, tomorrow. Remember; don't leave until I get there.'

She nodded, then Barker left.

As he went down the corridor to the door, he heard the voice of May Sullivan, or at least the part of her spirit that had remained behind to guard the two houses in which her descendants lived. She was talking to the beautiful thing, that was now helping Essa bring herself down.

He is concerned that he is accumulating too much energy?

The beautiful thing confirmed it.

Then, as he opened the door, and closed it behind him, May Sullivan spoke to him directly. She did this as Barker stared across the small carpark at the koala, who was straddling Bach's seat, hugging it with his claws extended, and rubbing his chest up and down.

It is far too late for such concerns. They are killing. They are preparing for an enormous perversion. You should have killed them all last time, when you had the chance.

THIRTEEN:
FLING

Fiif had been quiet a while now.

Carlton hadn't dared turn any lights on, but she hadn't moved. She'd just found a stool beside her at the kitchen bench and sat, in a direct line with the back door where she'd come in. She'd continued to cry, then she'd folded her arms and allowed her head to fall face-first into them, and cried some more.

She'd been wearing a black shirt, with a black V-neck sweater under the camel coat, and the little ambient light that was around them made her hair shine against the black; that which she was wearing, the darkness around her, and the black that was enveloping her spirit right now. Effectively, she had been softly spot-lit in her own private corner of Hell.

Carlton had picked up her coat and laid it gently across the stool beside her as he had taken the next one, leaving the space of the coat between them. Then he too had stared off into the darkness a while. He had known what they had to do next; but he was just waiting.

After about fifteen minutes she stopped crying and started sniffling, then after a few protracted huffs, she sniffed in, long and hard a few times. Then she had drawn in through her mouth, and exhaled, several long but increasingly less shaky breaths.

'He swept me off my feet...' Fiif finally spoke now, muffled but discernible, into her arms. '...I always wondered...' She looked up at the fridge, right in front of her, all of a sudden. '...is this what people mean, when that happens?' Carlton had already slid the box of tissues down before her, and poured her a glass of water. She made immediate use of the tissues. 'I mean...' She blew her nose hard; a real, honking, unselfconscious blast. '...money and grand gestures…' And again; a more sustained, cleansing blow. '…and romance and… *real fucking*…' She screwed up the tissue and threw it savagely into the kitchen sink. '… so you feel like you can never be apart?' She snatched another tissue and glanced at Carlton. 'Ever had that?'

'Not the money, but the rest. I was married a year. It started like that.'

'Huh…' She nodded, blowing again, more gently; obviously the first she'd heard of it. She reached out and gathered the glass in her hand, held it, then slowly brought it up to her lips and sipped a little. 'So, it was you.' She sipped again, then held the glass before her, staring at the soft, ambient light as it reflected. 'It was always you.'

'Fiif…'

'And now, no matter what I do…'

'Did you pick me to have an affair with?'

His own question surprised him.

Fiif shook her head. 'No. That happened. Like, for real. I stopped because I knew if I came back, I wouldn't…'

'You wouldn't leave again?'

She was silent.

Fuck. He couldn't believe it.

'You said it wears off; it must have worn off. Somehow. I mean, I saw you, and I thought; I hadn't thought about your bookstore in years. Years. And yet, I had gone in there every Wednesday, when I was working at the flower shop and had a half-day, just to see you, and talk to you. But that; that life, those experiences and desires, that affection, that was all just switched off like a light. I was falling for you, then Adrian just appeared. I remember thinking; he's a bogan. He's a good-looking bogan, but he's a bogan, a root-rat. He's had more stupid women than I've had hot dinners… probably, not even as a joke! And here I was, falling in love with him. Infatuated. Like; sometimes I would look at him and think, I don't even like you. But then, he would charm me into bed again and then, suddenly, we were *engaged*. And the wives of all his mates, and their mothers and their mothers' mothers; they all just… swept me up. And every now and then, I would remember… I would remember that he was horrible, and sexist, and racist, and homophobic, and that he didn't care about anything or anyone, just himself and money and having enough money to care about himself so that he didn't have to worry that he wasn't… respected, or feared, or worse, I suppose… and to make me into…'

Her mouth was drying and this time she gulped the water few times, then gasped at a series of new thoughts.

'…I mean; God! I must have had… *something*. Some degree of… I don't know? What could I have been thinking!? I don't care about platinum blonde!' She grasped some of her longer locks and held it up as though it were rags, then she clutched at her chest, her heart. 'I don't care about bigger tits! *I went under, Carlton. I* got these things put in! The best surgeon, the best everything, but… *cosmetic surgery.* Carlton, *people die.* For bigger tits? But I… *I couldn't refuse him.* All that stuff he said tonight, that I refused; there were three things, lesser things, that I didn't. But it was always; if he doesn't, I will lose… not him. But…'

She looked at her wrist.

They were more faded; half-gone now, as though her tears had somehow washed them off. Perhaps they had; perhaps there was an ink component after all.

'…it's bizarre, Fiif. The symbols. They go back to the cave. They're forgotten symbols; for more time than we can wrap our heads around, those symbols meant that you were a wife of a clan leader. The chief, the elder, whatever. They meant you were safe from… from rapes or beatings or starvation. A fucker like him shouldn't even understand them, let alone have access to them, or know they even exist.'

Fiif stared.

'So whenever I saw them, something in my primal mind told me I could never, ever lose his approval, or protection?'

'That's right. It's sick, but on a deep, deep level you couldn't resist the fucked-up bastard.'

'But after the fling, our fling; I learned how to *actually* fling. To throw those rocks. How did that get through?'

'You're gifted. Your intimacy with me switched you on. There are higher forces; guardians and guides. The reetrees, the symbols, they were blocking your connection with the Higher Realms. But once I was able to remind you of your former life, so to speak, somebody up there, out there, in there, they made an executive decision to empower you with a magical defence; they used my presence in your emotion again as the crack, and they forced in the thin end of the cosmic wedge. It looked to me as though you had perfect hand-to-eye coordination. Maybe even some kind of extra-strength. It'll be like my kali sticks. That will be your thing, to protect you, so you can do good.'

'Do good?'

'Too corny? Look, regardless, the irony is too big. Perfect throw? Can you catch as well?'

'I don't… I suppose? I always have been able…'

'Skills they'd kill for. Gifted, so you can get away from them. Someone, something, wants you away from him, because…'

'That storm?'

Carlton hummed thoughtfully 'Something has already happened. Last weekend, your friends; something is still happening, maybe? Still building? But, inevitable. That storm will be coming in some time tonight. And we need to know why.'

'Is that why *now*? Why I've been freed – *now*? And not before?'

Carlton took a deep breath.

'The agents of the Higher Realms will have done what they can. The timing matches with something bad that happened. Up here, in The Hills.'

'Timing?'

'Seven years ago. The good energy was… sucked right out of the whole city. Everything changed. Bad people took over. This might be just one of the results.'

'Me?'

'Your husband. A man like that being rewarded with occult power that is… not his to either possess, wield or dispense. And now, he's employing others. Working for something they call The Devil. That all started seven years ago. When a whole group of good people were killed, because they trusted the wrong person.'

'Who? Barker Moon?'

Carlton slid off the stool and picked up Fiif's coat, extending it to her gently.

'Come with me. Walk with me. We need to find out what happened.'

She allowed him to help her with her coat, and smiled gracefully when it was back on. Carlton returned the smile, then turned and went to the fridge.

'Provisions, perhaps…'

He opened the fridge, but pressed the button to dim the light.

'These Higher Realms…?' Fiif asked.

He glanced back over his shoulder at her. There was no automatic heating in Amanda's house, and it was becoming properly cold. She was till sniffling a bit, but it seemed that her tears had nearly dried, and although she could not see whether her eyes remained red, with her still-slightly-puffy eyes she had the open, almost innocent calmness of one who had, for whatever reason, recently gotten a lot of emotion off her chest.

But Carlton had seen this before. There would be more; she would remember other things. She would start to remember things he had repressed in her; at first things she'd been told she no longer liked. Foods, friends, TV shows, music. Her family, her friends. Her own opinions, receiving cunnilingus. Then she would realize that she had been told that she *did* like certain things, things she had not particularly enjoyed, or actively disliked, up until Zinco had arrived, and shown her the way.

That would be bad.

Sometimes very bad.

And then, she would realize, fully, that she had essentially been held captive for seven years.

And then she would want revenge.

'Higher Realms?' Carlton grabbed two of four bottled waters. 'Uh huh?'

'They're, like, where the Angels are?'

'Very high up, yeah.' He turned back to the bar and handed her one. 'Keep rehydrating.'

'Then, why can't they help us?' Fiif cracked it open.

'Help us how?'

'Well, help us. Not destroy the planet. Not kill each other. Not be greedy and psychotic?'

Carlton shrugged. 'Look, it's like... I mean, I'm not really that great at explaining all this shit, okay?'

'You've done okay so far.'

He was surprised to hear that.

'Really?'

'Well, considering nobody else had ever tried to explain all this to me, sure; I think you're the best woo-woo explainer I've ever sat in the dark and stolen food out of a close acquaintance's fridge with, for sure.'

She held his gaze.

God damn. She was just what he needed.

'I will accept that as a compliment and proceed.'

'We haven't got all night, after all.'

He gave her his most crooked grin. 'Well, the thing is, I'm not really sure I believe all that stuff. But; I've seen a lot of weird stuff, and I know that if you have the shit, the shit works.'

'Magic?'

'Magic.' He cracked his own lid and took a gulp. 'Sorcery, that kind of stuff. You have it; I have it; Barker has it...' Then he put it down, turned and opened the fridge again, again suppressing the light and holding the door with his shoulder as he rifled through. '...Cheryl has it in a different way, and the people who want Barker, they have it in the worst way.'

'But – why can't the Angels just *save us*?'

He started piling things in the crook of his arm. 'Because; and this is just what I'm told…' Carlton turned around again as the fridge lit up but quickly swung the door closed again. '…it's like we live at the bottom of the ocean.'

'The bottom of the ocean?'

He put a bunch of stuff down on the counter in front of her.

'Just, as an analogy. Right? In the spiritual world; we might be seen by some as living on the bottom of the ocean. And, there are bigger, wiser, more long-lived spirits, in the Higher Realms, in, other dimensions, right? If you like? And they have their own things going; The War in Heaven, angels against demons, Jehovah versus Satan, and all that; and that's just the dimension where all the Christianity stuff exists.'

He'd found a brown paper bag with some ripe peaches in it, and was adding an assortment of other things, Fiif presumed, for them to eat along the way. Two carrots, a block of almond chocolate, and an unopened pack of ham slices.

'I skipped dinner.'

'Jesus Carlton; how long are we walking for? Are we going up a black mountain where we have to throw a ring in the lava pit?'

'I need dinner but we have to move.' Carlton went to a pantry by the fridge, opened it and stared as he waited for his eyes to adjust. 'So anyway, it's actually really difficult for them to hear us up there, for the messages to get through. That's why people meditate. You have to get through the stultifying resonance of "their own things going on". And plus, they can only hear – us.'

'Us?'

'People like us. Psychics and metaphysicians, and the people who are switched on in whatever other ways work for them. Drugs, art, theatre, accounting, whatever. So if you need one of them to come down here, from, say, the upper atmosphere, where they live and breathe in rarefied air, if you're saying to them; please, please, please get into a diving bell, risk depressurization sickness, which in their case is contamination from our sick vibes and toxic spirits, please do that and come all the way down to the *bottom of the ocean*, to answer the request of me, *me-me-me*, a bottom feeder! And please, please, please, answer my prayer, my focussed intent, my wish, my desire, just for the sake of; you know, like, being nice. If you're asking all that, going to all the effort of getting heard, I mean; it had better be a fucking good request they're coming down here for, right? You know? As in; a request that you can't take care of yourself, by reading any, like, *any* of the reams and reams of occult and spiritual literature that's already been accumulated down here. I mean, it's like, the biggest rock star of the day is coming to your house, at the exact time you want, to answer a fan request – in person. What are the odds? You're sick? Well, welcome to Planet Earth. You're depressed. The human condition – next! You've spent ten years trying to figure things out, you've studied, gotten to know your own body and mind for yourself, figured out how spiritual energy works, how that works *in the rational world that doesn't want to acknowledge it*, what language other beings might speak, what symbols they use, or recognize and respond to; how to direct your 'hello!' into the great dimensional unknown to someone who might be willing to reply; if they can even understand? Then, right-oh. Now we might be onto something. Ding dong, saw your light on, thought we'd drop in. But remember one of the cardinal rules; be careful what you wish for! Don't blame God if these beings, whoever you may have attracted, actually *do pay attention*, but then set things in motion and you find out PDQ that there is a bloody good reason you don't have the thing you wanted. Too late to turn back now; better men than me have fallen prey to divine intervention. Or, maybe they decide to teach you a lesson about not asking for things you don't even need, or deserve; maybe they think they know better, and that's what they think is better for you, in the long run, over the sustained karma of all your lifetimes that *you can't see right now*! Or even outright *punish you*, for dragging them all the way down here and asking for help with things you could quite easily attain, or ascertain, or *ascend to* yourself with just a little more effort; quite easily sort for yourself with a little real-world application or nous. No, whatever you summon them up, or down, or through for, it had better be *really fucken good*, because chances are, that's what whatever is above them, actual, big-Gee God maybe, has left standing orders for the lesser-higher beings to do. *Teach you a lesson!* Christian God, anyway, which is what most people we know up here in the White Anglican Hills pray to by default, without even knowing half the time. But don't get me started on him.'

'Okay...'

'So, people like us, like me and Barker and Cheryl, and Heather...'

Carlton paused then.

'Heather.'

'Who's Heather?'

'Never mind...' Carlton gulped. 'What we did was, we educated ourselves. And then we tried... tried to bring them in to help us, after we'd proved we were worthy of help. Like, we wanted to stop the...'

Fiif was staring at him.

'...all that stuff I said before? The end of the world and evil and all that?'

'Well, yair.' Carlton scowled, and shrugged. 'spose that's what.'

'And, did they?'

'Did they what?' He laughed, mirthlessly. 'Look around! Does it look like we stopped anything? No. No, if anything, we made it worse.'

'Oh, Carlton. No, I can't believe...'

'Look, Fiif, here endeth the lesson, okay? For now. We really don't have time for this. We need to find your friends. There may still be time. Maybe we can talk on the way.'

'Time? Until what?'

'Until they're dead. Or worse.'

'Worse?'

'Trapped. Like you were. Against your will, without knowing, confused and bodiless and completely uneducated as to how to get around in a non-physical state.'

'But I wasn't…'

'No. But, it's possible.'

'To kill someone and have them still be your slave?'

'In all sorts of ways.'

'And not know, like I didn't know…' She looked at her wrist. It was still faded to about half way. '…about the retrees?'

'And the whole branch of dark magic they stem from. Exactly.'

'That's…' She watched him as he walked past the bench, heading to the back door. '…that's horrendous!'

Fiif followed him, but Carlton stopped short at the laundry corridor that led directly to the back door.

'What?'

He turned to her. 'You tell me. Can you sense anything?'

'Can I do that?'

'I don't know. Like I said; you tell me.'

'No.'

He could tell she hadn't tried.

'Imagine you're in a big space.'

'Do I need to close my eyes?'

'Right; again, it's; *you tell me.* It's *your mind.* Some people like a white void, like a big empty TV studio with nothing but white walls. Some people prefer a field, or to be standing in the middle of an empty stadium – an abandoned city or a desert, or a desert island. The main thing is, it's expansive, and there's nothing else in it. Nobody else there, but you.'

'Okay.'

There was something in a person's eyes when they… what did Cheryl call it? When they *went within.* They didn't have to close their eyes, just retreat. Kind of, mentally pull back and see things from a broader perspective. Fiif had that look now.

'I get it.'

'I can't do this. So if you can, it's going to be handy. There's nobody else. Right? You're fixed on that idea?'

'Yes... but...'

Good.

'But what, Fiif?'

'But there's two others.'

'Are they... do they look strange? Like, historical or ancient? Animal heads, or...?'

'No; but, there's someone else in the distance who might be...'

Her blue eyes were still open, although her vision was unfocussed. He wanted to kiss her. He'd never had that before; like, the urge to plant a surprise kiss on someone, all playful, but actually passionate. He suppressed it, and when he did, he felt shame. Not for the thought, but for suppressing the action.

'...don't worry about that person. The two others. Are they looking at you?'

'One is. One is looking for me. It's Zinc. He's... looking the wrong way. The other is... he's looking right at me. Oh!'

'Then we need to go. Come on.'

She was outside before him, closing the back door as gently as she could.

'Back fence.' Fiif commanded.

Carlton wasn't happy about that; Maz's trail went straight up the road. But he got it; whoever was watching was watching from the front. That was the thing about seeing psychically, the way she just had. It told you who was thinking about you, right then. And, who was seeing you, right then. She'd picked it up, right away.

She sealed the top two buttons on the camel coat then stomped across the tall, unruly grass to the old wooden fence at the back yard. As she did, she reached into one of the pockets and pulled out a thick wallet, which she resecured into her inside chest pocket, almost simultaneously tying her long, bright-blonde flow into a high, tight and neat ponytail, near-white in the moonlight. She took a second to examine the fence, then had one of her boots up and on the main horizontal support, with both hands on the top of a pole, one over the other. Then she was over, with a bump.

'Fuck!' Carlton heard, although softly.

He was right behind her, although he'd approached the corner and stood on an empty, overturned flower pot to gain easier height. Looking over, he was sure that she was okay, just standing at the back of a well-tended garden. He dropped down on the corner, over a mass of cherry tomatoes.

'What?'

She whisper-hissed back.

'I snapped a branch off this tomato bush…!'

'There's a dozen of them here, they won't care.'

'It's someone's tomato bush! Look at this garden! Somebody loves it!'

'Well, is there anything on it?'

'On what?'

'The tomato branch?'

'Well… *a tomato?*'

'Then bring it; we'll add it to the sandwich.'

She threw him a look but nevertheless put the tomato in her pocket. As she did, she spotted a chunk of rock under the dirt. It was easy to pull up from the soft soil.

'What are you doing?' Carlton demanded, still whispering.

Fiif closed her eyes. Carlton could tell; she was going within. Then she leaned back, just a tad, and tilted her whole body to the right slightly. Then she threw the rock, her arm curving as swiftly and gracefully as any baseball pitcher known.

Carlton held his breath as she opened her eyes.

They heard a dull smash of glass.

Quickly, they moved through the vegetable patch and across a lush, even lawn, then through an open, ungated carport and onwards, up the footpath and along the diagonal road on the other side, until Carlton stopped under a huge camellia bush, exactly between street lights, three houses up.

'Did that sound like a front window?' Fiif asked simply.

'What? Why did you do that?'

'I combined. The throwing and the seeing. The rock went straight to him. I threw it over his head. A warning shot.' She seemed suddenly disappointed that he would doubt this. 'It was accurate!'

'Then what did it hit, sweetheart?'

'I think…' Fiif leaned into his face. '…sweetheart, that he was sitting in a car. Right?'

Carlton felt his expression change, his features release with realization.

'Wow…'

'Right?'

'Wow. So now, if we see a car…'

'…with a shattered windscreen…'

They smiled at each other, knowing, then Carlton turned away and skipped past her. On the fourth block from where they'd come out, there was a huge rocky outcrop, a massive natural formation jutting to head-height in the middle of a small park. It was like a stone whale's head, frozen forty-five degrees as it broke the surface.

'Must mean something to the Indigenous people around here.'

Fiif put her hand on it as they passed. 'How come?'

'Or they would have just dynamited it when they planned the suburb. They didn't muck around back then in the seventies; it must be, like, a real landmark for them.'

'There's a plaque.'

'I know, I nearly tripped on it.'

'Thanks for the warning.'

She came up behind him. There were wattles surrounding the rock, and one giant gum, but they could see through to the street thanks to the one street light right at the end.

'My car's through there, in that cul-de-sac. Is our shattered spy still watching the house, or has he moved?'

'I think he's still there. He's furious, but, he's still there. I think it'll be hard for him to go anywhere for a while now.'

'And cold. Probably just a cop. Watching for missing persons.'

There were no barriers to the park other than the house-fences on either side so they went straight through. They kept low, just in case, like they'd seen in the movies, and Carlton opened the passenger door from the street side, low in the shadows of the night, maintaining a couching position as Fiif squatted beside him. He pulled out a backpack, dumped the paper bag of peaches and food inside it, then turned and signalled to Fiif that they should go back past the rock park.

Fiif didn't move. Now they were low, face-to-face. She whispered.

'You thought it back there too, didn't you?'

'What?'

'Carlton…'

'I was going to…' He shrugged as best he could, while crouching.

'There was an empty house, with a bed. We were alone. Adults. Attracted – adults. That's usually a one-outcome situation.'

Carlton smiled. 'Look, your friends… Amanda and Maz… if we started that… we'd never find them.'

'I'm glad you didn't. Everything that happened to me; it would have been impossible not to be consoled, like that, by you. But, everything that happened to me…'

She took a breath, as her left hand, gloved again, ran over her lips and chin.

'…everything, the last seven years, feels like it happened to someone else.'

'But –'

'I know. But it didn't. But Carlton, when that catches up…?'

'It'll be powerful.'

'…will you be there for me?'

He hadn't expected that.

'Will you make sure…' She looked him right in the eyes. He

could see now; she was going to be powerful. When sorcerers looked each other right in the eyes; that was something. That was crazy-mad, like it was crazy-mad now.

She would be another Emerald Tarragon.

Heaven help her.

'…will you make sure? Make sure that I don't kill him?'

He hadn't expected that, either. At least, he'd expected that would be what she'd try to do. But not that she would realize it so quickly; nor that she would request to be stopped in advance.

'I'll try, sweetheart.' He smiled, as best he could. 'I'll try.'

He moved quickly; kissed her on the forehead, then was away, past her, low still toward the park. He knew she would be confounded that they had not sealed that pact with a proper kiss, but… that couldn't happen.

She caught up with him on the other side of the whale's head, and they moved together up the street, Carlton now with his backpack over his leather coat, walking properly, nothing suspicious, just a couple on their way.

But she was already finding herself able to tell when he was anxious.

'What's the matter?'

He answered immediately. She liked that.

'Things in this city don't work properly. People who should meet and be together, don't meet, and when they do, it's like this; Fiif, you've been bottling up seven years' worth of magical energy…'

Carlton veered down a short side-street.

'This way…'

Carlton started down the street and Fiif fell in step alongside.

'So many side-streets…' Fiif uttered. 'What does that mean, what you said?'

Carlton wondered how to answer that.

For the moment, he didn't know how.

'I don't know, that's why…'

Her hand reached out for his, but he squeezed her fingers and quite deliberately let her go.

'We can't do that; you're too strong, even now. I need to keep my focus on Maz and Amanda.'

She said nothing and they kept walking.

People were always surprised with the Adelaide Hills; at how many actual streets there were, actually paved and lit, as though they equated The Hills with The Country. The genuinely urban parts were just like any other large suburban district; just more hilly, and a lot more bendy. But if you knew the back roads, as he did, as Maz had, you could get around on foot as well as you could get about anywhere else. If you knew the animal tracks, walk paths and hiking trails, and where there were gates or gaps in the fences, it could be even faster than driving sometimes. If you knew which empty blocks and abandoned paddocks went right through, which yards were the ones where nobody cared, which properties were the ones where nobody went or which owners just liked the fact that their property was a local shortcut, it could really be a fun experience, a challenge. It helped to know which refrigerated warehouse yards and giant storehouse carparks had no security, or which night watchmen would wave to you, as you passed through on a Saturday night, and which would chase you down and hassle you out and threaten to call the cops for trespassing. There were old train tracks that went through the forest, or cut through a housing estate, and dry creek beds you could duck and weave through; this was all local knowledge and passed down, walker to walker, without ceremony or secrecy.

But the real trick, the real rule one, was to look for anything that offered the elusive 'flat diagonal'.

There were others who could do this, who knew this, but Maz thought that he was the best; and being that was no mean feat.

Carlton squeezed his eyes shut.

Poor kid. The flat diagonal. That had been passed down the Hills walkers for decades, and he bet himself, just quietly, it had been the thing that had caught him.

A hill isn't a short cut. It's longer. The only thing that moves faster uphill is a bushfire. Look for the flat diagonals.

Carlton pushed forward along Maz's path, and his thoughts.

That night, Maz had thought that he had been learning something; something he had learned before, but had generally dismissed. Something that, whenever he was forced to re-learn it, would never fail to surprise him. And it was this; that there was always going to be another path.

Carlton agreed; although he was occasionally surprised by a new side road, or a forgotten shortcut, Carlton had liked to think he had a handle on this notorious warren he called home. He had good sense of direction, a good memory for the way the roads bent and swerved, for landmarks and local markers. Some of it was childhood, ingrained. Some of it was learned local knowledge, repetition through his teenage years. But it seemed tonight a truism that every now and then he, and Maz, could always be surprised by something like a field cleared after decades, or an old tree suddenly down, revealing some new aspect or clearing, maybe a property demolished or the sudden appearance of a new bridge; and there it was.

The elusive 'new path'.

Like Fiif had said, some time ago, Maz and a few of his mates had been involved in a pretty heavy car accident, just out of school. Carlton could feel it, still in the trail of Maz's energy; like supernatural encounters, some people brushed these things off and kept going. But for Maz, driving would forever more be equated with fear, not freedom. Since then, Maz had started to plan ahead. He had taught himself that, if he was going to drink, which was inevitable, he would drive half way and walk from there. Even walk the whole way, if it were close. A k or two, three. Twenty, thirty minutes. If he was too pissed to walk back to his car, he'd try his best to get a ride back to his car, or even back home, with someone sober. Or, someone more sober than him. Maybe even that rare someone who wouldn't, or couldn't drink much, but still went to parties. Then he'd sleep in his car, using the quilt and pillow he always kept in his boot, or pick it up the next day.

Carlton had learned the same thing at Maz's age. But he knew that it didn't always work out that way; some weekends you'd end up hitching a ride home with someone more pissed than you were, but you didn't realize until they started driving. Some weekends you were so pissed that even by the time you walked back to your car, you were still too pissed to drive, but didn't realize. Sometimes you did the right thing and crashed in the back seat, sometimes you were in a mood, or feeling lucky, and drove home anyway. But usually it worked out. Usually.

And, well, at least Maz was trying. Which was more than most.

'What's wrong?' Fiif asked. 'You're not talking. Is something wrong?'

Classic woman. He'd thought it was her that wasn't talking.

'Like they say; when your number's up, your number's up. Nothing you can do about that.'

'What?'

'They were walking along, and that's what he was thinking, right here.'

'He was thinking *that*?'

'He didn't like it. He was starting to be less and less *blasé* about throwing around quips like that. He was starting to knock on wood a bit more often. Especially since he'd met Amanda.'

Fiif stared at him as they under the street light. 'Are they dead?'

He knew she'd been watching his face for a reaction under the light.

Somewhere up ahead, there was a scream. It startled them, then they realized it was a very young girl, very excited. Far away.

Carlton could still feel Maz in his head. 'I think so. Probably. Maybe. Definitely something's happened; more than an hour's walk from here. Do you want to go back? This will take a while. I mean, I'm happy for you to come. But this isn't a romantic thing, this isn't going to end with you and me scaring each other into a passionate embrace, up against a tree on the side of the road, or rolling in passion in some field somewhere.'

'Jesus, Carlton. I understand.'

'I know you've just been through something terrible, but; if your powers are coming out this strong, you might be able to help, and help them. If someone, or something, comes after us, your hand-eye thing; that could save us both.'

She shook her head, right away. 'No, no, I get it. I totally get it. I'm in.'

She looked grim.

'So this is what I'm getting, okay?'

'Okay…' She stared straight ahead as they walked, her nose pointed dead-straight, her white-blonde ponytail bobbing.

'The older he got, and after he and his mates had been in that accident, it affected him. But he was thinking that… *tonight has worked out well.*'

They started walking again.

'How so?'

'Amanda doesn't live too far from the Dunfield Scout Hall… where Macka's twenty first… is it Macka?'

'Des MacDonald.'

'He was thinking it would only take half an hour, and he knew the roads. He thought they might stop and 'do it' on the way. Then it might take longer. He was thinking… is there a High School up here?'

It was a middle class section and the street lights were well maintained and regular, although almost every house was shrouded with thick bushes and trees. The only way you could tell there were houses sometimes were the driveways, and letterboxes, and even then sometimes it was unclear. Carlton knew that there were regulations up here, hard and fast, that all foliage was kept away from the power cables on the Stobie Poles, since several people had been killed in the bushfires that swept through here once a decade or so, like tornadoes in America's mid-west. The

219

bushfires had been thought, by some, to have been started by the power lines on the Stobie poles connecting with dry hanging leaves, or branches. You could still see the black tree trunks, between the new ones, here and there. For people who knew what they were, it was a constant reminder. Nobody who lived up here took any risks.

Fiif pointed up ahead. 'There.'

She was keeping up the pace very well. There was a high chain fence at the end of the road, which turned right. Suddenly there was a children's crossing, and a sports oval. The oval stood out like a canyon; a sudden great chunk of flat, green nothing.

'A flat diagonal. That's what Maz was thinking. This way.'

They walked a few houses along the fence, which had been designed to stop high-flying footballs and cricket balls from flying into the street, until it stopped after a second street ended against it also.

'Amanda's street. They came up here, and went across the oval, and through the school. He thought, if they cut through the High School, across the oval, then through the orchards, they'd come out somewhere along the bendy stretch of Stringybark Road.'

'Stringybark?'

Carlton knew what she was thinking. There were old houses up here that nobody ever went near anymore, that no farmer in this kind of recession, in this kind of new post-climate-change world, could afford to maintain. It was the kind of stretch where there were signposts to private roads and driveways heading off to nowhere, and not even the locals could remember where they led.

Carlton focussed. It was like having a story read. Like Maz's ghost was reading him the story of his own very basic chain of thoughts…

'He's thinking… he's saying to Amanda, that all they have to do is keep going until they hit the main road to Dunfield, and they'll be there. He says to her; no wucken furries.'

Fiif frowned. 'But…'

'I know. I know what he's thinking. Have you ever seen a Google map of all the towns around here?'

'I...'

Carlton pulled out his phone.

'Once again...'

There was reception.

'Look; it's like this. Aldgate, Stirling, Crafers, Dunfield, Verdale, Tennyson, Longbrook, Highheath and Garner Gully. You grow up here, you meet people from all those towns and it seems like they're just a stone's throw from each other. Like suburbs all next to each other down on the chequerboard plains. They even look that way on a map. But each one is separated by a series of hills and ridges and creeks that the local roads have had to navigate. Roads that are the only way through, that have been there since the olden days, day one, simply because it was, and had always been, the easiest way around.'

'But from a satellite, they actually are all quite close, really.'

'Sure. But on foot, if you're taking shortcuts, you have to know the ways through. Mostly Maz did, but in this case, he didn't. He's trying a short cut to somewhere he's never walked to before, from somewhere he's unfamiliar with.'

'But, surely that always ends well...?' Fiif stated, dry as burned toast, from somewhere deep and grim. She was finding her old self again. The one Carlton remembered from high school. Something she'd lost, he'd thought, until she'd seemed to regain it on their third dirty weekend together. At the time, he'd simply assumed she'd been loosening up.

'He told Amanda he knew his way around, and he did. Just, not from Amanda's house. Not this way. He thinks he does, but tonight, he's – I mean, that night, he was... unlucky. And while it seems like half an hour's walk, the way he's going to go, it's gonna take them half an hour the wrong direction...'

They walked on through the school, between the severe old nineteen-sixties government buildings and then along the wide lawns on the other side. Hills schools always prioritized sports. The buildings were eerily quiet, the kind of quiet that only comes with truly cold weather on a midweek night. Somehow, it didn't seem right to chat.

'Up there…' Carlton pointed. They came out on a street that seemed to define the final border between suburbia and bush. Just like that, and the rear school yard looked out on a long plain of orchards, and paddocks.

'He decided to cut across those orchards. You can see, the undergrowth has been cut back. It's a rise, not a hill, and a clear diagonal in line with the direct destination. It's new. Amanda's saying it wasn't here last time she walked through.'

'You can hear Amanda as well?'

He'd misspoken. He hadn't wanted to tell her. He'd wanted to protect her.

'Yeah. I can tune in on one at a time, but he's the loudest. He's certain, and proud. At least, he has certainty and pride, quite loudly, in his mind. He decided to go that way, thinking it would be quicker, showing off. Amanda agreed, and that was even better. He was thinking, he's three weeks into this thing with her, and they never seem to argue. She's never complained, and he's never felt like he wanted her to shut up.'

'It's always good when it's new.'

Carlton looked across the orchard.

'I think he really loved her. I think she was there too.' Carlton gulped, and was quiet for a minute. He was aware of Fiif watching him, of her growing fear. 'They ended up on Stringybark, but too far up. You still up for the walk?'

'Why do you keep asking?'

He smiled. Maybe it would be okay.

'When did you figure this out? That you could do this?'

'Ten, eleven. Puberty.'

'So; why don't you just pick up all these thoughts in the air all the time? All the ripples? There must be something dramatic happening in… I don't know, you tell me? One in ten of these houses each night?'

'Not murder.'

Her expensive black boots made terrible scraping sounds as she halted abruptly on the bitumen.

She just stared at him as he stopped too.

'I think that's what it is. We're… you're going to have to get the cops involved at the end of this. And keep me out.'

She broke the gaze and kept walking.

She didn't speak again until well along Stringybark.

FOURTEEN: WOODWARP

I

Outside 90mins.

How long ago…?

Barker sat on Bach. 'Don't go yet.'

– you saw me idiot!

She'd sent both those texts not long after eight, just after he'd gone into the Lion, and he hadn't checked his phone since. Now it was… Jesus he was more than an hour late, it was nearly eleven. Why hadn't he? He wondered. Maybe because seven years ago, not everybody had been so phone obsessed. Old Barker, the pre-Bridger Mansion Barker that symbolized the parts of his memory that were starting to return, certainly hadn't been. Old Barker, Returning Barker… (– was he? Was he really?) …just didn't think about that kind of thing.

This Barker tried to call her.

'Hey; are you still there? I'm sorry. Things have taken a turn. I need to know you're okay. Cheryl, it's starting. And it's bad. They might come for you to get at me. I'm bringing Carlton in. As of tonight, I think it's safer he knows we're here. Stay on the roof. I get why you're there – if you're still there. I'm coming now.'

The koala shifted. He had taken a seat on the back of the bike, and was sitting there, slightly tense, his heavy bottom back against the top box, back paws curled around to his front, front paws planted forward between them. He seemed well-balanced, and content, but as the bike was not Barker's officially, he did worry a little about the claws on the upholstery.

Barker got off and called Carlton as he paced the carpark.

'Craven; it's Moon. We're back, me and Chez. We've been

back a while but I didn't tell you because… look, you can probably figure that out. But I think we're safer in a pack from here.' As Barker spoke, he bent to pick up several of the smaller dropped branches. 'I'm staying at Mum's, on the shore, but I'll be at the Lion and Unicorn tomorrow morning, first thing. Cheers mate. Sorry for the lateness.'

He returned to Bach with the koala watching his every move. 'You okay?'

He extended the leaves. The koala accepted. Barker flipped up one of the side-boxes and quickly skinned some more braches, depositing them into the top box until it was nearly a third full.

'Okay. We're going, I think.'

Barker remained at the side of the bike.

'Bach, start. But be careful.'

Bach started her engine. The koala reacted, startled and seeming to tense as the bike roared and vibrated beneath him. At first Barker thought he would leap off and bolt for the safety of the highest limb on the Ghost Gum. But instead he quickly manoeuvred around on his bottom, a complete one-eighty, and locked his powerful back legs beneath the top box. Then he embraced the box itself, just like a tree-trunk, and sat still, staring over the top of the box, out toward the street.

Barker walked up to him as Bach idled and the bike's engine cranked down a few notches. His eyes followed Barker everywhere, and refused to unlock their gaze, even as Barker moved right in front of him and leaned down to stare the koala right in his brown, almond-shaped eyes. The catlike vertical pupils stared back beguilingly over his huge, black, spoon-shaped nose. There was a tuft of unruly hair that stuck out over his right ear, where the fall had split it. Barker reached up and touched the back of the koala's head. The koala seemed okay with that and as Barker scratched him there, as he would pet a dog, the koala's eyes narrowed a little.

Barker stopped.

He didn't know what that meant. He didn't know if they enjoyed being petted or even liked human interaction. And yet he remained there, clinging onto the back of the bike, despite Barker's proximity and the idling engine. Barker thought. One; the animal had been exposed to powerful, natural occult energies. And two; he was, according to Essa, much smarter than an average koala. And then thirdly; well, it had to be said, the koala had clearly somehow bonded with him.

Barker had an idea.

'Look, you can come along, but once you've had enough, you can move along of your own free will. Okay?' He spoke with a voice that was at once addressing the koala in a firm tone, but also addressing himself in such a tone. 'There are trees everywhere in this city. Climb one and someone will come get you.'

Then Barker realized he was also speaking, aloud and broadcasting, to whatever force had activated the tree to sacrifice itself for him; whatever force had also, somehow, maybe accidentally, maybe even as an accepted consequence or side-effect, brought this koala up to what appeared to be an almost canine level of intelligence.

As though in accord with the enormity of these thoughts; that it could even happen in the first place and, again, that it seemed to have happened in order to help him, thunder rumbled in the distance. He looked up at The Hills behind him, and for the first time sensed that something was coming. The terrible but wonderful cliché; *there's a storm coming*. But there was. There was a storm coming, in every sense of portent that the cliché implied. He looked back at the koala.

'You're not a pet, and I shall never treat you like one; you are a force of nature and you can come and go as you please. So the first place I am going to take you...' Barker sighed. He was already becoming attached to the dumb thing. '...look, I need to go there anyway, okay?'

He kept staring.

'You look like Arthur Lowe, do you know that?'

Bach followed Barker's orders.

She began at a slow speed and the koala remained clinging as they exited the parking lot, and remained firm but, so far as Barker could ascertain, essentially unfazed as they took the first of the corkscrews up. As Bach arrived at the straight, she parked just where the truck had fallen, returning now to the scene of the mystical crime. Barker removed his helmet as Bach dropped her stand. He gazed across the short drop. There was evidence, if you knew what to look for, but not a lot.

The truck driver and his niece must have first cleared the way for Kerry, Barker had assumed, up by the ghost boy's rock. They had made fast work of the remaining debris. It had been... what, a couple of hours? There were still a few large rocks right at the edge that they had been unable to get past the barrier, but mainly the stuff had all been pushed over the side.

And that was what Barker had been most afraid of.

He'd deployed that branch, empowered it, and left it.

He didn't remember much, and even though some of it was returning, he knew enough to know that this was poor form. Leaving magically activated items behind could have nasty consequences. There were things, and people, who came sniffing, had a sense for these things. They could sell them, or use them, or sell them to people who wanted to use them against you.

He couldn't see the branch anywhere.

'Okay...' Barker turned back to the koala. 'This is where you lived. In that forest up there; up the hill. Maybe the fall damaged your memory...' That had just occurred to him. '...damaged your memory too, huh...?'

Was the koala some kind of sign? From above? From below? He had forgotten The Below. The Beneath. The Earth Beneath, generally, to distinguish it from the Ocean Beneath. The Underground, The Underworld. The Inner Earth. People never thought of that; there were powerful spells made centuries ago to ensure it, and millennia before that to ensure those spells worked. But within the life of the actual planet, within the occult dimensions that were firmly attached to the planet that normal people rarely ever saw; between those and normal human oil and coal and Wi-Fi dimensions, the Inner Earth was just as relevant as the outer, as relevant as the Astral and everything that extended up and out from there. Had Nature, some power from the Inner Earth, acted to neutralize an abomination, as Kerry had suggested? Or had it acted to protect him? And now, sent him some sort of... what? Watcher? Guardian? Symbol? Living Totem? A Ward, even?

A familiar?

'Look, mate, you go back if you want. I have to find that branch, even if it takes me all night.'

As Barker continued to scan the side of the road in the moonlight, the koala continued to clutch the top box. But at the same time, the koala watched Barker's every move, with as seemingly intense an expression as his adorably blank grey-furred face could produce. Then, when the koala flinched and looked down suddenly, gazing down the edge of the hill, Barker noticed immediately. The koala had heard something. Essa had said; they had great hearing. Barker froze, a few steps from Bach, and waited. Then he heard it as well. He knew what it was immediately; the warped wooden man who had fallen with the truck was climbing back up the side of the ravine. Barker edged to the barrier and stared over. The truck's impact and subsequent fall had bent the barrier right to the ground, unearthing a solid wooden support that had been planted about half a meter back from the edge with a massive dob of concrete. And now, there it was, exposed. Barker stared over it. He could see the wooden thing, the trunk man. What the hell was it? His knowledge of occult lore had been enormous once; but even though his memory was returning, and conversely, even though he knew he probably might not remember what these things were, even if he had seen them before, something in his gut, in his chest, at the back of his neck told him that these things were some kind of new, some kind of contemporarily fashioned black sorcery abomination. It was slow, methodical; one hand then one foot, then the other hand, the other foot. As he watched, just a few seconds, he thought again; maybe not so slow. It was strong and determined and... he had hurt it. He could see its head, broken in half down the middle. It was bubbling. Something... like treacle. Thick, like – of course. Sap. It was hard to tell in the moonlight, but he was pretty sure...

The thing looked up and saw him.

Barker turned and went back to the bike.

The other side box had an emergency kit.

He flipped it open, the koala still watching. There it was. A thick yellow one. He flicked it. A long bright beam, strong. Returning to the edge, with the thing maybe only three or four body widths down, Barker shone the torch down at it, right in its sap-filled crown.

'Stop!'

Its hands were completely unaffected, not hurt or cut or bleeding, by its strong, firm grasp on the outcrops of rock, and the crags of stone it was using to make purchase and heft itself up.

'Don't come any closer!'

It looked up at him, into the torchlight. The bubbling sap was so thick it barely shifted as the thing's head tilted back. Barker shuddered. It had yellow eyes. Like amber, like bright sap, with weird black pupils. An aperture opened beneath them, where a human mouth would be.

'*Hhhhkkkkhhhh...*'

It was a weird, guttural hiss.

Barker blasphemed under his breath.

There was movement behind him as the koala shifted and dropped off Bach, onto the road, and came over. It went right up to the edge, beside Barker's legs, and looked over as well.

'That's not the way home, little buddy.'

The koala kept staring, then Barker saw it. The koala was

staring at the branch, the branch he had come down on, and the branch Barker had used to split the woodwarp's head.

Woodwarp.

The name had come… maybe he *had* seen, or heard of them before?

But it was climbing to get to the branch; Barker's branch. Barker's new…

'*Huck-kuh-kuh…*'

It had bark on it; leathery bark-like skin. It was a man, a humanoid, stretched out and withered. Had it… once been a man? Wood-warped? Into a man? Or a man wood-warped into… this thing? A man who had been *woodwarped*… as good as *murdered*. Woodwarped to death…

'*Kuh – kuh – kiii-iiill-uh…!*'

Barker kept the light in its face. It didn't seem to care. He could see now; beneath the bark… there were features. The thing was somehow mummified, dehydrated into… leathery old dry wood?

'What are you?'

Barker's request was part puzzlement, part horror, but also… this thing, he was starting to believe, had been human once. So in the timbre of his voice, within the inquiry, had been… *compassion*? This thing, converted and driven to kill?

'Don't touch that!'

He could see now, the woodwarp was going for his staff.

'Don't touch that! If you touch that… I don't know!'

The koala was becoming agitated. He started to cry out; Barker had heard this before. It could give you the willies in the middle of the night, and people unaccustomed to it could not believe it was a cuddly koala making the sound; but he did. A huge, burping, elongated grunt, then another, then another, longer, then finally a fully almost ape-like expulsion of territorial koala anger. Even as the sounds echoed forcefully, spectacularly throughout the valley below the ravine, even though Barker's new animal totem pal had pushed out his chest and become as animated and aggressive as he ever would, the woodwarp kept coming.

Barker looked about for the largest stone on offer. He couldn't find one; but there was the lump of concrete, just there. He saw what he could do; if he could push it, separate it from the twisted metal of the guard rail, or even shove it further to the side, its own weight would drag it over the edge, and probably take the rail with it. It would hit the thing, collide with it and send it back down. Immediately Barker dropped and started putting all his weight onto it, through his shoulder, his feet planted heavily on the slight rise between the edge of the asphalt and the dirt on the side of the road.

It was shifting. Barker could see over. Dust and dirt and bits of concrete were already falling into the thing's still-upturned face.

'*Kiiillll! Uhhhh-huuuhhhh-mmmmaaaah!*'

Barker paused. The giant cauliflower of concrete was almost ready to go. Another few good hefts. But he looked over. Was it going to say that? Was it really going to ask him to; *kill me*!?

The thing was there. The staff was lodged between two rocks, way too low, too precarious for him to climb down. The koala was leaned right over, still hooting his terrifying, territorial decree. For a second Barker panicked, thinking that his now-highly aggravated marsupial mate was going to try and climb down, take a swing, and his paws start arcing out, scraping the dirt before it.

'*Kiii-iiillll - hmmm-aaahhhh!*'

'You – want me to kill you?'

The woodwarp grunted, and lurched out and up for the long, straight, Ghost gum-white branch that, just a few seconds ago, Barker was sure was going to become the start, the replacement, the successor, to the staff that he had lost at Bridger Mansion, when *fucking Fenner Shilling* had –

Barker cried out. 'Don't!'

There was a power in his voice; the woodwarp shuddered, but it wasn't enough. The thing's long, withered arm arced right up and grasped the staff. The woodwarp shuddered even more. There were sparks from it; first white, then violet and lavender, electric blue and bright lime green. The woodwarp shrieked, then arced its hand right back, with the white branch extended as far as it could go. The koala was dancing about in the dirt at the side of the road now, no longer hooting, clearly furious but helpless to do anything about the woodwarp's steady advance. Barker couldn't lose both. He knew the koala was going to jump at the thing. His left hand shot out, open-palmed at the huge grey ball.

'No, mate! Stay!'

Immediately the koala jolted and turned to look up at him again, his huge brown eyes wide with shock. Then he scuttled over at lightning speed and plonked down on his bottom, right beside Barker's leg.

Okay. That happened.

Barker looked down. The woodwarp had the staff stretched out behind it now, right out over the ravine, with its other hand clutching an extended root like a rope handle. Its feet were planted solidly, its withered legs tense, and its wood-hollow mouth wide open, soundless, as the residual power shot through it, as it was frozen to the spot, as though a mountain-climber had accidentally grabbed hold of a live electric cable.

Barker thought he knew; the thing wanted to drop the empowered branch down the ravine, where Barker would never find it, but where the woodwarp could find it – later, whenever. Barker thought he had it pegged, thought that was its plan. But then, the thing stretched its arm back even further, as far as it could go, and with what sounded like a huge grunt, thrust its arm forward and released the staff in a mighty throw. The massive lob cast the branch in a wide arc, high up over Barker's head, where it collided with the rocky hill-face behind him and clattered down onto the other side of the road, sparking bright fireworks of violet, blue and green as it tumbled back across the old bitumen road to Barker and right up to the koala at his feet, who watched it roll up with a quiet, curious intensity.

Barker quickly turned back and looked down at the woodwarp, half expecting it to be mounting the ledge and coming over the top for him. But Barker only half expected that; the woodwarp was where his more knowledgeable half expected him to be.

It was still hanging on by one arm, feet braced hard against the ravine wall.

Then it – no, *she*, Barker saw, disgusted and totally appalled – *she* let go.

As she fell, Barker finally understood.

'*Kill!*' The thing that had once been a woman cried out. '*Him!*'

Barker watched as the woodwarp fell, vanishing into the darkness below. The she-thing was gone in a second, but her cry lingered as loud and long as had the koala's bellow, echoing through the whole valley, as the true horror of what was really occurring finally sunk in.

FIFTEEN:
FOREVER FOR AMANDA

I

Maz could still see a few kitchen lights, and living room windows, here and there, up and down, from the suburban homes that potted the hillsides and gum forests throughout the valley. The Hills were weird like that, sometimes, especially at night. You could be on a bendy road with craggy rocks to one side and a ravine down the other, turn the corner and find yourself suddenly in a dense suburb, the hillsides dotted with dozens of totally ordinary two bedroom houses, or a sudden, shallow valley comfortably but tightly populated. On a winter's night, when light played tricks with distance and scale, it could be ever weirder.

Maz and Amanda had walked back down Stringybark and come to a crossroads, then taken the main Dunfield road. Past here, Stringybark went all the way to the Verdale Pub, with nothing but a Gordian Knot of hillside backstreets on the way. Still, they had figured, even though they'd overshot, the shortcut across the orchard had saved them a good half kilometre.

'I never knew that shortcut…' Amanda confessed.

'I think that block's just been cleared. It looked like a flat diagonal.'

'A what?'

Maz shrugged.

'This guy, at the pub… he was older but he kind of…'

'What?'

'…he was okay, that guy. I could never really believe…'

Maz went quiet a second. He didn't feel like talking all of a sudden.

'You okay Maz?'

'Yeah…' Maz shook it off. 'Yeah, nah wuckers. This guy, he said, there were five rules to walking around The Hills. The first was, don't take a road that looks like a shortcut, if you don't know where it goes. In the city, walking is easy; head in the right direction and turn off any road that zig-zags in that direction. But in The Hills, in any hillside suburb, anywhere, like Los Angeles, Rio, wherever, you don't take a road unless you know where it goes.'

'Common sense.'

'You'd think. But the second was; look for the flat diagonals. Like what we just did.'

'We did?'

'Yeah. That cleared block was flat, and diagonally cut off in the direction we wanted. You can try a diagonal hill, but it will almost always take longer. Diagonal flats are gold. They can cut five, ten minutes off a winding road.'

'And who told you this?'

'That guy… can't remember his name now. I mean, I never bought any of that shit, the things people said about him.'

'About who? What things?'

They were walking uphill now, and Maz was becoming testy.

'That he went mad. That he killed…'

'What?'

'Don't worry about it. It'll just freak you out. You got that weed still?'

She let it be.

It wasn't until they reached the first blind hairpin that Maz had started to wonder if they hadn't taken a genuine wrong turn somewhere. But he wasn't going to say anything. He didn't care if they walked all night and never found the party. He liked just being with Amanda, alone. Doing something. He liked that he had never felt like this before, and would never tell anyone that he did now. It felt hot, secret, exciting. Things were going okay. He was at that point with Amanda that he'd seen other guys at, but had never actually been to himself. He was starting to think about her when she wasn't there, and listen to what she had to say when she was there. Sometimes he would even remember it later, or even the next time they were together. It was only now, that he'd reached that point himself, that he'd started to understand what he'd seen the other guys go through. Now he wished he hadn't been such a dick about it, because he was starting to understand.

It was the feeling that you were better off with her around.

That if she wasn't around, things wouldn't be as good.

Maz had started to make the effort.

II

Amanda was starting to think that Maz didn't know his way around The Hills half as well as he thought he did. She'd lived here all her life as well, after all, and knew her own part like the back of her hand. But once she strayed outside of that, it was a mystery to her.

This part was not her part.

This part was not anyone's part, really.

This road weaved through a low valley, alongside a creek that seemed to run through grazing blocks for livestock.

There was no cell phone reception here, but sound carried for miles and miles.

It was totally spooky, and it was freezing cold, getting toward Arctic, but still, they had a bottle to keep them warm. In her own walking career, she had learned that being a little bit drunk, and significantly stoned on top of that, would more than keep the cold at bay, so long as you forged ahead.

Amanda could handle her drink. She'd started hanging out at the local pub a few years before she was legally allowed, but up here in The Hills those sorts of laws didn't really mean much. The local cops didn't care, the adults turned a blind eye, and the kids just accepted that it was all okay so long as nobody ever talked about it.

She'd vomited from binge-drinking for the first time on her fourteenth birthday, and had grown accustomed to doing so every now and then in the years since. During those years, she'd learned the same lessons that her friends had. They'd helped each other through what she supposed, from a book she'd read once in high school, were called 'rites of passage', and her social life had profited accordingly.

Amanda and her group had each lost their virginity at sixteen, to young men they now regretted even knowing. They had each subsequently learned to adequately administer minor sexual favors to young men they liked but desired not to have full sex with, had held each other's hair back from the toilet bowl and thus each learned not to mix drinks, had each learned their respective levels for metabolizing different kinds of alcohol in similar fashion, and had each seen the others gain a steady boyfriend, thus learning to worry less about all of their previous concerns.

Amanda's group, of the several girl-gangs that hung out at the Pound and Silver, were connected through the hotel itself. They were a group of girls who individually did not come from any of the standard social tribes; the netball club; the younger girls who attended the local high school; the older girls who had graduated the local high school but remained in touch; the football and cricket WAGs. Amanda's group were the best looking of the local social left-overs. And there was something about that, to do with their non-affiliation with any specific tribe, that gave them fair standing amongst all the other female cliques. Because even Dezzie, the plainest of the five girls in Amanda's inner sanctum, knew how to turn it on. And people liked having good-looking people around.

So it was, and thus they were welcome, if not expected or even demanded, at any given show.

As it was tonight, as it had been forever.

Forever for Amanda was the time since high school had ended.

Forever for Amanda was about four years.

Carlton stopped.

Fiif turned back to him. 'What?'

They hadn't spoken since they'd left the school.

Carlton knew; she wasn't angry, but she was anxious.

'They were really late…' Carlton uttered. 'Amanda thought that because they were a relatively new couple, their friends still got a kick out of seeing them together. So unexpected, yet so 'under our noses the whole time', her friend told her. Dezzie? She said it was as though the fact that they were meant for each other had been camouflaged, but a few weeks ago, God ripped off the camouflage blanket.'

Fiif frowned. 'Dezzie didn't say that. I said that. I said that to Dezzie.'

'Well, Dezzie was stealing your material and using it on Amanda.'

Fiif scowled. 'We'll see about that. So why have we stopped?'

Carlton sighed, and shrugged. 'It's getting harder. They're…'

'Dead?'

Clearly Fiif was starting to get used to the idea.

'No. Well, I can't be totally sure. But the thing is, if they are, it's just so tragic. I mean they're so ordinary. So innocent. They're walking to their doom and they have no idea. They're just swapping a joint, and swigging from their bottle of Jacks… I mean, we just walked up three hairpins, right?'

'Tell me about it. Tell my heels about it.'

Carlton looked around. For quite some time there had been nothing but thick trees behind guard rails, and the flowing winter creek all the way along beside them. It was bubbling away, coming down fast from higher up, where the water was even colder. It was like a freezer; the closer you got, the colder it was; to fall in would probably mean hypothermia. Probably, in three seconds flat.

Then they had turned a corner, and come through the edge

of the forest, and walked along into a stretch of shallow valley as the road evened out. In the centre was a park filled with low shrubs, in the middle of which the road was centrally divided. The road to the left was short and bridged the creek. On the other side, there were houses, far back but visible, many behind tall bushes and trees. The road on the right was again short, this time branching out further, to the start of the valley incline, where there were more houses. Again, in the night and despite the full moon, tall trees and thick shrubberies made it difficult to see anything but the impression of homes; sometimes just the rooves, or the second floor windows. Once they'd walked past the streetlight that heralded the start of the town, there was just one more; right at the end of the park.

Carlton was sure he'd been here. Maybe never stopped, but been through here; they were just the normal line of quarter acre blocks to either side. Tasteful family homes and responsible native gardens marking their way. It was just the poor lighting that made the whole place look creepy as fuck. But that was The Hills; they were back in civilization, just like that, and he was grateful for it.

'On their timeline, the one I'm sensing, Maz's only just ready to admit he's overshot. He overshot, and they've walked half an hour in the wrong direction, just to make sure he was right about overshooting, before he said anything to Amanda. But part of him doesn't… didn't care. He prefers being alone with her, and lost, to being with her at a party full of people. They were in love, right at the start of it, and…' Carlton sighed. 'It's sad, that's all.'

Fiif was looking at him strangely.

'I know, I know,' Carlton sighed. '…we should get going.'

She didn't say anything, and they kept walking toward the second streetlight.

Carlton tried to gain his bearings.

There were creeks and ravines of all dimensions throughout The Hills, low and wide and deep and shallow, yet suburbia had

239

been built all around them. Although the two outer streets here were, from distant memory, lined with tasteful 'modern colonial' style houses, with their immaculate façades well-maintained, and although the village had clearly been planned with a picturesque central park, and possibly privacy in mind, all they had to do was just walk behind one of them and within a few strides there would be nature; inviolate rocks and immovable trunks, rampant bush and more creeks, more ravines, dips and peaks. Here in the divide between The Hills suburbs and The Country, it was like that. Chunks that could not be sub-divided, stretches that were too difficult to build on for any number of reasons. Carlton felt suddenly weird about that; as though for the first time in his life, although he'd considered it dozens of times over the years, he was genuinely realizing that The Hills weren't all they seemed.

Beneath the second of the only two streetlights, at the end of the main suburban stretch, the road divided; to the right it started up another steep incline, where there was an abandoned church, and some old houses at the top, then blackness and forest over a sharp rise.

'I don't remember that church closing...' Carlton declared, quietly.

Fiif smiled. 'You know where we are, then?'

He looked to the left. The road continued into utter blackness as the valley closed in, following the creek. The barriers started up again.

Yes, he did.

He hadn't put it together until now.

He'd never really put it together.

There was something about this part of The Hills that wouldn't allow itself to be put together.

'No; that's what Maz said to Amanda. He finally realized, when he saw that church, that they were lost. Because it's clearly been closed a long time, and last time he was here it was open. He's actually been lost out this way before. It's a classic Hills wrong turn, he remembers now. He tells her; 'Way back when we cut through the clearing, we should have kept going down to the next intersection. This isn't even Stringybark. It never was. It's Ghost Gum. We're gonna end up doing a huge circle.' And he's right. It's basically been the same road the whole time.'

'But it hasn't...' Fiif looked back and forth. 'Has it? I mean; we jumped a road. How can it be?'

Carlton's voice became a little more quiet, a little deeper. 'That... that's exactly what she said. And he tells her; absolutely, sweetie.'

'He called her sweetie?'

'He says; it's been the same road the whole time, it just wasn't the road we thought it was to begin with.'

'I don't understand.' Fiif looked back and forth again. 'Should we go back to the car? I mean; what you hinted at, about the flat diagonal? Someone wanted them to take that short cut and get lost, right?'

'I think so.'

'And now, we're following the exact same path? Asking the same questions and realizing the same things? Just like they did?'

Carlton could see the fear in her eyes as she looked at him directly, at length, for probably the first time since he'd suggested that Maz and Amanda might have been killed. He didn't like seeing the fear.

'It's okay Fiif. Give me a second and we'll head back. Okay?'

'I'm sorry. I still need to know what happened. It's just, we kept walking. The same way they did; up all those twisting little valleys because you think the next one is going to come out and you'll be somewhere, but it doesn't, and you're not. So you keep going, another one, then another one; and suddenly we... *they've* been walking half an hour in the wrong direction?' She looked around, doing a one eighty. 'What is this town?'

'It isn't...' Carlton looked around. 'I don't know how we got here.'

'We walked, Carlton...'

'Yes, but...'

A crashing slam made them both jump out of their skins; Fiif locked forearms with Carlton.

'Jesus!'

'We're in trouble, Fiif.'

'What?'

Carlton looked up the hill. The church door had crashed behind someone as they had departed. Now that person was standing in silhouette at the crest of the road before them, staring down. His legs were braced, and he looked tense, and angry.

'Who is that?' Fiif demanded rhetorically. 'We should call a cab, get it to take us back to the car, then bring the car back here.'

Carlton was surprised. 'You sure you want to keep going? I mean, it must be past midnight by now?'

'It's elevenish. We walked about an hour, but if we walk back, even mostly downhill, it will be past midnight.' He could feel her trembling, but braving it out. 'Will a phone work from here?'

'No. I don't think so. Fiif, you remember in the eighties, everyone from The Hills went down to the Greyside Roller Rink, every Saturday?'

'Sure... I mean... what?'

'You remembered it for a second, didn't you?'

'I...'

'There are places on the map that sometimes vanish. Brigadoon-type places. Things happen there, and they just close in on themselves. Greyside is like that; so is this place.'

'Close in on itself? How?'

'Will. Pain. Desire.'

'But what happened here...?'

'You don't want to know. But we won't be welcome here, and we might have a hard time leaving.'

'Go home!'

The cry chilled them both. It had come from nearby, and sounded like an older woman. But it was difficult to tell where it had come from; they had both instinctively looked up the hill to the church, to the silhouette man, but he was gone.

They heard a door, a heavy door like a front door open and close, nearby.

'Get out!' It wasn't a warning. It was an order. 'Get out!'

'I don't think they'll attack.'

'Attack?'

'Look, if you want to know what happened to your friends…'

'Why would they *attack*?'

'…I can try and follow the trail from here; or we can get out, now. It will be okay for a short while, long enough for me to follow the trail and find out. But if we leave now, the trail will be broken, and we may not get a second chance. We may never know.'

She squeezed his arms tighter.

'Okay; I can go deep, but it will be like a deep sleep. If you sense anything approaching; anyone hostile, anything at all, slap me, okay? Slap me as hard as you can.'

They heard another door open and slam closed, further away.

It was all the creepier for that; news was spreading.

'We might not have much time; are you sure?'

'Yes!'

She wasn't, but he kind of loved her a little bit now, for the bravery.

'Okay.'

Carlton sat where he stood, on the stretch of lawn between the split road, closed his eyes, and went deep.

'One more thing; if you hear children, you need to slap me as well.'

'Why?'

'Really hard. So fucking hard, okay?'

She knelt beside him. It felt safer.

'Why?'

'Because there are no children in this town.'

'Then how…?'

'Their parents…'

Carlton was drifting now.

'Carlton?'

'Their parents killed them all.'

And then he was gone.

SIXTEEN:
MAKEOVER

I

Hours now, and nothing.

This was not good.

This had never happened.

Well, not *never*.

It had happened.

But when it *had* happened, it had *not* been good.

Not good, not *ever*.

Never.

It was well past twelve now.

Two more strong mugs of World Casino lattes down, and restless.

Barker had started her on this whole 'mug of lattes' thing, because of his stupid curse. Still, the curse had saved them both. A lot. But Barker still called it a curse.

Hmmm.

But Barker's uncle, his curse, and his muscle tone, were another story. This right here though was a new story, and it was starting now; and that was not good either. People got hurt when a new Barker story started. When a new Barker story started, you knew; at the end, everyone would be changed. Some things would never be the same again. And not everyone involved would still be around to tell the tale; for better or worse.

The woman walked in, looked around the Aces High and locked eyes on Cheryl. Cheryl knew it was her. The entertainment she had given up on arriving. Shirley Swansong had finally sought her out.

'I thought you might still be here.'

Cheryl sat up straight.

'Why?'

'You're Cheryl Equinox, correct? White witch and permanent consultant to Barker Moon? Cohort of Carlton Craven?'

Is that who I am?

'And, you're Shirley Swansong?'

Shirley smiled. 'I pick up a lot of vibes, out there in the world. I come here to switch them off. You're using this bar up here to take meetings, but because of the same effect. I confess, I hadn't thought of that. That's very clever. Clients don't mind coming here?'

'Mine are gen-pop. They don't know the difference.'

Shirley smiled. 'Of course. Clever girl.'

Shirley was a small, slender, thin woman, maybe fifty, with a hive of blonde hair as big as her face. It was an amazing, striking look for this day and age. But she made it work; completely owned it, because she moved with such grace. Cheryl saw it as she crossed to the table. It wasn't poise, it was simply… this was her, and she knew who she was and, yes, she owned it.

'Will you stand up darling heart, so I can see you?'

Shirley's pale green eyes conveyed a sharp intellect, but also a wariness that had no doubt been earned by years of servicing clients within the world of the supernatural. Cheryl didn't see why not, and acquiesced. But Shirley didn't look at her body, not straight away. She maintained eye contact until Cheryl was fully standing, and only then did her eyes pass down over her clothes; down, right to her lace-up leather boots, taking everything in, then swiftly but with what looked like laser-precision back up again.

'Oh, that is a fine costume!'

'Is it? Barsia thought it was outdated.'

'Oh it is! Totally. But it is still very fine. My fee is five hundred. It includes three items of clothing from my van. My van is outside. I will make the recommendations, you may choose other garments, that wouldn't be smart, but it wouldn't be the first time.' She removed a pay-wave device from the handbag that was hanging unobtrusively by her side.

Cheryl felt as though she was somehow being stunned into agreeing.

'I'm waiting for a friend. Will it take long?'

'No. Not at all. I have been doing this for many years. I can have you looking new, the new you you'll be for the next... well, seven years, by the look of you?'

'Seven years? You don't even have to know my date of birth? Sun, Moon, Ascendant, all that?'

'I Googled you on the way up the escalator and worked it out on my app. Given that, and you standing right in front of me, I can see what I need to already; at least for now. As I said, many years under the belt. You stood with confidence, didn't break eye contact. I like that. Self-esteem is not your problem.'

Cheryl frowned and put her hand on her hip. 'No? What is, then?'

'Direction.'

Shirley's belt was wide, and black, with gold studs. She wore a tight tank top, with a long shirt and a shawl, a wrap-around skirt and simple white slip-on shoes. They all looked completely worn in, but then again, somehow still new. She might have been back from the markets, or the beach, or a week away somewhere. But she looked totally at home, relaxed and comfortable, and that allowed her to radiate a kind of easy-going feminine authority.

It wasn't even despite herself. Cheryl wanted to like her. And she did like her. She was slightly intimidated by her, but wanted to trust her; and if this was a spell, it was an extremely powerful one.

'I can afford that. But only just.'

'Only just is okay with me. If it's okay with you. Being more at home with who you should be, who you want and need yourself to be, will set you on a clearer path of abundance. Confidence, self-esteem, and being well-nurtured, these things lead to clear direction. Feeling comfortable in your skin, decorating your skin to add to that comfort; your personal grooming and clothing, are all part of that. But; there are a couple of things I need to check first. I know bathroom lighting is brutal and appalling, but can we adjourn in there, just so I can… assess the more intimate details?'

'I've had a fashion makeover before. You want to see my underwear?'

'For some girls, the right bra makes a lot of difference.'

'No biggie.'

Shirley folded her arms and assessed her again. Smiling warmly this time.

'Yes, I think I know exactly what will work for you.'

She spread her arm out and across, quite theatrically.

'Shall we adjourn to the unisex loo?'

Cheryl nodded and walked past her, pushing the door into the antechamber, then the second door into the bathroom. She heard Shirley push the first door behind her, then a thump. She turned around. There was something, a blob, on the door. It looked like thick ectoplasm, clear and sticky like transparent honey. Shirley was coming at her, and she didn't have time to react. Then she had her arm twisted behind her back, and a knife at her throat. Somehow she had missed that Shirley was taller than she looked. Shirley had spun her about to face to the full-length mirror, and Cheryl was staring at herself, immobile, her right shoulder in agony, with this woman leering victoriously over her left shoulder. Shirley was looking into her eyes as though she were insane, tightly clutching the slender-handled dagger, with a long, slightly warped but glinting blade directly across her throat. Cheryl could feel the near-freezing cold metal on her skin. She could feel blood trickling down, but she could see full-well, right before her eyes on her pale neck that there was no blood.

'Of course it was a spell, child! And of course, it is an extremely powerful one!'

Cheryl couldn't move.

'Who…?'

'Ssssh!' Shirley pushed the blade higher. 'Don't look at me! Look into your own eyes! Look into the eyes of the idiot child who ran when she should have stayed!'

'What?'

She couldn't help herself. She stared into the cavernous, sunken, shadowy pits; at the savagely sapphire blue within, at the tears welling, at the ghastly pallor of her brown and white and grey and pink tinges, of the mutation of Polish and Russian that was her heritage one generation back.

'You see?'

Wide cheeks, round jaw, button nose.

Black, sunken eyes.

Mouse hair.

Nothing to be done.

'Do you understand how things work, Cheryl Equinox? Do you understand your role? Do you understand why you have returned here, to this city? The wrong answer could very well result in your demise.'

'I... I thought you were an astrological fashion consultant?'

'I am.'

'You *are*?'

'Almost everybody's job is more than it first appears, darling heart.'

'That's...'

'Are you not so much more than Barker Moon's agent?'

'Barker knows I am.'

'Yes. You are a good friend to him. And a good friend for keeping your other platonic male friend out of this; but you have done him a disservice with that gesture of kindness.'

'I trusted Barker. Barker said –'

'Barker is acting out of fear; by the end of this night that will cease to be his modus operandi, or he will be dead. Others are seeing to him; now I am seeing to you.'

'Seeing to him?'

'Seeing to it that he acts out of courage, for life. Not out of fear, of death.'

'His life's in danger?'

'When has it not been?'

'Never in the past seven years.'

'But those past seven years all led to his returning here. He was always going to return, when the seven years had elapsed.'

'Elapsed?'

'It was always, it seems, going to take him seven years, to regather the strength it will take, to resummon his powers.'

'Re... resummon?'

She did not like the sound of that. Not at all. Not after what happened last time.

'Do you know child, that you are more than his assistant? He does, and brave Craven does, but do you?'

'He was broken. Truly broken. He fled, I went to find him. He would have done the same for me...'

'He saved you that night.'

'No, he got me out. I wasn't there when...'

'He is supposed to be the one with amnesia!' She spat at the mirror and missed. 'Amnesia!'

'I don't have –'

'You have been blocked as well!'

'No, I... have I?'

'How much of that night do you truly remember?'

'I...'

'Since that night, since he met you, Cheryl Equinox, and Carlton Craven, and let us not rule out Heather Holden; oh no! Never rule her out...!'

'Is he there now? With *her*? Is that where he is?'

'Oh no, it may be too late for that. Some of the greatest powers of light require trust between sorcerers, and once trust is broken, those powers diminish. Your friend Barker was always, always in danger of this night. And consequently, of these days, the here and now, after that; if indeed he survives this night. And so on, with the path ahead more perilous with each passing moment. Seven years again. Until his fate is resolved. *Not knowing exactly who to trust.*'

'Who are you?'

'You don't know?'

She didn't care as she gasped the witch's word out at the mirror. It was faster than light and took physical form as it bounced from the angle Cheryl had been calculating and smacked Shirley right in the third eye. She cried out and Cheryl's free hand clutched at her blade hand. She felt another weapon in her kidney, force and penetration, and knew she had been stabbed by a second blade.

Then again, then again.

She could feel the blood already pissing down inside her skirt, over her buttocks and down the backs of her legs.

'No!'

She summoned her will, hating herself for dying like this; in the World Casino loo, set up by a Black Prax in revenge for something *she didn't remember doing* at Bridger Mansion seven years ago. Her will welled up and she grasped the knife at her throat, kicked back and used the adrenalin of the shock to psyche-power Shirley back with maximum force. The little woman flashed lightning white and flew, careening backward, smashing into a stall door, then back again as Cheryl spun about and spat the physical force of her will out at her through her hands, her tendons, her trembling, tense fingertips. Shirley jiggled around like a machine gun victim, as though being shot by an automatic weapon against a wall in a gangster movie. Blasts of pure willpower, manifest in physical force; hate and regret and loss at knowing three stabs in the lower back like that, here, locked in with nobody knowing, shattered her body to death, would kill her within minutes now. Cheryl was going to bleed out on the dunny floor, but she was fucking well taking this bitch with her.

Cheryl stopped after one last triple energy-bullet blast impact as Shirley fell backwards onto the seat, her head slumped, her back already sliding down against tiled wall. Then she fell forward, straight onto the floor where she splayed, doll-like, out into the cubicle, over the floor-tiles, face down, arms out, like a dead drunk. Cheryl watched as the dagger and the knife that Shirley had used to kill her rolled forward out of each of her hands, then she moved quickly to take them. They were cold. Ice cold. Then she too fell; backward and against the nearest sink as her knees gave way, then down onto the floor, on her bloody buttocks, waiting for the rest of her vital fluid to pour down, past her, over the white tiles.

She was sure that she had killed Shirley.

Sure that she had succeeded.

She looked down at the knives.

No markings, but weird. Wavy blades.

Kind of like the ones they sell in games stores, that are supposed to look like elvish blades.

Then she knew; they were fake. Well designed, but fake.

Shit.

She leaned forward, but when she reached behind her, down past her skirt to her bum, her shoulder socket hurt more than the wound. The wound that… wasn't there.

But… Shirley was still prone.

The magic she had thrown at Shirley had been the strongest, most hateful… she had assumed she had nothing left to lose. She had held nothing back, given it…

Shirley started to cough. Like someone who had almost drowned, in one of those movies where it takes an impossibly long time to resuscitate someone from the bottom of the lake or something, but they do, and we buy it.

Cheryl sat and watched her.

'What are you? Are you alive?'

There was no way she was going to reach out and help, or touch her.

Cheryl started to stand, but managed only to crouch on one knee.

'Is that what you wanted?'

Shirley started to move. Using her hands, she pushed down on the floor like a weak push-up. All around her body, it was as though an invisible shell was starting to come clear, then crack. As it cracked, like a brittle baked-on white pastry, it fell and slapped on the floor, transforming to globs of ectoplasm.

'What is...?'

But Cheryl knew. Shirley had come to her with this already in place. Thick ectoplasm, magically solidified. In some places it looked maybe six or seven inches thick, in other places it was much thicker.

'Eyyyyyye.... cannnh...'

'What?'

'...showwww...'

'Any closer and I kick you right in the fucking face, you mad bitch...'

'...showww... yoooouhhh...'

She gave up, fell forward on one elbow and rolled onto her back, grunting.

'I... am not an old woman. But neither... am I young enough to ever, ever do something like that again...'

'What? Test a younger witch?'

'We wanted to know what you had. What you might have picked up in Sydney. But, you did not pick this up in the old rocks of New South Wales, or the weird plains of Victoria. Not even from earth-blood inner-north. This is all you. You have always been this.'

'I could have told you that.'

'What happened at Bridger Mansion changed so many of those who survived. And, so many of those... who did not.'

'There are angry ghosts at Bridger Mansion? Big fucking deal. That place is a Togic Moxic Central for this city. It's a cauldron of bubbling shit-lava for any witch who goes anywhere near it. You can keep it!'

'We intend to. But not as it is. It must be cleansed. But to be cleansed, the thing at the root of it must be killed.'

Cheryl felt her shoulders tense. 'It can't be killed, can it?'
'No.'
'Because; we stopped it fully emerging, didn't we?'
'We. No. He. He did it.'

Shirley rolled over again, face down, but this time she managed to stand. As she did, more of the ectoplasm fell from around her, from all over her, but now as it fell, it turned to a kind of caked, clay-brown mud.

'Earth and water....' Cheryl uttered.

Shirley's clothes were covered in it, but as she moved, as she stood, it seemed to lose all moisture and become plain dirt, falling off her in clumps and puffing out of existence, into finer dust across the white tiles. The wet ectoplasm there was already sand. Before long, before Cheryl's eyes, Shirley would be standing there, clean, in a clean bathroom, just as well-put-together as she had been, right before all this.

'Earth and water, turned to ectoplasm, and you caked yourself it it...?'

'Bath. We have health spas. Health spas with back rooms. With ectoplasmic mud baths.'

'We?'

Shirley smiled. 'We; they are not offering you this.'

'This?'

'What I am offering you.'

'And that is?'

'A makeover. You can keep the leather boots. They're gorgeous. But the rest...'

Shirley flung out a hand.

Cheryl was too slow, too spent to repel it. Her clothes were caught in a bright orange glow of spirit-fire. They burned, right off her as she stood there, helplessly patting them down, smacking herself, her slapping hands, desperately following, urgently trying to stop the progression of the orange lines, the fire that was destroying her clothes. The orange line crossed and consumed her garments like paper on fire; blouse, vest, skirt, belt, rings, necklace, beads, stockings, bra, undies and socks... leaving nothing but a thin floating ash. When it was over, Cheryl was left there, standing almost naked in her boots, her blue coat and her scarf.

'Well...' Shirley was impressed. 'That is something!'

Cheryl looked down.

'Why did you leave them...?'

'I didn't! It shouldn't leave anything at all! You must really adore that coat and scarf!'

'They go; right?' Cheryl demanded. 'They work?'

'Not right now. Not on the you, now. Mouse brown hair, pale skin; you look too...'

'What?'

'Nothing.'

'What?'

'Earthy. But; not in a good way. You look like a peasant.'

'A fucking – *what*?'

'There is a fine line between gypsy and peasant. Some can make it work, but you have to keep the energy going, mix it up a lot, or you look like you dress from an op shop because you need to. It starts to look stale, and old. Women who make that earthy look work, they have something. Something in the genes. It makes them look like a forest princess, not like they sleep in the park.'

'That's what – you think – I looked like?'

'No. No of course not. But it's under everything. *Threatening to emerge.*'

Cheryl immediately went defensive. 'The coat; it looked better on me. Everyone said. So Barker said it must have been for me. And Carlton gave me the scarf; the Christmas after Bridger. We were in town and we saw it, and I said I liked it, and he remembered and went back and bought it and gave it to me. Just before I went off, looking for Barker. It was the one kind thing anyone had done for me, since...'

'They protected you. Nobody knew you were there.'

'I was there.'

'I know.'

'But you don't think I remember everything – will you stop looking at me like that?'

'Darling heart, it's time to come out from under all those gypsy frills and goth layers. Turn; look at yourself. Slender, long-legged. Your mother was like this.'

Cheryl had no intention of opening her coat and revealing her naked person to this middle-aged stealth-witch, no matter her motives –

'My mother?'

'Your sunken eyes that you despise…'

'You knew my mother?'

'They are the mark of spiritual continuity. Of all your soul has seen and endured. They are the mark of a witch; a strong witch with a strong path of destiny.'

Cheryl couldn't help herself. She turned and looked at herself; stared into her eyes.

'You could have been a great beauty, if you had known how to bring it out.'

Cheryl looked at the woman; totally back to normal, in the mirror, standing behind her. Nothing but ash on the ground. The smell of some kind of Indian temple incense.

'I was seventeen when you were born. Your mother brought herself here, to this city, to have you born here. She was supposed to migrate to Perth, but a gypsy told her; Adelaide, the child would be needed.'

Cheryl frowned. She turned and opened her coat, like a flasher, so the mad woman couldn't see.

'I am not mad. But I am acting alone, against the knowledge of my coven. I am the oldest; I remember your mother. They claim that the gypsy forced her to make the move here. She had no choice in the oppressive magical patriarchy. It was this kind of male bullying that forced the hand of the witches, to come out into the open for the first time since the Christian purge. That was how it was; that is true. But that was not how it was for your mother.'

'She wasn't bullied to come here?'

'No. Ask her.'

'I talk to her on the phone, but I'll never go back to her Old Country.'

'She went back to get out of your way. This has been a Male Age. Two and a half thousand years. My coven all believe; the Female Age is coming. The Goddess is returning. But it is not so; the Age of Equality is upon us. But the balance; the balance of us all must be restored, and so the Goddess awakens, at last. And you must serve her, Cheryl Equinox. It was your mother's belief, her desire, that she brought you here and gave birth to you here in service of the Goddess.'

Cheryl stared down at her belly. Her skin was too pale, with too much of that weird grey-brown tint. Her belly was almost flat, but it wasn't. Her thighs; cellulite, no matter what she did. Stretch marks over her underarms.

'You are slender and well. You are fit, and healthy. Your mind is sharp, and your wits are keen. Your face is beautiful, your body attractive. We all see ourselves under the microscope of a psychotic teenager; the terror of puberty is an imprint that we have not learned to wipe away. But we will; in this new age.'

'I'm thirty-three and I still have good boobs.'

Cheryl snapped the coat shut and turned to face her attacker. 'You said five hundred?'

SEVENTEEN: GHOST GUM

I

Carlton watched.

'So, we've been on Ghost Gum Road the whole time?'

Maz shrugged. 'Sorry.'

Amanda looked at the bottle. The joint was finished, and the Jacks was quarter gone. But, now that she thought about it, there had been a pretty much endless parade of white-trunked Ghost Gums almost everywhere, all along the road, ever since the intersection. And she could see, thinking back, that it had been an easy mistake. Plus, the creek; Ghost Gum followed the creek, everyone knew that...

Suddenly, looking around, Amanda was struck with the notion.

They were in a forest that was much older than anything else around.

People might have built houses in it, and roads through it, but...

The roads still went through the forest. The bush, essentially. *The* Bush. The *Australian Bush*. Next stop, The Outback. The houses, the suburb; they had been built in this forest. The footpaths only *seemed* to be tree-lined. But really, from the reverse perspective, it was a massive forest, and they were on a slight, slender path that they could not break from; the only way through it.

The scale of things in her mind shifted.

From the perspective of the gum forest, civilization was... nothing.

They were nothing.

She was suddenly creeped out.

And cold.

She'd worn a coat, but not much underneath. She'd made the mistake of rugging-up too much for other outdoor parties or scout hall bashes during winter, then arrived and found it steaming hot, with a hundred people crammed inside one big room with no ventilation, and a giant bonfire outside. A good coat to get there, then to stand outside with, was all it took to avoid feeling like one tiny serve in a cannibal's buffet.

Carlton smiled within. Girl after my own heart...

'Any shortcuts?' Amanda smirked, trying to shake it off, pulling her coat tighter, sealing the lower buttons.

Maz looked around, doing the same. He didn't feel the cold as much; still, he had an old black duffle and a windcheater over his tight football-team tee, and he wasn't wearing long johns, just jeans.

'Sorry sweetie. Right now, I just want to take the most boring route there. Straight there...'

'Maz, even if we turn back now, by the time we get to the party, everyone will be gone. Do we just keep walking or – what?"

Maz laughed to himself.

'At least we've got each other.'

She smiled at him then, warmly, invitingly. That was such a nice thing to say, and mean it. And she could tell he'd meant it.

'If it rains, we're fucked though,' Maz warned sternly.

Amanda smiled. 'We'll live.'

Maz shrugged, pragmatic. 'If we get drenched through out here, on a night this cold...I wasn't going to say anything until I was sure but I'm pretty sure if we keep going this way, down here to the left, we get to Garner Gully. It's all suburbia through here, right the way to the Garner Gully main street. We'll probably get reception there, there's a phone tower on the roof of the pub. Hills Cabs run until one; we can probably be back at my place before then. I'll get the car in the morning.'

The implication was that she would sleep over.

She hadn't done that yet.

'Okay.'

Amanda kissed him again and they increased their pace. This was better than the plan she'd been working on. Her plan had been to drag him off the road and into the bushes, soon if not sooner, party or no party. She liked him on top of her, when she was high, and she liked it with the earth on her back. Not all the time, but… on a night like tonight. It was a kind of role playing. Like nerds did. But now they'd do it at his place. She hadn't even done it with him there yet, let alone stayed; he'd always come to hers and gone home after.

They walked a while, ten or fifteen minutes, holding hands, occasionally commenting on a big tree, or a possum on a wire, or the way the creek had reappeared beside the road again, rushing and bubbling and freezing cold. After a while the creek vanished again and they came upon a smaller fork in the road.

'This isn't…' Maz uttered angrily. '…I thought… this isn't Garner Gully…'

They were right under a street light but it still seemed pitch dark.

'Are we there yet?' Amanda asked in a whine.

Maz shot her look, then laughed. Amanda knew; any other girl would have pissed him off with a question like that. But he got that she found it funny, that she was trying to shake off a bit of a horror movie chill they were both no doubt feeling; that anyone of their generation would no doubt be feeling in this situation. That underneath it all, the fact that she could quip meant that she kind of liked it, the fact that they were out here, wandering together, on a wrong road, leading to a notorious fork where people became even more lost, but not really giving a shit because they were together.

Then she was suddenly struck with a flash of memory.

'Wait! Look; Halcyon!'

'Halcyon? Oh my God; how did we get…?'

'We took the wrong fork, like twice. Oh my God, Maz, we couldn't have taken more wrong turns if we tried!'

Maz frowned. 'It's so weird…'

'We shouldn't drink and walk. Next time, we wait until we get there, okay?'

He laughed. 'Okay! Fuck me; Halcyon Road! And this is, like, the start of it, too!'

'Or is it the end? I can never…' Amanda frowned now.

Carlton grimaced within.

If that was even a thing.

It felt like it was.

He could tell; if Amanda hadn't been drinking, if she hadn't been smoking, if she hadn't walked so far without thinking… she wouldn't have become so tired, so disorientated. Even if she hadn't been quite so giddy with new love, she would have seen it all more clearly. She had the ability. Carlton sensed that she did as strongly as he could sense her desire to be with Maz. Her ability to sense it; the spell, the lure, whatever it was. Carlton still wasn't sure exactly. But he knew now; he knew what was happening, that something was pulling them there.

'But…'

The feeling, the instinct, the inkling that was attempting to warn her, from deep within her spirit, to flee from a supernatural danger, was gone.

'…I have a friend whose daughter goes to primary school up here. I've picked her up once or twice. I know, that way…' She pointed right, and up, steeply. '…we take the hill now, but then the road goes all along the ridge and it's like… forever. It's a fifty-minute walk to Stirling, easy. This way, I know the way at least a little; the school's just through there. Then if we go down, through the Aldgate valley, we go up the hill on the other side; it's trading this steep side of the hill here for the lower side, through the valley at the end of the walk. You follow?'

'I think.'

'Either way, Stirling's on the other side of that hill.'

'The valley's longer surely?' Maz sighed. 'No. Never let me take another short cut.'

'You'll do better next time. And this isn't a short cut. It's a bit longer, but all together, not as steep. And I know the way.'

Maz had smiled then; Carlton saw real affection.

'There *will* be cabs in Stirling,' Maz nodded. 'And, the pub's open 'til two. We can get some Coke, take it home. But we should keep checking...' They both took out their phones.

'Nothing. You?'

'I've got one bar...' Maz uttered hopefully. He called up the local cab company and put it on speaker. There was the sound of terrible reception.

All they heard was: '... - cabs, hell −...?' The choppy voice vanished.

'Cabs Hell...' Amanda laughed darkly. '...that's about right.'

They walked on.

II

Carlton watched Amanda and Maz as they proceeded, in his mind's eye, down Halcyon Road.

Then he opened his eyes.

He saw his own fear, reflected back in Fiif's response to his expression.

'Oh God...'

Carlton didn't say anything.

'What...?' Fiif asked.

'Is everything okay?' Carlton asked smoothly. 'No children?'

'No; no nothing. It's all gone quiet.'

'Can you get reception?' Carlton asked. 'They're probably waiting to see what we do...' He looked around. The intersection still looked bleak, but the moon was higher and he thought he could see more. More houses than he'd thought, and further back from the side-roads. This was the second of Maz's three fatally bad decisions; the shuttered church had thrown him, badly. And the Jacks, and the weed.

'I tried while you were under...' Fiif took out her phone,

assessed it, then held it up. 'No. Nothing.'

Carlton gulped audibly. He hadn't meant to.

'Maz was raised Anglican. Strong, by his grandmother. Seeing a church shuttered up like that...' He looked up the steep street, right at it. 'How do we know it's closed?'

Fiif remained close by his side. 'The shutters...'

'We can't see them.'

It was Fiif's turn to gulp audibly, and hard.

'But, I did, I swear, when we first saw it...'

'What kind of church *wants you to know it's closed?*'

'I... I don't know.'

'We need to get back to the car. When I tune in now, it's strong. It's like... I *actually am* Maz. They took the wrong road three times. The thing is, if they were lured through here, all that way, from right over there, and ended up where I think they ended up...' Carlton squinted. 'I'm hungry...' He heard himself say. He hadn't expected them to walk this far, either. Maybe he wasn't thinking straight. '...maybe we can, I don't know...'

'What, Carlton?'

He tried to focus away from Maz. 'Look, here's the thing okay? The size of what's going on, is the same size as what's behind it. Okay?'

'Carlton, what does that even mean? Here, give me your...'

She didn't bother to finish; she just took the rucksack from the ground where he'd dumped it. He let her look through it for what he needed, like a tired kid.

'Something saw that Amanda had some kind of latent psychic energy. She was nowhere near awakened but she got insights every now and then. Enough to make her interesting. An easy target.'

'Target? For what?'

'Look, a lot of stuff in the world doesn't make sense. But a lot of stuff that doesn't, does at least start to, at least make more sense, if you study the rules and principles of mystical magic, and sorcery, and apply what you learn to the stuff that doesn't make sense.'

'That almost makes sense. Like... with the camouflage?'

'Camouflage?'

'Like; suddenly the planets align and two people who've been friends ten years are suddenly the real deal?'

Carlton shrugged. 'I'm not an astrologer. But if it is the way it's been explained to me, then the universe is a matrix and the planets can be seen as part of a massive symbolic engine. They rotate in ellipses and on angles and get in each other's way and cast blocks on each other's energies and influences, as much as they complement and intermingle. So I guess that, if that's true, then one day one moves out of the other's way and doesn't cast a shadow anymore, and the light of the universal energy suddenly gets through on that line, and shines down; then yeah, I can kind of believe that suddenly two people who've known each other a long time might get surprisingly switched on to each other, with that light. I mean, you and me, three weekends, then it's gone. That happens; nobody knows why. Now you're back and you're the most powerful adept sorcerer to come on the scene since ...'

Carlton suddenly looked away, into the darkness.

'What?' Fiif demanded. 'Go on! Since what?'

'Maybe it's part...' Carlton uttered, an edge of craziness in his voice. '...of a massive cosmic Rube Goldberg contraption. A cosmic contraption the size of a whole consciousness, of an entire planet...? But that's... what?'

'What?' He could tell Fiif knew that she'd been giving him a look.

'What's that look?'

'Nothing.'

'Really?'

'It's nothing.'

'I don't know if it means I said something you liked, or something you'll pay me back for.'

'I'm still listening, Carlton. You've become like a child for some reason.'

'Shall I go on?'

'Yes! Go on! Here! Eat this.'

'Well, that's why...' He took a bite. It was a peach. 'I think we should try to go back to the car; right now. Walk back, or...' Then he devoured the peach.

'What? Why?'

'Fiif; it's like...' Carlton gulped the peach down. '...we were talking about this before?'

'Talking about what before?'

'About how people wonder how you could control a conspiracy to kill Kennedy, or create a false flag incident and start a war, or create ridicule around alien visitations, or the fact that there's a worldwide network of black sorcerer bankers, or Luciferian trans-humanists, or Satanist paedophiles... they say you couldn't hide it, that there would be whistle blowers. Aside from the fact that there are, all it would take would be a consciousness, an intelligence, big enough to keep it all under control. Right?'

'I suppose...'

She slid the plastic sheath off the ham and handed him some, then saw there was half a loaf of bread in the bag.

'There's bread in here.'

'There's always bread in there.'

'Is it okay?'

Carlton seemed to switch away from her.

'A very powerful psychopath, right? A person without conscience, with the mind of an evil chess master, with enough money to keep paying people off, keep making them depend on it, until it's too late, and if anyone says anything...'

She handed him a hastily concocted ham and cheese sandwich.

'...it's ham sandwich.'

'It's what?'

'...too late. I get it. Anyone says anything, it's too late. It's too late. Wait; where's the tomato?'

She pulled it out of her coat pocket. 'How do I...?'

She rummaged around. 'Of course. There's a steak knife in with the bread.'

'It's okay.'

Carlton took the tomato from her and bit into it, then stuffed the sandwich in his mouth and chomped.

She stared at him, but he was staring into the distance, down the dark street, facing away from the boarded-up church, back at the road out of town that led back to the three corkscrew bends.

'What is okay? The tomato or this situation?'

'...you can't admit it, can't come clean...' Carlton kept chomping. '...because it's like prison. Or so they think. The thousands of people, of old-school men who don't tell their wives, old-school women who keep it from their husbands, paid off, just a few hundred every month, a few thousand once a year, by billionaires who don't even give a shit, who light their cigars, wipe their arses with that money, cash in the tree stump, monthly magazine delivery... clockwork, silence, as time passes, tick-tock, tick-tock and it's five, ten, three decades later, and that money has paid for junior's teeth, his education, the annual spree, the annual vacation you'd be crazy without now... and it's all over. You're not just living with it; you've lived with it. By this point, anyone idiotic enough to whistle-blow... well; whatever happened is so long ago, and affects so few people now, that nobody cares – and everybody thinks you're crazy. So, imagine...'

He swallowed and took another bite.

'Imagine what, Carlton?'

But he'd taken another double bite, and was chomping and staring off again.

'Imagine...' Carlton gasped finally, after a massive swallow. '...what a deity could do.'

'A deity?' Fiif handed him an open bottle of water.

'A very powerful demon or a demigod. One consciousness, a few orders of magnitude above ours. Right? I mean; a lot of people think we're basically going to be able to create an artificial consciousness, like that with… quantum computing? Within the next generation, some say. Powerful enough to read our patterns, predict our movements, our choices. Add it all up, take a stab at predicting bigger trends. So; take that idea over a few dimensions, that's not so hard to believe, right? That something could see The Vast?'

'See The Vast?'

'The Vast; the expanses of space-time…?'

'Space-time? But what's that got to do with…?'

'A state-sized cover-up takes a state-sized demon. A decent psychopath can control a political party, maybe even hold it a few years, with or without mystical influence. With a decent budget, even longer. A deity can manage that over a whole political party; where it counts anyway. Can do it for decades before it gets bored. That's nothing. But once you get into murder… more than one? Paying cops, paying witnesses, maybe killing a few more? There are rules; humans have a kind of built-in morality. This dimension has a built-in morality. Or rules, at the very least, about the taking of life. You can't just kill people who get in your way, not willy-nilly, not in the kind of civilization we have. I mean, primitive civilizations still do it; fascist civilizations still do it; but we all know it's absolutely wrong; we all know that's evil, right? It's hard-wired! Even the Mob, even the Gangs have some rules. You need something strong to back you, if you intend to break those rules, as a going concern. To keep the money coming in, to make the payments, to keep making the payments, to keep the people forgetting, and go along without even remembering what they're going along with. *To make the people forget…*'

Fiif had been watching him the whole time, listening.

'Carlton… what are you saying?'

'Think of it like; a big demon can, let's say, spread out through the sewers of a city, rise up and loom over it like omnipresent smog; see everything from a distance, a perspective. Comings and goings, patterns and routines. It can zoom in and hear, and see, and learn; what motivates people, what they want, what they're afraid of… it can find out; how much will it take to satisfy them? To keep them shut down? Stop their yearning, stop them being restless, stop them caring. And it remembers it all. All of it, like a spiritually bankrupt supercomputer.'

Fiif kept staring. 'Jesus. That sounds like Big Brother surveillance…'

'That's because it is. Just, a huge consciousness. Not a satellite array. But this is mysticism, you have to hold the metaphor, knowing it's a metaphor, but treat it like it's real, because it is, also, real. More real than anything, and a hell of a lot more real than a metaphor.'

'But, don't the Gods watch from on high? You said; the Angels? And the Demons look up from below? Isn't that how…?"

'All the higher forms of consciousness can see the city, all the people moving about. The really powerful ones can hold us all in their minds. Hold enough, see enough, know enough, to influence people; their minds at least. Most don't care to; they don't take an interest any more than we do when we pass a pre-school and watch kids playing.'

'Really? Not ants?'

'No, not ants. That doesn't hold. The things that can take an interest in us, even a passing involvement, do so because they can relate. Like a grandmother and a two-year-old. But, they can still relate.'

'So… we can communicate?'

'That's what Barker thought; that's what Barker did.'

'Christ, Carlton! Is… is that what happened at – ?'

'Think about it; you look in, into a school yard from behind the fence, and you think, isn't that nice, isn't that sweet; sometimes you hear them talking, understand something about what's going on, their social dynamic; but you wouldn't dream of interfering. Even if you hear one screaming out; most of the time, it's just kids screaming out. Kids scream; all the time. Over nothing. Nothing to us, anyway. It passes in a second. They don't even remember what the scream was for. Whatever the crisis is, the drama, it's gone and forgotten.'

'Yes…' Fiif nodded. 'I have nieces. Nephews.' She looked around. 'Are you sure it's wise to be talking about… you know? Children? After what you said?'

But it seemed that Carlton wasn't listening. Not entirely.

'Unless you see one of them really going at it with another, you know? Like with a rock or a knife; if there was blood? But unless they were doing actual harm, right then and there… there's no way, right? No way you'd ever dream of stepping over the fence, into the schoolyard, and interfering. And even if you did… before you could, they have their own guardians, waiting in the wings. It's all ordered, it's all okay, in its own way, on its own level…'

'So, the ones that do interfere…?'

'If you can make them listen somehow, really listen, and they don't ignore you or dismiss you or tell you to go away or even punish you for approaching them in the wrong way, then, they're like primary teachers, or parents of toddlers; there's a process, a hierarchy; there are rules about not interfering, and who can and why. Laws for where it's inappropriate, or might cause greater damage. Just like little kids.'

Fiif was stunned. 'That's really how they see us? Little kids in a playground? A bottom-feeder playground at the bottom of the ocean? Running around in chaos, stirring up the silt and the manta-rays, fenced into a playground?'

'Jump in without good reason, you'll be arrested.'

'But… then, how…?'

'Good parents and bad parents. That's what the deities are, the ones who intervene, anyway. Who decide to. But only where appropriate, *only with their own*, and maybe, maybe, when there is a strong, legitimate cry for help, and no-one else around.'

'So, they're connected to humanity somehow, aren't they…? You said, they relate? *Only with their own?*'

'Some of them come from this planet; like, the earth and the stone and the rocks and the wood, the fire and gas and clouds and air. Some were on the planet before we started appearing; some are a dimension or plane or two removed, but still came from here originally, evolved from here, and still interact. And some, *some* are much bigger; connected to our actual spirits, like, we're actually part of them, but, as though, we're… y'know, like, solidly focussed here.'

'Our…' Fiif was struggling, but not much; she was reaching for a term she'd heard, she knew. 'Our… higher selves? And what you said before. These are beings from the Higher Realms? Right? Is that…?'

'Yeah. As good as any word. Look; some of them can appear, some of them incarnate. They start to employ people, make them promises, give them power, help them gain influence, and their minions start going about, doing its bidding. The good ones or the bad ones; or the neutral and all stops in between. Sometimes they start to change things, alter the course of things; like the city, and the people in it, are just one big giant chess board. And maybe the demon, with the greater perspective, has powers a bit like mine, y'know? Like, being able to see into the past, and a little bit into the future sometimes; the ripples back and forth, who caused them, why and how. These bigger consciousness deities have a broader scope of vision, from on high, but those powers are much, much more powerful than anything I can do. They're able to see a society, and the way the city has evolved; I can see a few days, from two people intertwined. They can see everyone, for decades. If this is a demon –'

'A what?'

'Ignore that. Look; I see in real time, it sees in condensed time; all at once, so far as we're concerned. Reality; what's passed, the here and now, and potential; what's to come. It sees and feels and registers it all, everything, as patterns. It feels all the reverberations of all the people, the stronger the vibe the more influential the person, the more interest it takes. It knows all that. All the time. Like… like the way we know our way around the city. Our cafes, our shops, our parks. It knows its way around everything. Everything. The demons, and the demigods; they're so high up, their consciousness is capable of absorbing all these complex patterns of information and behaviour and routine, because that's what we are; creatures of habit and routine, and with that knowledge, those patterns…'

He started eating the sandwich again.

'What? Stop eating Carlton! What do they do with those patterns?'

'…they can start making moves.'

'Moves? Like; on the chessboard?'

'Through their chosen ones they start controlling more people, they start to have those people communicate, and create a network, and infiltrate society, choosing candidates for their high priests and priesthoods, their captains and corporate agents, and they have them bring in acolytes, and have them hire villains and thugs, and it all starts making money to hire more people, and pay people off; people who have no idea about any of this, but who take the money and keep quiet, because the money keeps coming and they rely on it now, they can't do without it.'

'Like what you were saying before. I get it! But that's just like… the Mafia?'

'Exactly, yes. Jesus, I mean, those old Italian Catholic networks are just as supernatural, just as demonic as anything, and they work hand in hand with organised crime!'

'But… why don't these things just – take over?'

'…they have! Look around! Nobody has a clue what's really going on, and everyone's too stressed out to even think about it. Everything's upside down and inside out. They've dug their tentacles in and they've been manipulating people since the dawn of time; our time, anyway. But there's not just one. They fight each other. People choose sides. We're in a very dark dimension here, this Earth plane, we're just coming out of a two-and-a-half thousand-year cycle of evil dominating.'

'We are? Why?'

Carlton spread his arms and shrugged hugely.

'I don't know! It's a giant cosmic machine! It's set up this way!'

'Okay, okay!'

She made a scoffing sound and looked back and forth down the road.

'I'm sorry, Fiif. With everything else, this is all too much…'

'No, no!' Fiif scoffed again. 'It's…'

She couldn't meet his eye.

'It's not something anyone should know this much about…' Carlton shrugged, lowering his tone. 'That was a real download. Somebody up there wants to bring you up to speed, really fast, Fiif.' He'd almost finished the sandwich, with just a corner remaining. 'I mean; you're involved in this now, it's found you out. Nobody needs to know that much in one hit unless…'

'Unless it's touched your life, right?'

'Or, someone you care about in some way. And then, you have to find out…'

She looked back at him, her beautiful gaze shockingly piercing.

'I have to tell you something…'

Carlton could see it coming, but he blocked it.

He didn't know why.

'Look, Fiif, there are good guys as well, okay? Me, for example, and… and Barker, and Cheryl. Remember Cheryl?'

'No…' Fiif scowled. 'You keep mentioning her like she's some sort of…'

'But it's hard, Fiif. It's not easy to get the traction. To make progress. Higher forces try and help us, but it's difficult. Messages don't get through; power dissipates; the wrong person gets the right information and keeps it for himself, uses it to his own advantage when it should be for a group. But things are changing; we're moving into a whole new age, a whole new thing, but it's slow, here in this time.'

Fiif was staring at him again, incredibly intense. Then her eyes narrowed.

'This is real, isn't it?'

Carlton shrugged. 'Umm, yair.'

'No, I mean; Zinco, he drugged me. Basically. Our whole marriage.' It was her turn to gaze off into the darkness. 'How do I know you're not…magically drugging me too?'

Carlton stared at her. 'Seriously sweetheart? You wanna throw a rock at me, see if I bleed?'

She took a deep breath and released it. Vapour flowed out, around the sides of her face as she stared back down the forked road again.

'These entities, these demons and dark gods, or whatever…'

'Yeah?'

'They don't just order people's actions, do they Carlton? If they get into society, manipulate our minds, our behaviour… our thoughts and motivations as well…?'

Carlton nodded. 'There are Demons now who use sorcery, dark sorcery, through marketing and mass media and by creating cultural memes. You must have seen some stuff, in your line of work…?'

'No, Carlton. That's what makes me think. I didn't see anything. At least, I didn't… react to what I saw. I'm going to remember a lot of what I saw, aren't I?'

'Maybe. But; look…'

He staggered a bit.

'Are you okay?'

'I don't know… what I said before; about you… did you…?'

She had him by the elbow, a hand on his back, but he slipped somehow and nearly fell.

'Jesus, Carlton…! If you have a freaking epileptic fit on me now, I have no idea what to –'

He started talking again as though she needed to hear it, quickly, before something bad happened.

'I heard what you said, Fiif. Of course…' He winced. '…but we can't know that. They see potentials; the greatest, maybe. But once the river is diverted, it's flowing in that direction and you'd have to literally move mountains…' She could feel him becoming weak. '…they want culture as their own, Fiif. But once they start

273

killing; once they know who to kill, and when, and who won't be missed; or when to take out the ones who will be missed, but know how to create a story around it that will make the murders go away, that's when you have something that is beyond dangerous…'

His knees were giving out.

'You need to sit down again!'

She pulled him further back into the bushes this time.

'Something that, if it targets you, can't be switched off with a remote, or a swipe. That something… is not to be fucked with. Because when a demon starts attracting people to feed on, just ordinary people, it means it's getting ready.'

'For what?'

'We never found out.'

'We? What…?'

'Because when it does that, that's a demon that can *see things coming*…'

'…and plan ahead?'

'Yes.'

'…but Gods and Angels do this too, right? You said – '

'They do. But like I said, the planet's moving through a lower vibration, an evil age. Just where we are, as the planets go round… it's a dark time. The end of dark time, but still a dark time. So, sometimes it can be hard to tell the difference between the Angels and Demons. It's like anything, like people, there's a spectrum; Pure Angels of Light at one end, Rank Demons of Darkness at the other; and all sorts in between. The Demons are going to fight harder than ever to maintain power at the end of this age. And this one might be making his final play to carry over into the next.'

Fiif nodded. 'You're telling me this, because of… what you said. Before. You think there's a Demon down that road, don't you? The road they took?'

Carlton nodded. 'We're not going down that road, Fiif. They were lured, probably killed. By something that knew it could get away with it. Something that will see us coming, too. Will have seen us coming from miles away, days away...'

'You talk like you know this one; like... Carlton?'

'I saw it.'

'Saw it?'

'But we all knew; when this town vanished. This was where it started. We just... had no idea...'

'This town?'

'...it doesn't appear on any maps. People forgot its name. I don't even remember its name. But the Demon took hold here first.'

'The Demon? Here? Carlton! Is this something to do with the children?'

'The children... aren't... children... any... more...'

'But there aren't any, Carlton!' Fiif hissed, louder yet trying harder not to be heard.

'They made it...'

'Made it? The children made the town?'

'Made it... so, when you pass through here...'

'What Carlton?' Fiif was exasperated now. 'What?'

'...you're...'

'You're what, Carlton?? We're – what? Where are we Carlton?!'

'Your Hell Cab is never coming...' Carlton scoffed. His eyes were distant, as though he'd suddenly contracted hysterical blindness. '...you're *already there...*'

'Carlton? Oh my God!'

She was sure that he heard her voice.

Heard her deep concern.

But this time he was totally gone.

And then she heard the children.

275

EIGHTEEN:
WHITE VAN WITCH

I

Nobody of course suspected that she was naked under the navy coat. The boots were high and the scarf suggested other clothes that went with it. They moved quickly; and at first, she had to admit, she felt a little thrill as she passed through the insane, infinite jingle-jangle of the poker machines, almost naked, nobody knowing. But then as they reached the escalators down to the first floor, she started to feel an unnatural chill. Right up her coat, down her collar, up her cuffs and into her bones as she pulled the belt and the scarf tighter.

'Hold on,' Shirley uttered in her ear. 'I know.'

She started to feel ill, distracted by what had happened and what was happening now; fleeing somehow, and without her usual rituals to protect her. Without the psychological and spiritual armour of her outfit, her full costume, to create a barrier against the appalling vibes of a city casino, late on a weeknight. She tried to ignore it completely, but the richness of the milks in all the lattes were churning in her stomach. Shirley had taken her, one arm around her, her palm flat on her back, the other in front, under her elbow, like a rudder and tiller, and was guiding her most of the way. She had a flash from someone else's random perspective that Shirley resembled a fast-acting madam who was whisking her prize escort away from some kind of messy scene upstairs, where the rich people played; then they were outside, on North Terrace.

'This way…'

Shirley's van was parked at the top of a bus stop, on the short decline from the casino at the main entrance to the Adelaide

Railway Station, a gap that led via footpath to the front of the World Conference Centre. A bus that would usually beep and take the van's number for parking illegally had just pulled up behind the van, just as they'd arrived. Cheryl was breathing easier now; she had held her breath for a lot of the walk through, down and out.

'Quick, in!'

As she opened the back of the van, she turned and waved at the bus driver, who was staring down at them as his passengers embarked.

'How...?'

'Get in!'

Cheryl stepped up, Shirley followed, and the doors were slammed behind them.

'It's a powerful glamour, but it doesn't pay to stand around tempting them to peer through.' Shirley handed her an unmarked bottle of water. 'Here. Proper spring water from The Hills.'

'So they just see it, and assume it's supposed to be there?'

'If they think even that. There are powerful forces at work in the human mind that filter out a lot of things. There's a fine reflective surface on this van, although it looks white, that reminds most ordinary people of one of the things that should be filtered out.'

Cheryl looked around. The van was lined down each side with racks of women's clothes. Beneath the garments, right up each side, were two lines of enormous wooden trunks, many with wide drawers, but some with old-fashioned heavy lids.

'Can you sense anything, darling heart?'

Cheryl looked up and down. 'There isn't anything here that's remotely the same as the thing hanging beside it.'

'Don't worry.' Shirley smirked. 'I know where everything is.'

Cheryl shrugged. 'Then you tell me.' She pulled her purse out of her coat pocket, flipped it open and flicked her card at Shirley. 'Be my guest.'

Shirley took the card and pocketed it as she leaned down

and opened a wide drawer. Inside were neatly stacked, unopened packages of unbranded, high-fashion matching bras and knickers.

'Here you go…' Shirley handed her a white set, in her exact size. 'The underwear is free. I didn't warn you I was going to burn all your clothes, it's only fair.'

'You didn't burn them, you disintegrated them. I can do that; but I was told we never should.'

'You were told a lot of nonsense by people acting out of fear. You never joined a coven did you?'

'I… not really. Before Bridger Mansion, technically I suppose I did. But I never went. They never seemed to care. And after? Well, nobody wanted to come near me.'

'Everyone assumed that anyone who walked out of that place seven years ago made a deal with The Devil himself. You didn't do that, did you dear?'

Cheryl stared at her. She wanted to say, no, of course I didn't. But Shirley had brought something home to her tonight. There were gaps. Slabs of extended time, that were probably just seconds, where all that she remembered was fear; acting out of instinct, out of survival, and that was all she remembered.

'That's all right, dear one. You don't need to answer. But did the thing at Bridger Mansion care if you obeyed the divine rules or not? Never destroy? It's all rot designed in Medieval times to protect us from the psychopathic lunatics who had control of political framework of the spiritual oppression network, and exploited it to their own fiendish desires. If they could prove we had destroyed something, then they could prove we had power. And then it was all over. Put your undies on now. It's all right. I'll turn my back, Modest Maureen.'

She moved her shoulder, pathetically, as though to suggest, *are you really such a prude?* Then Cheryl groaned, fed up.

'Okay!'

She removed the coat, then the scarf.

'Here you go!'

She didn't waste time slipping the knickers over the boots, however, nor to clip the bra in place very quickly. But it was enough for Shirley.

'Exactly like your mother. I picked your exact measurements, didn't I? Much better than that other thing you had, and the undies with the holes. We used to swim, your mother and me, in that dam, up in The Hills, near where your friend Carlton drinks. Pull yabbies from the mud and boil them with rice for supper. Yes, you have the body for what's required.'

Cheryl stood up straight, underwear all in place.

'What's required?'

'For what's to come.'

'Look; you obviously didn't do all of this for Barsia, did you? You obviously have a real life, and a genuine consultancy, for which people pay you good money for a, presumably, decent reputation and... satisfied results, but – '

'Overwhelmingly ecstatic results. *Overwhelmingly*.'

'Look, I don't know. Maybe that's true. Maybe you're a fence for illegal knock-off fashion Chinese importers. I don't care. But I know that you are not just... white van... Fashion Fanny!'

'That's for Modest Maureen, isn't it?'

'Who the fuck are you, Shirley Swansong?'

Shirley smirked and for a second Cheryl became a little scared again. She had to remember; she was trapped in the back of a van, and nobody knew; with an angry witch who was by no means as pure as the driven snow.

'I am a channel for the Goddess. The Goddess doesn't care what we think. How we perceive feminism or male patriarchy. She is an energy that is taking back the rightful share of the planet's energy, at the rightful time. But Cheryl, I truly have not come to threaten you. Or just to scare you. I needed to know what you could do. I came in armour. Proper magical armour. To see what you have. *What you can do*. I needed to see the look in your eyes; when you are afraid, when you realize you cannot hide the fear. I saw it. You are strong. I needed to see the look in your eyes when you thought you had minutes to live, and whether or not you would take vengeance. You fought back with lightning. You might have killed me if I had not gone back, before I left my home tonight, and added another layer of magical protection.'

Shirley saw something in her eyes that she did not realize she had conveyed.

'Oh yes. You are powerful, Cheryl. But you are good, and there was nothing wrong, nothing evil in taking down your own murderer. But you must learn not to use the male energies as you have. Your instinct went to zap, to the white storm energy of Zeus, and such. The Goddess will come to your aid if you call her, to use the wind and the water and the wild. Everything in nature can be employed by men and women, sorcerers and sorceresses, witches and magicians; whatever distinctions you desire to put on those titles. Anyone using the greater forces of nature; the supernatural, the majikal. But call on the Goddess, and the rain, the rocks and the soil will work with you, over anything else.'

Cheryl huffed. 'I'm not some kind of neo-hippy nature freak, Shirley.'

Shirley sighed, and for the first time looked truly disappointed.

Then Cheryl shrugged. 'But I get it.'

'You are a fourth generation witch, at the very least.'

Cheryl had no answer to that.

'What about Barker? What about Carlton?'

'Barker cannot be helped by you right now. But you can be helped, Cheryl. You can be helped. Now. By me. And that will help Barker, later. You know that your friend Barker has his staff. And your friend Carlton has his sticks. What protection do you have, darling heart?'

'Barker doesn't have his staff. It was –'

'That is being rectified.'

'What? How? How are you so sure?'

'To be honest, darling heart, I'm not. It's just the kind of thing that happens, when the people who have chosen a certain role walk off stage, only to reappear years later. You need your props, the ones you left behind; you need your potions and your poisons. You need to be told where your places are, ready for performance. If you are not properly prepared, you will be made to be properly prepared. Because the show must go on. Will go on. And you will perform. Because, that is who you are, why you came, and why you had to return.'

Cheryl found herself shaking now.

'I was born here. We all were. Up in those Hills.'

'And you'll die there, soon enough, in the grander scheme. There is a New Age of Spirit coming, and the evils of the former age will make one last grasp at clinging to power as the wheel turns full circle once again. All things are possible; it is possible that they will succeed, and propel themselves unwanted into this New Age. It happened on the last full turn; the interspecies predators, the psychopaths, weeded themselves into this age, riding on the spirit of the prehistoric apex predators, and created havoc. But you are here to make sure that does not happen again.'

Cheryl tried another tactic. 'What entity is speaking through you?'

'Nothing speaks through me anymore. Nothing needs to. But I know that the magic you require is rushing up the ocean road right now; up from the beach, across the plain, towards this north-western corner of the city. It is the great western wind this city has; the city is designed to funnel it, accept it, channel it, exploit it. It will not be stopped; and this time it is coming for you.'

Cheryl stared at her. She didn't know now whether to be scared or proud or... what?

Shirley removed Cheryl's card from her own pocket, and swiped it over her portable machine.

'Seriously? Now?'

'There will be no later.'

'What the fuck does that mean?'

Shirley kept staring at the machine; then it buzzed and

beeped.

'Terrific. We're all set.' Shirley handed the card back. 'Barker has been empowered physically to take the strain of the great spells that are his to command.'

'He didn't want that!'

'He needed it. It was a prize for defeating his first great enemy.'

'No, it…'

'Carlton stays in his warren, with the power of the network that surrounds him, man-made, natural and supernatural, and that makes him strong; as he will soon discover, or die trying. You can strike with white lighting, but that is not for you. Not as you employ it. Are you willing to accept the strength to make you an equal with your partners?'

'Am I… what?'

'You ran from here with Barker; admirable from the perspective of friendship but you should have remained. You should have trained, if not with me then another. Seven years would have seen it done. But now, seven years is coming, Cheryl. Do you accept?'

'What… what will it be?'

Cheryl realized that by answering in such a manner, that she had, if nothing else other than in spirit, just accepted whatever was coming.

'It will be painful, but it will be beautiful.'

Cheryl smiled, and tried to scoff, mockingly. Instead, it came out dead straight.

'What? Again?'

NINETEEN:
777 HALCYON ROAD

Maz and Amanda found themselves following the creek.

They had passed the high school, which was lit up like a mining operation, built upon and dug into the side of the hill, but as soon as they turned the corner and walked on behind some tall bushes, all that light was gone. They followed Halcyon Road as it dipped long and steeply into the valley, past some houses that looked very old, set back behind low stone walls and metal gates, then the road evened out and they started to sense that they were walking along the valley floor as the path closed in around the base of the hillside. The creek kept going alongside them, but the bed was deep and a good away from the road, almost into the hillside. They could still hear it bubbling and rushing, still feel the cold coming from it, but it just looked black and unforgiving behind a high natural hedge, and there was a bank of mist rising from it now, and a fog was descending. Soon the two would join and become indistinguishable, impenetrable.

Carlton was there with them. He could feel the cold, see the beauty of the rising mist and descending fog in the freezing cold suburban Hills valley; but he could also feel the fear that was rising in Amanda. He knew that Maz was oblivious now; hard to read now with half a bottle of straight Jacks in him. He was being carried along with them, but he did not want to go. He did not want to feel this, or go down this road. He did not want to know what happened next, even though he already did know, had already sensed it, streets back. He knew that his body was actually three days into the future from here, three fatal intersections back down the road, and that Fiif was either trying to keep his body upright as he staggered around, as though he were drunk, or had dragged his unconscious body to the side of the road and run for help. Or, if she was smart… and she was, he was pretty sure, she would have done that, found somewhere for him to lay down, and she would just sit with him, and wait.

Halcyon Road just kept going along the valley floor. On the other side from the creek, their left, was a long high stone fence, with rusty spikes all along the top. Amanda saw an occasional short-bridged driveway off to the right, through the thick, wild hedge and dormant blackberry bushes. These occasional exits would continue as driveways, up the steep hillside, then to house lights, way up but still uncannily bright, and magnified. Even as Maz pointed them out, Amanda saw as one of them went out, then another, as the presumably older residents of this well-established part of The Hills retired before midnight on a Saturday. Or was it even midnight? Amanda had lost track; she didn't want to know, didn't want to look until she was somewhere safe.

Safe?

Why had she thought that?

Why had she suddenly started to think… to believe, that they were no longer safe?

They kept walking. Maz had his arm around her now, and they were both slowing down. Even though the walk along the valley road was easy enough, with nothing steep and no hairpins, they had been walking for more than two hours. They were becoming more than just tired, and they had been hungry for some time. Only three of the street lights they had encountered so far were working, and even those had been obscured by low hanging willows. These enormous European aliens were fed, Carlton knew, by a lake on the other side of the stone fence. He also knew that the houses up the hill were all old, and all had terrific views of the valley. But they were all run down, owned by people who had lived in them for sixty years or more. Nobody would hear any sort of cry for help from the valley. And besides, people that age were more likely to secure their locks than open them to strangers claiming to be in peril, especially if they heard anything at this time of night. They might call the police, but by that time, even if any of the local police responded, it would be way too late.

Maz and Amanda walked on, now along the lowest point in the valley. There were great oaks and massive gums, with overwhelming willows, everywhere and on both sides, with no houses in sight, just the high stone wall which was virtually hidden by all of the draping branches. Amanda pointed out that it must have been the longest wall she'd even seen, but all Maz could talk about was what kind of pizza he was going to order, that they would eat in bed when they got back to his place. But it was empty now; Amanda knew that he would fall asleep in the back of the cab, the second he got in.

She stopped for a second as the road became an old stone bridge, just a short one, and took a few swigs of Jack Daniels to warm herself up. The bottle was well under half full now. She didn't care; she knew Maz could handle it enough to keep walking. It just meant that she would be eating by herself. That she could gorge on the leftover pizza without him seeing, and maybe just a little, secretly, check out where he lived. She looked back and forth up the road. It looked like an endless foggy tunnel, either end.

'I'm sure Stringybark Road's down there. Then up to Stirling.'

'It is. I used to ride my bike down this street when I was a kid. Like a long speed ramp. You shoot straight up the top of that steep hill we walked down, right back up to the school.'

Maz sighed after that. She could tell; it made him feel a little sad. In that way that happens when you realize childhood is gone, finally, never to return. She found herself sighing; it was a pity they would not have children. That they would never...

'But it's still a long way still,' Maz finished, startling her. 'Up a long, low gradient, then up Stringybark.'

'Sorry. We should have gone...'

'Nah, nah, you were right, the other way, over the ridge, it's like half as long again. We're okay. We're good.'

He pecked her on the lips then looked back and forth over the edge of the bridge.

'That's some cold water...' Maz uttered. 'Feel that cold!'

'I can!'

'Wouldn't want to fall into that!'

Rain drops started, only a few, but they were big.

Instantly, they both had their phones out.

'You got anything? I got nothing...'

'Yeah...' Amanda gasped.

'Really?'

'Yeah!'

She was already calling, already had it on speaker.

'Hills Cabs, hello?'

'Thank God!' Amanda couldn't believe it. 'We couldn't get reception all the way down Ghost Gum Road!'

'Talk to your provider sweetie, they all need more towers up here. It's all ancient rock under those hilltops. Granite and quartz. You sound cold and wet, my girl! Where are you? I'm going to need a street address so we can come get you!'

'Umm, we're walking... I'm not sure *exactly* where...'

Maz gave her a big smile. He followed the road over the bridge a little way, observing the rushing creek as it ran under the stone wall and into the property beyond. There was a brick arch built into the base of the fence, and spikes there too, pointing downward into the rushing water. These people really didn't want anyone getting in.

'I can't send a cab without a street address. Can you stand in front of a house?'

The rain was falling harder now. She hadn't seen any bridge driveways along the creek side for a while. They'd just have to keep going.

'Maz! Is there anything up there; any street numbers?!'

She couldn't tell if the person on the phone was an older woman or campish bloke, but whoever they were, they were reassuring. 'It's okay darling, no need to panic. You've got reception. Keep calm. We'll come for you.'

Amanda didn't believe it. In her mind, she just didn't believe it.

She had instincts, premonitions or something. Carlton couldn't sense her mind properly through the last two slugs of alcohol. But that was why it wanted her. That was why she was being led to her death.

Thunder cracked now, acute like an explosion.

The voice on the phone spoke again. 'Better hurry darling heart...'

'Seven, seven, seven!' Maz shouted.

Maz was standing only a few meters away. Amanda rushed down the bridge and across the street to him and saw that he was standing near a large wrought iron gate, set back from the street, inside the fence. It was huge and wide, each of the centrally parting gates at least five meters across, each was topped with spikes taller than he was.

But it was open.

It looked as though it had been open for decades; there was a gap, large enough for a car to fit through, maybe forty-five degrees. The gate had been that way for so long that the tyre grooves in the dirt of the driveway had actually curved to accommodate it, as though the owner had been old, and too frail to keep opening and closing it.

'Where's the number?'

'Here...' Maz pointed.

There was an old FOR SALE sign that obscured the street number, but Maz's eagle eye had spotted it, even though the three bronze numbers, screwed into the edge of the high stone fence, were obscured not only by hanging willow branches, but also by a huge, thick spread of ivy that almost blocked the pale grey stone of the fence entirely. Someone had clearly, quite recently, looked for the number as well, or Maz would never have seen it.

'Can we just stay out here?'

'The trees are dropping more water than the sky is!'

Maz tried to see beyond the gate as Amanda looked up. There was a canopy of oak and gum and willow and classic ivy and Salvation Jane and Jasmine and Wandering Jew, that started behind the gate and seemed to extend back, all the way along the drive, to where it curved, and all the way past that, into the whole property. But the thick canopy also extended out, over them and way past the gate, into and over the street. It was starting to pour water down onto them as efficiently as the now heavy rainfall would if they had simply stood out in the middle of the road.

Maz moved closer to the gap, using his phone as a torch. 'I can't see anything in there; it's pitch!'

Amanda peered past him, past the crooked gate. She tried to focus her vision with the torchlight, but was only moderately successful.

'It looks like a garden; it looks like it's been unattended for decades!'

'Emm, I think there's a house in there, see?'

The voice on the speaker phone startled them. It was breaking up, but still decipherable.

'Pam won't like it – you're too wet; she'll want to charge you doub – – on her way but she's coming in from Gully – good fifteen to twenty minutes away. Right up – other end of Ghost Gum. Can you find shelter? – get her to beep her horn and wait…'

'Okay!' Amanda shouted. 'Send Pam! Seven, seven, seven! Triple seven! Halcyon Road! Tell her if we're wet we'll pay double! We just want to go home!'

' – ssage understood, darling. Loud and clear! She'll be there in twenty! Stay dry darl'!'

'Are you sure!? Are you sure she's coming!?'

'Yes darl, I'm sure, you just…'

'Tell her we'll wait under shelter but run when we hear –'

'Hang on darli – you sure about tha – ? – – sure? Do you kno – – ere you are?'

'Sorry?'

'Sev – Sev – – ven… Halcy – Roa – ?'

'Yes! Yes, that's the address…'

'No, darling, I mean, are you sure you want to wait *there*? Do you know wh – eh –remeb – happ – at – Man – ? … der! – Sweetie? – there? – llo? – are – sup …'

Reception was lost. The phone beeped sadly as the call ended prematurely.

'What was all that about?' Maz frowned.

'Do you suppose the cab's still coming?' Amanda asked, redialling.

'Of course it is, you heard her; you offered to pay double!'

'Her? I thought it was… but she said…'

'They always say that! Come on; we might get out of the extra fare if we can find shelter and keep dry!'

'I got reception on that bridge, if I go back –'

'You'll get soaked! There's definitely an old house in there at the end of the drive, I can see it…'

'But what if…'

'It'll be some old widow, we can stand under the veranda and she'll never know…'

'I don't like it! I don't like this whole thing!'

'Me neither babe but we have to stay dry! If we get drenched and the cab doesn't come, we'll both get pneumonia!'

'But, Maz… look at this place!'

'I can't, there's a bloody great stone wall, all the way down the street! Maybe that's what's blocking reception? Look, I'll go in a bit; I'll look. Okay? You turn your phone off, we'll use my torch on the way up, yours on the way back…'

'But…'

'I'll be back in a second…' He kissed her. 'I'll look after you!'

Then he turned and went into the property.

'I'll just be a second!'

Carlton's heart stung at that point. Under these circumstances, that was so idiotic. There was nothing Maz could do to protect her once they stepped past the wall, through the gate, and onto those grounds. But it was just what Amanda, who was now fully frightened, needed to hear. She loved him, and it short-circuited not only her common sense, but her just-emerging psychic instincts as well. He knew that he could do nothing, absolutely nothing to help them at this point, but he wished more than anything at that moment that Amanda would, *would have*, just come to her senses, her sixth sense at least, and persuaded Maz to keep going, past the gates, along the horrible spiked fence, all the way down Halcyon. It was still another twenty minutes' walk to the end, then another twenty up Stringybark to Stirling. But it was better than staying here. Get wet and walk home, have sex with your boyfriend on the rug while your clothes dry on the heater... anything but...

Wait.

The epicentre of this was getting closer; Carlton was sure. They were dead. He could feel it. But, was there something else? Something... worse?

Amanda turned and looked at him.

He hadn't realized. He wasn't just seeing this on some recreated dream plane. He was there, actually there, last Saturday night, in spirit form. Disembodied and temporally dislocated, but actually there.

She looked right at him.

Don't – he mouthed the word. But it was as though his mind froze. Like he was trying to push his voice face-down through a pillow; a little give, then nothing. There was no way he could communicate, nor alter anything.

She kept staring.

'I see you, I think. Grampa? I see you, sometimes...'

Dohnnn...

'I feel like I'm safe when I'm with him. I feel like…' She winced. Carlton was perplexed. Then he realized; she was blinking away tears. 'Why do I feel like I have to go in there?'

The rain started coming down harder.

'Grampa?'

She stepped closer.

'Why do I feel like, no matter what I do…' Amanda gulped. '…the bad thing's already happened?'

'Amanda!'

She tuned to Maz's voice, inside the wall. Then she turned back to Carlton.

'Grampa?'

Carlton was frozen solid now.

'Grandpa, I have to go, I'm sorry…'

She turned and ran through the gates, into the grounds of Bridger Mansion.

TWENTY:
BOTANY GATE JUNCTION

I

As Bach entered the Adelaide suburban grid from the eastern foothills via the Nightmare Road for the second time that evening, Barker checked that the thousand bucks Clem had paid him was still in his coat pocket. He hadn't even thought about it during his encounter with the woodwarp. It was, held deep in an inside breast pocket, and that gave him a perverse satisfaction.

He had always intended to give it to Quaker.

But; were things lining up now, so that it seemed like he was being directed to go and see Quaker somehow? Which could possibly mean… that he had some room to manoeuvre, when it came to facing him?

After fighting the thing, Barker knew more than ever that he possessed no real command of his own powers any more. His faded memory meant he had to rely on instinct and sensations, inner guidance – and apparently, hopefully, some external, some might say supernatural direction – to light his way. But Barker of course was one of those people; one of those for whom there was nothing 'super' about it.

On the flipside, he'd been heading to the casino anyway. All night, it seemed, it had been his final destination; the money from the Lion had always been destined for Quaker, and it seemed that Cheryl was already there, still waiting with any luck. The last of her increasingly anxious messages had come through just an hour ago, but she wasn't answering now.

She'd be alright. The World Casino was one of the darkest places in the city, but she could handle herself. He'd just slip in there, to see and perhaps confront Quaker, collect Cheryl in the process of being chucked out, and possibly also see…

Her.

Emerald.

That all seemed… almost essential now. It just remained to be seen; had he been nudged there? Or lured there? And he could only tell by going.

It had even turned out that the road he was currently on, the road he had been on all night, really; Nightmare Road, and then its city-bound extension, down the long, straight stretch of Magpie Road, provided he kept to it, would take him directly there; directly through the inner suburbs, across the parklands to the city, and down the gaping yaw of North Terrace to the World Casino.

Bach kept going.

Magpie Road squarely crossed several other main thoroughfares on the Adelaide grid; he passed the first easily on a green light and by the time he came to the second, the suburban gums had already started giving way to more classically near-featureless urban spread of warehouses and factories, then flats and houses.

It must have been eleven thirty and there were very few other cars on the road. As usual, the majority of the traffic at this time of night were the roaring parade of interstate semi-trailers and road trains, tearing across the main thoroughfares at sometimes head-spinning speeds. A cop car passed on the green in front of him, then was gone. He looked back at Captain Mainwaring and flicked up the helmet visor. It was a bit hard, because he had the branch – the new, not-quite-yet-staff – shoved diagonally across his back, held in place by his tightly buttoned coat. He yelled over the engine.

'All good back there, Captain Mainwaring sir?!'

The Captain had remained with his back to Barker, hugging the top box, but didn't seem at all fussed by anything; not the woodwarp, the city, or the speed. Barker huffed. Another thing named that he probably shouldn't have named; but he really did look like Arthur Lowe, right down to the auburn fur.

The lights changed. Almost at the city now. Driving five, ten minutes, with the Ox making him feel horny on the bike, of course, but well within his limits of control. Both Kerry and Essa had been massive exertions of will, but not so much for abstinence of sex, or rather, the resistance of seduction, but for the syphoning off of the magical energy that a tryst with either would have afforded.

He folded his arms, flipped the visor up again and shouted back at Mainwaring.

'Okay. Okay; that red dress on Mrs Steward… I mean… wow. And the boobs on the nice vet lady, Captain! Did you see them? I mean; I think I did – extremely well!' He turned back to the road, but then back to Mainwaring again. 'And both of them; such lovely smiles!'

Some cars were approaching, out of the city, so he flipped the helmet down and put his hands back on the bars. Green again. Almost there. There was a hotel on virtually every major intersection in Adelaide. Most of them were two or three floors. He idled at the lights on the last one, The Maiden Magpie, noticing that the traffic was lightly increasing again; a few more cabs and ordinary cars, and more semis.

Nothing much was supposed to happen in any suburb on a Tuesday night, but Tuesday nights in Adelaide were known, in that regard, to be special in their own way. There was a particular kind of quiet, hours after everyone had already been indoors after nine o'clock, with half of them asleep, the other half mentally checked out before ten… that was almost completely Zen. Where, if you were still lucid, you were almost free to relax, and expand your consciousness unrestricted. That was, Barker knew, provided you didn't mind occasionally bumping consciousnesses with like-minded night owls.

Tonight though, things were stirring for that very reason; that they were not supposed to; because it was most perverse to simply start something hugely magically-toxic on the most innocent and therefore most corruptible night of all.

The Silent Winter Tuesday Night In Adelaide.

He was feeling it; he knew.

Suddenly he knew absolutely that he had been lured to the Lion, through Cheryl by another witch called Angela Lorre. To see whether he was ready or not. To face something unexpectedly powerful. Kerry Steward had been sent to track his progress, and watch that he was taken care of by the woodwarps; her suspicions as to her own intended demise notwithstanding. He was being tested and pushed, forced to remember and… reignite? Re-emerge?

He would have to do something.

Something he hated, and feared, and would rather swan-dive off a bridge before contemplating. On any other night, in any other city.

He would have to.

But not here, not tonight.

Tonight the forces were being summoned and the battle-lines drawn.

He smelled ozone and again thought, the classic: a storm's coming. He looked behind him. Facing away from the city, you could always see The Hills, looking up any of the main thoroughfares. Sure enough, it really was; physically and figuratively, a massive storm bank, like snow over the mountains, glowing and ominous white-grey in the moonlight.

The storm was coming, and he would be in its eye.

He had to watch now, as he approached one of its dark heart's bleakest corners, for anything. Third time's a charm; maybe the third time they would get him, finally take him out? Was that the plan? To test him, incrementally? Or send bigger and badder forces to try and take him out? One, then the other? Make him believe one, or the other? Try him, and turn him mad?

But something deep down warned him; no.

They are trying to force your hand.

And you must be ready.

So, once more, he tried to assess.

In his mind's eye, the city, the city that was the battleground, hadn't changed much since he'd been a kid. Sure, like many things, the veneer had slowly morphed over the decades, several times over by now and at least once since he'd been born. But the heart of his city, the city that had first existed in his mind, had not altered and did not change.

Could he use that somehow?

Could he use a ghost bike and a sentient koala?

How had he become this?

Did it matter?

Did he like it?

Did he like the thing that Barker Moon had become?

Bach took the green without Barker knowing now, and he sensed that she was fed up with the boring, straight suburban line of Magpie Road, after the insane fun of the corkscrew. She sped the last stretch before the parklands, responding to his mood, the simmering power of his Ox, his body overloaded with mystical power, over-thinking and getting angrier, burning faster. Finally, the end of Magpie connected neatly with the north-east corner of the Adelaide Parklands, as though it were a cord running down from The Hills and plugging in here, into the central grid, right at the north-eastern corner of the CBD. Maybe that was real? Mystically? After all, Barker had toured Europe in his twenties; he'd had stranger things explained to him, about how the mystical, occult energy of a city worked.

Maybe that was how it worked here?

He couldn't remember.

Or; could he? Was he remembering now, that that was true?

One thing he did remember though, just as a piece of history, was that the precise central checkerboard was one of the main reasons why Adelaide rated very highly on the worldwide matrix of occultism. The city had been blatantly designed and built in the 1830's upon a square mile Freemasonic grid pattern by the firm of a man named Colonel William Light, a name which also suggested that the city's pioneers had, for better or worse, Illuminati or even Luciferian connections. Therefore, regardless of whether or not the planners had intended it, weird things were bound to happen in Adelaide, anyway. A lot.

Barker was sure that before his amnesia, he had known all these things, all this occult knowledge, for a specific reason. But like all the other occult information of that kind he'd once stored, and exploited, it was now lost to him, and had been for seven full years. All Colonel Light's design really meant to him now, in any practical sense, was that the city of his birth was beautiful; surrounded for whatever reason on all sides by massive belt of lush green parklands, with a central square-pattern that was as easy to navigate as a chessboard.

Bach roared off again and soared through the north-eastern belt of the parklands. Barker gazed in and noted a sleeping bagman as the grassy expanse's sole occupant, huddled in a fortress of garbage-filled sacks beneath an ancient stringy gum, spaced in the darkness between two of the bright-white streaks of halogen-illuminated public paths.

It was somewhat ironic that during the flipside of Adelaide's annual calendar, within the high-summer months of January and February, this spread of parklands, and several extra acres south from here, across three massive parkland blocks, played home to more major events that many believed the city could comfortably accommodate; competitive horse trials; the infamous Adelaide Festival and its notorious Fringe; an international V-8 car race; and the world music festival, WOMADelaide. The city was insane during this time, and in recent years there had also been the inevitable, now-annual climate-change heatwaves, sometimes a full month-long, just to make sure everyone felt the condensed nature of the endless-carnival city with full, dripping, sweltering, war-of-attrition effect; two months with noise and tourists and drunks; colour and movement and traffic congestion and money, money rolling through like gangbusters. But by the end of March, the cold chill of the plains would settle back in. Adelaide's autumns and springs were getting short, and by the end of April... the old pauper was burrowed deeply, undisturbed and out for the count; dormant and oblivious.

The bagman's nest sat directly opposite one of Adelaide's most magnificent old hotels; a four-floored, multi-balconied colonial pub called the Botany Gate that faced the north-east edge of the city. Some of these old pubs on the central grid-rim were high enough to look over the gums and pines of the parklands and beyond. This one, on the very north-eastern tip; the T-junction corner intersection of East and North Terrace, was one of the oldest and tallest of all the South Australian pubs, and the views from the highest of the northern-facing, white-painted balconies well-alighted the stunning Adelaide Botanic Gardens.

As Bach stopped at the T-Junction lights there, Barker glanced at the huge iron gates to the garden on his right, then the pub diagonally to his left. Then, directly to his left, the old war memorial, for the Light Horsemen of World War One. The Great War, they had called it, The War to End All Wars. But then there had been another. Worse, some said. But in the first one, unarmoured men on horseback had faced machine guns, then tanks. They had been skilled and fearless, it was told.

There were a few people about here at the Botany Gate, with a respectable line of the city's distinctive fleet of white cabs lined up outside. Barker had stopped at the Botany once or twice, but he'd never lingered there much. He preferred the smaller suburban pubs, deeper into the city, or the crumbling old haunted things up in The Hills, like the Lion, or the Crow, even the Pound on occasion. He'd never been one for nightlife much, though. For a sorcerer, there was too much else to do. But he did like to know that 'the nightlife' was there, that the city's passion still burned, and that here, at the core of sleepy suburbia, amongst the people who constituted Adelaide's Tuesday night-life, the embers at least remained smouldering, albeit, most likely all within either this, or one or two other similar such buildings, pocketed about underground. Or, maybe this really was *every single person* in the general inner city who had wanted to drink tonight, or be around drunk people, or even party on this, the quietest of week nights... the hotel did look a bit to Barker as though a spaceship had landed. As though, for the spaceship's inhabitants, stepping outside of some kind of force field boundary of artificial atmosphere; maybe the vibrational limit of the beats from within, would mean a quick death.

...but probably most of them were just there to get laid.

Don't think about the Ox.

He frowned at himself. Get laid. Well... maybe, *there for the physical contact*, was a better way to express that thought.

And thoughts counted, Barker knew.

They mattered.

Don't – think – about – the Ox.

Especially if maybe some of the things that some of the people he knew said about him... were true? That, although he didn't clearly remember it, he was not just some kind of psychic, but some kind of...

...sorcerer?

But you were just thinking that – too much else to do!

That once, until one night, seven years ago, he had been a great one?

You almost remembered that at the Lion.

You almost remembered it completely... you think... up on the ravine at Nightmare.

He'd never quite faced the notion that he'd clung to; unconsciously, ignorantly, that he was afraid of. Afraid of 'Barker The Sorcerer' returning, and 'Barker Now' being... lost? Overwritten? Overcome?

Could they really be one and the same?

Carlton and Cheryl had been there, when the bad thing had happened. Carlton had tried to tell him some of it. But he hadn't been clear, and Barker had not been able to understand it. It had brought them closer together as mates, and yet, pushed them further apart. Cheryl had been there too, but she had not wanted to talk about it. She had thought that, for a time, she had lost consciousness there maybe, during whatever forgotten horror had gone down. But what she had retained; well, what was the point? Barker didn't remember, and it seemed actually couldn't remember. Even when he had been told things, and latched on to something, he had been told that minutes later he would not remember it again. As though what had happened there, at Bridger Mansion, had created some kind of incident-specific dementia. That everything to do with it – and he had no doubt – *bad things had happened*; he remembered not *what* exactly, but he did remember; *bad* – had been erased. Erased, along with all the magic he had ever used; all the big magic, the powerful sorcery that, again, he had been told, he had spent the best part of two decades accumulating and learning, practising and perfecting, and everything in his life, every event, person, notion and idea, that had anything to do with the big magic, had been made simply and completely inaccessible.

And then a trial.

A blur.

Occasionally someone would remember him from that.

The killer who'd gotten off.

But he didn't remember it at all, not at all.

Some random names, some blurred faces from the time, maybe… but; not linking up.

And then there was Heather.

Heather Holden.

Jesus.

Heather was still locked away at the –

He snapped out of it.

He wasn't ready to think about Heather again.

He was still at the lights.

Red.

There was no traffic.

He could see down North Terrace to the slight rise, where the university was.

Where his mother had made her name.

God, how his mother had hated Heather.

There was nothing coming toward him from the city; nothing coming along the T-Junction from East Terrace either. And the lights seemed to be taking forever to change.

As though on cue, a cop car pulled up next to him.

It was an unmarked cop car, but Barker knew.

'…okay…'

The passenger window slid down.

The cop turned and leaned from the wheel, across the passenger seat, to look up at Barker. He was a middle-aged man with a long face, accordingly centred by a long nose at the base of which was a thick and bristling black moustache. As with his short but slightly messy black hair, it was streaked with white here and there, giving him the look of a distinguished rogue. There was a twinkle in his grey eyes, and a mass of streaks; smile or stress lines, spreading out from the corner of each eye, along with a very long, square jaw, and a hard, almost lipless mouth from which he addressed Barker mostly through his lower row of long, unpolished teeth.

'G'day…'

Barker could barely hear, but read the greeting very clearly.

Barker nodded, without flipping the visor up. Then he tried something.

Bach; idle. Quiet.

Bach responded, down to a low purr.

The cop smiled, appreciative. His own car seemed new, and hummed very low. New, Barker observed, but for a shatter in the windscreen that covered most of the passenger's side, where it looked as though someone had lobbed a rock at it.

'Nice night.'

Barker nodded again.

'Bit chilly. But you get that this time of year.'

Barker remained still.

Then the cop smiled, a tight, knowing smile.

'You know you've got a koala on the back of your bike?'

Barker turned slowly, then feigned a not-quite theatrical recoil. Then he slowly turned back to the cop, and gave a really-quite theatrical, spread-armed shrug.

'And…a tree branch down the back of your coat?'

Barker reached back and felt it, again over-reacting, as though; *what's that doing there!?*

'Okay.' The cop flicked his hand. 'Visor up, thanks.'

Barker obeyed. He shrugged again, this time a little more apologetic, and tried to project his best charming smile while his face was all squashed in by the helmet.

'Ah,' said the cop.

Barker tried another angle. He gently fanned his hand, once across in the direction of the passenger window.

'This is not the biker koala you are looking for!'

The cop smiled again, and nodded.

'There's nothing for me here, I can be on my way?'

'Ah,' said Barker, loudly. 'So we're both adept at Jedi mind tricks?'

'Well; what kind of detective would I be?'

Both their engines idled.

Suddenly Mainwaring released one of his arms, turned slightly and flipped up the side box with the leaves in it, grasping a pawful and shoving them in his mouth. The box lid fell back of its own accord as the koala turned back to face the rear.

Both Barker and the detective stared at the koala a while after that, as though waiting to see what else it would do. It just chewed, sat and waited.

Barker turned back.

'There's a story.'

'I bet there is.'

'So, what do we – ?'

Mainwaring moved again, this time turning quickly and

facing the hotel, grasping the back of the bike with one hand, pushing both feet in and leaning out, staring like a sailor in a crow's nest, suddenly spotting unexpected land.

Barker and the detective stared along with the koala.

The detective frowned.

'That can't be good.'

A woman came stumbling out of the front door of the Botany, onto the East Terrace footpath. She was drunk and yelling, broadly and aggressively waving away someone behind her. The small crowd of smokers who were huddled outside, and a few people who had come out in a vain effort to hear whoever was on the other end of their phones, parted the way as a man followed, stomp-stumbling after her.

A young couple who'd had too much to drink, fighting over something idiotic.

Barker looked back at the detective.

The detective kept watching the hotel as he remarked openly;

'We've all done it...'

Barker turned back. They looked to be in their early twenties. She had a sleeveless bright-fuscia cocktail dress that was clinging to her, exposing her underwear-lines in the strong, chill breeze for which Adelaide was notorious, that was now picking up. He was wearing a black suit with a white shirt and no tie. This was either an event, or they'd come from one. Everyone inside and outside on the pavement ignored them but for brief glances of annoyance, but as the man followed the fuscia woman a few paces down the concrete footpath, toward the corner and closer to Barker, he reached behind his back and pulled out something from his belt. Something that glistened, shining silver.

A fucking *knife*.

Mainwaring leaped off the bike and ran across the road to the war memorial as Bach responded. She gunned through the red light and across the T-junction. Barker's thought had been to just come up next to the attacker, burn the back tyre around and startle him. He wasn't even sure if he knew how to do that, but he was sure that if he tried, someone would look, and see that there was a maniac with a knife. The woman would turn and see that she was being attacked. The man would back off, probably run. One of the smokers or phoners would call the cops, or the detective would get the gist and follow suit. But it seemed that Bach, who despite being new, who had been delivered or perhaps even bequeathed to him, with her pedigree clear but heritage unknown, just might have been, it turned out at this moment, raised and perhaps even born as, if not possessed by an urge to be, something of a savage attack bike.

The man spun about; not in surprise, at least not initially, but quite deliberately. As he turned to Barker and saw, startled now, that Bach was actually charging him, his dagger hand flicked out and he screamed something guttural and violent.

Bach skidded forward on her back wheel, as Barker had kind-of intended, but far more aggressively and at a much lower angle. Barker ducked instinctively but it didn't matter, the dagger flew past and slashed right over him. Bach kept skidding, screeching out a full one-eighty donut as a black limousine pulled up, completely out of nowhere, braking sharply and screeching to a halt beside the hotel pavement, right between Barker and the maniac as Bach's back tyre completed its tight circle and she came to rest right up against the shining black finish, only a centimetre short of a deep duco scratch.

TWENTY-ONE:
INSIDE, OUTSIDE

'I thought you said you saw the house just inside the gate?'

The gates had led directly to the distinct end of a driveway that had two garden paths leading immediately off to either side, but were so overgrown that they would have been impossible to traverse without garden shears. The rain was still penetrating the treetop canopy but when Amanda heard it crash down on the street behind them, back over the high, spiked stone fence, she realized they were better off on this side. Ahead, they could see in the moonlight, and the pale, willow-obscured glow from the closest street light, that the drive curved off slightly to the right for perhaps twenty meters, then curved back to the left.

'Come on…' Maz offered, somewhat bravely.

Despite the rationality of it being dryer on this side, Amanda was having second thoughts; more than that, she realized suddenly. She was having deep reservations now, right now, almost a real fear, about proceeding any further. But Maz was still holding her hand, and hurrying her along, so she didn't have much choice. As they trudged up the drive, their feet splashing in the puddles and the tyre grooves, Amanda could make out that the huge, wild garden was crazy with both European plants and native bushes. Some of the bushes were freakishly high, but at a minimum they were all monstrously overgrown, although they were still dwarfed amid massive stringybarks, several giant oaks and the willows along the fence.

When they followed the drive around, Amanda had hoped to see a house, or at least something that might provide shelter; a gazebo maybe, or maybe one of those old fashioned swing seats with a roof like a bus shelter, but instead there was only the continuation of the driveway. The whole path seemed more like a private road now, as they advanced through the rain down an even longer curved section, back to the left, that offered nothing but more of the mad forest.

Amanda tried to see past the wild garden, and could to a small extent; the grounds seemed essentially flat, perhaps undulating slightly into the distance, down to their left as the drive curved back around, as though sloping toward something from where the sound of the rushing creek seemed to echo back from the near distance. Unattended as it clearly had been for so long, the property's garden had probably become a kind of shut-away ecosystem all to itself, a mini-forest occupying a long stretch this side of Halcyon Road, that clearly extended several acres deep. But as they pushed ahead, and as more of the rain started to splash through, with her attention jarred every few seconds, and her focus constantly pulled by the sudden movement of nocturnal animals, all through the garden, disturbed, flinching and fleeing at their approach, Amanda continued to feel nervous to the point of near-panic.

Maz didn't let go.

She didn't protest.

They kept their footfalls to the relatively even tyre grooves as the moonlight faded even more beneath the thickening canopy of trees. For a while it seemed as though they were rushing down a tunnel of blackness with no end, a private road to nowhere that they'd had no business accessing, bordered by an impenetrable wall of trees and shrubs, and perhaps even an overgrown hedge on either side. Then even that faint suggestion of order, that remnant of human design and maintenance, simply gave out to some kind of intertwined, overgrown wall of jungle foliage, as the drive kept going, the long curve seeming to have no end. Amanda figured they must have come at least one hundred meters. Then they heard the rain increase again, blasting the canopy above. For a few seconds it didn't get through, then all of a sudden it penetrated and drenched them both in seconds; an instant, freezing cold shower, right through their clothes, to the bone, splashing and drenching and relentless.

The water flowed down Amanda's face and got into her eyes, affecting her balance momentarily as she regained her bearings. The possums, feral cats, rats and foxes they had startled on their way through all suddenly, simultaneously dashed for cover, and Maz swore as he almost tripped in a pothole. He pulled out his phone and activated the torch again. It caught the rain, and the path ahead was momentarily beautiful, icily bright and glistening. They could see that the tyre grooves were relatively even, but filling quickly with rain. Still, there were no more potholes. Maybe someone had taken care of things here after all?

They moved on, exchanging sour expressions that served as confirmation to proceed through what was becoming a high-arched tunnel, like a hallway in a cathedral, still shaking with scampering wildlife. They picked up the pace and when Maz's torch began to fade he turned it off and they quickly realized that the glow from the three streetlights, widely spaced as they were along the edge of the stone fence that was ten minutes behind them now, was now so faint as to be indistinguishable from what remained of the partial moonlight beneath the increasingly oppressive canopy. From there, they walked forward into near-total darkness a few seconds more, until Amanda's readjusted eyesight saw something, through the rain, up ahead.

The cavernous driveway now curved back to the right, completing a long S-shape, but in the distance was a vertical sliver of pale light. Her eyes further readjusted and she saw it was the end of the foliage wall, and of the canopy; the driveway from here was lined with enormous purple-headed agapanthus plants, but ended in what looked, at least from this distance, to be a clearing, down into which the moonlight, reflected off the clouds, was suddenly shining. There was more white gravel there, and a dull, white-painted façade of some kind.

Amanda felt relief; yet, some kind of grim inevitability had taken hold.

They were *almost there.*

They were both drenched again. She tried to smile at Maz but he looked angry now. She knew; Maz hated getting wet. He'd been one of those kids who, when their country-raised father had thrown him into the local dam, to sink or swim, had reacted by almost drowning and then never entering any significant body of water ever again. She had learned this when she had surprised him with their first, and apparently final, romantic bath, last weekend. He'd freaked out, stormed out, come back, calmed down, then cried and told her the whole sorry story. She had been tender with him, and promised to teach him to swim properly; that by summer, they would be able to make love in the ocean. They would even go somewhere special together to achieve this; a beach house or something, maybe even save money and get a beach cabin in Bali. Everyone knew someone who could loan a beach house, or a shack for a weekend, and everyone knew Bali was cheap. He'd responded well, and they'd had gentle sex for the first time; appreciative and nurturing.

'I did see something!' Maz announced, triumphant, confirming her own suspicions.

That would have been impossible, of course. But as they came closer Amanda realized yes, at the end of the driveway she could, maybe, actually see the facing corner and some kind of entrance. It was a huge old house. Maybe even a mansion. From the look of the corner, it seemed like a real Colonial classic, with three or maybe four storeys; certainly two balconies and an extended veranda.

There were pines too, toward the house, and giant elms.

They were there.

They'd made it.

Amanda could see that the drive didn't end, rather it branched off to either side and encompassed the house. The whole place looked ancient and unkempt. The walls were rough stone, but there was hard wood, and wrought iron that had been painted white at some point, but never repainted and now, where the veneer was visible beneath the dark and impenetrable ivy, with the same twisting, dormant vines of Salvation Jane and creeper-like wild Jasmine along with it, the old coating was cracked, like sun-baked mud, and stuck in a permanent pattern of peel that nobody had bothered to snap off. It was all over the wooden stairs and balustrades, the iron balcony rails and the rusting gutters, which were spouting rainwater like waterfalls, almost a complete curtain surrounding the house, running from every rusty corner and several points in between.

'What the…?'

'Under the balcony, Maz!'

They ran across the wide gravel drive, finally diverting from the almost-reassuring tyre grooves, which continued around the back. There was barely a gap between treetops and gutters; just enough for the moonlight to beacon down. They stomped across the gravel and directly up the front corner stairs. The drive was bordered by two more sections of completely untamed garden; barely bordering the jungle, a smaller but just as madly overgrown front garden of more agapanthus plants and a row of concrete troughs, interspersed with giant terracotta pots that might have been home to anything now; and opposite, along the house-front, a strip of roses and camellias in long concrete beds that were so high that from the drive they obscured the view of the windows along the veranda – a good two meters above the ground.

At the top of the veranda stairs stood an elaborate set of hard wood French windows, but the glass was shattered and the doors had long ago been boarded up, as though someone had been throwing rocks at the glass before kicking the doors in. It must once have been a beautiful setting for the owner to greet casual visitors; now it looked derelict and insane. Immediately Amanda turned right, instinctively away, and proceeded along the veranda, averting her gaze from the impossibly black front windows of the mansion as she moved, focussing down and out at the garden, at the driveway, and the forest from where they'd come. From here, the way back looked like the entrance to some kind of dark castle;

the pitch black hole bordered in silhouette by the high, pointed pines that they had not even seen from beneath the mad canopy.

Maz was following her now, hurrying along past the front windows that seemed impossible to gaze upon, as they quickly realized that their apparent shelter had been an illusion, and that the veranda was leaking like as sieve. The sound of the rain bucketing down on the corrugated iron above them made it impossible to speak. Wide ribbons of water splashed down in their path; even if they could avoid them, the puddles they created were spraying up like passing cars through drain water.

Below in the concrete beds, over the warping grey wood of the peeling balustrade, the huge rose bushes burst and twisted through the gaps, with the high but stringy camellias rampant behind them. The wide wooden stairway that led up to the porch was almost completely obscured; only the idea in her mind from movies and TV that *this was how these places were laid out* made her sure that there were stairs there, and they would lead up to a big front door.

Sure enough, the front door was set back about a meter. To either side there were angled windows that looked into two sitting rooms, and had once featured stained glass. They had long ago been smashed, but the elaborate wrought iron frames and lattice work had held, although someone had hopelessly installed cheap security bars over them at some stage. Their remains were on the ground before them, on the floor of the front door alcove.

Immediately Amanda could see; nobody came in through the front door anymore.

But the alcove was dry, a rectangular respite of about four square meters.

'We'll be okay here…' Maz grunted. He grasped and held Amanda, hugging her tightly from behind. 'Maybe someone lives here, but if they do, they live round the back.'

'You think someone's living in there?'

'Tyre tracks go out the back but don't come back round the house. It doesn't matter. I had a mate in Robe whose aunt had a big old limestone place like this, but in the end she couldn't afford to heat it, so she just used the kitchen out the back and slept in the next room. Had one of those big Aga ovens… fed it Mallee roots. Probably still there.'

'But…'

'Drifters and hitchers and off-the-grid oddballs used to take shelter in the front; sleep on the porch…' Maz shrugged. 'That's who's tried to break in. It's fifty square meters and six walls through there, to the other side, so we'll just stay here… wait for the cab to beep.'

'Maz, it probably took us ten minutes to get up this driveway…'

'She'll be five minutes more then. We hear it, we run. Run like fuck. Okay?'

'But…'

'We're wet babe. Soaked through. Once you're soaked through, it can't get any worse…'

They were dripping even as they stood there. She could feel her skin was cold. She was shivering for all number of reasons. Maz was as well.

'Maz I can't feel my feet…'

'What do you mean?'

'My feet are so cold… I can't feel them anymore. And my hands…'

Maz's hands came around and touched the back of Amanda's hands.

'Holy fuck, Amanda… you're like ice!'

Maz let go and turned around. He placed his hand on the front door of Bridger Mansion, and he pushed. The door swung open. It didn't creak so much as make a trio of sharp cracks. It was black inside.

'Fuck…'

Amanda turned. The doorway looked like that black monolith from that endless movie with the violent monkeys and the boring space station that everybody thought was so important. But it did… it looked so black in there, if it hadn't been for the door itself, angled in and catching the moonlight, you would have thought it was a solid black block. She couldn't cope any more. She was still shivering, she knew that. Uncontrollably. What had happened in that movie? Everyone had died, hadn't they? The space station had killed them all. But she had to get somewhere, get warm. The fear, the instinct to flee, was just background now, blended into grey against the rising panic of the far more physically specific fear that she was going to freeze to death. She felt like she was going to die. And now there were multiple ways...

How had this happened?

They had just been walking to a party, and... now she was borderline hypothermic.

Maz draped his arm around her. One hand was tight on her shoulder, the other gripped his phone as he lit it up. It came on bright, then instantly dropped to half power. They wouldn't have long. There was still hers, but she didn't even know what pocket it was in, and they still had to save it for the...

'Maz. We'll never hear the cab in here...'

'I don't give a shit, I've got a lighter, we can start a fire in the fire place and sleep here.'

'Fire...?'

'All these places have them. In every room, some of them. If we set the place on fire at least someone will come and find us.'

'I'm so cold, so hungry...'

'We need to warm up. Just a while. Then the rain will stop and we can go back out and call again...'

Maz sounded so confident. He was faking it; she knew that of course.

But one of them had to.

The phone torch illuminated a set of internal French doors with most of the glass intact. They opened into a short parlour, then a long, high and wide central corridor. To either side of the parlour were indeed the sitting rooms that Amanda had identified from outside.

'It feels warmer in here...' Amanda uttered.

It was all quite dreamlike now.

Everything was dark wood, with a deep red tint. Surrounding them was vertical, ceiling-height panelling, crossed high with row upon row of empty bookshelves in the sitting rooms, and elaborate nooks or feature-shelves around the parlour, then more into the hallway beyond. There was a tall, built-in cabinet to their left and a wide hall stand to their right, both built into the wall; empty-shelved, dark and sterile, yet somehow catching the glint of the torchlight and reflecting the edge of red in the deeply stained wood, as though there remained some rich sap beneath the treated timber. In the back of her slowing mind, Amanda knew what this suggested. There was no dust. Yet clearly, nobody ever came here…

'Jarrah…' Maz uttered as he looked around. 'Treated…'

Amanda looked at the beautiful warp of a knot, the classic twisted face. The panels were wide enough for the knots to start low and twist high, like stretched out mushroom clouds, or stare back from long horizontal triangles, right across a panel, like a blood-black version of one of those little grey, almond-eyed alien heads.

They moved on. The parlour was big and their footfalls creaked against the floor boards, yet Amanda would have expected them to crack and resound right across the room. There was no dust… on the floor… either…

The knots were everywhere in the dark wood.

Maz ushered her past the sitting room doors, through the parlour, and into a massive entrance hall, with a curved staircase up each side, and a deep landing that loomed above them so imposingly that they simply scampered though, as though they did not belong there, as though the master of the house was watching from above in dark disapproval. Beneath the landing, a square wooden arch sharply defined yet neatly decorated the beginning of a long corridor beyond, looming like the opening to a wooden mausoleum.

Maz stared again briefly at the wood, this time in the thick frame.

'…treated with what?'

He asked himself in a low tone, almost unconsciously perplexed.

Beyond, they slowed again as they stepped within the hallway now. Amanda saw a wide set of steps leading up to her right, then three doors to either side of the corridor. It looked stark, dark, and foreboding, like every big old house she had ever set foot within, but the strangest thing about it was that there was now a warmth to the wooden walls, a slight but discernible rise in temperature past the parlour threshold. She had a sudden image of a limestone block, lined on the inside with this weird dark wood, bound together somehow with wrought iron…

They kept walking, unable to resist now, walking down the long corridor with almost no creaks in the floorboards, toward the second beckoning block of upright rectangular blackness at the end. The hallway seemed almost as long as the driveway, and the phone's torch seemed to grow even dimmer as they came closer… but there was something else, another light, inside the end room; the central room, which was slowly glowing brighter to compensate.

Finally, Maz switched off the phone's light.

They could see without it.

The new light was that old kind of violet fluorescence, and it became clearer as they reached the doorway through another thick, doorless frame. This one was more elaborate, carved with wooden faces over the top; those theatrical masks, Amanda remembered, of comedy and tragedy. Then others, carved out of the wood, all the way down.

Neither stopped to look at them more closely as they entered.

The room was big and square. Every wall was panelled with that same dark wood. It might have been a weird cuboid space, right in the middle of the house, if not for the fact that the ceiling was two floors high. Around what should have been floor level of the higher storey was a balcony that ran, internally, the entire length of the room. Chairs lined the balcony, in scattered positions, as though they had perhaps some time ago been lined evenly for a performance on the floor below, but had since been pushed aside so that people could traverse.

The whole space was illuminated by four portable ultraviolet lights that looked to have been affixed, extremely carelessly, to the lower balustrades with their own looped extension cords. The odd, mild warmth emanated from four similarly placed patio heaters of the elongated-pyramid variety, glistening chrome behind their protective grilles, one each beneath an accompanying fluoro light. The vertical dark wood panelling went right around, up to and including the balcony, except for the wide facing wall where there was an empty fireplace, clean and disused for many years, bordered by small wooden door to either side.

As Amanda took it in, she noticed something very strange about the design. About two meters in, the floor was raised, maybe fifteen centimetres, as though the entire central area of the room had been designed for some kind of performance, or ceremony. Four more pyramid heaters had been stationed along the centre of each edge. Amanda stepped up, where the closest was facing away from them, into the middle.

Maz paused to examine the four power leads, trailing back to the house's original Bakelite socket, still clean, almost pristine, and totally functional.

'Oh God...' Amanda moaned. '...warm...'

She could see that they'd left a trail of rainy footsteps behind them.

'This is pretty weird...' Maz muttered as he stepped up beside her, unable to resist. They both stood there, side by side with their backs to the empty fireplace, being warmed. Through the still-open door, the long hall looked a mile long now.

'...maybe there really is someone living in the back part?'

Maz frowned and looked behind them.

'Is this a fashion thing? Like a photo shoot?'

'I… there aren't lights… but, maybe…? Or a movie set?'

'I don't want to call out…'

'I know…'

'Any second someone's going to come in and find us…'

She noticed Maz's attention was caught by a couple of small items in the middle of the strange, raised floor.

'What's that?'

Maz walked over. 'I thought I was crazy, but…'

'Maz, we need a change of clothes.' She finally relented and took off her coat. Her sweater wasn't quite wet through, but the coat was saturated, and she needed to feel the glow of the heater closer to her skin. 'Maybe they can help us? Just some dry towels?'

Maz wrenched his coat off as well, the wet material clinging to his shoulders. 'They already have…'

He sounded suspicious though.

'Amanda, there's a pile of stuff here. And some writing…'

He turned.

'Jesus; behind you! There's someone standing in the comer…!'

Amanda spun around. She'd been so drenched that her hair swung like dreadlocks and sprayed in the light and the warm glow like a shampoo commercial. Droplets of water sizzled against the radiators. She stood frozen for a second.

'No, no Maz it's just one of those knots…'

'It moved, Emm! I swear to God, it moved!'

'No it…' She didn't want it to be. 'It's, it's the… it's just the light…'

It wasn't.

Carlton had seen it too.

The giant wood knot on the panel in the corner of the room had moved.

Amanda and Maz stood still a few seconds, then the thing moved again. Amanda screamed over whatever shout of abject terror Maz had expelled.

Carlton felt his panic rise, but realized again, concurrently, that he wasn't actually there. That this had *already happened.* He didn't quite understand where he was situated; from where was he viewing this? In some kind of state of grace, or a state of invisibility at least, looking down from the upper corner of the room against the ceiling. Perhaps the north-east corner? And still, he hadn't realized somebody was standing below him, somebody physical, until they had moved from beneath him into the room; and another, and two more, each from the corners.

And that thing, the thing that had started them screaming.

It was just standing there, like a log.

Days ago, this had happened; days ago. There was nothing he could do.

But; the lectures he had given her, to Fiif.

Why was she here?

Why was she involved in all this?

Yes but, no. Not this. He couldn't have judged her that badly; that she had lured him here to a trap. But then, why was it starting to *feel like one?*

He had to think.

Amanda and Maz were clutched together in the middle of the room, frozen in terror but starting to move, starting to back away.

Think. In the grand scheme of things, he knew that an apprentice, like Fiif, not only appeared to the trainer, the instructor or the master, when they had required schooling in the arts. They also appeared when the master required a reminder, or a refreshing in the arts himself. So maybe, a lot of what had rushed out, a lot of what he had told Fiif, in such a hurry, had actually been...

Had he reached somewhere else now?

Had he somehow, through that circuitous path of roads and dimensional curves and cul de sacs that he and Fiif had taken this evening, that this insane sorcerer right here had laid down as a trap for unwary, unawakened psychics, come through the creepy dimensionally-warped paths along who-knows-where, to – another plane?

Somehow?

Had he reached that higher perspective?

Here, now?

He had, after all, not half an hour ago made himself become seen by Amanda, just as one of those 'higher' beings would appear.

Maybe he could do it again?

But back there, on the cold, rushing, rainy bridge, Amanda had been receptive. She had been frightened, yes, but also adrenalized toward seeking a sign. Now she was terrified beyond all comprehension. He would never get through; he could only watch as these terrible things unfolded.

And, while these things were going on below him, there were other things, just as bad.

Back, back... where... back, there...

But! But; she *had* seen him, hadn't she?

Amanda!

That was who he was here to save. Save Amanda for her, the one he...

She had seen him when she had needed to see *something*.

Would she be needing that now? Or would she be feeling forsaken, as though nothing could help her? How did fear work? It worked by making you feel wary, alert, unsafe.

It helped.

But when it was overwhelming, it clouded.

It hindered.

That was a human flaw, a side effect of the powerful brain chemistry that had been needed in the first millennia of evolved humanity, that had been exploited ever since by intra-species and extra-species predators alike. So now she would be feeling the peak of that; terror. Helpless, abandoned, and utterly terrified of her life ending painfully and horribly; she would be thinking of those she was leaving behind, who would look for her, have to see what remained of her and remember; this had been Amanda, my daughter, my sister, my friend, murdered horribly, tortured to the last, pleading for respite, or rescue, that would never come. The sudden invitation of Death's Door, swinging open in a sudden and unexpected breeze; an accident, a killer, offered nothing more than sharp fear and abysmal sadness and agonizing regret.

But there was, Carlton knew, that keyhole of hope, for those who at this time of dire peril were open to it.

That someone would be there, on high, watching at the time.

Perhaps someone who loved you. Perhaps, someone who could pretend to be that someone. If that was what you needed, right then and there, to manage.

If you were lucky enough for that to be real, right then, right here.

'The battery and the fuel...' One of the men spoke. '...as you so neatly put it, Mister Gong. How often they come in pairs of that combination.'

Carlton felt a shock of panic.

No; not Shilling.

No fucking way!

That scumbag, that utter prick, was dead!

And yet, Carlton knew that it was, indeed, that man, right there.

The most evil fucker he had ever known, right there!

Alive, the fucker!

Alive!

How?

How had they not fucking killed him?!

Carlton started looking now. Were there more? More of the traitors here, still alive? He saw seven others, occult practitioners, three men and four women. Eight in all, but there were more on the floor. Just bodies, around, from people who had come through, out of the four doorways, from other places in the house. Come in and collapsed, as though they had barely made it.

And there were more of those weird log things than he'd first thought, propped up, maybe six or seven about the place.

The seven other people standing around Shilling were all young and aesthetically pleasing in a fit, slender fashion, the way Shilling liked them when Carlton had known him. His wannabe actor-model-internet-star entourage, responding to his sexier-than-Crowley, less-overtly-insane-than-Manson, and more-charming-than-Ted Bundy vibe; the archetypal-post-millennial-cult-leader for fucking idiots who don't have enough toxic power in their post-millennial lives.

Or something.

Maybe he was just a sick cunt.

Carlton kept watching, looking for the others, the others who had killed his friends here seven years ago.

Amanda was trembling on the floor as Shilling came toward her.

'This is the one. Burley, you can have the man if you like.'

'Man? Boy, surely. Who else is here? Is there anyone else here to help me use him?'

'Why can't I move?' Amanda demanded from her knees.

'Find the women. They think they have left, never to return. Tell them, I am bringing them back. Now. I want them here before this starts. Then we shall see who is leaving for good.'

Who the hell was he talking about?

If he needed thirteen… there were four absent?

But again, he sensed something; there were more in the house.

The house had someone, or something, in almost every room now.

Why?

Why do this?

Why fuck with things, with people, like this?

It was the one thing Carlton had never really, truly understood.

Why did these maniacs behave this way?

When it was – so – *fucking* – *stupid*!

But… okay. Calm down and assess. What is happening?

Okay, it was a striking ceremony, to be sure. It was certainly not evil, not against any magical or spiritual laws, to enjoy or embrace beauty; Carlton liked to think he knew that better than most sorcerers. It was a fine thing in the eyes of the divine to be pleased or aroused by aesthetic attractiveness, to receive or dispense pleasure.

But it was, somehow, totally evil the way Shilling did it.

The way he collected and exploited and inevitably disposed of that beauty, these people, and for certain, the purposes for which he would deploy the power he gained from gathering them.

There was a slender, redheaded woman, and her equally slender partner, a man as lean as a liquid-metal Terminator. The eight switched in and out, fluid, but they always returned to each other, eye-gazing. Sometimes he would kick one of the hapless bodies on the floor, and they would groan.

Where had they come from?

There were a couple of goth girls, who couldn't stop pashing each other.

That was kind of hot until one of them punched another guy, a tall-dark-and-handsome, right in the face. There was blood, and he punched that other girl in the face; not the one who'd nailed him but her lover, and her nose was bleeding too, and then there was blood everywhere and the trio were kissing each other and smearing blood all over their bodies.

The tallest of the women, a great beauty, was the one to whom all the others seemed to defer when it came to their sexual favours. Carlton had seen her before, but could not place her exactly; she looked like someone who might have been on television, in a soap or something, as a younger woman. She might have been forty now, give or take, but she was lean, not an ounce of fat on her, and toned, with long, flowing dark hair and glorious rose-vine tattoos down her inside arms... although they might have been... Celtic knots? Or black lace patterns? He couldn't quite see exactly; but they would have looked totally ink-chic hot if it hadn't been for the circumstances, and they seemed to burst with red, blue and green richness whenever she opened her embrace, which was virtually all the time.

She seemed to be the hostess; perhaps in loose Satanic terms, she was even the altar. Regardless of what she was supposed to be exactly, she seemed to be important. She seemed to be the focus.

Shilling lay on his back for about a minute while she sat on his face and smeared herself all over him.

She had to be important, for Shilling to acquiesce to that.

Shilling had always been a total pig chauvinist, always insisting women keep to their place. Men on top, and all that crap. Cunnilingus was one of the many things know to be 'beneath him', ironically. Shilling was nude now, and he had what looked like a weird porn-star dick, a good nine or ten inches, freakishly pale white and tapered, like a wet, fleshy horn. Carlton had seen stranger in his time, online. Probably everyone had by now. But not by much. Carlton watched from his strange, ethereal distance as he stood again and surveyed his coven; watching the tall, dark beauty behind her back with knowing contempt, as though he were sure that, one day, she would indeed be put back in her place, on the bottom, where she and all her kind belonged.

Carlton was worried for someone else, however. While Amanda was just attractive enough to maintain a place here for the night, Maz was not; he was too brute for Shilling, and Carlton could see him eyeing him like he didn't belong.

The tall beauty went over to Maz as Shilling observed, hatefully, and grasped his face in both hands. Maz, delirious, drew a sharp breath.

The Faerie Queen!

'A pig! Or is he a dog? My darling you have brought me one of the local swine!'

Maz fell to his knees as the stark definition of her muscular legs expanded and spread, and she slammed each foot further out to her sides. Then she shoved his open-mouthed face forward, smack upon her gaping pink loins, and threw her head backwards in a low guttural cackle of what she surely felt was good-humoured satisfaction. Her neck seemed way too long for her body as she stretched it right back, ceasing her self-satisfied mirth, and allowing a long, rasping breath to escape. Again, the breath was too long to be completely normal, and sure enough a kind of bright pink gas, almost shockingly, independently neon, spiralled thickly from her throat, gathered in her open bowl of a mouth, then wisped up between her lips, over her pointed nose and into the air. Maz dropped to the ground as she released him without care, his skin noticeably more pale, the hair on his head falling out as her hands moved roughly through it upon release.

Carlton gasped.

That was powerful, *so powerful!*

She had taken his desire. His need, his urge; all the things within him that lusted, desired, loved and adored. She had sucked it out, and transmogrified it... into?

What?

The electric pink thing hung in the air above her, like some kind of weird tropical fish. A pink banana fish, trilling and throbbing, hovering and circling around her like a nervous pet.

The other six in the coven were turning in a circle now, with Amanda still staring at all the mad Black Prax fuckers like they were a ring of magical fairies or something. Maz remained on the ground, looking like he was in the final stages of leukaemia; but still gaping up in blind astonishment at the faerie circle that was shocking, but still enchanting and, bizarrely from Carlton's perspective, seemed to be less threatening to Maz with every pass.

Amanda had started to glow as well, as the room started to fully glow, a dull shade of conversely bright violet.

Shilling finally came up to Maz and pulled his hair back. His voice rang out once more, his slender white hand still clinging to Maz's scalp.

'The woman, almost always the battery! To be drained! The man, the fuel! To eventually become run down! That we should all be both, and more, never occurs, is never even known or desired to be known!'

Shilling suddenly yanked Maz's hair fully back, pulling out clumps but maintaining a shallow grasp, then swung his whole body down, as though he were a python, opening wide to devour him head-first.

He shouted full in Maz's face.

'Gimmee fuck-een foot-ee, moyt!'

Then he slammed Maz's head hard into the wood floor. Maz's skull rebounded like a half-flat basketball and he collapsed to his side, but groaned a little. He had actually played footy; he'd had worse, but he was bleeding from his now-bald upper scalp. The blood started to seep into the floor, and seemed to vanish as though the hardwood was some kind of absorbent sponge.

With that, Carlton snapped out of his own fog and back into things at hand.

It was easy to go with the perverse flow of it.

But this was not a performance.

This was real; this was Shilling's new coven, or at least part of it, and they had started a larger ceremony that appeared to have been building for days, perhaps weeks or maybe even months. Or maybe, most horrifically; this was all part of the same ceremony that Shilling had started, all those long seven years ago.

The thought filled Carlton with such dread that he almost vanished, almost lost himself in the ether of whatever dimension he'd stumble-slid into. For a second he thought he would lose himself entirely, then he realized that the less focussed he was, exactly here and now, the more likely it was that he would lose purchase, and remember where he really was, and where his body was, where he *should* be, and just… zip right back to…

But no, no, not yet.

He had to try, to see through the ugly brown-purple bruise-fog, the smog-mist that was all through the room now, the streaks of dark blood-red, swirling in this atmosphere of evil; but minutes seemed to pass yet again, even as he had thought that, remembering that the woman, the woman he now wanted again, the woman who was his lover now, if he wanted her; she who wanted him, needed him now, and even more so, was in ever greater danger, the longer he remained here.

But they had come, they had both come, for...

Amanda was quivering now.

Naked in the fog on all fours.

She was glowing that ethereal purple, all over; Carlton knew what this meant. Her ethereal energies; her psychic, spiritual, otherworldly powers, whatever you liked, were being drained. The body restored them naturally, but usually a day's store came out with the breath of sleep, or was employed reaching the astral dimensions in dreams, or the inner-earth dimensions for nightmares, only then to be naturally replenished as part of the body's natural biorhythms, from sunrise, while in waking. This was a perversion of that process; awful to behold, to have that inner core artificially stimulated, against your will, and to be drained like this. To have the energy stolen so that it could power whatever blood magic Shilling was working in tandem.

This was rape, by any definition, and he'd come too late to prevent it.

Ghastly, that some deep reservoir had been activated within Amanda, a power she might not have even been required to acknowledge or expected to access, however the light-forces worked, until she was a mother perhaps, or a spiritual teacher, or who the hell knew what. And that she remained there, like some kind of half-arsed, doped-up animal, being milked, the violet pouring out of her open vagina; just a disgusting, disgraceful, profane parody... some sick combination of a human night club smoke machine and impromptu-hippie natural childbirth.

Holy crap, someone was going to pay for this.

Amanda was drenched in sweat, her eyes glazed over. And yet she was still, Carlton sensed, vaguely searching for Maz, her love. Already lost. But he remained intact, out of her sight but nearby, still drained and concussed on the floor.

How could this stop? Was Shilling going to murder them all? No; Carlton could see, the others, the orgy going on that was fuelling Amanda's sick spiritual syphoning, they had all been through this. Shilling did not murder, apparently. At least, not quickly. Amanda would remain. She would be part of that orgy-entourage as they drained the next initiate, the next night, and the next, and the next, and so on, and on. On and on; but, *for what?*

It didn't matter.

There was magic that could dispel this.

Carlton knew it.

Enough to…

No, not enough. Enough to give it a go, nothing more. He wasn't strong enough, not like this, not from a distance like this; whatever distance actually meant from wherever the hell he was.

See?

How could he?

And even if he did, what would that serve?

He needed to leave, and come back, come back *now*; the now back with Fiif. In the hope that they were all still alive, Shilling's cult-captives, now, after three days and presumably more and more, and crazier and crazier of this already batshit-crazy occult shit, still going on, on and on for every one of those days that had lapsed in between this, the past, and the now…

He would have to come back, back to Bridger, with Barker and Cheryl and…

But; the reality of the situation was permeating his mind.

Jesus.

…they would have to bring, just, whoever the fuck else they could find.

Because Shilling was back.

Fenner Shilling – wasn't dead.

He was – back.

Only two people had ever stopped Fenner Shilling before.

One was insane, the other was magically impotent.

Only, now it seemed… they *fucking hadn't.* They hadn't stopped him. Then; *what had it all been for?* These past seven years?

Holy fuck!

Maybe he should, right now, do something? Do whatever the

hell he could?

There was dispelling power, sure. He could summon some of that, throw it in, but at this point who knew what it would do, if anything? The amount he would be able to summon from here was... no.

Pointless! And could he, from here? There was no answer. *There was just try.* He'd never summoned anything, disembodied from a higher dimension. He'd never met anyone demonstrably powerful enough to do that, besides maybe Barker and Heather in their heyday, nor had he read any of the grimoires or spell books that possessed such information.

He'd never thought to.

He'd only ever wanted to understand stuff. Just, know at was going on behind the curtain once the little old man had fucked off.

No, no, he had to get back, back to Fiif.

He had to do what he could now, in the now.

The real now.

Sadly, before he could witness anything worse, he began to retreat. But then he realized, he couldn't. Not because he didn't want to.

He couldn't move.

There was noise now, again. It sounded like... it sounded like what it was, exactly what it was, and what he had forgotten; where and when he was. It was Saturday night. Last Saturday night. It sounded like a rowdy, Saturday night crowd of blokes, just out of the pub at closing, or off for a pizza, or simply all blind off their faces and rocking up at... a party. They had been told there was a party here.

Jesus, what was Shilling going to do to these guys?

They were really drunk by the sounds. Monosyllabic and fired up. Truth be told he had never minded guys like this; but he knew Cheryl and Barker did. He knew that to them, that kind of wild, drunken whooping, rather than sounding like a gang of ordinary

327

blokes blowing off steam, signalled to them the approach of savages. That they should flee in the other direction post-haste. That these primitives would hunt them for being different. Hurt, torture or possibly even kill them.

These were not the sort to seek shamans.

But Carlton didn't have that programming; at least, not that initial reaction. The sounds of drunken male revelry just made him smile, and remember good times and maybe even join in, or open a beer and start a session himself.

He understood his friends though; it was just the mind. Just the brain, and how your genes popped out. Whether your genetic patterning had enough of the different, the diversified, or the unique in it, that was located outside of the main code, or pattern, or whatever the fuck it was... string, or something? Anyway, enough of that in it, to justify the installation and activation of the 'other' gene, that made you afraid of the herd. So, to be genetically predisposed to be afraid of the herd, there had to be enough 'other' for your being to register, as a whole greater than the sum of parts, that people like you, in your ancestry, had been culled by frightened villagers often enough throughout the rest of history, to make you stay away from revelling villagers as going concern. Just as Barker had told him that he had been drawn to 'the other' his whole life, Carlton had needed to be pulled, kicking and screaming toward it, and sorcery, and where, he had to admit, he now belonged.

But, these guys... what the hell were they doing here?

'There was no need to bring me a pig, my cock!' The tall woman declaimed at Shilling. 'I have summoned a whole herd!'

How had she done this?

They started to filter in.

Three, then two more, then three more, all through the rear doors.

They were all wearing their Saturday night pub clothes, a style which Carlton firmly eschewed but was so painfully familiar with that he found it almost endearing; polo shirts and jeans, rugby tops and track pants, all utterly nondescript. They were all so pissed at this point that they had not had the sense between them to throw on a sweater or windcheater, heaven forbid some kind of jacket or coat. They were bronzed specimens, and did not feel the cold. The piss had anaesthetized them to it, a fact they would all no doubt find hysterical whilst simultaneously taking great pride in it.

'Beer...'

Several of them had been saying this from a distance. Almost like old-fashioned cinema zombies. He saw that they were shuffling more than they usually would, even extremely drunk, and that their feet were wet and muddy. There were suburbs out there, but also ravines and a few paddocks. They had not come wandering across at twelve-thirty, maybe even later by now, on a Saturday night, uncoaxed. It was a long, hard trek from the country pub, the one where he had to assume they had somehow magically been lured from. Something very strong, very powerful and primal had summoned them in their vulnerably binge-drunk state.

'Beer.'

'Tits.'

'Beeuh.'

'Tehts!'

'Fucking!'

'Fah-king!'

'Beeuh.'

'Tehts!'

'Fah-king!'

Somehow they had been reduced to their primal desires. As they entered, a dozen now, and then a few more, they staggered around the chamber like characters from a comedic satire, and yet... real.

Magically lobotomized bogan zombies.

It was utterly tragic.

Carlton could see from their looks, from their eyes, that they were not just drunk but under some kind of powerful influence; as good as drugged and hypnotized. The tall woman had spiked their drinks, perhaps, with something that reduced them to… well, what she'd said. A herd. Pliable with magic from a distance.

She approached the closest as he wandered through the fog toward her, and placed her hands on his broad, athletic shoulders.

'Tehts! Fah-king! Fah-kii-iing! Fah-king tehhhts!'

He went slightly limp and dropped to his knees, and then her equally as athletic loins were mashed into his drunken face, just as with Maz. Again she threw her head back, but this time there seemed to be a greater lengthening along her neck; definitely and freakishly so. The man, who could not have been older than twenty-five, was dropped unceremoniously, pale and shedding, limp on the wood, as the second of the electric pink eels slid up from her throat and took flight with the first. Then, as the others in the coven swirled around her, groping each other but focussed and fascinated, she took another of the drunken young sportsmen, and another in quick succession. Her pets were not all the same shade; the next was very bright pink but the one after that almost cherry red.

Shilling cried out, raising his hands to the sky.

'What are you doing!'

It was impossible to tell if he were excited, overjoyed, furious or all of those; he certainly seemed to believe she had been fantastically audacious.

'What are you doing!'

She grasped her fourth footballer, thrusting him so hard into her vagina that her lips seemed to spread wide enough to encompass his entire face.

'They shall have their hundred heads! They shall have their hundred heads!'

Shilling seemed to catch on.

'Yes! Yes! Yeeesss!'

Carlton tried to run, then.

He tried to recoil.

The vibration of the room descended in that instant, seemingly upon Shilling's will, and total approval, into something with which he was completely unfamiliar, with which he never intended to become familiar, and which he never desired to see again. There were sparks shooting across the bruised clouds before him, ejaculate of some kind, and more of the pink and red and now purple eels. The new ones though were erupting from the electrical storm before him like reverse-meteors, or bulbous blob fireworks, up from the ground, that somehow settled to become slithering sky-snakes, blasting up from a white core and turning deep orange and blood red, then swirling about with the pink and red, until there were a dozen of each and Carlton was so disorientated, so ill within his vision and mind, that he would have done anything to be free, to get back, to be away and anywhere, anywhere, fucking anywhere else.

'There is someone here with us.'

Shilling looked up. The voice had come from a woman.

It had been shock, and now all the streams, the pink slugs and fire-snakes, streaked up from below and came for him, stopping all around him, in a circumference about an arm's reach from his vision, staring in with…

Jesus!

Faces! They had tiny – *almost human faces!*

Peering with rage and suspicion and, most horrifically, some kind of rudimentary, surely self-conscious intellect, they were clearly outraged at his psychic presence.

'Freyanna cannot know I'm here!'

'Freyanna will be dead in three weeks! Up there! Who – is that?'

'He has come through your insane maze; through the astral from Argent! I can smell those foul fucking children even from here!'

'A clever one!'

The sorceress was rising, levitating. Carlton could almost see her face.

'Is it Moon?'

Shilling scoffed from below. 'Surely not!?'

'He has the shadow of Moon over him! But Shilling... he is days in the future!'

Still she hovered low, beneath him where he couldn't see.

'Then it is Moon's bumbling accomplice! The astral tracker! Following the moon-scent of one of these plebeians!'

'What shall I do with him, Shilling?!'

'Prevent him from leaving! More bait for Barker Moon!'

'I shall pull him fully through! Snap his spirit off his faraway body! Disembody him!'

'Kill him! Rip his soul from up there and bring it down to me! Let Moon come for the captured soul of his hopeless companion! Finally! Let him come! Let – him – come!'

With everything he had, could be and ever was or would be, Carlton kicked back.

TWENTY-TWO:
ONE

Stationary now, jolted back to an upright sitting position and fully adrenalized, Barker ripped off his helmet. Vapour jetted from his mouth and nostrils. He was furious at himself, at the maniac, and especially at the chauffer, whom he could not see through the tinted black windows.

Suddenly Barker realized that the traffic lights were out. So were the street lights. Around him everything seemed pale, almost colourless; washed out in a kind of anti-neon fog. With a light hum, the rear, black-tinted window of the limousine gently lowered. A man sat there. Sitting on Bach, Barker was looking right across at him through the window, almost even. But even as he stared angrily into the vehicle, Barker suddenly felt as though he might as well have been a bottom feeder, staring in through a porthole in the Deepsea Challenger. The man within seemed unfazed in the extreme to Barker's presence there, completely preoccupied by some kind of tablet device on his lap. Then Barker realized he was wearing an almost invisible headset; listening to something with a dead-eyed intensity. Just as Barker realized this, the man blinked several times, very heavily.

'Well that *is* quite good…'

The man's voice was baritone and articulate, with a musical edge.

'…hah. Really, quite good.'

Then he noticed Barker out of the corner of his eye.

'Oh. Hallo…'

At first, Barker thought he might have been listening with the latest transparent headset from Japan or something, but then he saw that it was something else entirely; part of a larger device, a

333

net of gossamer that had been attached all over his scalp, like an EEG net that was somehow... alive.

The man looked a healthy sixty, with his thick white hair in a timelessly immaculate cut that was lush and lustrous; his severe cowlick side-part swept into a fixed but elegant low-curving coiffure, arcing up behind his ear, with the other side short and aesthetically, sharply angled back. The man pulled the net from his head without displacing a single white strand of hair, then let go of it in front of his face. Now it just hung in the air before him, like some kind of beautiful, glistening, miniature deep sea squid, weightless and peaceful.

'Who – ?'

'Sorry... are you Barker Moon?'

The gravelly edge to his voice seemed scarred from centuries of smoke, yet his voice remained silken, the smooth tone eroded over a river's age of wine, and carved deep with brandy canyons. It must have been long ago, because Barker had the impression that in this age, this... incarnation? This dimension? Regardless; here, he was totally sober and razor-sharp.

'Perhaps...' He held up a thin white finger and smiled, wry. 'Don't answer that.' He grinned a touch, slightly crooked. 'Obviously you are. Or I wouldn't be here to see you, would I now?'

The man placed his white finger in the middle of his wide, thin, delicate lips.

'I had to intervene...' He let out an apologetic wince and smiled serenely. '...please don't be angry with my driver, he's really a very good man. Gotten me out of all sorts of...'

He seemed to realize that Barker was still staring at him, irrationally furious. He removed his finger and shook it lightly in the air.

'I told him; do what you have to, just put a stop to that blade...' The man laughed a little, friendly but wary, as though awaiting Barker's reaction. 'Are we okay? Are you okay? Do you need to take a moment?'

Barker examined him again; he was indeed pale, British pale to suit his informal high class British accent, but he had been tanned, deeply, once. Barker thought he recognized him suddenly, then thought he recognized him again as someone else, equally as suddenly. Then he was distracted from any kind of specific recognition as he saw that beneath his stylish clothes the man was muscular, too; as though he had once been fully toned but was now content with being simply graceful... then another aspect; he had that sharp but androgynous male beauty that was appealing to everyone, the kind that went with those immortal levels of pure, idolised charm, levels that could mesmerize stadiums...

'There...' The passenger smiled again, wider. 'It's been so long. Since we last saw each other. I'd wanted to come earlier but I was afraid. I didn't want to blow your mind, before it's time.' He gave a little shrug. 'In the very least; not permanently. Perhaps that can't be helped.'

As Barker's eyes drew accustomed to his presence, he suddenly found the man spellbinding to behold.

'You're... a deity. Some kind of... twentieth century... Rock God?' Barker deduced.

As he came to realize who he was talking to, the wry grin became more of a slightly crooked smile, edged with dissatisfaction. The Rock God's eyes were a bright, clear grey, but ringed with darkness.

'Not the Rock God...' He smiled again, as though all this were the least of it. '...but a major aspect. Enough to have free rein...'

Barker tried to see more closely again; there was a shimmering black and white scarf, a black silk waistcoat and a crisp white shirt. They looked brand new, but were the apex of timeless style. Although, the light within the car was strange, and Barker couldn't truly see much. The upholstery might have had some kind of harlequin pattern. What the deity's face told him though, was that this was some kind of great archetypal spirit, a force from the great days of Berlin, Paris and New York; art and trend, darkness and sophistication, cabaret, music hall, beat, glam, punk, new wave, pop and progressive. Barker could immediately feel at least three household names from three totally different eras, and a dozen more weaved through behind them. Then the Rock God slipped his glasses down the bridge of his immaculately aquiline nose and their eyes met. Barker hadn't even realized that he'd been wearing glasses; they were frameless, round and, like his other tech, virtually invisible. The clear grey beamed out as through the sun had streamed through behind storm clouds.

'We've met before... somewhere...?' Barker uttered.

'Everybody's seen me before, sometime, somewhere.'

'No... not the ones you've influenced, not the ones who channel you, not even the two or three who...'

'Yes?'

'In my mind I can barely distinguish... but there are two or three... who *were*, who *are* you, aren't there? In this mystical, celestial form? The *actual you*?'

The Rock God raised his hand and traced a symbol.

'That's it, Barker. Very good.'

The symbol came to life, maintaining integrity in thin air. It floated, glistening like weightless mercury. It was as though a plane, or even a pane of air before him had become solid, like glass, but just a very thin membrane. Where the Rock God had traced his finger, the membrane had broken, and whatever was behind it had shone through to create the shape of the symbol. The symbol held for a second or two before dissolving like fine sand, then a bolt of time, of memory, or experience seemed to hit Barker and he remembered a concert. In England, at the Brixton Academy.

'You saw me that night... me and him; we were genuinely one, for a few nights, back then...'

Barker caught his breath; he had always remembered it but now it seemed as though it were just last week. Still fresh; still vibrant and echoing...

It was too much. Barker stared at him. 'Brixton…'

Brixton nodded. 'That's fine with me.' He smiled; crooked, knowing, but with a remote, casual kindness. 'And you are Barker. Barker Moon. A fine name, my friend. That is what you will always be, here on this plane.'

Barker's head was spinning a little. 'What do you want…?'

'You, Barker.'

This was a bit startling.

'No, not that. Heavens, no. Barker, you did something seven years ago and it's time you made it right.'

'I don't remember.' It was reflex now, along with how adamant he was about it. 'I've started to think I never will…'

Brixton smiled. 'We'll see…'

When he smiled, his voice became more nasal, as though highlighting the fact that he had earned the smile; his jaded, tired, friendly-trickster smile, through the relief of kicking all sorts of powdered habits, not just in recent decades, but many down through the millennia.

'Now listen. There can only ever be one Barker Moon, of the kind of Barker Moon that you are. Just as I can only ever be Brixton once. Maybe for a very long time…' Brixton laughed, as though reflecting back on a crazy, melancholy life well-lived. '… but, just once. Understand?'

'Sure. Gods live longer, but when they're gone…'

'…they're gone. Well… maybe not gone, exactly. Same with humans. I mean, vessels are created on every plane. The big consciousness sends down whatever kind of soul energy, or soul love, those vessels attract; whatever their egos emerge as demanding or requiring. When that variant of soul consciousness hits the vessel, it starts a record.' Brixton smiled, a little cheeky, a little wise. 'And whether that's written in grooves or waves or bits, it exists and can be experienced.'

'My vessel's a human body. Yours seems to be a limo.'

'Oh, I'm plasma or ether or quantum matter or something. Held together by will; I am when I'm like this, anyway. It's only on your material plane where they insist on so many labels to make things work that all of matter matters. Everything defined by the low sciences on your plane stops making sense once you step off it. Almost every conscious life form on any plane expects the entire universe to conform to their labels at first; it never does. It's why there are so many planes, and barriers. You were quite good at negotiating those barriers at one time.'

'So I'm told.'

'Oh, I wasn't told, I saw you do it. Do you remember the song?'

'No...' Barker frowned. 'What song?'

'Don't worry. You will. One way or another. At the beginning and the end all is one, so nothing is ever really forgotten.'

'Or lost or dead or gone...' Barker growled. 'I've heard this one.'

'I've heard them all. Several times now,' Brixton nodded sympathetically. 'Very difficult to come up with anything new, with all the limited variations you have here; the tiny range humans can see and hear. It's why it's all got to change. Or at least; why so many of you have to change.'

'People don't like changes.'

'Changes can make the familiar seem strange. They frighten people, but they must be faced, no matter how strange.'

'People are strange, if you ask me.'

'Most people are rather dull, unfortunately. But your kind of people are indeed strange. But you may also be the answer. There are three solutions to the current state of discord on this plane, Barker. But to understand what they are, you need to understand what this plane is. Do you understand that Barker? Do you understand that, to begin with, there is only this time once? Here and now, once?'

'Sure. You only live once, and all that...'

'No, not that. I told you. The subtle difference. Take it from the top now.'

'Barker Moon only exists once.'

'That's right. Well done, sunshine. It's true, others may have had that name; your uncle for one. But you are you, only once, this Barker Moon. There is only one go round for the cosmic forces to create this planet, in this part of space-time, to create me, create you, for us both to *emerge*; to have this conversation… "Brixton", talking to "Barker".'

Brixton nudged his head forward, in a way that suggested Barker look behind him.

Barker glanced back over his shoulder.

Barker's body was lying on the road behind him, bleeding out onto the asphalt, the dagger embedded deep within him.

TO BE CONTINUED…

Barker Moon will return...

And in fact does.

In...

Saga of The Urban Sorcerers –
Book Two: The Reckoning of Emerald Tarragon

www.GalexyTales.com

(OR SEARCH "GALEXY TALES" AT AMAZON...)

"Last Season on... *Barker Moon!*"

The character of Barker Moon came into existence in a television pilot script for a two-hour telemovie/backdoor pilot (along with a very detailed concept document) in around 1989. The series was to be called *Barker Moon*, and that version, as finalized sometime in the mid-nineties, would most likely have been produced by Network Ten. This novel is a massively unpacked and greatly expanded version of the first half of that final two-hour pilot script, which had the title *Once Summoned.*

This is by no means Gospel, and happened pre-email (we were still posting scripts in the mail) but this is how I remember it...

The extremely handsome *Neighbours* actor, now wildlife photographer, Dan Paris, was always the favourite to play Barker Moon, and probably would have if the series had gone ahead. He would have been great, I think.

But there were a lot of versions, in that regard. Also courted was bad-boy Aussie thespian Jeremy Simms, who was keen, but had just started his own theatre company. In keeping with the bad-boy theme, the role was apparently seriously considered by a surly but brilliant young actor, then virtually unknown, by the name of Russell Crowe, who decided to wait and see how his new movie *Romper Stomper* would work out.

Three very different shows, right there.

The pilot was in consideration by several Australian networks, and optioned (from memory) by at least two production companies, but as stated above, it was quite some time ago; one network required that the female lead character, Emerald Tarragon (see the next book in the saga for more on what happened to her) should absolutely, definitely have red hair, mainly because of a very popular character in a new show called *The X-Files*, that at the time was kind of starting to catch on a bit.

After Dan Paris had expressed firm interest, Kiwi actress Simone Kessell was the front runner for Emerald Tarragon (a very handsome couple). Kimberley Davies and Tammy MacIntosh were also considered at various stages, for different Barkers, and were apparently interested.

Bardot singer and Australian household-name Sophie Monk was looking to begin her acting career, and had come aboard to play Cheryl. Michael Caton, a national treasure who at the time was hot off the classic Australian social satire, *The Castle*, had agreed to play Detective Parry, which was what we think made Seven sit up and take notice. We were after the late, great Jon English for Fenner Shilling. It would have taken some doing, we were told... but we had begun to try!

In the earliest version of the series, Heather Holden had been Hector Holden, a role that the fabulously intense and wonderfully eccentric Barry Otto had agreed to play. Things evolved however (the series was seen to require a romantic interest for Detective Parry, whose role had suddenly expanded) and while we were super-keen on a post *Ab Fab* Joanna Lumley for the now-female 'Heather' Holden, we had only just started the process of courting her agents when Ten... or it might have been Seven by then... (but don't tell Seven that Ten were still interested) put us into turnaround.

(Word was though, Joanna Lumley was quite interested, but not so sure about coming to Australia for four months a year.)

So what happened?

Well, after probably three serious circles of the airport with who knows how many Heads of Drama, and developing and pitching other series in between, almost a decade had gone by, and after all that time, *Buffy* was catching fire, and as much as we love that series too, we simply weren't prepared to start all over again with all the characters as teenagers operating out of a high school.

After all, whoever heard of school-aged sorcerers, eh?

Network Ten had been looking for a locally-produced companion show to air with *The X-Files*, and eventually settled on a dark cop show, *Murder Call*. Then, *The X-Files* kind of faded away. Seven were keen on a series of TV movies (and technically still are, I suppose!) but never committed. The ABC liked it, but didn't have the money.

There are various expressions of interest from agents, in a box somewhere, along with all the scripts.

So there you go.

Who knows what might have been?

Probably not this novel, for a start...

Still, there was a lot of development done on the *Barker Moon* series. Its two touchstone series were the late-eighties game-changer, *Wiseguy*, and as development proceeded, the sci-fi classic, *Babylon 5*.

Consequently, this book represents just the tip of the storytelling iceberg; *Saga of the Urban Sorcerers*, née/aka *Barker Moon*, has a beginning, middle, and end, with plenty of potential for magic in between.

I never forgot the Barker Moon universe, and I'm overjoyed now that I get to re-summon him, his companions and his world, and give them each their own tale.

And with an unlimited special effects budget, too!

I hope you enjoy them - thanks for reading!

Alex James
(...exhausted, on the plane back from Sydney Supanova, June 2016.)

Novels by Alex James:

THE ASCENSION SEQUENCE:
VOLUME ONE
The Pandora Sequence
VOLUME TWO
Book One: The Pandora Inheritance
Book Two: The Pandora Arcana (Pre-order)
Book Three: The Daughters of Pandora (Pre-order)

THE CHRONICLES OF THE TERRAGUARD:
Book One: Maker of Rules

AMAZON SEVEN SAGA - VOLUME ONE:
Book One: Mission Queen
Book Two: Queen Renegade
Book Three: Intergalactic Ingenue (Pre-order)
Book Four: Princess Executor (Pre-order)

SAGA OF THE URBAN SORCERERS:
Book One: The Summoning of Barker Moon
Book Two: The Reckoning of Emerald Tarragon
Book Three: The Shaping of Cheryl Equiniox (Pre-order)

DARK STREETS SAGA:
Book One: Agents of Fear
Book Two: Avatars of Wrath (Pre-Order)

Venus IA

www.GalexyTales.com

(or search "GALEXY TALES" at Amazon!)

Acknowledgements

Enormous thanks and all my love as always to Melissa Sheldrick.

Huge thanks to Michal Dutkiewicz for the wonderful cover – this book changed its structure and length, and elements of story several times over the course of 2015 and 2016, resulting in a frustrating number of minor changes for the cover design. It was a bumpy road, but I am very grateful.

Thanks and gratitude to Adam Dutkiewicz for the formatting.

Gretel Newman-Sugrue was way ahead of me in regard to her suggestions, as usual.
I am so glad my fridge broke down.

Thanks again to everyone who helped.

Raechel Carroll – brilliant and amazing!

Anne Ruwolt – amazing and brilliant!

Special "you know what you did" thanks to - Stan James, Gennie James, Chris Collings, Angelina Collings, Darren Koziol, Gillian Koziol, Adam Vale, Tom Kafa, Kay Leanne, Travis Pollard, Melissa Stokes, Alexandra Champion, Regan and Nicole, Mario Kukec, Karen Carlisle, G.R.Thomas, Stacey Logan, Kimberley Clark, Andrew Irvine, Kylie Chan, Mark Custance, Walter Rhein, Michael Lickorish, Nat Karmichael, Sam Elsegood, Nick Talbot, Claudia Ienco, Zoe Clare, Dave de Vries, Petra Elliot, Lucia Stanzel, Greg Gates, Matthew Pilkington, Anthony Fagan, Cherie Davy, Veronica Gaunt, Peter McNamara, Pat McNamara, Greg C. Grace, David Bradley, Dan Foley, Big Pete Wagner, Jon James, Chris James, Mike Cooper, Haley Snook, Dave Baker, and Joanne Bouzianis-Sellick – for heaps, going way back!

And really, really many, many thanks to all the cosplayers who pose with me, all the people who've bought my books at cons and expos, and to all the people who come back! I love the people who come back!

About the Author

Alex James is a writer who lives in and is inspired by Adelaide, South Australia.

Alex studied European History, Classical Mythology, Film Studies and Screenwriting under the Communications and Liberal Studies banners at the University of South Australia.

Between 1992 and 2005 he wrote many, many, many outlines, treatments, concept documents, bibles, pilots and screenplays, for just about every active Australian production company there was.

From 2008-2014 he was an in-house writer for Angel-Phoenix Media, who published his first two e-book novels, *The Pandora Sequence* and *Venus AI*, both of which were launched at the 2013 San Diego Comic-Con.

Alex's most recent works are epic novel sagas which include *The Saga of The Urban Sorcerers*, *Amazon Seven*, *Dark Streets*, *The Chronicles of The Terraguard*, and *The Ascension Sequence*.

He publishes via his own independent imprint, Galexy Tales.

www.ingramcontent.com/pod-product-compliance
Lightning Source LLC
Chambersburg PA
CBHW060934120726
47910CB00002B/328